the
lighterman

the
lighterman
simon michael

URBANE
Publications

urbanepublications.com

First published in Great Britain in 2017 by Urbane Publications Ltd
Suite 3, Brown Europe House, 33/34 Gleaming Wood Drive, Chatham, Kent ME5 8RZ
Copyright © Simon Michael,2017

A CIP catalogue record for this book is available from the British Library.

ISBN 978-1-911583-00-4
MOBI 978-1-911583-02-8
EPUB 978-1-911583-01-1

Design and Typeset by Julie Martin
Cover by Julie Martin
Image © Terence Donovan Archive

Printed and bound by CPI Group (UK) Ltd, Croydon, CR0 4YY

RBANE
Publications

urbanepublications.com

MIX
Paper from
responsible sources
FSC® C013604

Praise for the Charles Holborne series
The Brief and *An Honest Man*

"Britcrime at its very best – completely unputdownable."
thebookmagnet

"Will keep you up for hours. It will play on your mind and you'll be dying to know what happens next."
https://aloverofbooks.wordpress.com/

"A pure gem and kept me turning the pages constantly. Brilliant characters, excellent plotting and overall an indulgent, absorbing and enjoyable read."
@BookwormDH

"A gripping yarn from beginning to end… On a par with Lee Childs and James Patterson (5 stars)."
Amazon reviewer

"Addictive reading; I couldn't put it down. A brilliant read (5 stars)."
Amazon reviewer

"… gritty, gripping and utterly compelling. Highly recommended."
Leah Moyse, Independent Blogger

"Move over Martina Cole, you're going to have company on the bestsellers lists (5 stars)."
Amazon reviewer

"...In weaving Holborne's adventures around legal London, Michael evokes the "pyramid of steaming cholesterol" of the all-day breakfast at Mick's, and the "damp sheep pen" smell of Bow Street Magistrates' Court. Michael writes excellent dialogue too... on this form Michael should cast [Holborne] in more adventures."
Law Society Gazette

"These are confident novels, sharply observed, packed full of rich, authentic dialogue. Pacey, yet measured, they weave complex legal scenes with light, credible domestic and professional moments where characters are fleshed out and the central hero is exposed, both for good and bad."
Bookends and Binends

"...well out of the ordinary and far into the realms of seriously good storytelling... superlative courtroom drama..."
New Law Journal

"Chilling suspense and climactic surprises."
Publishers Weekly

"An exceptional novel by an exceptional writer. Charles Holborne is an utterly convincing and compelling fictional creation – I came to have the same sense of attachment to this honourable yet beleaguered barrister that I have for characters such as Philip Marlowe or Maigret… an exhilarating…reading experience."
Mark Mayes, novelist and poet

"Gripping and utterly compelling…Brilliant! A must read."
RC Bridgestock, authors of the best-selling DI Dylan series, and consultants on TV series Happy Valley and Scott & Bailey

For Kay, Alastair, James and Roxanne

prologue
september 1940

Luftwaffe Hauptmann Heinz Schumann releases his bombs at 03:45 hours. His Dornier 215 is in the middle wave of the attack and although several of the escorting Messerschmitt 109s have been shot down, the approach has been easy. The cloud cover as they crossed the Channel had melted away, and the bomber squadron had simply followed the meandering line of the Thames, deviating slightly every now and then to avoid the puffs of smoke from the anti-aircraft fire and then returning to its course. Ahead of Schumann, clusters of incendiaries continue to rain onto the city, dropped by the leading bombers in his formation. As each new cluster falls there is a dazzling flash followed by a flame soaring up from a white centre, turning the underside of the barrage balloons silvery yellow and throwing up great boiling eruptions of smoke. And as each burst of black smoke clears in the breeze, the great river reappears, a black snake in a brightly-illuminated landscape of uncontrolled fire.

As he releases his payload, Schumann is able to look down and obtain a perfect view of the U-shaped bend in the river known by the Britishers as The Isle of Dogs. He watches the bombs drop, becoming tiny black dots before they are swallowed up by the great orange and yellow tongues of flame which leap hundreds of feet into the night air, as if making futile attempts to lick the belly of his Dornier. The Port of London is burning to the ground, and to Schumann's eye it is both terrible and beautiful.

It takes the 1000 kg bombs 42 seconds to hit the ground. This is what happens on the ground during that period of 42 seconds:

Hallsville Junior School, Agate Street, Canning Town is heaving with over 600 East Enders – men, women and children – awaiting evacuation. Almost all of them are homeless, their houses and schools having been destroyed in the first few days of the Blitz. Some have gathered together a few treasured possessions; some have a cardboard suitcase or two; some, recently dug out from collapsed buildings, have nothing but the nightclothes they stand in, their modesty covered by borrowed blankets, soot and building dust. Almost all have lost family members and the majority carries injuries. These are the walking wounded of working class London.

New dazed families continue to arrive at the already overcrowded building but, despite all, spirits remain reasonable for much of the day. Then, as the hours pass and the promised transports fail to materialise, muttering turns to anger, and anger to shouting at the hopelessly overrun authorities. They are sitting ducks, they protest, with no air raid shelter to protect them and another bombing raid inevitable. By early afternoon a blind eye is being turned to the dozens of East End servicemen who desert from nearby postings to slip into the school and spirit their families away.

The unrest turns to barely-contained panic when the air raid starts. Children shriek with terror and cling to their mothers' legs as the bombs scream down, shaking the ground with each impact, and the drone of the oncoming Luftwaffe planes goes on, and on, and on, wave after wave, dulling the senses, making it impossible to think beyond the thundering engines and the rising hysteria.

40 seconds.

Harry Horowitz, tailor and furrier, lately of British Street, Mile End, and his wife Millie Horowitz, milliner, huddle at the very end of a corridor at the back of the school with their boys, Charles aged 14 and David, 12. Despite the noise of the German planes, the bombs raining down all around them which shake the entire building, and the thick dust-laden air which catches in her throat, Millie's lifelong debilitating anxiety is focused mostly on David. Her younger son had been running a fever when dragged out of their damaged home two nights earlier, and he now lies in her arms, sweating and shivering uncontrollably. Crouched next to them on the floor of the narrow corridor are four other families, one being that of Millie's best friend, Sarah, who along with her husband and three girls had arrived earlier that afternoon to claim the last remaining floor space just inside the door leading out to the playground.

30 seconds.

Another bomb – one in fact released by the plane

preceding that of Luftwaffe Hauptmann Heinz Schumann – screams down towards Agate Street and for a few seconds every adult in the school building holds their breath and falls silent. It lands with an almighty impact and the entire building shakes violently, but it misses the school, destroying instead the row of buildings on the opposite side of the road. Pieces of masonry and shrapnel ping off the cobbles of Agate Street and several heavy pieces of debris crash into the school roof at the front of the building.

'That's it,' announces Harry. 'We're leaving.'

Harry Horowitz is a short, dapper man, always perfectly turned out in a three-piece suit, a watch chain across his slim torso. He works long hard hours in his little East End factory which produces high-quality fur coats, stoles and hats for the carriage trade. When he returns to the family home, invariably late and tired, he speaks little, preferring to sit in his armchair by the coal fire in waistcoat and shirt-sleeves and read the newspaper from start to finish in silence. Everyone knows that Millie, sharp-featured and sharp-tongued, wears the trousers in the Horowitz household. However, few realise that on the rare occasion when Harry put his foot down, Millie always complies without a word. She stands and lifts David to his feet, turning to her friend.

'You coming, Sal?'

Sarah looks up at her husband, who nods his assent.

The nine East End Jews grab their pathetic suitcases and shoulder their way through their terrified neighbours and friends, shouting their apologies over the drone of the aircraft and the explosions all around them, and emerge through the door into the playground.

15 seconds.

'Run!' shouts Harry, as he leads them across the playground.

10 seconds.

Charles hesitates, looking back down the corridor as the rest of his family hurry outside into the orange tinted, dust-filled, cacophony of the air raid. Further down the corridor, into the bowels of the school and just outside its combined gymnasium and hall, is another East End family. The Hoffmanns live only thirty yards from the Horowitz household and their house had, like that of the Horowitz family, been almost completely destroyed in the raid two nights before. The two families often queue together with the same ration books; eat the same sparse food; speak essentially the same language in their respective homes, and have much in common besides. But they never speak beyond an occasional nodded greeting. The Hoffmanns, although refugees from Hitler like many in the surrounding streets, are not Jewish, and Millie and Harry Horowitz's social circle does not include non-Jews. Their lives revolve around their home, their business and their synagogue. The Hoffmanns are, simply, "*goyim*" – of "The Nations" – and accordingly outside the circle. But the Hoffmanns have a daughter, a slim, fair and blue-eyed girl of fourteen, named Adalie. Unknown to either set of parents, while walking back from school every evening Charles Horowitz and Adalie Hoffmann have become friends. They have shared their thoughts on their teachers, their homework and on Hitler. And at Adalie's instigation, they have shared several sweet, chaste, kisses.

So Charles lingers for a second or two, trying to catch a last glimpse of Adalie, and as a result very nearly loses his life. The rest of his family have stumbled across the rubble-strewn playground and are disappearing through the rear gates of the school. Outside on the street the air glows, backlit by orange flames on all sides; the fires of hell.

The shriek of Luftwaffe Hauptmann Heinz Schumann's bomb fills the air as Charles, having given up his quest, races across the playground after the shadowy figure of his mother, the last of the party to disappear through the school gates ahead of him. Charles reaches the gates and takes two steps up Agate Street.

Impact.

The 1000 kg bomb scores a direct hit on the school. Charles is blown off his feet and finds himself sailing eight feet into the air, the explosive pressure drop making him feel as if his eyeballs are being sucked out of their sockets. He lands in an adjoining garden, destroying the rhododendron bush which breaks his fall, and suffers a bruised back and a cut to his scalp from a piece of flying masonry from the school wall. Everyone else in the family is unscathed. Although winded, Charles manages to roll back onto his feet in a single movement and continue running.

Harry Horowitz, soft-spoken East End tailor, has saved the lives of his family.

Later that day the government places a "D Notice" on

the event, preventing accurate reports of the number of casualties to avert a collapse of morale in London. Officially 73 people died. Locals know that of the 600 or so men, women and children in the building, over 450 were killed instantly, many more in the hours thereafter, and almost all of the survivors suffered injuries. The Hoffmanns were blown to unrecognisably small pieces.

Four days later the Horowitz family members unfold stiff limbs and climb down the steep steps of a bus in the centre of Carmarthen, and are introduced to the farmers who are to take them in. Four weeks of regular enforced chapel attendance later, Charles runs away and jumps on a Great Western milk train to London where he spends the next, and best, years of his life, running wild on the rubble-strewn streets and the one artery the Luftwaffe never managed to close: the River Thames. He never forgets the beautiful Adalie.

chapter 1
1964

Charles Holborne stands outside the basement cells of the Old Bailey, wearing his court robes but holding his wig by the tail in one hand and his case papers in the other. He hates the wig, its feeling of containment, its smell of horsehair and the sweat it generates in the febrile atmosphere of the courtroom, so he only ever dons it at the last moment. He's also wryly aware of the faint vein of vanity in his personality that contributes to his dislike of the object. The attractive curly black locks that, whatever he does, persist in falling over his forehead, would be hidden by the wig.

Holborne is 38 years of age. With wide dark eyes and an olive complexion, and built like a bull with massive chest and forearms and tree trunk legs, he looks more like an Italian truck driver than the eloquent and precise barrister he is.

As he waits, he examines the huge metal straps and studs of a centuries-old oak door, the original door of the Old Bailey, preserved from the 1907 re-building and now set as an ornament in the corridor wall. As he invariably does, Charles wonders how many men have passed that slab of oak on their way to a 30-year stretch, transportation to Australia or to the gallows.

Heavy footsteps approach from behind the iron door leading into the cells and Charles turns. The wicket clangs open and Charles's nose is assailed by the smell of fried bacon and toast. His stomach rumbles in response; breakfast two hours before consisted of a mug of cold tea, forgotten and then swallowed in two great gulps as he pulled on his raincoat.

'Yes?' asks the custody officer through the bars.

'Hello, Bob. I'm here to see Ninu Azzopardi.'

'Hello, Mr H, sir,' replies the custody officer in a cockney accent. 'The prison van's only just pulled up. Do you want to come in and wait?'

Charles checks his watch: just before 10. No time to go back to the Bar Mess for another – and hot – cup of tea.

'Any chance of a cuppa?' he asks.

'I'm sure we can manage something for one of our regulars,' replies the officer. The wicket clangs shut and Charles hears a large metal key from the ring attached to the officer's belt being inserted into the lock. The door swings inwards and Charles, whose broad shoulders almost fill the narrow space, shuffles sideways past the other man. The door closes behind him and the inner door made of steel bars is opened. Charles leads the way to the desk and signs in without being prompted.

'Take conference room one,' directs the officer, pointing with his pen to a small windowless conference room. Charles looks down pointedly at the half-eaten bacon sandwich sitting on a greasy sheet of paper next to the ledger which records legal visitors' entrances and departures. He looks up again hopefully into the face of his friend. Charles has known Bob and his family for almost twenty years, since long before either of them was on the right side of the law, and long before Charles changed his birth name from Horowitz to Holborne. The appellation "Mr H" had started as Bob's joke – he'd initially refused to use Charles's anglicised name – but it had stuck.

'Yeah, I expect there's a bit of bacon left, too,' he says, good-humouredly.

Charles smiles.

'You're a prince amongst men.'

'So you always say, Mr H,' says the custody officer, drily. 'It's one sugar and brown sauce, ain't it?'

'In the right places, yes. Try not to put the sauce in the tea.'

'Oh, you didn't like that then?'

'Not to my taste, I'm afraid.'

Charles walks into the converted cell and throws his papers and wig onto the tiny table which is, as always, screwed to the floor to prevent its use as a weapon. He sits on the wooden bench built into the wall and leans back against the white tiles, noting that they must have been scrubbed recently of their usual covering of colourful graffitied commentary on the Bailey's judges and their parentage. He detects one faint, part-scrubbed, comment on the wall opposite and leans forward to read it: *"Only 157,680,000 seconds to go, THEN I'M OUT!"* Charles smiles and tries unsuccessfully to calculate how many years the unfortunate mathematician had received.

He listens to the familiar echoes from the basement cells as keys jangle, men are moved and toilets are flushed. He loves the Old Bailey. He feels perfectly at home here, relaxed and at the top of his game and, unlike any other barrister working in the building, he knows almost everyone by their first name. Over the years, he has made it his business to know the prison escorts, the ushers and the court clerks, to remember their names and the names of their loved ones and, if volunteered, details of their lives. Charles knows that these are the people, more than the judges and lawyers, on whom the Lord Chancellor relies to make the administration of justice run smoothly. He also knows that the usual display of barristerial arrogance or, worse still, failure even to notice the existence of these essential functionaries, is a guarantee of everyday friction and unnecessary difficulty. He long ago learned that asking after a court clerk's sick mother can smooth the odd listing difficulty, as when chambers' clerks are over-optimistic about a guvnor's ability to be in two courts at the same time; and a few minutes of banter with a court usher is a small price to pay to get an urgently-required Court of Appeal precedent run down from the library to Court No 2 at short notice. Charles's interest isn't manufactured. He likes these people; he feels at home with them – more than he does with most of his professional colleagues. He grew up on the same streets of the East End, shared the same privations during the War and, despite his present profession, still speaks their language. Not so long ago he used the same East End boozers, went to the same football matches at West Ham and queued to swap his ration coupons for the same scarce vegetables, fish and bread. He knows only too well what it is to be poor.

Louder clanging metal and voices can now be heard from the far end of the corridor, and Charles stands to greet his client. He has known and represented Maltese-born Ninu Azzopardi for over a decade. Charles was in pupillage when he received his first brief to defend the good-natured little man, on that occasion for stealing a lorry from the quayside at Hasties Wharf, a lorry Ninu had supposed was full of Canadian timber but which was in fact, on closer examination, completely empty. It had been a plea and Ninu received a sentence of two months' imprisonment. Several further briefs featuring Ninu arrived on Charles's desk over the years as Ninu and Charles learned their respective trades, with contrasting degrees of success. Charles developed a growing reputation as one of the brightest junior criminal barristers of the post-War generation, until a charge of murder against him caused a temporary, but almost fatal, setback in his career. On the other hand, while Ninu's crimes grew bolder and more ambitious, sadly, his ability to complete them without detection didn't improve. He nonetheless remained stubbornly optimistic. Once caught, in Charles's hands his acquittal rate was approximately 50:50 but he was seemingly undeterred, either by the 50% in which Charles was unsuccessful or by the increasingly severe sentences he received. More than once Charles suggested that the little man should try another line of work, but Ninu's round face would crease into an enormous smile and he'd shrug. 'I no good at anything else, boss,' he'd say.

'You're not much cop at this either, Ninu,' Charles would answer, but to no avail.

Charles's present instructions, which had arrived on his desk from a well-known firm of solicitors two days before, are slightly different to Ninu's usual lorry thefts and warehouse burglaries. Ninu had been lifted by the Dirty Squad – the Obscene Publications Squad – while collecting envelopes stuffed full of money from bookshops in Soho. Charles's instructions are that Ninu will plead guilty to three specimen charges of conspiracy to extort, on the basis that he was collecting money destined for other unnamed officers in the same squad, but otherwise Charles's papers are strangely reticent about the circumstances of both the offence and Ninu's arrest. Charles is looking forward to obtaining further instructions from his client. Hence the pre-hearing conference in the cells.

Bob enters bearing a chipped plate on which rests a bacon sandwich and a mug of steaming tea. He places them both on the table. To Charles's surprise he pushes the door almost closed with his foot and turns to Charles.

'Got a bit of a problem with your client, Charles, I'm afraid,' he says, keeping his voice low.

Charles frowns. 'What's that?'

The custody officer makes a twirling movement with his forefinger against the side of his temple. 'Gone a bit funny.

Says he's going to kill himself. Prison guard says he was weeping all the way from Pentonville. I've asked if there's a police surgeon in the building.'

'Ninu Azzopardi?' asks Charles, in disbelief. 'I don't believe it. He's a simple soul, big smile, always cheerful.'

Bob shrugs. 'What can I tell you? They're bringing him along now. We'll have to leave the cuffs on.'

As if on cue the door opens and a little olive-skinned man in his early forties enters wearing handcuffs, flanked by two prison guards. He is manoeuvred to the chair at the table. One of the prison guards places a hand firmly on his shoulder and forces the man to sit down. He complies without making eye contact with anyone in the room, his manacled hands in his lap and his shoulders slumped. Charles notices that one hand is heavily bandaged and blood is seeping through the dressing.

'Alright?' asks the prison escort.

Bob nods. 'I think we can cope from here,' he says, and the two prison escorts shuffle out.

'Hello Ninu,' says Charles, offering his hand. The Maltese doesn't look up. Charles looks over to Bob. 'Alright if I have a few moments with him?' he asks.

'Yes, but leave the door open. I'll let the court clerk know there may be a delay. We won't take him up till he's been assessed.'

'I doubt there's a surgeon available,' comments Charles. 'And I can't let him enter a plea if there's doubt about fitness to plead.'

Bob shrugs. 'We could probably get the case put back to

this afternoon, but after that he'll be sent back to Pentonville to be produced after an assessment.'

The custody officer slips out of the room, leaving the door slightly ajar. Charles regards his client, looking for eye contact, but Ninu continues to hang his head. Charles notes that his eyes flick briefly to the bacon sandwich before settling again on his lap.

'Here,' says Charles, reaching over and trying to tear the sandwich in half. The bacon inside makes the division impossible, so Charles takes a single bite out of it, puts the rest back on the plate, and pushes the plate towards his client. 'I bet you've not eaten yet.'

As if in confirmation the Maltese's stomach grumbles and Charles sees a trace of the smile that usually illuminates the guileless face.

'Go on, take it,' encourages Charles, swallowing, and Ninu reaches up with his manacled hands and grabs the sandwich, taking a large bite. 'Shall I get some tea?' asks Charles. Ninu nods, mouth full.

Charles stands and goes to the door. The custody desk is deserted. Charles returns to his client.

'Bob's not there. I'll ask in a minute. You can have mine,' he says, pointing to the untouched mug. 'Now, Ninu, what's going on?'

Ninu is licking his fingers, the sandwich quickly consumed. He looks up slowly into Charles's face. 'I'm in big trouble, boss,' he says, his mouth still full of bread and bacon.

'Tell me.'

Ninu reaches for the mug and takes a sip of steaming tea to clear his palate. 'My Angelina's not been well … *defijenza ta hadid* … how you say, iron missing from blood, you know, tired all the time? She begs me not to do another job. So I ask around and the Messina brothers said they have some work up West, just running errands, collecting stuff from their dirty bookshops, you know?'

Charles shakes his head. 'They're trouble, those boys. I've had dealings with them.' The Messina brothers, also from Malta originally, were heavily involved in prostitution and pornography in Soho. They'd carved out their territory with violence – firebombs and knives – and had a reputation for brutality matched only by the Richardson brothers.

Ninu shrugs. 'They promise me, no trouble, and it kept me in London so I could look after Angelina. It was fine for a few weeks, just moving stock, driving a van to and from Lowestoft, that sort of thing. Then a man comes into the shop on Frith Street. He says he's there to collect an envelope. I hand it over to him. That goes on for a few days. Then the brothers give me a handful of envelopes to deliver …'

'To coppers?'

Ninu nods again. 'I think. But it's a set-up, or something goes wrong. I'm waiting for one lot to turn up and then others – other coppers – arrive and arrest me. They say they're Dirty Squad too. So I don't know if I'm in the middle of two lots, you know, fighting over their share, or the second lot's clean and onto the first lot.'

'Clean?' snorts Charles with derision. 'There's not an

honest bobby amongst them.' He nods to the other man's damaged hand. 'Did they do that?'

Ninu shakes his head. 'No. The Messina brothers. One held me down and the other put a bayonet through it. But it not get better.'

'Why did they do it?'

'They don't believe me. They think I was working with some of the Dirty Squad on the side, and I got a cut. They want all the money back – a grand – and if I don't get it they kill me. And hurt my Angelina.'

Charles sits back in his seat to consider this information. It wouldn't have surprised him if Ninu had indeed received a backhander for being at the right place at the right time, but as he frames a delicate question to ascertain if the Messina brothers' suspicions are accurate, Ninu's little face creases in the middle and tears well in his eyes. Charles reaches into his jacket pocket and comes up with a clean tissue – standard equipment when visiting remand prisoners – and he pushes it across the table. He changes tack.

'I need to ask you an important question before we go any further, Ninu. You do understand, don't you, that by pleading guilty you'd be accepting that you knew what was in the envelopes, *and* who they were going to?' asks Charles.

Ninu nods, picks up the tissue and blows his nose loudly. 'Sure,' he snuffles. 'I'd be putting the Dirty Squad in the frame.'

'Which would make Soho a rather dangerous place for you.'

'Is already dangerous for me.'

Charles nods and sits back again. He wouldn't want to be caught between The Dirty Squad and the Messina brothers either.

'Today's been listed for plea. Are you ready to enter a plea today?'

Ninu looks up and shakes his head vigorously. 'No, boss! I need more time.'

Accused men often delay entering a plea. The prison regime is much more comfortable on remand – they can wear their own clothes, have more visits, be supplied by family with food and smokes – but the price of delay is a longer sentence. The sooner the accused pleads guilty, the greater credit he gets. Charles suspects why Azzopardi wants to delay arraignment, and it's nothing to do with home cooking, but he's not sure what's up the Maltese's sleeve. Charles studies the little man's face intently, and plays a hunch.

'When did Angelina last visit?'

'Two, three weeks, maybe.'

'Why so long?' Charles leans forward, his elbows on the table, and keeps his voice low. 'You've sent her away, yes?' There's no response. 'Ninu, you can trust me. Nothing you tell me goes outside this room, you know that.'

'She has family in Sicily. They'll never find her there.'

Charles leans back again on the bench, satisfied he understands. 'Got it; you need to buy time.'

'When I plead, they deport me, yes?' Azzopardi had barely escaped deportation the last time Charles represented him.

Charles nods. 'If you still have no papers –' and Ninu shrugs, his hands spread wide in eloquent gesture, '– then very likely. But of course you can't enter a plea ...' begins Charles.

'... if I crazy man,' finished Ninu. 'I see psychiatrist first, yes?'

'Yes, I get it. That can take days, even a week or two. But I can't lie to the court, Ninu, you know that. If you're just faking to get an adjournment ...'

'I'm not faking Mr Holborne!' and his face creases again and tears start to run down his cheeks and land with little splashes on the wooden table. If it's an act, it's a good one, thinks Charles; the man looks genuinely distressed. I suppose being caught between two squabbling groups of Dirty Squad police and a gang of Maltese pornographers who've already run your hand through with a bayonet would tend to cause depression, concedes Charles to himself. And I'm no psychiatrist. So, let's leave it to the experts.

'OK,' concludes Charles, 'if those are your instructions. It's not my job to make psychiatric assessments. And I'd be amazed if they can find a police surgeon for a mental state examination this morning.'

And for the first time since he entered the room Ninu Azzopardi's face brightens up. 'That's fine with me, boss.'

•

An hour later the hearing has been adjourned and Ninu, humming quietly to himself, is back in the Old Bailey cells awaiting transport back to Pentonville where he will eventually be psychiatrically assessed. Charles returns to the robing room to change into his day wear. He pushes open the doors and the familiar smell of leather and stale coffee greets him. Charles makes his way across the newly-laid thick carpet, past the bookcases laden with frayed leather-bound books and the comfy armchairs to an enormous polished table in the centre of the room. It is covered with glossy black oval wigs tins, each bearing the name in gold lettering of the barrister whose wig it houses. They resemble a shoal of black fish glinting in the sunshine filtering through the floor-length net curtains.

It's still before noon and the place is deserted; all the other barristers in the building are engaged on their cases. The two robing room attendants sit in their cubbyhole drinking tea and reading newspapers. From the small transistor radio sitting on the table between them Charles can hear Roy Orbison telling his faithless love that *It's Over*.

Charles takes off his wig and places it delicately in his wig tin. Unlike all the others around his, inside the lid of Charles's tin is the name of the wig's manufacturer, "Ravenscroft". Mr Ravenscroft was a well-known wigmaker who in the 19th century joined forces with a Mr Ede, at that time the proprietor of the oldest tailoring business in London, founded in 1689. The partnership thus became "Ede and Ravenscroft", but the sole name "Ravenscroft" inside Charles's tin demonstrates that his wig must date from 1850 at the latest. At the time of his call to the Bar, Charles couldn't raise the money to buy a new wig. He was forced to acquire a dust-covered, sweat-stained second-hand wig through unofficial channels, in this case, a long-retired High Court porter who Charles had befriended on the terraces at Upton Park. It cost almost as much to have it professionally cleaned as it would have cost to buy a new one. Before Charles had his name printed in gold lettering on the outside of the tin, it bore the name "Drake, Esq." the name of a barrister who, later in his career, became a notorious hanging judge. While Charles is aware that his Jewish ancestry goes back in unbroken generations for five thousand years, he finds great difficulty identifying with it; on the other hand, there is something about the thread of English history represented by this wig and its tin which appeals to him much more, and still makes him fiercely proud to be a member of the Bar. He carries that pride to this day, notwithstanding the anti-Semitism and class prejudice displayed to him by some members of his honourable profession since he was "called" by the Middle Temple in 1949.

Charles replaces his wing collar with a clean newly-starched Windsor and tries to force the collar stud through the stud holes. It's always difficult with a freshly laundered collar as the launderers' starch tends to close up the holes, requiring the stud to be pushed forcibly through a sealed buttonhole. As he pushes, the brass neck of the stud snaps off the mother of pearl stud and falls somewhere inside his shirt.

'Shit!' curses Charles quietly. He is focused on fishing inside the shirt and so doesn't notice as the robing room door opens silently. A young man steps into the room. He's young and very pretty, with a wide voluptuous mouth and thick straight hair swept up from his forehead held in place with a large dollop of glistening Brylcreem. He wears a grey suit and well-polished winklepicker shoes. Had Charles noticed the young man he might initially have identified him as a junior clerk sent to collect his guvnor's papers from the robing room at the end of a case, but closer examination would have made him doubt that first impression. The suit is much too expensive for a junior clerk and the man seems unfamiliar with the room, as he stands just inside the door scanning the rows of lockers and the dressing tables with darting pale blue eyes, as if to get his bearings. Had Charles looked very carefully, he might also have noticed that the young man has something in his hand, half-tucked into his cuff, something that glistens like polished silver.

The man's casing of the room complete, his eyes land on Charles and he moves immediately. In three silent steps, he halves the distance between the oak swing doors and Charles's back. As he walks he allows the silver object to drop completely into his right palm and, with a precise click, the blade of a flick knife springs into place.

Concluding that the stud has fallen out of his shirt and is somewhere on the floor, Charles bends down to look under the table. He's still wearing his gown, and it's suddenly pulled up over his upper body and he finds himself enveloped in black material.

'Hey!' he shouts, imagining for a moment that one of his more idiotic colleagues is horsing around. He stands up blindly, trying to fight his way out of the cloth that restricts his upper body, but his arms are being pulled above his head. Less than a second later he hears voices and the tension on the gown is suddenly released. It takes him a few seconds to get his head free. Three barristers have entered the double doors, laughing loudly and chatting. Charles whirls around: there's no one else in sight.

'What's the matter, Holborne?' asks one of the barristers, looking at Charles's dishevelled gown and white face. 'Can't find a way out of your gown?'

The others laugh and Charles flushes.

'Someone just …' he starts. 'Did you see anyone leaving as you came in?'

'Yes, a young chap pushed past us,' replies one of the three. 'A clerk, I think.'

Charles barges past them and throws open the doors. One of the young barristers elbows another and they all smirk. The corridor outside is deserted. Charles returns to the robing room, slightly embarrassed, his thudding heart slowly subsiding into a normal rhythm. Could it have been a practical joke? Of course it could, he reasons; probably was. But he has had the sensation of being watched over the past few days and, once, he could have sworn he was being followed. A nagging doubt remains, buzzing away in the corners of his mind like a persistent fly trapped behind a window. He tries to swat it away and starts to pack his bag, but it's still there. And it's linked to a name: Ronnie Kray.

chapter 2

Charles shoulders his robes bag and pushes open the doors of the Old Bailey, stepping down the marble steps into bright sunshine. He squints and scans the street, but apart from two suited young men disappearing through the doors of the pub opposite, it is deserted. Charles checks his watch: still only 12:20, and forty minutes until he is to meet his brother for lunch. This will be their third such meeting since Charles re-established tentative and awkward contact with his family. David is an accountant and, since his recent promotion, finds himself in the firm's Ludgate Circus office twice a week. Encouraged by the ease and convenience of a quick lunch which doesn't have to be mentioned to their mother, for whom Charles's name still provokes persistent bile, David and he have begun to rebuild the close relationship they enjoyed as boys, until Charles's last year at Cambridge; until he committed the unforgivable sin of Anglicising his name and "marrying out" and was as a consequence wiped – apparently forever – from the Horowitz family history. When Millie and Harry Horowitz learned of their eldest son's betrayal they sat *shiva* – tore their clothes, covered every mirror in the house, and recited prayers for the dead for five days.

And then they acted as if Charles was dead.

The venue for today's meeting is special: David is to be Charles's guest at Middle Temple Hall. There, David will be able to eat lunch – as kosher as possible for the observant brother – under the same double hammer beam roof that saw the first ever performance of *Twelfth Night* in 1602. He may even be able to take his coffee from "the cupboard" a table made from the hatch of Sir Francis Drake's Golden Hind. As they eat on long trestle tables surrounded by judges, benchers and barristers, Charles will be able to point out the stained glass windows and the heraldic shields of former members of the inn, including Sir Walter Raleigh. Charles remains very proud of his membership of the Inn, an institution that symbolised to him the very best of the British establishment – a place where he expected merit, industry and integrity to be rewarded, regardless of race, creed or background. His "call night" had been one of the proudest moments of his life, more so even than when decorated with the DFC for valour as a Spitfire pilot. Although he would never have expressed the thought or even admitted it to himself, he had expected being a barrister to qualify him as an English gentleman; he'd no longer be an outsider; and he'd be worthy of marriage to Henrietta, the daughter of a viscount.

He was, of course, entirely wrong; it changed nothing. Indeed, as he was to learn over the next few years, in many ways it made things worse. On his call night, only Henrietta was there; all the other pupils were supported by parents, siblings and friends. That his parents and brother had not been present still saddens Charles. So, although the shine of his "honourable profession" had tarnished somewhat over the intervening years, Charles is now finally able to offer David a glimpse of that to which he had aspired. His younger brother had been out of his life until recently. Charles is unaware that David, still faintly susceptible to the childhood idolisation of an older brother – especially one who can handle himself in the boxing ring – has followed Charles's career surreptitiously ever since Charles's name was banned in the Horowitz household.

Charles walks swiftly across Ludgate Circus and up the slight incline of Fleet Street towards the Temple, scanning the street and alert to sudden movement in his peripheral vision. But the day is warm and the people on the street so apparently innocuous that his pace gradually slows and he begins to think that the odd event in the robing room was, after all, just a prank by a chambers colleague. He'll probably return to chambers after lunch to find the clerks grinning at him as he is teased by a couple of the junior barristers.

Charles passes the entrance to the Old Bell Tavern, which claims to be one of the oldest pubs in London, allegedly built by Sir Christopher Wren to house the builders reconstructing St Bride's Church after the Great Fire, and turns left into Tudor Street. He finds himself facing the back of a brewer's dray and the pavement blocked by a pile of barrels. He skirts the sweating and cursing drayman and continues along the cobbles towards the entrance to the Inn. The wind picks up as he walks parallel to the River

Thames and overhead, between the buildings, a handful of seagulls wheel and screech.

As Charles enters the Inner Temple he looks, as always, to his left along Kings Bench Walk to assess the river. The wind is really picking up now, and the white-flecked waves of the incoming tide race one another westwards. Charles slows to watch a group of barges, three tied abreast with one behind, inching downstream past Temple Gardens against the elements. At that moment the tug captain looks to his right, as if staring straight at Charles, and Charles is tempted to raise his hand in greeting. Instead he smiles to himself, turns, and walks on past Crown Office Row towards Middle Temple Hall. He greets the uniformed official guarding the door and descends the stairs to the cloakroom, where he hangs up his robes and deposits his briefcase. He washes his hands in the adjoining lavatory, nodding at one or two barristers of his acquaintance, and then returns upstairs to sit by the entrance and wait for David.

David arrives exactly on time at one o'clock. Charles signs him in and they go into Hall for luncheon, finding two spaces facing each other across the trestle table towards the far end of Hall. Over the next ten minutes there is a mass influx of barristers. The Hall throngs with them, many still in court robes. They compare cross-examination notes, exchange chambers gossip and order quick lunches before returning to their trials.

The uniformed waitress approaches their bench. David chooses a salad and a glass of water and, so as not to offend his brother, Charles follows suit, with only a minor pang at having to decline what looks, from the meal served to his neighbours, to be excellent rare roast beef and Yorkshire pudding with lashings of gravy, roast potatoes and pigs in blankets.

While they wait for the meal to be served, Charles regards his younger brother across the table as David takes in his surroundings. David is taller, slimmer and blonder than Charles, and unlike Charles does not look Jewish or even Mediterranean in appearance. Superficially he would fit in perfectly with some of Charles's more thoroughbred English public school colleagues but, as an Orthodox Jew, he wears a head covering at all times, and having left his hat in the cloakroom with Charles's robes the black skullcap covering the fair hair at the back of his head is very obvious, and draws frequent glances from barristers and judges passing behind them. He seems oblivious to the scrutiny, but Charles feels an uncomfortable tension in his chest as he is torn between fierce protectiveness and a contrasting envy of his younger brother. Unlike Charles, David has never been uncomfortable in his own skin. David is Jewish, and proud of it. His life revolves around his new bride, Sonia, his Jewish home, his synagogue where he prays standing next to their father, and the firm of consultants where he is employed. Almost half the partners are Jewish and several are members of the same synagogue as David himself. He has never wanted anything more and finds it difficult to understand Charles's sense of dislocation.

Charles points out various features of the institution of which he is so proud, but has the impression that only half of David's attention is on his explanations. Sensing that something is wrong, Charles falls silent and waits for David to raise it. However, by the time they have finished coffee David has said nothing significant and Charles is impatient and slightly disappointed that the lunch hasn't been as successful as he had hoped.

'*Nu?*' he asks. 'What's the matter?'

'Nothing.'

'You seem a bit preoccupied, Davie. Is it Mum and Dad?'

David shakes his head. 'No, they're fine – or at least as fine as normal.'

'So …?'

David chews his lip for a moment and then looks up into Charles's dark, almost black eyes. 'I'm not sure how to tackle this, Charlie. I don't want to offend you.'

'Davie, you couldn't offend me,' reassures Charles with a smile. 'What's up?'

David takes a deep breath. 'Well … I'm worried about you.'

'Why?' asks Charles with some surprise. 'I'm fine. The press are finally off my back, work's beginning to build up again, I've got a new girlfriend … What could be wrong?'

'Well, let's start with the girlfriend. Her name's Sally, right?'

'Yes.'

'And you two have been seeing one another, what, six months?'

'About that.'

'And before that it was Rachel.'

'And your point is …?' asks Charles, smiling. He expects to be chided by his rather conservative, religious, younger brother about his modern lifestyle. He suspects that both David and Sonia were virgins on the night of their wedding, and he knows that his parents – and probably David – would disapprove of sex before marriage.

'So, two girlfriends in the space of a year since Henrietta's death.'

'Ah,' says Charles with a smile, satisfied that he now understands. 'You're fretting over my promiscuity. It's 1964, Davie. Things are changing – at least outside the Jewish community they are.'

David pauses for a long moment before answering and, when he does, he fiddles with his empty glass nervously, looking down at the old polished table.

'It's not that at all; that's your business. You were married to Henrietta for thirteen years, Charlie. Yes – ' and he holds his hand up to forestall Charles's intervention ' – I know things weren't good when she died.'

'Exactly. That's why the police thought I had a motive for killing her.'

'But you loved her, didn't you?'

David looks up and his penetrating light blue eyes lock onto Charles's.

'Yes, of course I did.'

'You wouldn't be able to tell.'

'What the hell do you mean by that?' demands Charles, his voice rising slightly.

'I'm sorry, that probably sounded a bit brutal. What I mean is: I've seen no suggestion that you've mourned her.'

Charles lowers his voice. 'You may have forgotten, but I was on the run from the police at the time,' he whispers hoarsely.

'I know that. And then you got involved in that Robeson trial, which is where you met Sally.'

'No, that's not right. I'd known Sally for years before then. But it was during the trial that we started ... seeing one another.'

'I'm not criticising your morality, Charlie. It's nothing like that. I'm just worried for you. I don't think you've dealt with your feelings about Henrietta. You seem so ... *normal*. And that's not normal. The woman you loved was murdered. You were charged. Most people would be devastated by that, emotionally wrecked. But you've just gone about rebuilding your career, forming a new relationship – two relationships in fact – and I'm just worried that somewhere down the line this is all going to hit you pretty hard.'

'What are you, my rabbi? It's not my fault I've had two relationships,' remonstrates Charles, defending himself. 'Rachel Golding left me for some other bloke in New York!'

David puts his hand gently over his brother's forearm. 'I know, I know. But that's not the point. You fell into another relationship with Rachel within days of Henrietta's death— '

'That was just circumstance! She was helping me, while the police were looking for me! She was all I had, remember?'

Charles immediately regrets the aggression in his voice, but the intensity of resentment he still harbours at having been cast out by his family has taken him by surprise; he thought he'd long since come to terms with it. He realises from David's sideways glance that they've been overheard by the barristers next to them. Charles rounds on them and they look away hurriedly, one of them blushing.

'Let's get out of here,' mutters Charles and he climbs off the bench. David waits in the entrance while Charles pays the bill and collects his robes and David's hat and raincoat. They walk together towards a bench on Fountain Court. The earlier sunshine has been replaced by dark clouds scudding across the sky and it looks as if it will rain soon.

'I know you mean well, Davie, but I think you're worrying about nothing. Henrietta and I had been drifting apart for years. Yes, I still loved her, but I couldn't make her happy and I knew we'd reached the end. So I'm not going to feel the same as if we were still in a loving relationship.'

'Have you asked yourself why you didn't make her happy? You must have loved one another so much at the start. Look what you both gave up to be together.'

'Of course I've asked myself!' says Charles, his temper rising. He controls himself with an effort and lowers his voice again. 'Look, I've got a lot to do, and frankly I've no time for this.'

As he answers, Charles wonders why he doesn't mention to his brother that he still hears Henrietta's voice. Not just in his imagination; her voice suddenly comes out of thin air right next to him. Being the logical and unemotional man he is, after the second or third occasion Charles had visited a library, found his way to the Psychiatry section, and looked up "Hearing Voices after Bereavement". He was reassured to find that it was quite common. He had closed the books, satisfied, and expected it all to stop in due course. It hadn't; now, months later, when his life seems otherwise to have reached a new "normal", Henrietta's voice still intrudes, usually with some acerbic comment on Charles's behaviour. Even so, Charles refuses to believe he's having auditory hallucinations; that would mean he's ill and needs help and, as he tells himself, psychiatric illness is the last thing on his mind. He likes the joke; it's just a pity he can't share it with anyone. Furthermore, there is another reason why he doesn't want to mention Henrietta's running commentary on his life: he likes it and doesn't want it to stop, and David would assuredly recommend medical intervention designed to stop it.

'Please don't be cross with me, Charlie,' says David softly. 'I love you, and I'm only concerned for your well-being. But will you think about what I've said? I know that circumstances brought you and Rachel together but almost as soon as she's gone, different circumstances bring you and Sally together. There's been no gap. No time for you to grieve over Henrietta. No time for mature reflection. It's as if you're still sprinting for some finishing line.'

'I don't know what you mean.'

'Well, I've probably expressed it badly. But please think about it.'

Charles sighs and shakes his head. Then he shrugs. 'Okay. I'll think about it.'

'Good. And thank you for lunch. I've never eaten in such splendid surroundings.'

Charles offers his hand to David, but instead of grasping it David wraps his arms around his brother and pulls him into a warm embrace. 'You know where I am, if you need me,' he says quietly into Charles's ear. He steps back. 'Same time next week?' he asks.

'Sure – assuming I'm in court in central London. I'll come to your office canteen next time. They do kosher food, don't they?' asks Charles, trying to restore some normality to the conversation. 'At least I'll know you'll be able to have something more than salad and a glass of water.'

They part on the steps leading down from Fountain Court, David walking back to his office via the Embankment and Charles returning to Chambers. Contrary to his promise, he doesn't actually think about his conversation with David, pushing it to the back of his mind. Now there are two flies buzzing about there, both contributing to his irritability.

chapter 3

Charles side-steps a black cab pulling up outside Middle Temple Hall, crosses the cobbles of Middle Temple Lane, and ducks under the arch into Pump Court. The courtyard is small and bounded by tall 17th-century buildings and, for that reason, is sometimes rather gloomy, but the sun is at its zenith and today the courtyard is warm and beautiful, with golden shafts of sunlight illuminating the small manicured garden at its centre. A workman in Middle Temple overalls kneels on the grass with a trowel in his hand as he weeds the borders, and two young women sit on a wooden bench in the sunshine eating sandwiches, their heads together, giggling and whispering furiously. The click–clack of court shoes on the flagstones – Pump Court is used as a short cut from Middle Temple Lane into Inner Temple – and birdsong are the only sounds, and it is difficult to believe that 20th-century Fleet Street, with its lorries and buses thundering past, is no more than one hundred yards to the north.

Charles emerges into Church Court and crosses the courtyard, passing Temple Church on his left. A gaggle of robed barristers who have just finished luncheon descend the steps from Inner Temple Hall and turn to their left, walking swiftly towards Fleet Street and the

High Court to resume their cases. They resemble a murder of crows with their black robes flapping behind them. One notices Charles, and waves as he jogs after his companions.

Charles walks under the tall plane trees, their leaves fluttering in the light breeze off the Thames, and looks to his right across Inner Temple Gardens to the river. As he often does, he silently thanks the fates for allowing him to work in such beautiful surroundings. He knows that few, especially those with his start in life, are fortunate enough to have an occupation that fires them with enthusiasm every morning and allows them to work in surroundings of such historic tranquillity right in the centre of one of the world's great cities.

Charles climbs the worn stone steps of his chambers and pushes open the heavy outer door. The door is almost three inches thick and Charles has often wondered how much of that is actually timber and how much made up of the layer upon layer of paint applied over the last three hundred years. He passes beneath the arched doorway ascribed to Sir Christopher Wren and runs, two at a time, up the slightly irregular wooden steps to the first floor. Shafts of early afternoon sunshine slant through the sash windows behind him, picking out motes of dust on the ancient staircase.

Charles pushes open the door of the clerks' room on the first-floor landing. It is reasonably quiet at this time of day, with most of the barristers in court and the telephones relatively silent. Barbara, Chambers' senior clerk, a fierce redheaded woman in her early 40s, sits at the largest desk in the corner of the room from which she can survey the whole of her domain. She appears to be working on Chambers' accounts, as her desk and the wooden floorboards around her are hidden beneath piles of ledgers and unpaid fee notes.

At smaller desks sit the junior clerks, Jeremy and Jennie, known by the barristers compendiously as "JJ". Jeremy is a bright eyed and slightly over-enthusiastic young man in his early 20s who in Barbara's opinion will make a fine clerk eventually if he learns to calm down and think before opening his mouth. Jennie, in contrast, is thoughtful, methodical, and painfully shy. Although she has been in Chambers longer than Jeremy – it is almost two years since, at age 16, she was appointed to the post room – she still cannot look senior members of Chambers in the eye without blushing. She is standing by the barristers' pigeonholes explaining to another young person their purpose, and pointing out the name of each barrister above each opening. As Charles approaches his pigeonhole to see if any new briefs – and more importantly, new cheques – have been delivered since he last looked, Jennie turns around.

'Oh, hello Mr Holborne, sir. I was just showing Clive how the pigeonholes work,' she says, just about making eye contact.

The young man spins round. He's in his late teens and very fashionably dressed, with drainpipe trousers, a dark tweed Hepworth jacket and a narrow tie. He has an open, slightly spotty face, and reddish-brown hair. He sticks out his hand confidently.

'Allo Mr 'Olborne, sir,' he says in a strong cockney accent.

Charles smiles. Barristers and clerks do not usually shake hands, but Charles disdains such hierarchical protocols and he likes the young man's confidence. He places the accent as Plaistow, maybe Poplar, and it is one with which he is very familiar. He accepts the young man's offered hand, and grips it firmly.

'Charlie 'Olborne, at your service,' he says with a mock bow and reverting to the cockney of his youth. Charles's voice is not what the young man has expected and Charles sees doubt and confusion cross his face. 'No, don't worry, Clive,' reassures Charles in his normal voice. 'Just teasing. I used to talk exactly like you, but these buggers eventually beat it out of me.'

'Language please, sir,' calls Barbara from across the room, without looking up.

Clerks are not supposed to have favourites in Chambers. It causes the competitiveness between the barristers fighting for briefs to erupt into outright hostility and has been the cause of many a set of chambers splitting up. But if Barbara has a favourite, it is Charles Holborne. He's easy to deal with, has none of the airs and graces of some of his colleagues, and he's a good team player. If Barbara is left at five thirty in the evening with a difficult plea in Leeds for a pain-in-the-backside solicitor, she knows that she can always ask Mr Holborne to take the case. He's a safe pair of hands, good at his job and pleasant both to the professional and lay clients. She also likes an underdog, and if there was ever a barrister who was an underdog, it was her guvnor, Charles Holborne.

The door behind Charles opens and another barrister comes into the room. He is in his fifties, short and spherical in shape, the buttons of his waistcoat straining to contain a protuberant potbelly. He wears a black jacket and striped trousers with a razor-sharp crease in them and always smells of expensive cologne which, in Charles's opinion, is applied too liberally.

He interrupts the conversation and calls directly across to Barbara.

'Well?'

'I did say I would call if there was anything, Mr Knight.'

'So, nothing then?'

'I'm sorry sir, but no.'

The man takes a couple of steps towards Barbara's desk and points at her in a faintly accusatorial fashion. He looks as if he is about to say something but thinks better of it. He spins on his heel and walks back to the door with that light dancing tread so often incongruously associated with heavy men. He's about to disappear through the doorway when Barbara calls after him.

'I know that Mr Hamilton-Rudd was looking for someone to devil those Admiralty papers for him,' she suggests. 'If you're at a loose end?'

'I'm not devilling for him. He's ten years my junior!'

Charles smiles at his colleague in what he hopes is a sympathetic way – he knows only too well what it's like to be out of favour with solicitors – but it produces precisely the opposite reaction to the one he expected.

'I don't know what on earth you're smirking about!' says Knight in a low voice, but one heard by everyone in the room. 'You … you …' but it appears that an epithet fails him and he gives up, slamming the door behind him.

There's an uncomfortable silence in the clerks' room, broken eventually by Clive's hesitant question: 'Devilling?'

Charles answers. 'Yes. It means working on papers for another barrister. The work will go out in the other barrister's name after he or she's checked it, and that barrister will be paid for it as normal, but they will pay the devil an hourly rate for their work. It's something we all do at the beginning of our careers, and sometimes later when things are quiet. I always take it if I can; you often learn something new in a field of law you don't normally have time to study. Anyway …' Charles cranes his neck forward to see if there is anything in his pigeonhole and is disappointed to find it empty, 'after that interesting interlude, I shall leave you in peace. I have an Advice to draft.'

Charles winks at Jennie, making her blush – which was his purpose – and climbs the stairs to his room on the second floor of the building.

chapter 4

It's ten in the morning and the Regal Billiard Hall, Eric Street, in the East End of London is in almost complete darkness and appears deserted. None of the lights over the fourteen billiard tables is illuminated and the bar area is dark, the little light that penetrates through the dirt-ingrained windows just picking out the optics and stacked glasses. The hall reeks of stale cigarette smoke and beer. It is possible to detect, faintly, the sounds of traffic outside on the Mile End Road.

The one point of illumination in the room comes from a small desk lamp with an underpowered bulb in it resting on a small coffee table. In a comfortable but tattered armchair next to the table sits a fleshy man in his early thirties wearing heavy black-rimmed spectacles. He sports a clean freshly starched white shirt tucked into dark blue trousers held up by blue braces – he calls them "suspenders", in homage to the American film gangsters he emulates – and a red silk tie, held in place by a heavy gold tiepin which matches his cufflinks.

Through his dark-rimmed glasses, the man's heavy-lidded eyes appear almost completely closed as he focuses intently on what's in his hands: in the left, the recoil spring tube of an Erma-Werke Luger semi-automatic pistol; in the right, an oily cloth which he has used to clean every part of the pistol. The recoil spring tube is the last component to be cleaned; the other dismantled parts of the pistol lie neatly spaced on a lint-free cloth on the coffee table awaiting reassembly, glinting dully in the yellow light of the desk lamp.

By the side of the chair lies a large Alsatian dog, asleep with its head on its paws.

There is no noise that a human might have detected but the dog's ears suddenly twitch and it lifts its head, looking round towards the swing doors at the back of the hall. A few seconds later there is a thump as something heavy and metallic is deposited outside the doors. The man's hands become still and he lifts his head.

'Terry?' he calls.

There's a pause and then one of the swing doors opens. The Old Bailey robing room interloper puts his head around the door. 'Morning Ronnie. I'm just giving Stan a hand with the barrels.'

The man in the armchair studies the young man from under heavy lids, noting the boyish features, the long dark lashes, the full lips and the sheen of sweat on the slightly flushed cheeks. His fisheyes travel dispassionately down the boy's body.

'Well, stop that and come over here,' he orders quietly.

'Sure.'

The door opens fully and the young man walks across and stops a respectful distance from the table. Like Ronnie

Kray, one of the notorious twins warring for rule of London's underworld, he's in shirt sleeves and suit trousers, but he wears a brown storeman's coat to protect his clothing. He stands off to one side, with only the bottom of his coat, his knees and shoes in the circle of light, awaiting orders.

'Don't stand there like that, it's creepy,' says Kray without looking up. 'Get a chair and sit down so I can see you.'

The young man does as he's told and brings a hardbacked chair into the circle of light. He scrapes it on the floor, causing a sharp noise which echoes around the empty billiard hall, and sits, slightly higher than Kray but with his elbows on his knees, watching intently as the pistol is reassembled. Kray's hands move deftly, demonstrating a skill born of repeated practice, and within a few seconds the pistol lies complete in the centre of the cloth on the table, as if waiting to be picked up and used. The young man's handsome face is outwardly calm, but the nervous flicker of his eyes as he follows Kray's hands and the shallowness of his breathing betray anxiety. Kray leans back, satisfied, and examines his fingernails for oil.

'Now,' he says conversationally. 'What the fuck happened?'

'I tried, Ronnie, honest I did,' says Terry in a high-pitched voice. 'I told you, he's never alone long enough. His gaff's only a hundred yards from his office.'

'Chambers,' corrects Kray.

'Sorry, chambers. He's always with other briefs as he walks to the Bailey. And he's been prosecuting for the last few weeks so he's surrounded by Filth. Plus, I think he's wise to me, 'cos he's started acting strange.'

'Strange?'

'Yeah. Like, last week, I followed him down Fleet Street, and he stops to tie his shoelaces, so I'm forced to keep walking past him. As I'm going past I see he's wearing slip-ons! So after a couple of paces I turn, but he's legged it down that alley, right? By the Old Cheshire Cheese? By the time I get back to the alley he's disappeared altogether. Must have sprinted right to the end 'cos the pub was closed. I'm telling you, he's as fit as a butcher's dog, that brief.'

'And yesterday?'

'I promise you, Ronnie, I did just as you said. Kept an eye on his court and as soon as he left, followed him to the robing room. You were right – the place was deserted – and I got to him but some other briefs turned up before I could do nothing. So I scarpered, like you said: don't get caught.'

Terry finishes speaking but Ronnie Kray, known within the Firm as the Colonel, continues to stare just past his left ear, somehow looking at him but not looking at him. They say he can read minds, Terry reminds himself, and he freezes his face into a bland expression, pressing his sweating palms into his knees and holding his breath. Like many of the members of the Firm, he hates talking to Ronnie without Reggie present. Reggie Kray is no less hard, but you can usually reason with him; he's at heart a businessman and will always look for the profit in the violence. But Ronnie … well, sometimes Terry thinks Ronnie's unhinged even when he's *not* depressed and dosed up on booze and pills.

Ronnie gets these ideas into his head and nothing can shake them. And sometimes he'll go completely overboard, just lose it, and then even Reggie can't restrain him. In fact, it's in just those circumstances that Reggie's most likely to back up his twin brother, even if there's no profit or even logic in it. It's as if that weird bond between them, a sort of competitiveness never to let the side down, will always trump Reggie's business sense and his sense of proportion, whatever the cost.

'Okay,' concludes Kray, his fisheyes sliding further off into the middle distance. 'Fuck off then.' Terry gets up. 'Oh, yeah: what did you do with the shooter?'

'I took it back to Fort Vallance for safe keeping.'

Terry takes two further steps towards the rear to the building, but then hesitates. He turns. 'Do you want me to keep following him?'

Kray pauses for a moment before answering, without turning round. 'Give it to the end of the week. If you can get him by then, I'll give you an extra monkey. If not, jack it in, and we'll think of something else. And remember: not a word to Reggie, got it? Now, go on, fuck off.'

chapter 5

Charles opens an eye and focuses on the alarm clock beside him: ten past six. He groans inwardly and slides carefully to the side of the bed, taking care not to wake Sally. His feet hit carpet and he sits up on the edge of the bed. He pulls to one side the net curtains covering the narrow floor-to-ceiling window and looks down into Fetter Lane. The road is usually quiet on Sunday mornings but at just past six o'clock it's completely silent, with no traffic at all.

Charles turns and looks across at Sally asleep next to him. Her face is buried in the pillow and her shock of shiny black hair in its short bob is splayed across the white linen. Her right shoulder is visible above the sheets and Charles finds the temptation to bend and kiss it, to wake her up and snuggle into that warm delicious-smelling body, to be so strong that he almost gives in to it. He resists, looks again at the clock, and asks himself if he is likely to get back to sleep with the light streaming in. He has had a bad night, counting the hours. He decides it's a waste of time trying to sleep, so he stands quietly and pads around the end of the bed, again resisting the temptation to tickle the single white foot sticking out of the covers.

Charles pulls the bedroom door closed behind him and

goes to the tiny cupboard in the one square yard space mendaciously described as an "elegant hallway" in the estate agent's particulars. He reaches in and takes out a green army rucksack, a relic of David's conscripted military service which ended in 1952. In it Charles keeps a clean towel, shorts, socks, singlet and training shoes. The rest of his boxing kit, including his gloves, boots and head guard, he leaves in his locker at the gym. Charles changes into his sports gear and repacks the rucksack with clean underwear, a pair of slacks and a clean but un-ironed shirt taken from the laundry basket in the kitchen. He gulps down a glass of cold water from the kitchen sink and slips out of the apartment, closing the door with a faint click behind him.

Charles steps onto Fetter Lane and turns left and left again onto Fleet Street. He starts jogging, his spirits lifting in the cool morning air. It's a mile and a half south to the gym in Elephant and Castle, a pleasant run over Blackfriars Bridge, and he can usually cover the distance in fifteen minutes.

The Kennington Institute was built after the War on the site of another London boxing landmark, the Rupert Browning Youth Club. Over the years, the Rupert Browning had been responsible for training many of the East End kids who went on to have successful pro careers. Charles was taken by his father and uncle to join the club at the age of thirteen in 1939. He still remembers the day in 1943 when he was first introduced to the Kray twins, then still ten or eleven years of age, on the day they started training there. For a short time, he and the brothers even shared the same trainer, an ex-pro called Charlie Simms. Both twins were good lightweight boxers; Ronnie, brave to the point of foolhardiness and a bit of a slugger, and Reggie, equally brave but also a very good technical boxer – so good that most informed observers thought he had the makings of a champion.

Having crossed Blackfriars Bridge Charles jogs down London Road towards the roundabout at Elephant and Castle, breathing heavily but still comfortable. He squints to avoid the sunlight reflecting directly into his eyes from the windows of the newly-completed six-storey Castle House. He looks down and focuses on the small section of pavement before him – his feet entering and leaving his field of vision, with their regular thud-thud, thud-thud. A London bus sweeps past southbound, and in its diesel-fume wash a flotsam of grease-stained chip paper and other refuse is blown across his path. Charles extends his stride, leaps over the larger pieces and keeps running.

Five minutes later he sprints the last hundred yards down a narrow service road, skirts a burnt out Austin van, and pushes open the large doors covered by greasy chipboard at the back of the gym. He is welcomed as always by the familiar blend of stale sweat, mould and liniment. He walks down a short corridor to the changing room. Sweat-stained wooden benches line one wall facing a bank of grey-painted lockers. Above the benches is a rogue's gallery of faded black and white photos of young men in typical boxing poses. Second from the end is one of Charles himself, aged 14, wearing around his neck the golden gloves of a London Schoolboy Champion.

Charles opens a locker opposite his own photograph and takes out his boots and gloves.

''Ello, 'ello, 'ello,' says a gravelly voice from behind Charles. 'Couldn't sleep again?'

Charles turns. A man in his early 60s in stained jogging pants and a grubby white T-shirt leans in from the corridor, a dripping mop in one hand. His nose is flattened and he has the characteristic cauliflower ears and scarred eyebrows of an old boxer.

'Morning, Duke,' replies Charles. 'No. Don't know what's up – that's four nights in a row. I could do with a few rounds. Anyone available?'

'What, at this hour? Nah, I'm the only one in.'

'OK – heavy bag, then.'

Charles puts on the rest of his kit, clangs shut the locker door, and walks further down the corridor into the gym, pulling on his gloves. The room is in almost complete darkness, the only windows being inaccessible pigeon dropping-covered skylights set in the asbestos sheet roof. Charles hits the lights and most of the fluorescent tubes flicker into reluctant life.

Still warm from his run, Charles immediately starts working on the heavy bag in the corner of the room. After a few minutes Duke enters carrying a striped mug of tea, and he leans against the wall watching Charles punch, every now and then offering advice: 'Use your full range Charlie you're just taking it easy!' 'Left your feet at 'ome 'av yer? Get back out of contact range, you lazy fucker!' 'Get that hand back up after the hook! You're leaving yourself open – plus you'll never get a third shot off!'

Charles does six rounds on the bag, the first two on jabs and hooks while he works up a really good sweat, the third on southpaw, the fourth concentrating on head movement, and the last two at fight pace, fast combos while keeping his footwork fast and loose. By the end it is almost quarter to eight, and he knows that Sally will soon be stirring. He steps away from the bag, undoing his left glove with his teeth and just managing to catch the towel thrown through the air to him by Duke.

'Not too shabby, Charlie – considering you don't train enough, you're 'alf a stone overweight and yer mind's somewhere else,' says Duke.

'Thanks mate,' replies Charles. 'I've got to run. Someone waiting for me.'

'Yeah? Is that Robeson's girl?'

Charles looks up, surprised. 'You know about her, then?'

'The 'ole fuckin' East End knows about her. You can't keep nuffink a secret round 'ere, you know that. You two still an item then?'

Charles walks towards the doors, towelling down his matted chest hair, wanting to bring the conversation to an end. 'Got to move, Duke. See you Wednesday.'

Ten minutes later, hair still dripping from the shower and rucksack over one shoulder, Charles emerges onto the roundabout at Elephant and Castle. A bus which would take him to within a few hundred yards of Fetter Lane is approaching, but instead Charles hails a taxi. 'Fetter Lane,' he instructs the cabbie, 'but via Old Compton Street.'

'Whatever you say, guv.'

The streets are still empty and within twelve minutes the cabbie is waiting outside Patisserie Valerie with the engine running. Charles exits the shop at a jog, warm paper bag in his hand, and gets back in. Eight further minutes, and he's walking through the doors of the apartment building on Fetter Lane. He runs upstairs, picking up his Sunday paper from the reception desk as he goes, opens the apartment door and put his head round the door jamb. He smiles. Sally's still asleep. He steps into the kitchen, puts the kettle on the stove and places the two freshly-baked croissants into the oven to keep warm. He makes a pot of coffee which he places on a tray with two cups, milk and the croissants. He tucks the newspaper under his arm and carries the tray quietly into the bedroom, laying it on the end of the bed and sitting down carefully by Sally's side. She has turned onto her back and is still asleep. Charles watches her chest rise and fall. He's aware of the dark outlines of her brown nipples through the thin cotton of her nightie and feels blood start pumping to his groin. He lowers his mouth to hers and kisses her gently.

'Morning,' she mumbles.

She half-opens her eyes, shading her face from the sunlight streaming in through the window. 'You already dressed?'

She reaches up to touch Charles's dark curls. 'And showered, I see.'

Then she smells the coffee. 'Ooh, coffee.' She struggles to sit up, and bashes the pillows behind her into a shape to support her. 'And croissants! You have been busy.'

'Very nice, Charles,' says Henrietta's dry voice beside Charles's head. 'You never brought me breakfast in bed.'

Sally reaches across, takes one of the cups of coffee and sips. 'Hmm, lovely.' She glances again at Charles. 'Shame you're dressed though.'

Charles grins. 'Easily remedied,' he says, ignoring Henrietta and undoing his belt.

•

It's an hour later. Faint tinny sounds of pop music courtesy of the Light Programme emanate from behind the closed bathroom door, and Charles can just make out John Lennon's wailing harmonica on *Love Me Do*. He pushes his chair back from the table in the lounge, puts down the newspaper, and steps quietly to the bathroom door, inclining his ear to listen for the sounds of water running. Satisfied, he walks the two paces to the window overlooking Fetter Lane. He pulls back the curtains slightly and scans the street: deserted. There had been a man loitering in a doorway twenty minutes before. Charles had been unable to see his face from above due to the brim of the man's hat, and he could easily have been waiting for a bus. In any case, the doorway is now empty. *Easy Beat* is extinguished as the transistor radio in the bathroom is turned off, and Charles swiftly resumes his seat and picks up his cup. He hasn't said anything to Sally about his "problem" with Ronnie Kray and doesn't want to worry her. The bathroom door opens and Sally steps across the hallway into the lounge.

'More coffee?' asks Charles, reaching for the now replenished pot.

Sally's hair is tied in a towel and she wears Charles's white towelling dressing gown. Charles on the other hand is wearing a woman's pale blue silk bathrobe with a word in Japanese embroidered on the back which, Sally tells him, says "Happiness" but could just as easily translate as "Idiot". The garment was Sally's, but he'd been forced to start wearing it when she commandeered his more suitable bathrobe. Sally has told Charles many times that he looks ridiculous – huge square hands, hairy forearms like great hams, and a heavily muscled neck emerging from a woman's silk robe – and has asked him to buy her a second towelling one to match his. But, for reasons he has avoided examining, he hasn't managed to find the time to do it yet.

Charles looks up at her and pauses, coffee cup in hand, marvelling again at his luck. Sally is petite and slim, a little over five foot in height, and his towelling robe is huge on her, hiding the contours of her body as it wraps round her almost twice. It hangs only a couple of inches off the floor and that, together with the towel wrapped round her head which accentuates her large round eyes and small features, make her look childlike. Charles knows that this waif-like vulnerability is deceptive; underneath the robe is a demandingly hungry body. He finds the contrast irresistible, the thing about Sally that attracts him the most.

Whatever she does, she commits herself to it totally. He's never met anyone with such a full-blooded enthusiasm for life – a complete contrast to the anxious, "keep your head beneath the parapet", attitude of his family. Sally disdains diets, demanding proper meals – three courses, wine with each, and a dessert – and despite being half Charles's size will match him course for course and drink for drink. When they play games, Monopoly on wet afternoons or football in the park, she plays to win, perfectly happy to cheat, trip him or foul him if necessary. And when they make love … Charles feels as if he's being carried away in a tidal wave. Her selfishness, her demand to be satisfied, inflames him and – though he would never admit it even to himself – scares him slightly. Despite her small stature, Sally is the strongest and most determined woman Charles has ever met.

He stands and goes to her, wrapping his great arms around her, squeezing the breath from her chest, nuzzling his face against her neck and luxuriating in the smell of her freshly washed skin. The knowledge that this wonderful young woman's soft curvaceous body is a mere towelling belt knot away, is *there* and available to him, still seems miraculous to Charles. But not this time. As his kisses descend in inch by inch increments towards her supraclavicular fossa – the velvet depression between her clavicle and her neck, the name of which he learned specifically because he loves hers so – he feels his erection growing again, and he runs a hand down the curve of her back and starts rucking up the bathrobe to reach for the soft globes of her buttocks, still hot and slightly damp from the shower. Then she grabs his wrist.

'No,' she says simply. 'I want to go out.' Charles stops but doesn't release her immediately. 'Seriously, Charlie. Let's do something.'

She pulls herself away from him and his erection, now freed by the distance between them, protrudes through the front of the inadequate robe. He looks down and demonstrates his predicament with both hands open.

'Tough. You'll just have to save it. Get out of that ridiculous gown and get dressed.'

'What, this?' asks Charles disingenuously, making himself decent and twirling round like a model. 'I thought it made me look elegant.'

'It makes you look like a Sicilian boxer in drag. Now fuck off and put some clothes on.'

Charles bends and plants a kiss on the end of her upturned nose. 'I'll get changed then.'

He disappears into the bedroom. The apartment was never intended for occupation by more than one person, and with a double bed in the bedroom there is only room for one person to move around, so Sally sits on the settee and picks up the newspaper, leafing to the section on business. Sally is now the senior clerk at the Chambers where Charles once practiced – the youngest senior barristers' clerk in the Temple. Confounding all the predictions, she'd made a great success of it, increasing both the turnover of the set and the number of clients in a year. But the longer hours meant that she could no longer care for her ailing mother, and she'd been forced to employ an ex-nurse, Betty, as a carer. Despite Sally's fears, the two older women got on instantly, becoming in a few short months more like friends than carer and client. That had started Sally thinking. She knew several elderly people in the same situation as her mother, all War widows with distant families and a bit of money put by. So Sally had interviewed and hired three other carers, all mature women with nursing experience acquired in the War, to carry out home visits in the East End and surrounding boroughs. It was a novel idea, and it worked. Sally is now looking to expand what she has named "The Domestic Care Agency" and, for the first time in her life, she finds the business news of interest.

'What do you fancy, then?' calls Sally from the lounge. 'Can I meet any of your friends? Or your family?'

Charles doesn't answer, so Sally follows him into the bedroom. He's sitting bare-footed on the edge of the bed in his slacks, his enormous chest about to disappear into his vest. He stands and starts looking under the covers for his socks.

'Look at me, Charlie,' she orders softly from the doorway. He avoids her gaze for a moment longer. 'I've told you, Charlie. I won't put up with this. It's been over eight months since Dad's trial. In all that time I've met none of your family. You never even mention them. I've never met any of your friends – and don't give me that line about not having any, 'cos we both know it's balls. I used to be your clerk, remember?'

She approaches him and reaches up, turning his head towards hers, and holding his face firmly between her hands to keep him focused on her.

'You know how much I love it here – our own little world. It's sexy, and special, and I was perfectly happy curled up in your pocket for months. But now I want to be part of your life.' Charles doesn't answer, and his eyes drift off hers and over her shoulder. 'You're ashamed of me, Charlie Holborne, aren't you?' she asks.

'No. I'm not ashamed of you.'

'Then why am I still a secret? Why do we never meet in the Temple? Why do we never go anywhere? This is turning into a tacky affair. I want more.'

Her voice is calm and there's no sense that she's nagging Charles, but he hears the intensity in her tone and knows how much this means to her. Charles takes her tiny white hands from his face and holds them together in front of him. He closes his eyes and kisses her fingers tenderly.

'This isn't a tacky affair. You know that's not me.' But there is an unspoken "But" after these words, and they both hear it.

At the start there had been an unspoken accord between them to keep their relationship quiet. There is a taboo against barristers having relationships with barristers' clerks and, more immediately, the press were still looking for more angles on Charles's life to fan the public interest in the East End criminal barrister framed for the murder of his titled wife. So they'd both been anxious to avoid further publicity. Furthermore, the physical attraction between them was so overwhelming that in the first few months they'd preferred to be locked away in their private cocoon. They never strayed far from Fleet Street, grabbing hasty meals to rush back to the flat and tear one another's clothes off. But that was then. Charles's face has not appeared in the newspapers for months and Sally hungers for a normal relationship. Charles is finding it difficult to understand his own reluctance.

'You have to give me some time, Sally. I'm finding this very difficult. It's not only the professional thing. I'm old enough—'

'To be my father, yes, you say it all the time. It's not actually true. You're only thirty-eight.'

'And you're barely twenty-three.' Mirroring her earlier gesture, Charles takes her soft face in his hands and stares deep into her light brown eyes with the tiny golden flecks around the pupils.

'Sally, twenty years from now I'll be just short of sixty. That's old. Bits'll have started falling off. You'll still be in your prime. I don't want to be constantly looking over my shoulder, worried about all the young bucks trying to get into your knickers.'

This is a familiar refrain and she knows that, despite his jocular tone, it worries him. She reaches up and brushes the hair at his temples with her fingers, failing to get the few wiry white hairs to lie down with the sleek black ones.

'That's in twenty years' time. Who knows what might happen by then? What about *now?* We're together *now.*'

'Listen to her, Charles,' orders Henrietta.

But Charles can't answer. He hates to admit it to himself, but the age difference is only part of it. He's worried at the gossip that's bound to fly around the Temple – just after it's all died down. The Bar is the province of upper class, well-heeled, Oxbridge graduates for whom dating a clerk would be akin to walking out with one of the domestic servants. At the same time, Charles is ashamed of his embarrassment. He acknowledges dimly to himself that he's at risk of acting out the very class snobbery he so loathes when it's directed at him. And then there's the Jewish thing. Charles is not interested in his parents' religion – its weird rituals, its adherence to five-thousand-year-old dietary rules – but having just managed some form of rapprochement with his parents, what would be the effect of introducing them to yet another *shiksa* as his life partner? Another ten-year silence?

And then … then … what about what Davie said? Could this reluctance be about Henrietta too?

So for some months Charles, never good at disentangling or understanding emotions – especially his own – has placed the knotty problem of his relationship with Sally on the back-burner, hoping that somehow it would resolve itself.

He looks into her eyes and smiles. 'I've never met your mum,' he offers.

A slow smile spreads across her lips. 'Are you suggesting you should?'

'Why not? Have you told her anything about me?'

'Have I? She's bored to death of me banging on about you. She's even started saying she doesn't believe you exist 'cos she's never met you.'

Charles shrugs. 'Well, then …'

Sally pulls his head to hers and lands a wet kiss smack on his lips, releases him as suddenly, and runs back to the lounge. 'I'll give her a ring!' she calls. Then she reappears in the doorway, frowning. 'You sure about this? Sunday lunch in Romford, with my sisters, their blokes and a baby? Bit of a baptism of fire.'

'Compared to meeting my family, it'll be a walk in the park.'

chapter 6

When she's not with Charles at Fetter Lane, Sally still lives with her mother in the narrow terraced house in Romford in which she and her sisters grew up. Sally lets herself in by the front door, and steps back to let Charles precede her into the hall. The home smells different to that in which Charles grew up in Mile End – no Jewish cooking – and it has none of the paraphernalia to be found in every Jewish home, but otherwise it's instantly familiar to him. Almost identical to his childhood home on British Street, it has a narrow corridor with a "best" lounge opening off to the left and a staircase on the right; at the end of the corridor is a kitchen which has been extended into what was once a scullery and coal shed; and upstairs, there will be a main bedroom and a room for Sally and her sisters to share. He also knows that when this house was built it would have had an outside toilet at the end of the garden but he suspects, rightly, that an inside bathroom and toilet have been installed in an extension over the top of the scullery sometime since the War.

Sally closes the door and leads Charles to the end of the short, tiled corridor. From behind the closed kitchen door facing them come gales of laughter and an indistinct tangle of conversations. Sally put her fingers to her lips and listens for a moment.

'Ready?' she asks quietly.

Charles looks up from examining a notebook hanging from the kitchen door jamb. He recognises Sally's handwriting in some of the entries and realises he is looking at a handover record for Mrs Fisher's carer.

'Ready,' replies Charles with a smile.

Sally opens the kitchen door quickly and the conversations from within are instantly snuffed out. Facing Charles is a woman in her late forties or early fifties, who Charles guesses is Sally's mother. Around the scrubbed pine kitchen table also sit two young women and a man in his late twenties gingerly cradling a young baby. Charles smells roast meat cooking – lamb perhaps – and boiled vegetables.

'Mum, this is Charles Holborne. Charlie, meet my mum, Nell Fisher. Next to her is my sister, Michelle – that's her husband Frank looking likely to drop the baby – and next to Frank at the end is my baby sister, Tracey.'

'I'm nineteen,' clarifies Tracey, 'nearly twenty, and I'm married.' Charles can see her resemblance to Sally. She too is very pretty, though taller and slimmer and her black hair is worn longer and at this moment is tied in a ponytail.

Frank stands and awkwardly extracts a hand from under the baby which he offers to Charles over the table. He is tall and thin, with thick brown hair cut in a severe horizontal line across his forehead. Charles shakes his hand.

'How do you do?' they say simultaneously.

'You haven't introduced me to the most important person here,' says Charles, indicating the baby.

Michelle laughs. 'That's Denise,' she says.

Charles leans forward and puts his enormous stubby forefinger into the baby's curled hand and feels her grip it. He lowers his head to the baby. 'Hello, Denise,' he says softly. 'Six months?' he asks, looking up at Michelle.

'Five,' says Frank with unmistakable pride.

Charles sees an enquiring glance flash between Michelle and Sally. 'You don't have kids, do you?' asks Michelle.

'No.'

'But you seem to know about them …' says Michelle. She is fairer than her two sisters, of larger build, and looks more like their mother.

'Not really,' says Charles. 'But I like them. Especially at this age.'

'You never told me,' says Sally, with surprise.

'I've never told you lots of things,' replies Charles with a twinkle in his eyes.

'Ooh, that sounds mysterious!' says Tracey.

Charles holds out his hand across the table toward Sally's mother. 'Mrs Fisher,' he says.

He detects a slight hesitation before she answers and there is a guarded look in her eyes, in contrast to the open and curious welcome of the younger members of the family.

'Mr Holborne,' she replies, taking his hand. 'Take a seat. Can we offer you a drink? There's sherry, and some brown ale.'

Charles pulls out one of the two remaining chairs and sits

at the table. It is set for Sunday lunch and Charles guesses from the smell of silver polish faintly detectable under the roast dinner that he's looking at the best cutlery, not often used other than at Christmas and other special occasions.

'It's Charles, please, or Charlie,' he insists. He nods at the mugs dotted around the table. 'And I'd quite like a cup of tea too, if that's okay.'

'I'll do it,' offers Tracey, getting up. 'Want one, Sal?'

'No thanks. Mum, what's still to be done?'

Sally puts her bag down and starts working around them, putting the finishing touches to the meal, and it becomes clear from the conversation around the table that Nell Fisher has a problem with her back which makes standing and walking very difficult.

Sally keeps one ear on the conversation, concerned lest Charles feels awkward, but she needn't have worried. It's as if he's known her family for years. He speaks their language, contributing effortlessly to discussions about the dog races at Walthamstow, the state of Romford market and the chances of West Ham winning the FA cup under Ron Greenwood. She smiles to herself as she makes the gravy. Charles is as much at ease with her family as he is with his colleagues in chambers and the judges before he pleads his cases. She notes that even his accent has changed subtly. There's no hint of the precise speech he uses at work; he speaks simply, using familiar vernacular expressions, and there's a faint echo of cockney that she hasn't heard before.

When she first came to know Charles, when he was a guvnor in her chambers at Chancery Court, Sally thought she'd never met anyone so at ease in any social or professional situation; he always seemed to fit in effortlessly. It is only now, some months after their relationship began, that Sally is beginning to appreciate that in fact the opposite is true: despite all his social ease, Charles doesn't fit in at all. He doesn't feel as if he belongs *anywhere*, and so he hides beneath a series of shifting masks, one thrown up after another with a magician's sleight of hand. He's a chameleon. And now, like a magician's assistant who has learned to see past the smoke and mirrors, Sally can glimpse flashes of a bewildered and slightly lost little boy. It is *that* Charles who makes her heart ache and with whom she thinks she may be in love, not the slick social performer who can mimic a dozen accents and even unconsciously alter the way he walks depending on the company.

The dinner table is noisy and boisterous with lots of teasing and laughter, and even Mrs Fisher thaws a little. A call comes from Tracey's husband saying that there's been a problem at the bus depot where he works and they should start lunch without him, and so the meal is served. After the main course, Charles and Frank go out into the small backyard to have a cigarette. Charles had managed to give up smoking completely, but the events surrounding Henrietta's death and his run from the police led to him start again, and he hasn't been able to shake the habit since.

Frank offers Charles a Rizla and some tobacco and they each roll their cigarettes in silence. Charles looks up to see Frank studying has face. Frank strikes a match against the kitchen wall and offers the light to Charles. Charles inclines his head and inhales, watching the end of his rollup glow red. He looks up, taking the cigarette from his mouth.

'Yes, Frank. I do remember you.'

Frank smiles wryly. 'Yeah, thought so. Thanks for keeping schtum. Sorry about the "Charlie".'

'It's my name. You're not my client anymore.'

'Still feels odd, *Mr Holborne*.'

Charles nods backward to the kitchen. 'What do they know?'

'Michelle knows I had some trouble a few years back and that I did some bird, but that's all. The others don't even know that.'

'You straight now?' asks Charles.

'On my honour. Been working as a stevedore at the Port of London for three years. Meeting Michelle made the difference. And now we've got the kid ...'

'I'm pleased for you, Frank. It's not often that my ex-clients turn things around. Good for you.'

'Yeah, well, I didn't get on with being inside. But please – not a word to the others. Nell's very protective of her girls, and we get on fine at the minute. It would upset the apple cart if she knew the truth.'

Charles nods. 'I shan't say a word.'

The two men smoke in silence, listening to the women's voices drifting through the kitchen window and the more muffled voices of the families living on either side of the Fisher household who are also at Sunday lunch.

'You're not what I expected at all, Charlie.'

'What did you expect?'

'I dunno. A lot posher for a start. You was the proper barrister when we met … well … professionally.'

'Yeah, well, I grew up in the East End.'

'And maybe I was expecting … well … someone less straight. The press did you no favours.'

Charles laughs briefly but without humour. 'You don't have to tell me. Murderer, robber, con artist – I was called all of them.' Frank remains silent but his brow contracts into a frown and Charles can see him struggling with something else. 'What's up, Frank?' he encourages. 'Spit it out.'

'We've heard a lot about you from Sally over the last few months. She's pretty smitten, you know?'

'So'm I.'

Frank studies Charles's face. 'Yeah? Well that's great. But you probably noticed that Nell's a bit cool towards you.'

'Maybe, yes. I'm a lot older than Sally, I'm Jewish, I'm a barrister – and I have a history. I can see why she'd be protective.'

'None of that would bother her. She … well … *we*, was worried about the connection with the Krays.'

Charles shakes his head. 'There isn't any connection.'

'Well, it turns out there was, so far as Harry Robeson was concerned.'

Charles sighs, wondering how much Frank actually knows. The previous year Charles had represented a high profile criminal solicitor, Harry Robeson, on an indictment for conspiracy to rob. Unknown to Charles at the time, Robeson was Sally's father. Also unknown to Charles at the time, Robeson was the Kray twins' legal fixer, an important cog in the machine which laundered and reinvested the proceeds of their criminal ventures. Robeson's eventual conviction and incarceration had caused Ronnie Kray such fury that he had put Charles on his "List" – a list of people to be *"dealt with"*. But nothing had happened in the following months and, at least until the last week or so, Charles had begun to think it was either an empty threat or that The Colonel had bigger fish to fry.

'Harry Robeson was up to his gills with the Krays, but he was just my client,' he explains. 'I had no idea at the time that he was Sally's father. I've got no other connection with them.'

Frank pauses again, still obviously chewing something over. 'Please don't be offended, Charlie. You've got to understand that Nell and the girls have got no men in their lives 'cept me. No one to look out for them, understand? So I do me best, right?'

'I understand.'

'Well then. The word on the street is that you was working for the Krays and you fell out with 'em. And that's why you're now on Ronnie's List. Is it true?'

'Is that what everyone's been saying?'

Frank nods, and Charles detects embarrassment and a flicker of fear in the other's face.

'Where did you hear this?' asks Charles.

'Loads of people are talking about it. At the Stow, up the Lane, everywhere.'

'Does Sally know?'

Frank shrugs. 'I've not talked to her about it personally, but I can't see how she wouldn't have heard the same as everyone else.'

'Right.'

Charles pauses and stares at the weeds growing from cracks in the concrete at his feet. He drops his fag end and grinds it out, his heart sinking. Yet another difficult issue to be addressed with Sally.

'Do you think I really need to worry?'

'I'm sorry to say it, mate, but I do.'

Charles casts his mind back a few days to the time he thought he was being followed, and then, more recently, to the event at the Old Bailey robing room. So Ronnie's in earnest. But what to do? He couldn't spend the rest of his life looking over his shoulder. Report it to the Filth? Against his nature, and old habits die hard. If he had no love for the police as a teenager, his experience at the Bar had only made him more cynical still. So many of them were bent, at least in the Met, and he wouldn't trust them as far as he could spit. And in any case, half of them were still convinced he'd murdered his wife and the other half thought he was on the Twins' payroll. He didn't see much help coming from that quarter.

'From what I hear,' he says, 'you can't exactly reason with Ronnie.'

Frank considers. 'I've not had much to do with the Firm,' he replies. 'They financed that warehouse job where you represented me and handled the stuff afterwards, but I only met the brothers once, and made sure I kept me mouth shut while everyone else did the talking. But I think the only way you might get through to Ronnie is through Reg. He's got a better business head and if you can persuade Reggie, he might get Ronnie to see reason. But even then, not always.'

The conversation is interrupted by Michelle's head emerging through the kitchen window. 'You two coming in for sweet? Our Tracey's made a trifle!'

'And it's me first!' adds Tracey's voice from behind her.

'Coming,' calls Charles. He leans his head towards Frank's. 'Will you keep me informed if you hear anything?'

'Will do. But watch yourself, Charlie. You can't afford not to take this serious.'

chapter 7

Charles turns off Fleet Street and walks swiftly under the arch and onto the cobbles of Old Mitre Court. Unusually, the gates into the Temple – normally left open during daylight hours – are closed. Then Charles remembers a notice in Chambers alerting tenants of the Inn of the possibility of some delay today. On a single day each year the Inner Temple exercises its legal right to control entry and exit, thereby preserving the private nature of the thoroughfare.

Charles takes his place in a queue of lawyers waiting to enter the Honourable Society of the Inner Temple and watches with a faint smile as a sweating man in uniform opens the door to each barrister in turn and then closes it again for a couple of seconds before letting in the next. Charles waits patiently for the half dozen or so barristers ahead of him in the queue, almost identical from the rear in black jackets and black and white pinstriped trousers, to be let in. The weather has suddenly turned warmer, and Charles takes off his overcoat and folds it over his arm. He's happy to wait and let the spring sunshine warm his face.

'Good afternoon, sir,' says the official as Charles approaches the gate.

'Afternoon. And a very nice one it is, too,' replies Charles cheerfully. 'It's Richard, isn't it?' Charles has met the official on a handful of occasions, but he's a relatively new employee at the Inn.

'That's right, sir.'

Charles steps down into the Temple as the gate clangs shut temporarily behind him. He walks through the arch into King's Bench Walk. The Temple has not quite fully donned its spring garb, but the tall plane trees are almost in full leaf and Charles can see a scattering of yellow from the few remaining daffodils on the manicured green sward sloping down to the Thames.

He resists, as he does most afternoons, the enticing smell of toasted muffins from the Inner Temple common room as he passes the corner of Crown Office Row and heads towards Chambers. When Charles first started at the Bar the common room had been the regular haunt of a large group of pupils just out of military service, and butter-laden toasted muffins and tea had been an afternoon ritual. Pupil barristers would gather for an hour or so to discuss the horrors of their pupil masters' personal habits, their unreasonable working demands – which often included such tasks as polishing their shoes or collecting their snuff or laundry – and the incomprehensible cases on which the pupils had been set to work. They would blow off steam and horse around as if they were still at university or, as in Charles's case, at an RAF dispersal hut waiting to scramble, minded by a rota of indulgent middle-aged tea ladies. Several of the young men then starting in practice still carried physical and psychiatric injuries from the War, and the tea ladies – all of whom had served themselves – were more like nurses or nannies than waitresses in their ministrations to their young battle-scarred charges. In 1950, shortly after being called to the Bar, Charles had been present at Chelmsford Assizes when a colleague still suffering from combat stress took refuge under the barristers' bench when startled by a clerk dropping a stack of books behind him. The barrister concerned climbed out from under the bench, puce with embarrassment, but the evidence had continued without a word being said by anyone in court. Everyone present, including the ex-marine on trial, had understood.

Charles climbs the stone steps to Chambers, passing the board on which his name has risen by reason of increasing seniority to halfway up the list. He hadn't intended going into the clerks' room, knowing that it was the busiest part of the day and having already received his brief for the morrow, but as he goes past the door he hears his name shouted.

'Sir!' calls Clive, squeezing between two barristers returning from court.

'Yes?'

'Message for you,' he says, handing Charles a folded piece of paper.

'Thank you,' replies Charles, turning to walk up the stairs to his room. He flips open the message, pauses, and then calls after the young man who has disappeared back into the clerks' room.

'Clive?' The youngster reappears in the doorway. 'Who took this message?'

'I don't know, sir. It was on my desk when I got back from tea.'

'This isn't Barbara's writing, is it?' asks Charles.

'No sir. She's been out all afternoon. And I asked JJ, and they didn't write it or see who left it. Perhaps one of the other members of chambers? Some of the younger guvnors do tend to pick up the phones, even though we've told them not to.'

'OK, thanks.'

Barristers are not supposed to pick up the phones. They're not to expose themselves to the risk of discussing such grubby matters as their fees or whether they're available for court on a certain date. Instead they're supposed to remain cosseted in their ivory towers and reach deep insights into the law, while their clerks actually run the business. Charles finds this 19th century demarcation of duties ludicrous, but he's in the minority in his dangerous modern thinking.

Charles re-reads the message: "*Message for CH: Tried to reach you while you were at the Bailey but must have missed you. Need to talk urgently. I'm in Ct No 10. S.*'

Sally. They often meet at the Magpie and Stump, the pub in Old Bailey so close to the court and so popular amongst lawyers that it's acquired the nickname "Courtroom No 10". Whatever her reason for needing to speak to him, it must be really important for her to abandon her desk at this time of day: Daily Cause lists to be checked, tomorrow's briefs to be assigned and the phone ringing constantly with calls from solicitors needing a barrister the next morning. Charles turns on the stairs, pushes through the doors and walks swiftly towards the Temple's Tudor Street exit, still carrying his coat and court robes.

It takes him ten minutes to reach the Magpie and Stump. He pushes open the door to the saloon bar and stands just inside the threshold. It takes a few seconds for his eyes to adjust from the bright afternoon sunshine to the gloom of the smoky bar. The pub has only been open for a few minutes. A group of keen legal drinkers is in the process of ordering drinks, but there's no sign of Sally. Charles notices but does not mark the man sitting in shadow in the panelled booth immediately behind the door. The man watches as Charles walks through to the public bar. It's deserted. Damn! Charles curses to himself; he must have missed her.

Charles turns right out of the pub and is about to return to the Temple when he spots a red telephone box fifty yards away down Bishop's Court, the narrow cobbled passageway to the side of the pub. He hesitates for a second but then decides to ring Chancery Court, his former chambers where Sally still works, to see if she's returned.

He walks down the gloomy alley towards the red telephone box, the ancient buildings on each side leaning over the cobbles and cutting out much of the light, fishing awkwardly in his trouser pockets for change. As Charles opens the door his nose is assailed by the acrid stench of urine and stale cigarettes and he's reluctant to let the door close completely behind him, so he jams his foot against the door near to its hinge while he tries his jacket pockets. He's hampered by his overcoat, still folded over his left forearm, and his red barrister's bag, a large triangular cloth bag with a rope drawstring used by barristers to carry their court robes. He looks at the damp and fag-end littered floor of the telephone box and decides immediately against putting the bag down. Instead he opens the loop of the rope drawstring and hangs the bag around his neck so it's bumping against his chest. At least he now has one hand free.

So engrossed is Charles in searching for change that he's completely unaware of the silent approach of the young man who has followed him from the pub. Then he feels a sudden blow in the area of his right kidney. Charles's initial thought is that someone else has tried to get into the telephone box behind him and has merely bumped into him, but then as he turns to explain to the impatient newcomer that he's about to make a call, a searing blade of hot pain shoots from the area of his belt up his ribcage. Before Charles has any time to work out what's happening the young man lunges at him again, and Charles sees a shiny flick-knife covered in what he realises, with a hollow shock in the pit of his stomach, must be his own blood. The knife is coming straight towards his abdomen. Without conscious thought Charles rotates his right arm at the elbow, sweeping his hand down in an arc as if he was blocking a low blow in the boxing ring, and knocks the attacker's hand against the wall of the telephone box. With the man's guard down, Charles's first instinct is to bring his left arm round in a hook to the other's exposed right cheek, but there's no space to move his feet or swing his arm, so instead he delivers a power jab from the back foot, the overcoat on his left arm flying up and forming a momentary curtain between the two men. Charles can't see where the blow lands but hears a satisfying crack and, as the overcoat falls between them, he sees blood spurting out of both nostrils of his attacker's nose and dripping onto a clean white shirt front.

Any hope that Charles has seen off his attacker disappears as the man steps back, slightly crouched, and throws the flick knife from his right hand to his left and back again, trying to distract Charles as he seeks a target for his next lunge. Charles is still cornered in the telephone box. His mind is entirely calm, totally in the moment, and he waits, balanced lightly on his toes, for the attacker's next move. With the back of his hand, the attacker wipes the blood running into his mouth from his smashed nose, pauses for a split-second and feints right. The knife flashes through the air from right hand to left and comes again at Charles, aiming now at the centre of his chest. Charles raises his right hand and feels the blade going through the sleeve of his suit but he has done enough to deflect it and he hears a metallic thud as the blade strikes the wig tin hidden in the cloth bag hung around his neck. He sees the puzzlement on his attacker's face and in that momentary hesitation Charles throws jabs, left and then right, both scoring points against the attacker's head. The blood on the other man's nose is now smeared across his upper cheek and Charles watches as an angry red welt appears above the attacker's left eye.

Charles sees uncertainty on the attacker's face and,

simultaneously, hears a woman's shout from the top of Bishop's Court. The attacker looks sharply over his left shoulder and as he does so Charles has enough time to take two steps forward, his guard raised. The telephone box door closes slowly behind him. Now, freed of the constraints of the telephone box, he's able to move. This, above all, is what gave him his reputation in the ring and his string of successful bouts – extremely fast footwork for so big a man, together with complete balance.

Charles yanks the bag from around his neck and starts swinging it above his head in a fast circle to keep the attacker at more than arm's length. The attacker sways backwards – once, twice – to avoid the swirling bag and snatches another glance behind him. There are people running towards them. He makes one last half-hearted attempt to strike Charles – a horizontal slash with the knife held at full distance from his body – but it's just to gain time, as he immediately steps sideways and sprints off southwards down Bishop's Court, away from Old Bailey and the onrushing witnesses.

The entire attack has lasted less than a minute, during which not a word was spoken. Charles lets the bag drop, feeling suddenly sick, and aware that his surroundings are fading to white.

'Catch him!' he hears, but the words seemed to echo from the bottom of a well and he remembers nothing further.

•

Charles draws a deep lungful of air and finds himself inhaling ammonia. He chokes and coughs and his eyes sting, and he lifts his head to get away from the bottle being waved under his nose.

'Stay still, Mr Holborne,' commands an unfamiliar voice.

Charles is lying on his stomach, his face pressed into cold cobbles. He allows his head to drop back. His back is cold and he starts shivering violently. He realises that his tunic shirt had been pulled up to his shoulders.

'We've not met before,' explained the voice. 'I'm the matron.'

'Matron?' croaks Charles. 'From the Old Bailey?'

'That's right.'

'So you're the famous Mrs Hamlin?'

'So they say.'

'How do you know my name?' asks Charles shakily, aware that he's burbling only to stay conscious.

'It's stitched on your bag. You're very fortunate we were working late. There's an ambulance on its way and the police have been called, but I want to look at this knife wound, so lie still and be quiet.'

Cold fingers probe gently just above Charles's belt line. 'I think you've been extremely lucky. The blade's skidded off your leather belt. You've got a deep three-inch flap of skin and flesh, but it's still attached, and the blade missed both the kidney and its main vessels. Still lots of blood, but I think they can reattach the flap. I'm going to press down hard to staunch the blood loss now. This may hurt.'

But it doesn't hurt, because Charles loses consciousness again.

chapter 8

Charles is escorted into Snow Hill Police Station through the beautiful central doors beneath the five-storey leaded bay windows. A young officer hovers by each elbow in case he should need assistance. He had been loaded into the ambulance and taken to hospital before the police had arrived at the scene. When officers did eventually turn up at St Thomas's Hospital, Charles was in theatre being stitched under light anaesthetic, and they departed again. The hospital had planned to keep Charles in overnight, but he woke to find himself on a public ward and felt vulnerable, so after a terse exchange with the registrar on duty, Charles had signed the disclaimer forms and discharged himself. He was about to hail a taxi when the two coppers returned and offered to take him back to Fetter Lane via Snow Hill where he could file a report.

Charles is shown into an interview room and given a grubby mug of lukewarm tea. He waits for fifteen minutes and then the door opens and an officer in plain clothes enters.

'Mr Holborne?'

'Yes.'

'I'm DC Miller of the City of London police.'

Charles starts to stand, offering a hand, but the anaesthetic has now worn off and every movement hurts. He wonders if he's made a mistake by leaving hospital, and sits down again gingerly. 'Sorry,' he says. 'I'm a bit sore.'

'Not to worry, sir.'

Miller takes the seat opposite Charles and opens a manila file containing blank statement forms. 'Now, this shouldn't take long. I just need some basic details of what happened.'

Charles looks at the policeman opposite him. Miller is in his late twenties, perhaps early thirties, tall and fair, with thinning hair and light brown eyes. 'Please don't think I'm being rude,' offers Charles, 'but I would have expected a more senior officer to take a statement from the victim of an attempted murder.'

Miller looks up from the blank statement which he has begun to complete, and smiles, a slight frown distorting his fair eyebrows. 'Attempted murder? Don't you think that's a bit … well … exaggerated?'

'Have you been told about my injuries? I've got thirty stitches in my back where he sliced a half-pound steak off me, and he was trying to knife me in the chest.'

Miller pauses, weighing his words before speaking. 'I don't want you to think I'm minimising what happened, sir – I'm sure it must have been very frightening,' he placates. 'But let's take your evidence and we'll decide what to make of it. But in all likelihood it was an attempted robbery.'

'Robbery?' repeats Charles in astonishment. 'He didn't try to take anything.'

'Well, sir, did he have the chance? Maybe he was just

trying to frighten you with the knife when you started hitting him. I understand you have boxing experience?'

'Yes, I used to box, but …'

'And the witness, Mrs …' Miller pauses while he sifts through the papers to find the name, 'yes, Mrs Hamlin, she says she saw you throwing some very effective punches at the offender.'

'I'm telling you, Mr Miller, this was no attempted robbery. He stabbed me in the back before I even turned round to defend myself.'

'Which would be completely consistent with attempting to disable you while he stole your wallet or your coat, for example.'

'Possibly,' concedes Charles, 'but someone's been following me for weeks, and there was a strange event in the robing room at the Central Criminal Court a few days ago.'

'Really, sir? A "strange event"? What was that, then?'

Charles relates the event when his robes were pulled over his head, but the hint of a smile on Miller's face tells him immediately what the police officer thinks.

'I don't mean to be rude, but doesn't that sound more like a prank – perhaps by one of your colleagues? Are you really saying you think that was a murder attempt?'

Charles considers, and is forced to admit to himself that, on retelling the story, it does sound weak. 'Taken alone, perhaps not,' he concedes reluctantly. 'Although if it was one of my colleagues, why would they run out of the room to avoid being seen? But there *has* been someone following me, and if you add that to the robing room, and now this, surely you can see there's a pattern?'

Miller puts down his pen with exaggerated patience. 'Did you report being followed, sir?'

'No. There didn't seem to be enough … enough evidence … to make it possible for you to investigate.'

'No. Precisely. There was nothing to investigate when you thought you were being followed, and nothing to investigate when this joker, whoever he was, pulled up your gown.' Miller shrugs and stares at Charles with the same slight mocking smile. 'You're a barrister, I understand Mr Holborne?'

'What of it?'

'Well, if you were to put those facts before a jury, would you expect them to be satisfied so they were sure that those events had anything to do with what happened this afternoon? Ask yourself this: did anyone know you were going to be in the area of Bishop's Court this afternoon?'

'No. Well, only my ex-clerk who I was trying to meet.'

'And would he have told your attacker where you were going?'

'It's a "she", and no.'

If, of course, Sally left the message in the first place, thinks Charles. He'd not managed to speak to her yet. He'd almost called the house in Romford before he left the hospital but he doesn't like to call in the evenings, and risk disturbing her.

'So the chances are this was an entirely opportunist attack. And in any case, who might want to murder you?'

The Kray twins, Charles almost says, but even as his mouth opens, something makes him hesitate before speaking. It had taken Charles months to persuade members of his profession that he had not been in the pay of the Krays during the Robeson trial and there are still those, especially in the police, who suspect him of having got too close to the organised crime gang. Telling DC Miller that his name was on the Colonel's "List" was going to stretch the policeman's incredulity to breaking point.

'Look,' continues Miller, picking up his pen again, 'I do understand that people in our position – involved in the criminal justice system – make enemies. But that's a long stretch to an attempted murder in broad daylight. Anyway, shall we take the details of what happened, get your statement down in writing, and leave it till later to decide what charges might be brought – if we ever catch the man? I'm sure you should be lying down – I gather you lost a lot of blood.'

The "if we ever catch the man" was ominous; it was obvious that Miller thought an investigation would be a waste of time. Charles draws a deep breath and is aware of a sudden increase in the throbbing pain in his back. He'd been given some painkillers by the hospital before he left, and he feels in his pocket for them, swallowing them with a sip of cold tea.

'Yes, okay,' he concedes wearily. 'Let's do the statement. Then you can show me some mugshots and I'll see if I can pick the man out.'

'Let's just get the statement out of the way first, sir. My

sergeant and I can then decide on the best way to investigate thereafter.'

So Charles gives a complete statement of what happened from the time he left the Old Bailey until the time of the attack. It takes a further hour and by the end he's exhausted. Miller offers a patrol car to take Charles back to Fetter Lane, and he accepts.

Charles is led out of the building and to a waiting car. Back in the interview room, DC Miller finishes tidying away the papers. Another policeman enters the room, an older man with small black eyes, a sharp pointed nose and a short bristly moustache that seems only tenuously attached to his top lip.

The newcomer takes a roll-up cigarette out of the corner his mouth and spits a flake of tobacco onto the floor. 'Well?' he asks.

'As you predicted, Inspector. He reckons he's been followed for some days, someone had a go at him in the robing room at the Central Criminal Court, and today they tried to top him.'

'Did he mention the Krays?'

'No sir. There was a moment when I think he was going to, but he thought better of it.'

The face of the older man, Detective Chief Inspector Wheatley, twists into a thin satisfied smile. 'He's only got himself to blame for the company he keeps.'

'I suppose you've had dealings with Holborne before?' asks Miller respectfully. 'The Heavy Squad, I mean?'

'Oh yes,' replies Wheatley. 'He's that Jewboy cunt who

murdered his aristo-totty wife. I was in charge of that one – before I joined the Flying Squad. And don't tell me he wriggled free, 'cos I know. As I said to your inspector, that doesn't mean he didn't do it.'

'I remember the case, sir. So, what would you like me to do?' asks Miller, his deference for the Flying Squad DCI plain in his voice.

'I'm not your guvnor, Detective Constable, and you don't take orders from me. Inspector Collins will have to decide. But I'll have a word with him.' Wheatley put his hand on the door handle. 'If it was me, I wouldn't waste any time on Charles Holborne.' He spat Charles's name as if it was bile in his mouth. 'A bent brief's a dangerous thing. And if the Krays are cleaning house ... well ... I'd be inclined to let them get on with it.'

DC Miller nods. 'Thank you, sir. I get the message.'

chapter 9

Billy Hill climbs the opulent gilded staircase of the Clermont Club, Mayfair, towards the first-floor landing. As he passes the brass plaque on the wall, so highly polished that it could be solid gold, he pauses to examine his reflection. He lifts his tinted glasses, folds them and slips them into his jacket pocket. Beneath the interlocking capital "C's" which form the club's logo, and slightly distorted by the embossed name of the club beneath, he sees a fit, solid man in his early fifties with dark hair receding only slightly from a tall regular forehead. The hairline hasn't moved much in the last twenty years, for which Hill is grateful. He prides himself on looking like Humphrey Bogart and, once he mentions it, most people claim to see the resemblance. He makes an unnecessary minute adjustment to his silk tie, fastens the middle button of his new Pierre Cardin jacket – a bit too modern for his taste, but Gypsy insisted that his old suits make him look middle-aged and that, as she knew, was the clincher – and resumes his climb up the carpeted stairs under the chandelier.

Two men await his orders at the head of the stairs, large intimidating men in dark suits. Both are discreetly tooled. Billy Hill doesn't need their protection. He is the acknowledged boss of Britain's underworld, with so many notorious criminal successes under his belt that he's almost a legend. His reputation for violence, especially with a knife, is equally celebrated among the *cognoscenti*. He's wont to give guidance to those favouring retribution with a blade: "*Strike down the face – never across or upwards. That way, if the blade slips, you'll never risk hitting an artery. Slicing an artery usually ends up with a body. And murder's a mug's game.*" But Hill is as cautious as Ronnie Kray is unpredictable, and when Ronnie's in one of his depressions, as now, he can be completely irrational.

Hill wishes the twins hadn't chosen The Clermont for their first outing since Ronnie's most recent relapse, especially with The Big Edge only into its third week. Aspers and Burkie had assured Hill that this was a winner, but even they had been astonished when the first fortnight raked in over £100,000. Hill, ever the prudent businessman, knew it was too soon to be counting chickens. No suspicions had been apparent at the tables, but when dukes and earls lost fortunes, and fortunes had indeed been lost, questions usually followed.

Hill reaches the head of the stairs, his two thugs waiting patiently with their hands clasped in front of their belts. A waiter bearing a tray full of cocktails slips past them and speeds silently downstairs.

'Have they arrived?' he asks.

The men both nod. 'They're in the club room,' says one.

'Alone?'

'There was a coupla geezers having a chinwag by the

fireplace a while back. I've not checked since,' says the other.

'Okay,' replies Hill, as he leads the way across the landing. He opens the door and enters the club room. It is a beautifully appointed, high-ceilinged room, with a large chandelier, original paintings on the walls and comfortable armchairs in small groups. The principal light is extinguished and the effect of the several table lamps is to create two or three discreetly illuminated areas. Hill scans the room quickly. The twins, immaculately dressed as always, are seated in the far corner with their drinks. In the opposite corner, largely hidden from the door in a high-backed armchair, is another distinguished-looking man sitting forward in his armchair whispering with great intensity to another, younger, man whose expression suggests that he's being berated and doesn't like it.

Hill enters the room. He nods in greeting to the Kray twins but approaches the other two men. He bends to speak quietly in the older man's ear.

'Sorry to disturb you Lucky, but d'you think I could have the room for a moment? A bit of business, you understand?'

The man addressed turns his face toward Hill. He's in his thirties, with an enormous moustache that dominates his face and eyebrows that almost join in the middle of his brow.

'Yes, of course, Billy. We're done here anyway.' He stands.

'But my Lord …!' protests the man to whom he has been speaking, half-rising at the same time.

'Not another word!' hisses Lord Lucan, rage barely suppressed in his voice, and he strides out of the room without a backward glance. His companion scuttles after him and one of Hill's two bodyguards follows him out, leaving the other to plant himself heavily on the inside, his back to the closed door.

Hill crosses the room towards Ronnie and Reggie Kray. They both stand. After a decade or more of mentoring the twins, Hill can no longer be caught out by their occasional trick of pretending to be each other, but he is still amazed at the resemblance between them. The similarities are not only physical: they think so alike – no, more than that, Hill corrects himself – they seem to *share the same thoughts*. Their ability for unspoken, and to anyone else, undetected, communication is genuinely eerie, and never more apparent than when they are required to make instant decisions, whether in the context of business or violence. Hill had been present on many occasions when the boys couldn't possibly have discussed a proposed course of action in advance, and yet they would burst into synchronised movement, two cogs in a perfectly meshed machine, without any apparent communication between them. In Hill's opinion that was what gave them their edge over the rest of the new generation of ambitious strong-arm boys: people were frightened of their uncanny communication and the extent to which they were prepared to back each other up – to the death if necessary.

Hill shakes hands with each of them in turn and sits on the couch facing their two chairs.

'Drink?' asks Reggie, always the slightly more urbane and communicative of the two.

'No, thanks,' replies Hill with a wave of his hand. 'I want to get back to the tables as soon as possible. How can I help?'

Reggie speaks again. 'What happened to that mate of yours, the Irish geezer, Marrinan?'

Billy's eyes narrow. 'He was no mate of mine. He caused me no end of grief; worse since he was disbarred.'

'Is he still knocking about?' asks Reggie. 'We might have a job for him.'

'Don't waste your time, boys. I hear he died in a car crash a while back.'

'Is that right?' asks Ronnie.

'So I hear. But he's so slippery, I wouldn't believe it till I'd seen the corpse myself.' Hill smiles, briefly. 'What do you need a disbarred barrister for, anyway? Is this still about Charlie Horowitz?' Neither of the twins answers, but both stare at Hill. 'Fine. None of my business. But I'd have thought you'd got more important things to waste your time on. He's harmless.'

'Really? He got Harry Robeson banged up,' says Ronnie, with surprising force.

'The way I heard it,' replies Hill, calmly, 'that was down to Robeson himself. He copped a plea at the last second. You can't blame a brief for that.'

'That ain't the whole story,' says Ronnie.

Hill shrugs in apparent agreement. He doesn't need an argument with Ronnie Kray tonight. 'Sure – it never is,' he says in a conciliatory tone. 'I knew Horowitz a bit, y'know? During the War. He wasn't always the shining light of – what do you call it? – yeh, probity. Before his little dad came back and gave him a thick ear at the back end of '42 he was a bit of a jack-the-lad.'

'We know that,' says Ronnie. 'I fought him once on the undercard at Wembley in '51.'

'Nah, it weren't him,' corrects Reggie. 'It was that other Jewish kid. Horowitz was in the weight above.'

'Whatever. I'm going to have him – whatever he fucking weighs,' says Ronnie emphatically, his voice rising again. 'He's an arrogant cunt what needs teaching a lesson!'

Hill's eyes flick quickly from Ronnie to Reggie and back again, and shrugs, holding up his hands in submission. 'Okay. Whatever you think's best. But Marrinan's not going to help you. If you need to get close to Horowitz, Holborne, or whatever he calls himself now, you'll have to come up with something else. Sorry boys.'

He gets up to leave. 'I'll send some more drinks up.'

As he walks towards the door, his bodyguard's hand resting on the handle, Hill turns and pauses, head cocked to one side and his intelligent eyes glinting like those of a corvid. The Kray twins regard him patiently, waiting. There are few people in the London underworld Ronnie and Reggie Kray actually respect, but Billy Hill is one of them. He's clever, thoughtful and, since his release from prison for a warehouse robbery in the late 1940s, had made a fortune through his various criminal enterprises, never being caught.

'Who are the people who get closest to barristers?' he asks quietly, almost to himself.

The twins think. 'Coppers?' suggests Ronnie.

'Closer.'

'Clients,' says Reggie after a moment's consideration.

'Exactly. And where? Inside, that's where. Where legal visits are ...'

'Unsupervised,' finishes Ronnie, sitting back in his chair thoughtfully.

The door is opened for Hill and he's about to step outside when he turns again. 'If I wanted to shiv a brief, I'd find someone already banged up on a murder charge, someone bound to go down. I'd offer to find him a top-class brief and then look after his family. What'd he have to lose? You can't be hanged twice. G'night gents. Have a nice evening.'

Hill disappears through the door but as it's about to close his head reappears. He's wearing a smile. 'But I'd avoid the Chemmy tonight, if I were you. Got a feeling it might be another good night for the house.'

chapter 10

Detective Sergeant Cyril Jones, known throughout Soho as "Moody's sergeant", pinches out his roll-up and slips the remaining inch in his top jacket pocket. He knows it's a disgusting habit and his guvnor says it makes him stink, but he's calculated that it saves him at least half a crown on snout and Rizlas every week. That amounts to over ten quid a year, or the price of a weekend in Bognor. And despite the fat brown envelopes that he receives every week from those kings of pornography, Humphreys and Silver – his share of the licence fees paid to the Dirty Squad to turn a blind eye – Cyril Jones has always been careful with his money. Known for it, in fact.

He listens as keys jangle in the corridor outside the visiting room. A few moments later the prison guard escorts a man into the room and shoves him into the chair opposite Jones.

'Thanks,' says Jones, and the guard leaves without a word, closing the metal door behind him with a clang.

Jones examines the man before him. He's in his thirties and he is strikingly good-looking. His face and the top part of his neck have been bronzed by sun and wind, though Jones can see white skin below a "V" of suntan. Thick honey-coloured hair, with lighter highlights caused by exposure to a lot of sunshine, falls over a level brow beneath which are deep-set light brown eyes, a straight nose and a strong chin. He would not have looked out of place on the billboards for the American Saturday matinee films which Jones sporadically attends when he succumbs to the dreariness of his two-room flat in Shepherd's Bush. However, Jones knows that this specimen of perfect manhood is no film idol; he has read the contents of the manila file now closed on the table between them.

As a remand prisoner, the man is entitled to wear his own clothes, consisting in this case of a sleeveless leather jerkin over a shirt with rolled sleeves revealing power-ful tattooed arms with tight knotted muscles; high-waisted baggy blue trousers held up with a frayed leather belt; and a flat cap perched back on the crown of his head. The tanned face and lithe build speak of hard physical work.

'What do you want, copper?' asks the young man. 'You're not Waterguard.' His bright eyes appraise the policeman from between narrowed lids.

'Hello, Merlin. You don't mind me calling you "Merlin" do you?'

'I don't give a fuck what you call me; what d'you want?'

Jones reaches into his jacket pocket and pulls out a packet of Players. He doesn't usually smoke them himself – rollups are much cheaper – but cigarettes are universal currency inside, and he knows that Merlin will need them to buy soap, shampoo, perhaps even protection. He can also see from the tar stains on the index and middle fingers of Merlin's right hand that he's a heavy smoker. He reaches over the table and offers the packet. Merlin looks from Jones's face to the cigarettes and back again.

'Go, on take one,' urges Jones. 'In fact, take a few. It'll cost you nothing.'

After a momentary hesitation Merlin reaches over and takes a handful of cigarettes from the packet. He puts all but one carefully in his shirt pocket to spend later, and flips one neatly into his mouth. Jones smiles, takes one himself, strikes a match, and lights them both.

'How're you finding it inside?' asks Jones. Merlin doesn't answer, but stares hard at the policeman. 'No one giving you any ... trouble?'

Merlin continues to stare, his brow creasing slightly as he tries to understand the hidden depths present in the question.

'Suit yourself,' says Jones, drawing a deep lungful of smoke and sitting back on the hard, wooden chair. 'Right. It says here,' he points at the manila folder with the cigarette, 'that you killed an Assistant Preventive Officer as he was conducting a search of your lighter. Is that right?'

Merlin turns his head away and he looks up at the barred rectangle of sky in the wall above the sergeant's shoulder. 'If that's what it says,' he replies in a disinterested voice.

'It does. It also says that you confessed to murdering him. In an interview under caution.'

Merlin resumes his steely-eyed glare for a second, but then looks away without response.

'You're going to be arraigned in a fortnight,' continues Jones. 'Pleading or fighting?'

'I don't have to tell you that,' says Merlin lazily, still focusing on the patch of sky-blue in the institutional green of the interview room wall. He lowers his head slowly to look again at the policeman and spits a flake of tobacco onto the table less than an inch from the other's hand. 'I don't have to tell no one that, 'cept my brief.'

'Quite true, son, quite true. But your brief's surely told you your chances? I mean ...' and Jones pats the folder gently with his fingertips, '...you're no fool. You're banged to rights. You know it and I know it.'

Merlin examines his nails as if disinterested. Jones smiles; it's a decent act but he can read suppressed fear in the young man's pursed lips and tense eyes.

'And you know what that means. Waterguard are coppers – weird boat coppers it's true – but coppers all the same. And you was resisting arrest. So either way, you're gonna swing.'

Merlin suddenly stands, the chair rocking and falling backwards to the floor. 'Piss off!' he says, and he bangs on the door. 'I'm going back to me cell.'

'Up to you son. But I'm trying to do you a favour here. I'm offering to get a decent brief for you – not just some tosser you've never heard of, assigned under legal aid. I'm offering to make sure your mum's looked after if the worst occurs. Not just for a while, but for the rest of.' The metal door opens and the prison guard is standing outside. 'Sure you don't want to discuss it?' asks Jones, still in his seat.

Merlin pauses. 'It's alright,' he says to the guard. He turns and rights the chair, settling back in his seat at the table. The guard closes the door again.

'Who are you?' asks Merlin. 'And why would you help me?'

'I'm Detective Sergeant Jones of the Obscene Publications Squad.'

The young man's brow screws up in puzzlement. 'The Dirty Squad? What on earth would you want with me? That's not my game.'

'We know that. I'm just a messenger. Let's just say you've a got a guardian angel on the outside who's prepared to throw a lot of effort at your defence. If you get off, well, that's your good fortune. But ...' and Jones leans forward intently, pointing so that his index finger is only two inches from the bridge of the other's nose, '*but*... if you're convicted we need you to do a little job for us.'

'What sort of job? I'll be banged up, won't I? Waiting on the hangman. Not exactly available for work.'

'You'll be in exactly the right place for this little job, believe me. And when it's done, your mum – Beatrice, isn't it? – will receive a very large sum of money; enough to see her through to the end of her life. Where else you gonna get an offer like that? Eh?'

The young man stares hard at the policeman and blows smoke straight at his face. Jones doesn't flinch.

'Think about it, Merlin. She's in bad health, I hear; got no one but you. How else you going to provide for her after ... well ... once you're gone?'

Merlin takes a final deep drag of his cigarette and slowly stubs it out in the foil ashtray on the table. 'How can I trust you? I don't know you from Adam.'

'You don't have to trust me, son. Wait till you see the brief we've got lined up. He's one of the top barristers in practice. If you've any chance of an acquittal, it's with him.'

'I don't see the catch.'

Jones smiles slowly and shakes his head. 'That's the beauty of it, son. There ain't a catch. It's a win–win.'

Merlin sighs deeply. 'Okay. If I was to be interested, just what's the job you want done at the end of this?'

•

An hour later the prison door clangs shut behind a satisfied DS Jones. He pauses to light up the stub end of his rollup and then walks back to his private car, a light blue Morris 1100, parked around the back of Brixton Prison. He appears to be in no hurry. He opens the door, sits in the driving seat and leans back, his eyes closed.

Fifteen minutes later a tall man with thinning grey hair brushed across a domed head walks around the corner from the front yard of the prison. He wears a raincoat buttoned up to the neck which, had it been noted by anyone, might have appeared odd as the weather was warm and there had been no rain for several days. He approaches the Morris 1100, places a hand on the door handle of the passenger door, scans the empty pavements quickly and slides into the passenger seat. As he does so, his raincoat parts slightly around his knees, and a flash of blue prison uniform serge is visible.

the lighterman

A hurried whispered conversation occurs in the car and a fat brown envelope is passed from DS Jones to the prison officer. Without a further word the recipient of the envelope leaves the car and walks swiftly away. The entire exchange takes less than sixty seconds.

chapter 11

The front door at 178 Vallance Road, a small terraced Victorian cottage in Bethnal Green, opens and closes as Reggie Kray steps into the narrow hallway. The noise of his entry is drowned by the rumble of the Liverpool Street-bound train whose tracks run almost directly behind the terrace's backyards. As the street falls silent again Reggie hears his mother, Violet, talking quietly to someone in the kitchen. He hangs up his jacket and opens the kitchen door.

Ronnie Kray is sitting at the kitchen table in his shirt sleeves. His hands are clasped around a tumbler of amber liquid, full almost to the brim, and Reggie's eyes flick to the almost empty bottle of spirits by his brother's elbow. At the table are their mother and older brother, Charlie. There is tension in the room. Violet shares a look with Reggie, her eyebrows raised with a fractional incline of her head towards Ronnie.

Reggie pulls out the remaining chair from the table and sits down. 'Sorry I'm late, Mum,' he says.

Violet gets up. She is in her mid-fifties, short and stocky with her brittle blond hair cut fairly short. 'That's all right dear. We kept yours warm.'

Violet takes a kitchen towel and removes a covered plate

from the oven. She places it in front of Reggie and goes to collect some cutlery. Reggie nods towards a cardboard box of pills on the table next to the bottle of spirits.

'Not feeling too good, Ron?'

If Ronnie Kray hears the enquiry, he doesn't answer.

'We've been trying to persuade him to take them,' says Charlie. 'It's the pills the shrink gave him last month.'

'Don't wanna fuckin' take them,' mumbles Ronnie, head down and staring unseeing at the table top. 'I ain't fuckin' mad.'

His voice is slurred and Reggie guesses that his brother has drunk almost the entire bottle of spirits since the early afternoon when he stood up without a word and walked out of the billiard hall. His mood had been on the wane for several days.

'No one said you are,' reassures Reggie. 'They're just to help you stay calm.'

'Well I ain't fuckin' taking 'em.'

Violet places a knife and fork and another empty tumbler in front of Reggie and resumes her seat. 'There's a brown ale left if you want it,' she offers.

Reggie reaches for the bottle of spirits – brandy, he now sees. Ronnie's hand moves towards the bottle as if to grab it but he doesn't complete the movement.

'Can't I have one?' asks Reggie.

Ronnie shrugs. 'Help yourself,' he slurs.

'I called Rose,' says Violet. 'She should be here soon.'

Reggie pours himself a slug of the brandy, picks up the knife and fork and starts eating the meat loaf, gravy and boiled potatoes on the plate in front of him. The room descends into an uncomfortable silence. Reggie chews for a moment and then points at his twin brother with his fork.

'I got something that'll cheer you up,' he announces. Ronnie doesn't answer. 'Did you hear me, Ron?'

Ronnie Kray lifts his head slowly, as if struggling against the gravity pulling it towards the table. It takes a moment for his eyes to focus on Reggie. 'What's that then?'

'That brief we was talking about. The one you're anxious to sort out. The word from the Temple is he's starting a week-long trial at the Bailey next week. You might want to have a word with that chap at the prison; get transport arranged. Wednesday or Thursday maybe, late afternoon.'

It takes a few moments for the words to percolate through Ronnie's alcohol-fuddled brain. Then he nods slowly. 'Yeah, that is a bit of good news,' he says, an uncertain smile just touching the corners of his mouth.

•

Charles eases himself into the hot water of the bath with a sigh. He can hear Sally in the kitchen making them both a cup of tea. A moment later she prods the bathroom door open with her toe and comes into the steamy bathroom. She holds out a cup to Charles, who takes it, and she sits on the edge of the bath.

'Do you want me to have a look?' she asks.

'It feels as though it's falling off,' replies Charles bending forward so that Sally can see the dressing on his back.

'Hang on a sec,' she says, placing her cup of tea on the

floor and kneeling by the side of the bath to look more closely. Her fingers explore the edge of the dressing. 'It's curled up at the edges. It's a bit grubby.'

'They said not to touch it until today.'

'What you want me to do?'

'If it looks as if it's going to come off, just peel it off carefully.'

Sally picks at the one remaining corner still adhering to Charles's skin, and slowly lifts the dressing off completely. 'Jesus, Charlie! This is much worse than you let on. There's got to be, what? twenty stitches here.'

'Thirty, I was told.'

In not wanting to worry Sally with his suspicions – at least until he has a plan, a course of action to follow – Charles has been selective with his account of the attack outside the Old Bailey, repeating the police theory that he was the victim of an attempted robbery. He has made no mention of the phone message left, presumably by his attacker, in Sally's name.

Sally gets a flannel and carefully washes the dried blood off Charles's back. She runs a finger gently along the fresh pink scar. It looks fully healed but she knows it still hurts when Charles moves, as she hears his breath catch when he bends to pick up his bag or put on his shoes. 'Have you heard anything more from Snow Hill?' she asks, concerned.

'No. I need to chase them.'

'Yes, you do,' replies Sally emphatically.

She gets off her knees and returns to her position on the edge of the bath. She appraises Charles's naked body in the water. Sally has had boyfriends before Charles, but that's what they were – *boys* – compared to this powerful, very masculine man. They haven't had sex in the two weeks since the attack due to Sally's fear that the movement might open Charles's wound. It's been their longest period of abstinence since their relationship began and both are acutely aware of it. Sally slides her hand into the hot water and caresses Charles's penis, staring into his eyes. He keeps his eyes locked onto hers, enjoying the sensation, the light touch of her fingers and the blood pumping to his groin. He rises in little jerks out of the water until he is fully erect.

Sally breaks off eye contact and looks down. 'Glad to see everything's still working,' she says with a smile. 'I was beginning to wonder. Fancy a gentle test drive?'

chapter 12

'I shall remain in court, gentlemen, but please feel free to leave.'

Charles and his opponent bow to Mr Justice Fletcher and start gathering together their papers. The movement causes Charles to wince slightly, but today is the third day he has managed without painkillers, and he hopes to start training again at the weekend.

The usual courtesy requires that the judge should never be left in court without barristers present, and so counsel whose cases have finished will wait patiently in their seats until the next case is called on or the barristers in that case arrive to take their places. Fletcher however, a straightforward Yorkshireman with few airs and graces, is not such a stickler for protocol, and if he has paperwork to do will frequently do it at the bench rather than retiring to his chambers in the bowels of the court. He often excuses any members of the Bar whose cases have finished.

That is, however, the extent of Fletcher's humanity. He is known throughout the legal profession as the most prosecution-minded judge on the South-Eastern Circuit. When one prosecutes for the Crown before Mr Justice Fletcher it's like sailing with a flood tide and the wind in your sails. He agrees with every point you make for the Crown, praises the police officers for their professionalism and makes frequent asides to the jury as to the manifest credibility of the prosecution witnesses. On the other hand, defending before him is like wading thigh-deep through a swamp into the teeth of a gale. Every Defence point is met with scoffing or barely concealed irritation; cross-examinations are interrupted frequently to prevent Defence counsel building up a head of steam and to afford helpless prosecution witnesses time to think; answers are even suggested to questions to which no ready answer can be found; Defence witnesses are mocked and undermined from the bench; and the Defence case prompts frequent looks of sarcastic disbelief, shared knowingly with the jury. A judge's summing up is supposed to focus on the law and summarise the evidence without telling the jury what it should decide are the facts. Nonetheless, judges still have enormous power to sway a jury and indicate what conclusions should or should not be reached, and Fletcher invariably uses that power to destroy the defence case and commend to the jury the Crown's version of events. Barristers and solicitors could often be heard in robing rooms and Bar Messes bemoaning their fate when listed before Fletcher, and wondering out loud when the old bastard was likely to retire. He is now well into his 70s, the most long-serving judge to sit at the Central Criminal Court, but there seems to be no end in sight.

As to the cause of his partisanship, he is reputed to be a member of the same Masonic Lodge as many senior police officers but, in Charles's opinion, the explanation is much simpler. Fletcher is old-school, an integral part of the establishment. He views the police as an essential bulwark against the disgusting tide of immorality sweeping the country; he categorically refuses to believe that any police officer could be as corrupt as most defence advocates know is in fact the case.

Charles has watched with detached amusement the discomfiture this trial has caused his Lordship. Charles's client faces indictment of two counts of false accounting in a position of trust, a charge which would normally guarantee Fletcher's ire notwithstanding the fact that the sum allegedly appropriated is as modest as sixteen shillings and sixpence. Unfortunately for the judge this accused is a senior staff member at the Colonial Office, a lay magistrate and the treasurer of his golf club; a man of unimpeachable reputation and as upright a member of the establishment as one could hope to meet. Fletcher's wish to "put the boot in" to someone facing charges of this type appears to be equal and opposite to his wish to defend someone who is clearly a very decent fellow. As a result, extraordinarily, Fletcher has been conflicted into relative silence. He has let the advocates get on with their respective jobs with barely a word for the last four days.

Charles's case is not quite complete – the final Defence witness, a character witness from the accused's Army days has been delayed – but at quarter to four on the fifth day of an interminably dull trial in Court 4 of the Old Bailey everyone present is pleased to be offered an early adjournment until the following morning.

The jury having already been excused for the rest of the day, the other occupants of the already half-empty courtroom rise. A handful of journalists had attended for the first couple of hours on the opening day, hoping to hear tales of corruption by government officials but, having listened to the prosecution opening, had decided that the case was of no great interest to anyone. One by one they had slipped out to find something more interesting for their editors. Except for the accused's wife and people sheltering from the sporadic rain, the benches reserved for the public have been largely empty.

Charles's opponent, a dour but not unpleasant northern Irishman named McKenzie, stacks his books and puts them under his arm. As he sidles out of the barristers' bench he leans towards Charles.

'Finish tomorrow?' he asks under his breath.

'Oh God, I certainly hope so!' whispers Charles with feeling. 'My speech'll take ten minutes at most.'

'Same here,' confirms McKenzie as he starts towards the courtroom doors.

There is a sudden commotion from the dock. The accused, on bail throughout, has already left the courtroom, and Charles turns to see what's happening.

A tall uniformed guard with thinning grey hair stands in the dock, having come up the steep stone stairs from the cells below.

'Application for a dock brief, My Lord!' he shouts. A

handsome young man wearing a flat cap appears behind him, manacled to the guard's wrist.

Charles whirls round as McKenzie disappears through the court doors with a regretful and rather guilty backward glance at him. Charles has been caught. As the only barrister left in court and still in full robes, professional etiquette requires him to take the case and represent the unfortunate prisoner, whatever the charge may be and whatever other commitments he might have.

Mr Justice Fletcher puts his pen down and leans forward, a mock sympathetic smile on his thin features. 'Bad luck, Mr Holborne,' he says with malice. 'You appear to have acquired a new client.'

Charles's heart sinks; a docker! The institution of a dock brief was centuries old and for a barrister with a busy practice like Charles it was a thorough nuisance. Barristers can normally only be instructed by solicitors, but in rare cases where an accused is brought to trial without representation he can chose from any of the robed barristers in court to defend him – for the princely sum of one pound three shillings and sixpence, to be paid in advance by the prisoner.

'What's the charge on the indictment?' asks the Judge of the gaoler.

'Murder,' replies the gaoler. 'Of a Waterguard,' he adds, 'and while resisting arrest.'

This further information is all-important. Since the Homicide Act 1957 came into force most types of murder are no longer punishable by hanging, but murder of a police officer and while resisting arrest remain two of the exceptions. So, this unfortunate prisoner faces the rope; not something to attempt without legal representation. The thought flashes through part of Charles's mind that it's surprising for the gaoler to be so well-informed about this particular remand prisoner's case, or for him to be so apparently gleeful about the possible death penalty, but he pushes the thought aside as he reaches for his Archbold, the criminal practitioner's Bible, to look up the legal aid provisions applying to prisoners without means.

'Then why wasn't the prisoner given a Defence Certificate under The Poor Prisoners' Defence Act?' asks Fletcher, clearly thinking along the same lines. 'He'll be on trial for his life.'

'Sufficient means, I understand, my Lord. And a full confession.'

'But Your Honour!' shouts the accused man from the dock.

'Be quiet, you,' says the judge. 'You'll have your chance to be heard. What about legal aid?'

'If I can assist, my Lord,' offers Charles. 'You may find some help at paragraph 409 of Archbold, the 1962 edition.'

'Thank you, Mr Holborne. Just give me a minute.'

Judge and barrister each read the relevant paragraphs in silence. After a couple of minutes the Judge looks up at Charles again. 'It appears that the examining justices had a discretion which, one must suppose, they exercised against the prisoner.'

'Yes my Lord.'

'Very well. I'm not disposed to overturn their exercise of discretion. I won't start hearing the case this afternoon, but be prepared by tomorrow morning.'

'My Lord, this man is on trial for his life! How can I possibly –'

'You've heard my ruling Mr Holborne. That's enough. I expect to have this man arraigned tomorrow afternoon, Monday morning at the latest. Who's for the Crown?'

At that very moment the court doors burst open with a bang, and a dishevelled barrister almost runs down the aisle. Charles knows him well: Collin Montgomery QC, a charming and pathologically absent-minded barrister who was forever misplacing his wig, his place in the depositions and his notes. It makes little difference: he is brilliant, with or without notes, and is one of the foremost silks favoured by the Crown in heavyweight cases. He is also fun to work with and completely straight; he doesn't believe in the cunning employed by many prosecutors: no gamesmanship, no withholding of evidence, no taking of bad legal points and no sleights of hand; he has no need of such trickery.

'Ah, Mr Montgomery,' says the Judge. 'Are you for the Crown?'

'Please forgive me, my Lord,' gasps Montgomery. 'We were in another court and were only given a couple of minutes' notice that the prisoner was being brought up for arraignment. My junior –' and he looks around desperately to the back of the court – 'is apparently somewhere else. I thought he was behind me.'

'Not to worry Mr Montgomery. Mr Holborne will put you in the picture. Now ...' and Mr Justice Fletcher looks across at the dock. 'Stand up young man. You've heard my decision. Mr Holborne is an extremely experienced and, if I may say so, talented advocate, and you couldn't have chosen better had you the choice of the entire Bar.'

Charles knows that this hyperbole is not to be taken seriously and is entirely disingenuous. Fletcher's only purpose is to justify his decision not to grant legal aid or allow greater time for the accused's defence. If the prisoner has confessed to killing a Waterguard, that is enough for Fletcher. A short trial followed by sentence of death are all he deserves.

'What's your name?' demands Fletcher.

'Me birth certificate says Isaac Conway. But I'm generally known on the River as Merlin.'

Charles whirls round, looking at the prisoner in the dock for the first time. 'Good God!' he exclaims, not entirely under his breath.

'I'm sorry Mr Holborne? Is there a problem?' asks Fletcher.

For a moment Charles is utterly speechless, but when, after a few seconds, he has gathered his thoughts and closed his mouth, his first impulse is to tell the Judge that he cannot possibly represent this accused. He even draws breath to say the words. But then he registers Merlin's eyes: wide-open with shock and containing a silent intense plea directed at Charles. In that split-second Charles makes a decision which will affect the rest of his life. He turns, and by the time he faces the Judge again his face is calm and composed.

'Nothing at all, my Lord. If your Lordship will give me permission, I'll go down with the prisoner immediately and start work.'

chapter 13

October 1940. The Blitz. And 14-year old Charlie Horowitz is forcing himself to think, despite the cold, his chattering teeth and the fear that he may faint at any moment. For a few days after he crept back into the East End under cover of the blackout he'd tried to live in what was left of the family home on British Street. The scullery still stood – although roofless – and Charles had rummaged cautiously through the timber, dust and rubble and had found some tins of food. Astonishingly, there were also two intact glass jars of his mother's favourite pickled herring. They had been blown off their shelf clear through the larder door and had landed on what had been his mother's armchair. The thick green glass of one was cracked but otherwise both were undamaged except for a coating of fine powdery dust. They looked so comical sitting side-by-side in his mother's accustomed seat – a sign that her spirit still ruled the house – that on discovering them by the light of a flaring match Charles had to suppress first a shiver of shock and then a spasm of laughter.

A roof beam from the living room had come down at one end but it remained propped at an angle, creating a triangular hole through which an agile fourteen-year old could crawl into a small recess formed of the rear wall and the collapsed sideboard. With a blanket and pillow recovered from the roof of next door's outside lavatory – where they'd landed after the bomb struck – Charles had been able to construct a cosy if rather dusty den, where he stored the personal treasures rescued from the rubble: his mother's handed down silver Sabbath candlesticks which, he knew, were so important to her; his three-bladed penknife, given to him by his father for his twelfth birthday; a photograph of David and himself holding hands and squinting into the sun on the beach at Southend taken several years earlier; and, of greatest importance to him, a photograph of his first girlfriend, Adalie, whom he prayed, without much hope, had survived the direct hit on Hallsville Junior. For the first few days he had even been able to drink, as metallic-tasting water trickled down from a bent and pierced lead pipe that formerly ran to the kitchen sink.

Charles would spend the nights curled in what he referred to as his "hole", listening to bombs dropping all around him. The Anderson shelter in the garden was buried under a ton of masonry and he knew that if he took shelter in one of the underground stations he was certain to be asked why he was alone and what had happened to his parents. That would inevitably mean a return to Wales, and a month of that had been quite sufficient. Teased constantly for supposedly possessing horns and a tail – which the local schoolchildren assured one another in overheard whispers were the hallmarks of Judaism – and publicly ridiculed by the teacher for his inability to explain the Holy Trinity, he had at first refused to attend the school and then, when forced to go by his father, had picked fights with anyone who dared stare at him in the playground. After several days of torn clothing, bloodied knuckles and half-hearted beatings by his father, the school and the Horowitzes tacitly agreed that Charles's formal education had probably come to an end. After a further few days of boredom hanging around the farm, regarded sullenly by both farmer and farm animals, Charles had had enough. He had slipped out one moonlit night, crept across the fields, and jumped on an eastbound train as it paused to take on water. His only regret had been forgetting to leave a note explaining his absence to David.

At daybreak Charles would wipe his hands and face with a cloth dampened from the dripping pipe, dust off his clothes and, when sure he wouldn't be heard or seen, wriggle out of the hole to go foraging. British Street itself was deserted, all other families having been evacuated from the dangerously unstable buildings. He calculated that on the busy Mile End Road, a main artery into the City, the fire officers, ARP wardens and other volunteers making up the Civil Defence teams would probably be too exhausted and overrun to worry about asking questions or checking his identity, but he took no chances. Instead he would turn south and cut across Bow Cemetery. The cemetery too had been hit by German bombs. Each morning there were new craters with bits of coffin and white bones pointing accusingly at the morning sky through the mounds of soil and clumps of disturbed turf, and many of the headstones were blown far from their original positions. They lay like scattered dominoes, broken, chipped and scarred by shrapnel.

Charles would then turn towards Limehouse and the River. Several streets close to the river had also been evacuated but had thus far remained undamaged, and he had no trouble getting in and raiding larders and basements.

However, after six days the mains supply at the end of British Street was shut off, and the trickle of water in the hole dried up. For two days Charles managed to fill empty milk bottles from houses in other streets but then he began to feel ill. He lay in his hole, shivering and doubled up with stomach cramps. He crawled out to the garden several times to empty his bowels, and crawled back again, exhausted. Then, late that night, he was woken by torchlight shining into his flushed and feverish face. A new incendiary bombing raid, through which Charles had somehow slept, had set alight houses at both ends of the street and as Charles crawled out he found himself in the centre of a bustle of activity of firemen and ARP wardens. He was moved out of harm's way, wrapped in a clean blanket and given a cup of tea, the assumption being that he'd been dug out of a house that had just been damaged, and that his family was still buried. Ten minutes later his stash of treasured possessions was discovered and he had no choice but to admit that he had been living alone in the remains of the family home. As his belongings were handed to him in a paper bag by a tired and humourless ARP warden, Charles gave his name, date of birth and former address to his captors.

That had been over an hour earlier and long after the "all clear" sirens had sounded, but Charles is still sitting on the pavement, shaking, his back against slightly, but today ambulance, wrapped in a blanket smelling of moth balls. The cramps have subsided, but his whole body cries out to lie down. Every now and then he looks up to watch the firefighters dousing the flames further up the road. Finally one of the firemen (the one who had handed the cup of tea to him with a wink over an hour earlier) approaches. Charles's heart sinks as he sees the fireman in conversation with a tall young police constable in uniform. Charles stands unsteadily, holding onto the ambulance for support. The fireman is covered in dust and soot and looks as if he's been down a mine, but his teeth gleam white as he smiles and introduces the constable.

'Charlie, this is Constable Archer. He's going to take care of you from here on. Best of luck, son!' he says shortly, and he turns and jogs back to rejoin his colleagues.

'Okay,' says Archer. He looks down at Charles and then reads from his notebook. 'Charles Horowitz, born 4 December 1925. Formerly of 26 British Street, Mile End. Is that right?'

'Yeah,' says Charles, his voice shaking and uncertain.

'Come over here and sit down,' says the constable, pointing to a dwarf wall outside a demolished house. They both sit, and the constable takes off his helmet and rests it next to him.

'And your parents – Harry and Millie Horowitz, of the same address, but presently evacuated somewhere in Carmarthenshire?'

'Yeah.'

'But you don't know exactly where?'

Charles shakes his head. 'It 'ad cows,' he says despondently.

'Don't get cheeky with me, sunshine. Don't you think we've enough to deal with without a runaway schoolboy?'

Charles flushes briefly, chastened, but tries to explain. 'I weren't trying to be funny.'

The policeman looks at the exhausted and dirty youngster, his pale face and febrile eyes, and nods. 'Got any family left in London?' he asks more gently.

Charles shakes his head again. 'I've been trying to think. I don't think so. Me mum 'ad two older brothers. But one went to live in South Africa and the other one she don't speak to – not for years. I dunno where he lives, or even if he's still in the Smoke.'

'What's the name of the brother who didn't emigrate?' The constable takes an inch of pencil stub from behind his left ear and holds it, poised to write, above his notebook. It's almost pitch dark except for the moving loom of an anti-aircraft searchlight behind the row of destroyed houses, and the constable angles his notepad to get some light onto it.

'Uncle Jacob. He worked on the river.'

'On the Thames, eh? What, waterman? Lighterman?'

'Dunno. Why?'

'Reserved occupation – he may well still be in London. Surname?'

'Cohen. But I ain't seen 'im since I was a kid. And he changed his name … "Conway" maybe?'

'Jacob Conway. And where does he live?'

'I don't know. It was near the river.'

The constable finishes scrawling. 'Righto, son. I'll make a call and see what we can find out.' He stands, and hesitates, considering Charles carefully. 'You're going to stay put, right? You're not going to do a runner on me, are you?' checks the constable.

Charles shakes his head. 'Nah – knackered. Not feeling too kosher.'

'No, you don't look right. You need a proper bed and some food.'

•

Constable Archer had returned with an address and informed Charles that a police car was on its way to take them to Shadwell, but after waiting for almost another hour he had concluded that the bomb damage in Mile End Road was probably preventing the car from getting through, and so they are now walking. Charles fears with every step that his knees will give way, but fortunately Police Constable Archer is not a chatty man and Charles is left to grit his teeth and concentrate on putting one foot in front of the other. Archer only speaks once on the journey.

'You know where we are now?'

Charles looks up and recognises the street immediately. 'Yeah. Cable Street.'

'Were you here?'

Charles knows immediately to what the policeman is referring. The Battle of Cable Street had already become part of East End folklore, especially among the Jewish population. Like many children growing up in the East End, Charles had listened attentively to the frequent impromptu street corner meetings of the Labour Party, the Communists and Moseley's British Union of Fascists. It was inevitable that he, like all the kids from the surrounding streets, would become aware of political events. He'd actually been in Levi's the poulterers, collecting a chicken for his mother, when the bricks thrown by two Black Shirts had come through the window, covering all the customers inside with shards of glass. It had been in the papers. And although his parents had strictly forbidden him to go anywhere near the route of Moseley's planned march – everyone knew it was a deliberate provocation to which there was bound to be a response – like every other boy in his *cheder* class he'd slipped out of his Sunday school lessons that morning to watch.

'I was ten.' Charles glances up at the tall man walking slowly by his side. 'And yeah,' he concedes. 'I was 'ere.'

'So was I. I'd only been in a few months.'

They continue walking in silence for a while. When Archer speaks again, what he says surprises Charles. 'Frightening, wasn't it?'

Charles looks across at the young policeman, trying

to judge if he's genuine, and concludes that he is. 'Yeah,' Charles confesses. 'I got caught in the crush at Royal Mint Street. Couldn't get me breath at all for a bit. Thought I was a goner.'

'I lost my helmet. Well, in truth, it was taken off me. By your lot. Lots of us did. But that was all; no violence, not even angry words. Symbolic I suppose. The Commies – well that was different; a right bunch of thugs.'

The policeman pauses, searching for the words to say something further. 'But I did get a new respect for your people, that day. The Jewish community, I mean.'

Charles doesn't know how to answer so he remains quiet, and they walk on in silence.

The sky over the jagged wrecks of houses – silhouetted broken teeth in the gums of a wrecked East End – lightens from black to blue as dawn approaches. Every now and then they are forced into detours by bomb disposal crews and firemen, and the journey takes another hour.

It is almost full daylight when they arrive at a narrow, four-storey, grey terraced house on Juniper Street. Charles can smell the salt air from Shadwell Basin, just behind the houses, and a squabble of gulls fight over something small and dead in the gutter.

Constable Archer stops at number 16, Charles behind him, and bangs on the flaking wooden door. They hear shouting and clattering from somewhere inside but no one comes to answer the knock. The policeman knocks again. This time footsteps are heard approaching the door, and it opens a crack.

'Yeah?' says a boy's voice. The door is only open a couple of inches and the hallway beyond is in darkness. It's impossible to see who is speaking.

'I'm Police Constable Percival Archer, and I'm looking for a Jacob Conway, or Cohen. Is there anyone of that name at this address?'

There's a pause and then the boy behind the door evidently turns away. 'Dad. Dad! There's a copper 'ere to see you.' The door opens wider to reveal a skinny boy in a vest, short grey trousers and bare feet, aged between ten and eleven. The outline of someone approaching from the back of the house can be seen and then the door opens fully. A man in his mid-forties blocks the doorway. He is stocky with prematurely grey hair. Charles doesn't recognise him but, as he looks more closely, Charles notices a definite resemblance to himself: a similar build – a very broad chest with muscled forearms sticking out of the rolled up sleeves of his shirt – and although the hair is grey, it falls in curls over half the man's forehead in just the same way as Charles's black curls do.

'I'm Jacob Conway,' says the man, suspicion in his voice. His eyes move from the police officer to Charles behind him and back again, and in that split second of eye-contact Charles thinks that he detects a flicker of recognition.

'Do you know this young man?' asks Constable Archer, stepping back slightly.

Conway narrows his eyes and starts to shake his head slowly. 'Not sure I do ...'

'He says you're his uncle. His parents are Millie and Harry Horowitz?'

Conway leans forward, examining Charles more carefully. 'So ... you'd be ... Charlie?' he asks.

'Yeah,' confirms Charles.

'In that case,' says Conway, 'I do know him. Or at least, I know of 'im. Last time I saw 'im was shortly after his *bris*. But what's the problem? I've got to leave for work.'

'Can I come in for a moment?' asks Constable Archer. 'We don't want to be discussing this on the pavement.'

Conway hesitates but then steps back to let the policeman enter. Charles follows, Conway's eyes on him throughout. 'Go in the front parlour then,' he says, 'on your left.'

They file in, followed by Conway and the young boy. They are in a dark room full of heavy furniture. An enormous Marconi wireless set, as large as a sideboard, takes pride of place in the corner of the room, a standard lamp and several chairs in a semi-circle around it as if awaiting the start of a broadcast. Before Conway can shut the parlour door completely it's pushed open again and an older man enters. He's short and wiry, almost completely bald, with a sun-bronzed pate and arms. He has deep wrinkles around his brown eyes which seem to dance with mischief. Charles puts him in his late sixties, but his movement is quick and agile and he looks very fit for his age. He perches on the arm of an armchair just inside the door, careful not to disturb the embroidered antimacassar, and smiles at Charles.

'And you are, sir?' asks Archer.

'I'm not important,' replies the older man with a Germanic accent.

'That's my father-in-law,' explains Conway. 'He lives with us. Now, what's the problem?'

'It's this young lad, here –' starts Archer, turning towards Charles behind him. He is just in time to see Charles folding up on the floor and his paper bag of possessions hitting the wooden boards. Charles's knees have finally given way. Archer and the boy leap to catch him. Charles isn't unconscious but the room is spinning and its colours have suddenly bleached white. He's helped onto a couch where he collapses, clammy and breathing heavily.

'What's the matter wiv 'im?' asks the boy.

'I'm fine,' says Charles, but the words are mumbled and he can't focus.

'He was evacuated with Mr and Mrs Horowitz to Wales, but he ran away. As far as I can tell he's been living rough in the remains of British Street for about a week. He's been looting food and I suspect he's eaten something he shouldn't. Bit of bed rest and feeding up and he'll be right as rain.'

'P'raps he should be in hospital,' suggests Conway sceptically.

'There isn't a bed to spare in any hospital in London,' replies the constable. 'You know that.'

Conway sighs. 'Yeah. But we can't look after him. I don't mean to be unkind, but we've a full house 'ere – and as he says that, as if to prove the point, the parlour door opens again and a rangy fair young man of about seventeen enters, followed by a middle-aged woman. 'And – save for the boy – we're all out at work all day. Can't he go back to his parents?'

'I suppose he can, but not till he's a bit fitter. And it'll take days to make the arrangements,' replies Archer. 'I'd have to make enquiries about when the next train of evacuees is going to Wales.'

The woman intervenes. 'It's little Charlie isn't it?' she asks, peering at Charles over the top of her glasses.

'Looks like,' confirms Conway. 'Not so little now.'

'Jake we can't send him away,' says the woman. 'What would Millie say?'

'I don't give a stuff what my sister says,' replies Conway in a quiet but vehement tone.

'Yes you do,' says the woman softly. 'And you can see the poor boy's not well.' She turns to Charles, still lying back on the couch, and addresses him in a sing-song voice as if he was a toddler. 'Do you remember me, Charlie? Auntie Bea? Do you want something to eat, darling? I've got some chicken soup from last night.'

Despite feeling dreadful and a bit put out at being addressed as if he were a child, Charles smiles. You can't ever go into a Jewish household without being offered food. It doesn't matter what time of day or night or what crisis might be unfolding, somehow there is always some chicken soup, fried fish balls, salt beef, herring – *something* – left over in the larder.

'Yes, please.'

As he answers, Charles notes himself moderating his

cockney accent. He doesn't want to be sent back to Wales. His accent becomes stronger when he's on the streets of the East End because it goes with the tough image he cultivates, but right now he's presenting Millie Horowitz's well-behaved, well-brought up lad who can be trusted to join the Conway household.

'Of course you do,' said Aunt Bea. 'I'll put the gas on.' Before she leaves she puts her hand on her husband's arm. 'Jake: he's got to stay here, if only for a few days.'

The father-in-law stands and places himself in front of Charles. 'You don't recognise me, do you boy?'

Charles shakes his head. 'No, sir, sorry.'

'You did meet me once. I'm your great-uncle John. John Joseph Milstein. Can you stand up?' Charles levers himself cautiously out of the couch, still unsure of his balance. His great-uncle John walks around him, noting the broad shoulders and thick neck. 'He's strong, Jacob.' He lifts Charles's arms and feels his biceps. 'He's got your build. Do you exercise boy?'

'I box. At the Rupert Browning.'

Charles sees an approving glance on his great-uncle's face and a look passing between him and Conway.

'We could do with another pair of hands, Jake, since we took over Milton's barges,' says Milstein.

'But what's he know about the work?' replies Conway.

'He can work with me,' offers Milstein.

'Jonjo, you ain't had an apprentice in twenty years!'

'About time I had another one, then.' He turns to speak directly to Charles. 'Do you want to stay in London?'

'If my choice is going back to Wales, yes. Definitely.'

Milstein looks over at his son-in-law. 'Alright?'

Conway shrugs his reluctant assent. His formidable wife and her father making common cause? He knows when he's outgunned.

'Right, Charles Horowitz,' says Milstein. 'It's hard work, and there's people being killed all the time. It's not a cushy number. Your cousin Milton was cut in half by a load of Russian timber last month, and we're a sitting target for the Luftwaffe. We can't run for the shelters like everyone else; we work through it. So we can't afford passengers. Still want to stay?'

Charles nods. 'Yes please.'

'So, where's he gonna sleep?' asks Conway.

'He can bunk up with me,' says the seventeen-year-old, speaking for the first time. He steps forward, hand outstretched. 'I'm your cousin Izzy. But on the River everyone calls me "Merlin".'

Charles looks up into the wide brown eyes of an extremely good-looking young man with fair hair. He is three or four inches taller than Charles and stands with a slightly stooped posture, as if he had recently shot up in height and is still resolving the resultant self-consciousness. His smile is warm and genuine, although at the same time Charles detects something slightly mocking about it.

'Pleased to meet you, Merlin,' says Charles, also with a smile. He takes the outstretched hand and grips it firmly, and a lifetime's friendship is thereby cemented.

chapter 14

Charles is not permitted to follow Merlin and his gaoler through the dock and down the steps into the cells. He excuses himself to the Judge, walks back through the court and then descends the flights of stairs to the main hallway. He continues down another flight to the basement. The five or six minutes it takes him to reach the conference rooms in the cell area allow him a few moments to think.

For almost two years Charles and Merlin had been inseparable, often in one another's company twenty-four hours a day. They worked, under different Masters, for the same lighterage firm from dawn till dusk on the River, spending their wages up West together in the same dance halls and bars, and returning home to share Merlin's freezing bedroom in the roof of the house on Juniper Street. When, in 1942, Harry Horowitz turned up unannounced on the Shadwell doorstep and grabbed his son by the ear, dragging him back to the Horowitz family's new digs in Burdett Road to resume his education, the two cousins remained firm friends. After Charles joined the RAF in 1944 he wrote two letters every week, one to David and his parents and the other to his adoptive family in Shadwell. Aunt Bea would read Charles's letters out loud round the kitchen table after the Conway family finished tea and before the Marconi was warmed up for the BBC Forces Programme and Aunt Bea's favourite, *Ack-Ack, Beer-Beer*. Charles's letters to Shadwell, even when censored, were always more detailed and funnier than those to his close family. He was happier and more at ease with them than ever he was in his parents' home. The Conway household was chaotic and, compared to that of the Horowitzes, untidy and grubby; but his aunt, uncles and cousins seemed to give him permission to be less anxious, lighter of heart and more generous of spirit than did his own parents.

It had been the entry of Henrietta into Charles's life in 1948, his second year at Cambridge, that marked the beginning of the cousins' drift apart. Charles's romance with Henrietta had been unexpected, intense and exclusive, and had caused his life suddenly to veer off in a new and unanticipated direction. Having realised that success as a barrister was going to be hard enough to achieve even without an obviously Jewish surname, Charlie Horowitz had become Charles Holborne shortly before meeting Henrietta. Always a superb mimic, he swiftly shed the clipped cockney accent and adopted the languorous speech patterns and argot of the profession and class to which he aspired. As he and Henrietta became closer, they each revealed more of their past and found commonality in their strained relationships with their respective parents, but somehow Charles edited out of his history the two years he spent on the Thames as a lighterman, the criminality and the close bond with Merlin and his family in Shadwell.

A tough East End Jew-boy made good – top of his school, RAF hero, scholarship to Cambridge – well, that was one thing; a tough East End Jew-boy with a criminal past, including some moments of uncontrolled violence which he still did not fully understand – that was something else altogether. Thus did Charles absolve himself on those increasingly rare occasions when he took the events out of the memory box where he had buried them, turned them over in his hands momentarily and then closed the lid firmly again. At such times Charles reassured himself that he'd had no choice if he wanted to pursue his new life and love; Henrietta would never have understood. In that, as in so much of his understanding of his late wife, he had been wrong. Although the daughter of a Viscount, the Hon Henrietta Lloyd-Williams was never a snob nor a racist. Indeed, it had been Charles's air of dangerous bellicosity, his tendency to take risks and the very exoticism of his Levantine heritage that had so attracted her. As she was wont to point out, she'd known he was a Jew before falling in love with – and then marrying – him. Charles heard this oft-repeated reassurance; he never actually listened to it.

So, over the space of one short Michaelmas term Charles's contact with his family in Shadwell came to an abrupt end. Merlin and Aunt Bea in particular continued to follow his exploits. They knew when he was called to the Bar and took immense pride in the fact that Charles was the first member of their family ever to join such an honourable profession; they saw the belated and cursory announcement of his wedding to Henrietta in *The Times* and took the cutting to their local, the Prospect of Whitby, to show it to all their friends. On the face of it they were proud of Charles and would be heard to say that, of course, his life had changed and it was hardly to be expected that he would bring the daughter of a Viscount to their little terraced house in Shadwell. If Merlin or any other member of the family was hurt at having been discarded so completely, they never mentioned it.

So, it is with mixed feelings and some foreboding that Charles waits for the gaoler to open the solid steel door and admit him to the cells. The door is eventually opened by a different gaoler, one whom Charles does not recognise, and he takes Charles through the formalities strictly by the book. Charles gives the process only half his attention, noticing, as his details are being written down, that his heart is beating slightly faster than normal. He is shown into one of the tiny cells that has been converted into a conference room. On the other side of the table waits Merlin. The lighterman rises as Charles enters and pushes back his flat cap so it perches on the back of his head. Charles stands on the threshold for a moment and the gaoler remains behind him. Realising the gaoler is still there, Charles glances over his shoulder.

'Thank you. I need to speak to my client alone.'

Charles takes a further step into the room and the gaoler shuts the door behind him.

The cousins regard one another steadily for a moment. Merlin's face is contorted with conflicting emotions which, for an instant, confuse Charles. He had expected bitterness at the prolonged estrangement, probably anxiety and, perhaps, desperation. Instead Merlin evinces genuine joy at seeing Charles, love even, and something Charles interprets as relief. But there is something else, a hesitation about Merlin's eyes that Charles cannot identify. At that second however Charles is so pleased to see his cousin again and so full of empathy for Merlin's plight that he dismisses the discordant note and launches himself at the handsome lighterman, wrapping his arms about him in a great bear-hug. Merlin reciprocates, and they hold each other for several seconds.

'I can't believe it's actually you!' breathes Merlin into Charles's ear, his voice breaking in his throat. 'I'll tell you, I'm right up against it here, and of all the people in the entire world I wanted to see, it was you! And here you are, Jonjo!'

Charles hasn't been called "Jonjo" in over twenty years. It's the tradition on the River for nicknames to be passed down the generations. Izzy's father and grandfather had the nickname "Merlin" and so when Izzy started his apprenticeship he became "Merlin" too. Charles's father, Harry, was neither a waterman nor a lighterman, but once apprenticed to John Joseph Milstein, known all his life on the river as "Jonjo", Charles became "Jonjo" as well. The name brings to Charles's mind impossibly hard work in all weathers, the constant risk of death from above and below and long, lazy days of summer aboard the barges being towed up and down the Thames. The best time of his life.

Charles releases Merlin and gestures to the chair

opposite. 'We haven't got long,' explains Charles. 'I need to know the whole story, and quickly.'

The cousins each take a chair and Charles gets out his blue counsel's notebook and pen.

'You ain't changed a jot,' says Merlin, evaluating his cousin across the table. 'How long's it been? Fifteen years?'

Charles answers immediately, having already been thinking about it. 'Yes. Your dad's funeral.'

Merlin nods. 'Yeah, must be right.'

'How's everyone else?' asks Charles.

'Grandad – Jonjo Milstein – he died a coupla years back, in 1960. Heart failure they said. Still, he was 75, so a fair innings. I never hear from me kid brother from one end of the year to the next, but 'e seems to be doing okay over there.'

'Yes, I heard from my Dad that he'd emigrated. And your mum?'

'Not too clever, I'm afraid. She's got emphysema. Can't breathe properly. Coughs 'er guts up every time she moves. I'm still at home, so I do what I can for her. She often talks about you.'

Charles, perhaps oversensitive to it, thinks he detects gentle chiding in his cousin's voice. He changes the subject abruptly. 'We better get on with this; we can catch up later. So: murder?' he asks, busily unscrewing the top of his fountain pen and checking it's full of ink.

Merlin nods again.

'But why haven't you got a solicitor?' asks Charles. 'I haven't heard of a dock brief on a capital charge since the

1940s. Weren't you offered legal aid at the magistrates' court?'

'I wasn't really with it in front of the beaks,' explains Merlin. He turns his back to Charles and points to the back of his scalp. 'Vermeulen gave me that.'

Charles half-stands and extends his hand towards the back of Merlin's head. His fingertips encounter a golf-ball sized lump under the wavy hair. He explores it gently and Merlin winces. It's soft and soggy. 'Who's Vermeulen?' asks Charles, sitting down again.

'A cunt of a Waterguard, a PO. He was in the police wagon when I was being escorted to the Mags. I didn't see it coming.'

'I think you'd better start at the beginning, Izzy. First: where are the prosecution depositions?'

'I left them in the cell at Brixton. I didn't think I'd need them today.'

Charles's heart sinks, but he's careful not to let it show in his expression. 'Okay,' he says. 'I'll apply to the Judge for an emergency legal visit and go through them at the prison. How thick are they?'

'You what?'

The question would be familiar to any advocate. The thickness of the papers gives a clue as to the number of witnesses and therefore the complexity of the case. Without instructions from a solicitor, prosecution depositions, defence witness statements or even the indictment so as to know what charges are faced by his new client, a barrister instructed on a docker is fighting with both hands tied behind his back. Some barristers enjoy the challenge; without instructions and no affirmative case to put on behalf of their client, it can be fun to be more "creative" with the defence than if trammelled by precise instructions as to what the accused says actually occurred. In this case however, if convicted, Merlin almost certainly faces the hangman; this is not a case where Charles expects to have any fun.

Merlin holds up his right hand, his forefinger and thumb about half an inch apart. 'Not that much,' he says. 'As you know, my reading's a bit iffy, but I got through 'em in an hour or so.'

'Good,' replies Charles. 'I might just be able to get my hands on one of those new xerographic machines and makes copies,' he adds quietly, almost to himself.

'You can have mine,' offers Merlin. 'I ain't gonna need them.'

'You will. I need you to read them tonight and write your comments on them, line by line, word by word. Where you agree, where you don't; understand?' Merlin shakes his shaggy head. 'You've never heard of a dock brief, then?' asks Charles.

'A stevedore's solicitor?' jokes Merlin, laughter in his brown eyes.

Charles ignores the poor attempt at humour. 'Izzy: focus on this please; it's really important. A dock brief means I have to work without a solicitor, which makes preparing your defence difficult. And instead of weeks or months to prepare for the trial, we have tonight – the weekend if we're lucky. We're both going have to work bloody hard.'

Merlin whistles softly. 'Blimey,' he says, but almost immediately his countenance clears and his familiar smile reappears. 'But I've got you ain't I, Jonjo? I see your name in the papers all the time, Charles Holborne wins this case, Charles Holborne wins that case. If anyone can get me off, it's gotta be you, right?'

Charles fixes his eyes on Merlin's and speaks intently. 'I'll do everything I can, you know that. But ...' Charles shakes his head to himself, deciding not to worry Merlin any further by telling him any of the stories about Fletcher. 'Let's just get on with it. Start at the beginning: what happened?'

Merlin draws a deep breath. 'Okay. Some years ago I was rummaged by an APO called John Evans. It was just before I got me ticket, while I was still with Union Jack. Remember him? The *ganzer macher* up the Pie Shop?'

'Of course I do,' replies Charles.

Union Jack: barrel-shaped – almost as wide as he was tall – ruddy red cheeks and a monk's fringe of thinning hair bleached almost white by the sun; a pipe permanently clenched between stained teeth; and an enormous booming laugh which could be heard from one bank of the River to the other. Everyone on the River Thames was familiar with Union Jack and his laugh.

Union Jack Carver came from a family of lightermen and tugboatmen who'd worked the Thames for generations, as far back as the 16th century according to Thames legend. He'd spent his life on the River and he knew every wharf, jetty and landing place from Teddington Lock to the

Thames Estuary. He was indeed the *ganzer macher* – the bigshot – at the "Pie Shop", the rivermen's familiar name for Watermans Hall, the ancient institution which hosted the Courts of the Company of Watermen, Lightermen, Tugmen and Bargemen of the River Thames. His working name was Jack and he was a *ganzer macher* in the union; so, of course, he became known as "Union Jack".

'I was apprenticed to him when Dad got hisself injured,' says Izzy.

'Yes, I remember. Your dad almost lost his hand.'

'Right.'

Charles smiles in recollection, and nods. 'Is Jack still alive?'

'No. I'm coming to that.'

'Okay, carry on then,' says Charles.

'Well, this was after your dad took you off the boats and back to school. Although I hadn't got me ticket, I was all but qualified and Jack would leave me to it for much of the time. We'd towed up on the tide and delivered a load of copper from Tilbury to the Royal Albert Docks. We were six barges, three abreast, and he left me there while he took two up to Isleworth. So I was moored up by some buoys waiting for the tide. I was knackered, I'd done twenty-six hours straight. You remember what it's like.'

Charles remembers it well. The Thames is the "Larder of London", with wharves from Waterloo all the way down to Greenhithe. Even in the early 1940s when he was working with Merlin, and despite the depredations of the U-boats and the loss of merchant marine vessels, there were almost one hundred lighterage companies on the River employing over three thousand lightermen. There was a constant stream of huge boats in the docks from all over the world waiting to be loaded or unloaded, and the lightermen were so busy they would frequently work twenty-four or even thirty hours straight even when there were no German bombers anticipated. When another air raid was expected the activity was frenetic. They received double rations due to the long hours of strenuous work which, for an ever-hungry teenager like Charles, was very welcome, and there was so much overtime available that the lightermen became known as "The Weekend Millionaires." With most able-bodied men in the forces and so much money in their pockets, they became very popular with the young women at the dance halls. Despite being in his mid-teens, Charles was a big strong lad who'd been shaving for over a year when the Blitz started and he could easily pass for eighteen, which he did, taking full advantage of the pleasures that that afforded him.

'So,' continues Merlin, 'I'm asleep, when the next thing I hear is footsteps above me 'ead. Thought for a moment that it was Union Jack coming back – lost me sense of time, right? But, next thing – some other bloke's legs appear down the hatch. Legs in uniform. He was bloody surprised to see me, but 'e says he's an APO out of Harpy Waterguard Station.'

'Didn't you think that a bit odd?' asks Charles. 'Don't the Waterguard usually come on board on the Upper Coast, or has it all changed?'

'Nah, you're right, it was odd, but I didn't think much of it at the time. Anyway, he says he's going to rummage me and I thought "Fair enough." I weren't concerned. It weren't a custom barge with booze or nothing, just an ordinary hatch barge, and we was empty. I thought I might get back to sleep, so I left 'im to it. So, he comes down, looks around for a few seconds, and then the bastard claims he's found a hollowed-out bulkhead with bottles of brandy. He's staring at me with one in each hand. I swear, Jonjo, I knew nothing about them.'

Charles can't quite suppress a grin, despite the seriousness of Merlin's situation. The Preventive Officers' job was to prevent smuggling, and their rummage officers, usually based on a station moored in the River called Harpy Waterguard Station, were specialists, trained in the design of ships and every nook and cranny available for hiding contraband. They circulated amongst themselves detailed descriptions of vessels involved in smuggling, together with "copycat drawings" which illustrated where contraband was likely to be concealed. The drawings showed every hollowed-out bulkhead, hidden engine room compartment and accessible instrument panel on every type of small vessel plying its trade between the oceangoing ships in port and the wharves where they discharged. Charles smiles because, even if Merlin had been innocent on this occasion, every now and then he and Charles did help themselves to booze destined for bonded warehouses to make the return journeys and the long periods of waiting between the tides more agreeable. The life of a lighterman is characterised by intense, physical and very dangerous work in all weathers, twenty-four hours a day, interspersed with prolonged periods of boredom – waiting for the tide, for others in front of them to load or unload, or for a tally man to give them the go.

'And that's another thing. They normally rummage in teams of two, but this one was alone,' continues Merlin. 'Anyway, he orders me to help him shift the bottles onto his launch – there were about six or eight – and off he goes. Couple hours later Jack comes back and I tell him all about it. At first he don't believe me, but then he says he knows someone in the Waterguard and he'll have a word, you know, see if he can find out what's going on.'

'Do you think Jack was in on it?' asks Charles.

'Union Jack?' replies Merlin, eyebrows raised. 'Never. I'd swear on me life. I knew him since I was tiny, two or three. He was me godfather! Straight as a die, one of the most decent men I ever knew. A few weeks after that, he was dead.'

'How come?'

'We was on Millwall Dock, unloading a huge consignment of tins of salmon from Canada. There was four of us, ten or twelve barges in all. We'd almost finished and Jack was on the quayside. One of those grain vacuums was above him, and it suddenly discharged several ton of grain, right on 'is nut.'

There is silence in the cell except for the sound of Charles's pen nib scratching on his notebook as he writes furiously, trying to catch up with Merlin's story. His neat angular handwriting now covers five or six pages. He looks up.

'Was it an accident?'

Merlin shakes his head in disbelief and shrugs. 'That's what the coroner reckoned.'

'There was an inquest, then?'

'Oh, yeah,' replies Merlin cynically. 'It took ten minutes. Accidental death.'

Charles lifts his head and stares, unseeing, at the tiny square of light above Merlin's head which penetrates through the grubby light-well at pavement level. It is darkened briefly every few seconds by the shadows of passers-by, unconscious of the dramas unfolding literally beneath their feet. Charles ponders the information Merlin has given him for a few moments. Then: 'Okay; interesting. Let's move on to how you come to be here.'

'After that first time when the APO came aboard, I got me ticket and two of me own barges. One of them was Jack's old Belgian barge – remember all that lovely paintwork inside? A few months later and I notice that every now and then things are out of place. I couldn't work it out, but eventually I realised someone must be coming onboard. When they're empty we usually tie the barges up overnight by the buoys. They're not locked – you never expect anyone to nick 'em. But it means anyone with a boat can get aboard. I was getting suspicious, so one day I was on a three-day trip to the River Medway, four barges. After I discharged I took the Belgian one into a dry dock run by a fella I know, and we took it to pieces. We found four hidden compartments, all stinking of spirits. So, then I knew what was going on.'

'This Assistant Preventive Officer was using your barge to smuggle booze?'

'Brandy. Yeah. It was clever. It meant I was taking all the risk. If I got rummaged by someone else it would all be down to me, and saying I knew nothing about it wouldn't get me nowhere. So I decided to catch him. I'd tie up the barges every night, wait till it was dark, and then sneak back and sleep on board. It only took me a week before I caught him.'

'And?' For the first time Merlin avoids Charles's gaze. 'And?' repeats Charles with heavy emphasis, guessing what's coming.

Merlin pulls a face, and shrugs. 'Yeah, well, you know me. I told them I wanted my cut. I said I'd even run a few trips for them.'

'Them?'

'I never met anyone except this APO, Evans, but more than once he let slip he was working with others, more senior people. I got the impression he was the junior partner. My stuff was small beer by comparison. You know what was going on round that time.'

'Are you saying he couldn't have done this without his superiors having known?' probes Charles.

'Certain of it.'

Charles makes some further notes. 'Did you run a few trips for them?'

Merlin gives a wry smile. 'Nah. Tried to persuade him,

but he said it was a Waterguard enterprise – no outsiders. Shame; it would have been a nice earner. But after that he would leave me a few bob each time he used the barge. Just enough for a couple of drinks to keep me sweet. He used to call it "rent". I always knew when he'd been there.'

Charles shakes his head slowly, more in sorrow than in surprise. He and Merlin had got up to quite a bit of mischief when they worked together. The younger lightermen and apprentices used to play cricket on the empty barges. When they were moving fast, for example when towing up from Tilbury, tugs would race, with apprentices surfing behind the barges on gratings. They also held illegal bare-knuckle boxing matches on the barges, on which large sums were wagered. When Merlin realised how good a boxer Charles really was, he cajoled Charles into letting him become his unofficial manager, and Charles had several successful fights from which they each made more than a week's wages. There was also minor pilfering but, as far as Charles could tell, almost everyone was at it, so he didn't pass judgement. He was having too good a time: he exulted in the freedom of being on the River, so far away from his restrictive, anxious parents, and for the first time in his life having money in his pocket and girls on his arm. He sensed even then that it was different for Merlin. His cousin was a comical and likeable rogue, but he always had his eye on the main chance. What started off as a bit of petty thievery slowly changed. Merlin's dishonesty became more serious and Charles found himself being drawn into more carefully-planned criminal enterprises, here a stolen lorry, there a bung to a tally officer to turn a blind eye to goods being lifted. And then, finally, there was the incident at the warehouse at Saint Katharine's docks. Thereafter Charles wanted nothing more to do with the darker side of Merlin's ambitions. When his father finally did turn up, Charles was very sorry to leave Shadwell and his unofficial apprenticeship on the River, but his disappointment at having to return to school was also tinged with relief.

'Anyway,' says Merlin, returning to his story, 'one day the rent payments stopped.'

'Why?'

'Well, he ... had something on me.'

'What?'

'Don't know.'

Barristers practising in the criminal courts day in, day out develop a sixth sense for truthfulness. It's by no means infallible and Charles had been taken in by a plausible liar more than once, but Charles had learned to rely on his instincts. And there is something about Merlin's tone, the increased intensity of his gaze – as if challenging Charles to disbelieve him – that rings a false note.

'Is that true, Izzy? Do you really not know?'

Merlin chews his lower lip for a moment and a wry grin spreads over his face. 'That's the problem, ain't it, Charlie? You know me too well.'

'Look, Izzy, nothing you say to me – in this room or anywhere else – goes any further than between the two of us. It's called legal professional privilege. It doesn't matter what you say to me, I can't tell anyone anything. There's one exception: if you admit to killing this bloke I can't put forward a positive case suggesting you didn't. It's against the rules; I'm not allowed to mislead the court. Therefore, I couldn't call you to give evidence. But – and this is important – I'm still allowed to test the evidence of the prosecution witnesses, and if it doesn't come up to scratch, you have to be acquitted, whether you did it or not.'

Merlin doesn't answer. Watching his face is like watching fast-moving cloud shadows flowing across an undulating landscape. Charles sees uncertainty, relief and fear cross the handsome face in quick succession, reflecting an internal debate. He can't decide how much to divulge, thinks Charles, whether he can trust me; where the truth, once uttered, might lead.

'What …' ventures Merlin eventually, 'what – just saying, you understand – but what if I killed him, but it was self-defence?'

'Then it's not guilty.'

Merlin hangs his head, and all Charles can see are the gold locks swinging as his cousin rocks very slightly on the chair. Eventually he looks up again. 'I need time to think this through, Charlie.' His face is almost apologetic.

'Of course,' reassures Charles. 'Of course,' he repeats. 'But, as I said, we have no time to mess about. I'll come to Brixton as soon as I can and collect the prosecution depositions. We can talk again then.'

Without a further word, Merlin stands and bangs on the door, signalling that the interview is at an end. Charles is surprised but he nonetheless closes his notebook and screws the top back on his fountain pen.

'I have to ask, Merlin: do you have one pound three and six?' he asks diffidently.

'What?'

'I'm so sorry, but my professional rules require that you pay me one pound three and six for the dock brief before I take the case.'

Merlin looks astonished. 'What, you mean that unless I have the money you won't defend me?'

Charles is now very uncomfortable. 'Those are the rules. I'm not supposed to. But ...' Charles hesitates briefly before reaching a decision which he knows, if revealed, would land him in hot water with the Bar Council. As he answers, part of him wonders if this is the first compromise to which he'll be forced, and whether he'd been wrong after all not to mention his relationship with Merlin and decline the case.

'Forget it,' he says. 'But, if anyone asks, you paid me. Okay?'

'I wouldn't want you to get into any trouble,' says Merlin with some bitterness.

'Forget it, I said. I don't like breaking the rules, but in this case ...'

Merlin nods slowly. 'Fair enough.'

They hear the gaoler approaching from the corridor outside, keys jangling. Merlin turns again to Charles. 'I've got a question for you, Charlie.'

'Yes?'

'When you was on the run from the law over Henrietta's

death, why didn't you come to see us? We would've helped you, you know that. No question.'

'I know,' confesses Charles. 'I did think about it. But I hadn't seen any of you for over a decade.'

'So? We're family. We love you.'

Charles is shamed by Merlin's frankness. 'I was embarrassed. I felt guilty at having let our friendship die.'

Merlin looks at him, astonished. 'Die? What *are* you talking about Charlie? Nothing died.' He stabs his forefinger at Charles just as the gaoler swings the door open. 'You're a fuckin' idiot,' he says, walking out of the conference room.

'Yes,' says Charles, raising his voice at Merlin's receding back. 'I know that now.'

chapter 15

Charles pushes open the door to the tiny flat in Fetter Lane. The smell of frying bacon greets his nose and immediately makes his mouth water. Sally, only three or four yards away in the kitchen, hears him enter.

'I'm in here!' she calls.

Charles throws his robes bag and papers from the day's part-heard trial onto the couch and puts his head round the corner. Sally is still in her formal working clothes, but her dark pleated skirt and waisted jacket are covered by a pink flowery pinafore she bought specifically to use at the flat.

'Bacon?' asks Charles.

'Gammon steak,' says Sally over her shoulder. 'Special treat.'

Charles grew up in a kosher home where eating pork would have been unthinkable, but he developed a fondness for bacon and eggs in the RAF and now pays little attention to the dietary rules which strictly govern his family's life.

'Fried eggs or poached?' asks Sally. 'I bought some carrots, too.'

Charles doesn't answer. 'Charlie?' calls Sally.

When Charles still doesn't respond, she takes the pan with the half-cooked gammon steaks off the gas and comes into the lounge. She finds Charles slumped in the armchair, his elbows on his knees and his head in his hands. She perches on the arm of the chair next to him.

'What's up?'

Charles continues massaging the back of his neck with both his hands, draws a deep breath and replies without looking up. 'I got a dock brief today.'

Sally knows that this wouldn't be cause for celebration for any busy barrister, but she realises that there must be more to this story, so she waits patiently.

'The bloke's charged with murder of a Waterguard while resisting arrest.'

'Waterguard?'

'They're a sort of river police, basically Customs and Excise men. Which means the rope if he's convicted.'

'Blimey.'

'And guess who the judge is.'

'The Recorder?'

'Worse.'

'Not Fletcher?'

Charles nods. 'He's given us till the morning to prepare. But that's still not the worst of it.' He looks up. 'I know the accused; he's my cousin.'

A moment passes as Sally absorbs the information. 'Jesus, Charlie,' she says softly. 'Who is it?'

Charles has never before had cause to speak about this period during the War when he worked as an apprentice lighterman, and so he explains about his time in Shadwell and his relationship with Merlin.

'You can't possibly represent him, can you?' asks Sally when he finishes. 'Surely, you're not allowed to.'

'I don't think there's any rule preventing a barrister from representing a member of his family,' replies Charles, shaking his head slowly, 'but I know the Bar Council would say it's not wise, and I should certainly tell the judge about the potential conflict. And I didn't take the fee either – which is definitely a breach of my rules.'

Sally kneels in front of Charles, her hands on his knees, trying unsuccessfully to make eye contact with him.

'I've never known you break any of your professional rules before now,' she says gently.

'So?' replies Charles, looking up now, the suggestion of a challenge in his voice.

'I'm not having a go, Charlie. I would've done the same. I'm just saying it must have been hard. I know how much those things mean to you; the integrity.'

Charles draws a deep breath and his shoulders slump. 'I'm sorry. Yes, you're right. I watched myself do it and wondered what was happening. But, honestly, Sal, I didn't feel I had a choice. I value the law immensely, you know I do. I try to live by it, when no one else swimming in this sea of effluence seems to give a shit.'

Sally notes Charles's language with surprise – she has never heard him swear in front of her before – but says nothing. He speaks calmly; he doesn't appear angry, merely resigned.

'Not the gangs, nor the Filth – not even the judges. But I do. But … *but* … in the end my loyalty to Merlin – Izzy – was stronger. He's in the worst possible trouble, and I'm all that's standing between him and the hangman.'

'I know. You made the right call,' she says, trying to reassure him. The frown on his face tells her that she's not been completely successful. 'Are you hungry?' she continues.

Charles looks up. He takes her little white hand in both of his paws and kisses it tenderly several times. 'Yes,' he answers.

'You go get changed, and I'll finish the cooking.' She stands and makes to go back to the kitchen but Charles holds onto her hand.

'Can you stay tonight?' he asks.

'Betty can't go in tomorrow so I was going home to get mum up before coming in,' she says regretfully. Then she sees the disappointment on Charles's face. 'You look like a little boy who's broken his favourite toy. Oh, go on then. I'll call Tracey and see if she can fill in for me.'

Charles smiles with gratitude. 'Thank you.'

He remains slouched in the armchair, desultorily watching Sally's rear as she returns to the kitchen, gathering the energy to get up. He hears her striking match after match trying to get the gas ring to light again. It's been causing problems for a week or more. It finally "whumphs" loudly into flame and Sally lets out a small inarticulate exclamation as she jumps back.

'You need to get this thing looked at,' she calls. 'It still doesn't light properly. Can you get someone to look at it tomorrow, maybe, before we go?'

'That's the other thing. This weekend's looking a bit dodgy, Sal,' calls Charles.

He hears the gas extinguished again and wonders briefly what the gammon's going to taste like when it's been treated this way, when Sally re-emerges from the kitchen, a scowl on her face.

'No. You're not cancelling again?' she demands.

Charles stands and approaches her, planning on stroking her hair to placate, but Sally's head jerks back and she stays out of reach.

'It's been in the diary for weeks, Charlie,' she says, her face contorted in an eloquent plea. 'I'm really looking forward to it. And you know full well the trouble it's taken to arrange mum's care for a complete weekend!'

They had been invited to spend the weekend with one of Charlie's RAF friends who had recently moved with his wife and young son from London to Brighton. Charles thought it would be easier to introduce Sally as his girlfriend to someone outside the law; who would have none of the prejudices and preconceptions about barristers' clerks and their guvnors. He had proposed driving down late on Friday night once the traffic had cleared, returning Sunday afternoon. He fully expected the false accounting trial to finish on Friday but, even if it didn't, he would have finished his speech and have a couple of days relatively free of work. Sally's sisters had rearranged their weekends –Tracey's new husband had even changed shifts – to make sure Sally had cover and was able to go to the seaside with her new beau. Sally had been bouncing with suppressed excitement for a fortnight. An entire weekend of being a normal couple – and by the seaside!

Charles spreads his hands. 'Fletcher is threatening to arraign Izzy tomorrow. I don't think he'll have time, but that means Monday by the latest. I've only got the weekend to prepare his defence.'

'Can't you get an adjournment?'

'I'm going to try, but you know what Fletcher's like. I can't take the risk he'll say no. I've got to be ready to start on Monday, whether he gives me more time or not.'

'This isn't fair Charlie.'

'It isn't fair to Izzy, that's for sure. His life's at stake.'

Sally purses her lips and Charles can hear her draw breath heavily through her nose as she tries to control her temper. She hates the way that he is always able to come up with a perfectly reasonable excuse for breaking arrangements. There is *always* a good reason, and of course this is the best reason yet, but the result is always the same. She is somehow made to feel guilty and unreasonable for making demands on Charles's time and is left frustrated and impotent. For month after month she's been kept in Charles's demarcated compartment labelled "Love Life", a butterfly pinned inside a glass case, and she is sick and tired of it.

Charles watches Sally's shoulders rise and fall as she draws a further deep breath to calm herself. She reaches behind herself to pull apart the bow tied in her pinafore strings. She tugs it over her head and offers it to Charles.

'I think I will go back to mum's,' she says simply. 'I'm not hungry anymore.'

She turns towards the doorway into the lobby to collect her shoes which she usually slips off on entering the flat.

'Oh come on, Sally, you know I wouldn't cancel if there was any choice!' protests Charles. He follows her out to the lobby as she bends to put on her shoes. 'What else can I do? I can't tell my cousin "*Sorry you're going to hang, but my girlfriend wanted a weekend at the seaside*."'

Sally stands up and reaches for her coat hanging inside the hall cupboard. 'Course you can't. I get it. You have to work this weekend, and he needs you more than I do.' She turns, straightening her coat collar, and looks up at him. 'I'm not being ... What's the word, like childish?'

'Petulant?'

'Yes, petulant. I really do understand, Charlie. You've got no choice, and you've got to focus on your cousin's case. But it's hard for me, too. There's always a reason – time after time. And they're always good reasons, but somehow I *never* win. I'm always at the bottom of the list,' she replies, shrugging sadly. She shakes her head. 'Maybe this ain't going to work,' she finishes, the stress allowing the cockney accent to show through the recently-acquired RP veneer.

'Don't go now,' he says softly, 'please.'

'Sorry, Charlie. I don't want to be here at the moment and you've got work to do anyway. I'll give you a bell tomorrow.' She stands on tiptoe and places a kiss lightly on his lips. 'See ya,' she says, a strained smile on her face. The door opens and closes, and she's gone.

•

It's early afternoon, the following day. Charles had tried ringing Sally early, before she would've left Romford, and received no answer. He also tried at Chancery Court before heading out for the Old Bailey to be told that she was in a meeting and couldn't come to the telephone. He gives up and goes to court.

By ten thirty the last witness in the false accounting trial is still a "non-attendance" and, having exhausted his very limited patience, Mr Justice Fletcher orders the barristers to get on with their closing speeches. They each take considerably more than the ten minutes predicted – never trust a barrister's time estimate because he invariably underestimates the degree to which he likes the sound of his own voice – but the Judge makes up time by summing up in just over an hour – almost straight down the middle – and the jury retires to consider their verdicts shortly before lunch. By three o'clock, having considered the evidence over sandwiches, they return unanimous not guilty verdicts on both charges on the indictment, and Charles's client is discharged. Fletcher, obviously keen to get away early on a bright Friday afternoon, rules that Merlin's arraignment will occur on Monday morning first thing, at which time Charles can make any applications he requires. Charles takes that to mean that the door is still open a crack to a possible adjournment after Monday if he needs more time.

Charles spends the afternoon working on papers in Chambers, finally forcing himself to address a matter that has been demanding his attention for several weeks but which he has been avoiding: signing the deeds to dispose of his former matrimonial home with Henrietta in Buckinghamshire. It feels, finally, like the end of a chapter. He half expects one final acerbic comment from Henrietta as he signs the documents, but if she is still looking over his shoulder from somewhere on the other side, she keeps her counsel to herself.

On Saturday morning Charles presents himself at Brixton Prison just before ten o'clock. For the first time in his career he does not have to queue to get in. The order of Mr Justice Fletcher addressed to the deputy governor has facilitated an emergency legal visit, for which Charles would otherwise wait days, if not weeks. Charles shows the order and his identification to the prison officers at the entrance and is shown inside.

At the same time, on the far side of the maze of grey brick Victorian buildings making up the prison complex, Merlin is taken off association and is escorted back to his cell by a tall prison officer with thinning grey hair to collect the prosecution depositions. The landing is relatively quiet and the door to the cell is open. The Brummie drug dealer with whom Merlin is sharing lies on his back on the bottom bunk, reading a magazine. The cell smells of recently-opened bowels.

The prison officer nudges the reclining prisoner with his knee. 'Piss off, you.'

The young man looks over the top of his magazine and, without a word, rolls off the bunk and leaves the cell. The prison officer put his head out onto the landing to make sure no one is within earshot. He turns to face Merlin.

'Here,' he says, holding out his hand.

Merlin looks down. On the officer's palm is what remains of a steel comb. The teeth have been removed and the remaining shaft has been sharpened into a wicked shiv with a triangle-shaped pointed blade approximately three inches in length. Merlin stares, unmoving, at the implement in the other's hand.

'Well, fucking take it!'

Merlin's hand moves forward slowly and picks up the weapon. He tests the point, and draws blood from the pad of his forefinger. 'Stick it up your sleeve,' orders the officer. Merlin sucks the swelling pearl of blood from his finger and does as he is instructed. 'Right. Come on,' orders the guard, turning on his heel impatiently.

Merlin follows the officer out of the cell but then, as he goes through the door, he turns and sweeps his cap off his head and spins it in an arc back into the cell, watching it land safely on the top bunk.

·

In the suite reserved for legal visits Charles places his notebook and pens, two packets of cigarettes, a wad of tissues and a pad of lined notepaper on the desk. The prison officer in charge, an enormous redheaded man, as broad as Charles and at least six inches taller, returns to Charles his driving licence and a copy of Fletcher's order and, without a word, Charles slips off his jacket and hands it over. He drops his keys and loose change into a metal bowl offered to him by a second officer and, unprompted, stands with his legs apart to allow a third, a bony man with an unpleasant body odour, to frisk him. Charles watches over the head of the man engaged in stroking the inside of his thighs as the senior officer feels through the folds of his jacket, paying particular attention to the collar and cuffs where items such as razorblades can be secreted.

Charles's jacket and belongings are returned to him and he is shown into a conference room. It is one of several, and all the others are empty. Two of the prison officers unlock the steel barred doors and disappear, leaving only the redheaded giant sitting at the desk doing some paperwork. The visiting area, usually full of cigarette smoke, raised voices and squabbling children, is unusually quiet. The only sound is the scratch of the officer's pen on his ledger, and the faint sounds of association continuing some distance away, behind several walls. The unaccustomed silence makes Charles feel uncomfortable.

A few minutes later he is startled by a knock on the door. The door opens.

'Conway, to see you, sir,' says the huge prison officer. There's an unpleasant intonation in the way the officer uses the word "sir" as if it were spelt "cur". Charles glances sharply at the man's face but he avoids eye contact, ushers Merlin into the room and closes the door swiftly behind him.

Charles extends his hand to shake that of Merlin but the lighterman ignores it. He tosses a small bundle of papers onto the desk and, rather than taking a seat opposite Charles's, sits on the wooden bench built into the wall as far from Charles as he can get.

When they last met, Charles had been worried that Merlin was too blasé about his situation, but now his cousin's mood seems to have flipped completely. Merlin looks unusually pale and there's a faint sheen of perspiration on his tanned forehead. The thought enters Charles's mind that perhaps Merlin has mental health problems. Who knew what had been happening to him over the last decade?

'You okay?' asks Charles.

'I'm just tired,' replies Merlin, glancing at Charles but looking away again quickly. He swings his legs up onto the bench and lies flat out. 'You ever tried to sleep in one of these places?'

'Not a remand prison cell, no, but a police cell, yes. I remember it well. On one occasion, I seem to recall, I was with you.'

That produces no response and so, with a further prolonged look at Merlin, Charles slips off his jacket again, hangs it over the back of his chair and sits down to start work. He picks up the first deposition and turns it over. Then he flicks ahead several pages.

'You've not annotated them. You were going to mark them up for me so I know exactly what you say about every allegation of fact.'

'Yeah,' says Merlin, in a disinterested tone. 'But then

I started reading them again. And I thought, "What's the point?"'

Charles draws a deep breath and considers carefully before he replies. 'I understand. I'm sure it's not as bad as you fear. But I'll read them first and if I agree with you there's no point, I'll give it to you straight.' Merlin shrugs in reply. With a final worried look at his cousin, Charles turns over the first page again and starts reading.

INDICTMENT
Murder, contrary to common law
STATEMENT OF OFFENCE
Isaac Conway did on or about 4 November 1963 murder
John Huw Evans

No surprises there. Charles turns to the evidence.

Deposition of Vincent Vermeulen
Occupation: Chief Preventive Officer, HM Waterguard
Address: Harpy Waterguard Station, Custom House
Pier, Custom House, 20 Lower Thames Street, EC1.

Magistrates Court Rules 1952: This deposition of Vincent
Vermeulen, Chief Preventive Officer, Her Majesty's
Waterguard, Harpy Waterguard Station, Custom House Pier,
Custom House, 20 Lower Thames Street, EC1, was sworn
before me, Ralph James Nesbitt, Justice of the Peace, on 6

November 1963 in the presence of the accused, Isaac Conway, at the Thames Magistrates' Court.

Signed: Ralph James Nesbitt Esq.

Signature of deponent: V. Vermeulen

Vincent Vermeulen WILL SAY AS FOLLOWS:

I am employed by HM Customs and Excise as a Chief Preventive Officer in the Waterguard, presently stationed at the pontoon customs house moored on the River Thames opposite Custom House Pier, known as HMS Harpy Waterguard Station. My duties include the application of the current regulations relating to lawful allowances of tobacco and alcohol and the collection of Customs and Excise revenues on such goods as exceed the permitted allowances. To prevent goods being imported into the country in breach of customs regulations we conduct searches of vessels on the River Thames. The officers stationed at the Harpy are responsible for the Upper Coast of the river between London Bridge and Teddington Lock, the tidal limit.

On 3 November 1963 I was minuted for duty on the Harpy. The Waterguard stationed at the Harpy include specialist "rummage teams", teams trained in the detection of hidden contraband aboard vessels. Teams would usually start from east to west on the north bank of the Thames, and return west to east on the south bank, investigating any vessels of interest.

I was aware of an ongoing investigation by Assistant

the lighterman

Preventive Officer Evans and other personnel stationed at Harpy into the activities of the accused, Isaac Conway, a lighterman whose working name on the river was "Merlin". It had come to the notice of the Waterguard from information received that the accused may have been involved in smuggling spirits.

I started my duty that night at 11 pm and noted that the station's vehicle, an Austin Mini, had been taken out by APO Evans earlier that evening. I required that vehicle to carry out my own duties, and anticipated APO Evans's return by the start of my shift. By 03:30 hours on the morning of 4 November 1963 he had not returned nor been in touch by telephone, and I became concerned. I knew the route he would have taken to reach the buoys where the accused had been under surveillance, and where he often tied up his barges overnight. I accordingly took the launch and travelled to where I hoped to find the accused's barges. I found them moored at Isleworth Eyot and they were in darkness. Before investigating the barges further I tied up the launch on the western side of the river to investigate the area of Bridge Wharf Road. I there found the Waterguard's Austin Mini parked at the corner of Mill Plat, a few hundred yards from the barges. It was locked and the lights were extinguished. I took the launch across the river to the barges. I could see light emanating from one of the hatches, and I descended the steps. The accused was asleep in the bunk at the far end of the barge and was in a state of undress. I questioned him informally as to whether he had seen any officers of the Waterguard that night, and he denied having done so. I noted that the accused had bruises on his face and neck and I asked him how he came by them. He informed me that he had been in a boxing match the previous day. It is known on the river that lightermen and watermen will occasionally engage in illegal boxing tournaments on board barges, and at that moment my suspicions were not aroused. Accordingly I reboarded the launch and commenced a search. I proceeded upstream towards Twickenham.

At around 05:30 hours, less than half a mile from the accused's barges, I saw something in the water floating just off one of the small islands in the middle of the Thames. On further investigation I realised that it was a uniformed body. I was able to snag the clothing of the deceased with a boating hook, and pull it into the shallows. At that point I recognised the body as that of APO John Evans. I called for assistance from the Waterguard and from the police. While I was waiting, I became concerned that the accused might leave the vicinity and I returned to Isleworth Eyot, and reboarded the accused's barge arriving at 06:10 hours. He was still in bed, but awake and apparently very distressed. He was crying and almost incoherent. I cautioned him and he made no reply. I arrested the accused on a charge of suspected murder and conveyed him in the launch to HMS Harpy where I placed him in the secure room usually used for seized or detained goods.

At 07:14 hours I conducted an interview of the accused under caution. A true and accurate record of the interview is now produced and shown to me marked "VVI". I handed him over to the officers of the Metropolitan Police at 07:40 hours.

Signed: Vincent Vermeulen

RECORD OF INTERVIEW UNDER CAUTION OF ISAAC CONWAY

This interview of Isaac Conway consisting of 1 page in length was taken by me Vincent Vermeulen on 4 November 1963 at 07:14 hours at HMS Harpy Waterguard Station Custom House Pier, Custom House, 20 Lower Thames Street, EC1. [Caution administered]

Q: Do you understand?
A: Yes.
Q: Do you know APO Evans who works out of this station?
A: Yeah, I know him.
Q: How do you know him?
A: He's rummaged barges and tugs where I've been working.
Q: Did you see him tonight?
A: Yes.
Q: Did he come aboard a barge of yours moored at Isleworth Eyot on the River Thames?
A: Yes.
Q: What happened?
A: I was trying to get away. We had a fight and I killed him.
Q: What did you do with his body?
A: I threw it in the river.
Q: I am ending this interview now to await the arrival of the Metropolitan Police.
A: Okay.

Charles finishes making notes on Vermeulen's statement. So far as Evans's body was concerned there were a dozen ways it could have got into the river without any link to Merlin at all. The location of the Austin Mini was an uncomfortable coincidence and Charles would need more information to establish if other circumstances – other suspects perhaps – might have brought Evans to that part of the Thames, but the alleged confession was hardly impregnable. What was Vermeulen doing interviewing a murder suspect instead of leaving it to the police? That in itself raised questions, if not suspicions. There were no other witnesses to it, and Merlin hadn't signed it as correct. There was no obligation for Vermeulen to get Merlin's signature, but it would have proven that Merlin said the words attributed to him. Most importantly, the interview contained no detail that proved it came from the offender. Charles knew that, whereas it was virtually impossible to extricate oneself from a confession which contained detail that could only be known to the accused himself, this interview was typical of those vague confessions made up by over-zealous investigating officers determined to secure a conviction; known in the trade as "a verbal."

'Didn't you tell me that Evans's superior officer was involved in the smuggling?'

'Yeah.'

'And that would be Vermeulen?'

'Probably.'

Charles makes another note and continues reading.

Deposition of Adrian Peter Keeley
Occupation: Assistant Preventive Officer, HM
Waterguard
Address: Harpy Waterguard Station, Custom House
Pier, Custom House, 20 Lower Thames Street, EC1.

Magistrates Court Rules 1952: This deposition of Adrian
Peter Keeley, Assistant Preventive Officer, Her Majesty's
Waterguard, HMS Harpy Waterguard Station, Custom
House Pier, Custom House, 20 Lower Thames Street, EC1,
was sworn before me, Ralph James Nesbitt, Justice of the
Peace, on 6 November 1963 in the presence of the accused,
Isaac Conway, at the Thames Magistrates' Court.
  Signed: Ralph James Nesbitt Esq.
  Signature of deponent: AP Keeley

Adrian Peter Keeley WILL SAY AS FOLLOWS:

I am employed by HM Customs and Excise as an Assistant
Preventive Officer in the Waterguard, presently stationed
at the pontoon customs house moored on the River Thames
opposite Custom House Pier, known as Harpy Waterguard
Station. My duties include the application of the current
regulations relating to lawful allowances of tobacco and
alcohol and the collection of Customs and Excise revenues on
such goods as exceed the permitted allowances.
  On 3 November 1963 I was on duty at Harpy. At
approximately 05:45 hours the following morning I was

preparing to finish my shift when I received a call on the radio from my superior officer CPO Vermeulen concerning something he had found floating in the Thames. He requested me to proceed by land to Bridge Wharf Road Isleworth where he would meet me with the Waterguard launch. I travelled immediately to Isleworth in my private vehicle, and parked behind the Austin Mini used by members of the Waterguard for patrolling the Upper Coast. I walked down to the river where I saw CPO Vermeulen flashing his torch at me. As a result of information received from CPO Vermeulen we boarded the launch and allowed it to drift with the current until it reached the island known as Isleworth Eyot where I saw two barges tied to a buoy. We boarded one of the barges and CPO Vermeulen instructed me to conduct an immediate search for contraband goods and weapons, or any signs of a struggle or fight. I found nothing of concern. However, during the course of my search I could find no boathook, which surprised me as it is a standard piece of equipment to be found on all small vessels working the river.

Signed: AP Keeley

Deposition of Rueben Steffan Burch
Occupation: Home Office Pathologist
Address: 36 Harley Street, London, W1.

Magistrates Court Rules 1952: This deposition of Rueben Steffan Burch, approved Home Office Pathologist, of 36 Harley Street London W1, was sworn before me, Ralph

*James Nesbitt, Justice of the Peace, on 6 November 1963 in
the presence of the accused, Isaac Conway, at the Thames
Magistrates' Court.*

Signed: Ralph James Nesbitt Esq.

Signature of deponent: RS Burch

Rueben Steffan Burch WILL SAY AS FOLLOWS:

*I am Dr Rueben Steffan Burch, and I am on the Home
Office List of approved forensic pathologists covering the West
London area. At approximately 06:30 hours on 4 November
1963 I was telephoned by Sir Ian Pears, HM Coroner for
West London, and asked to attend Bridge Wharf Road,
Isleworth to examine a body which had been brought ashore
shortly before. This is not usual procedure, but after speaking
to Sir Ian about the unusual circumstances I was persuaded
to attend. I arrived at the scene at 08:00 hours and was
met by Chief Preventive Officer Vermeulen and Inspector
Dennis Prentice of the Metropolitan Police. On the Thames
riverbank, I was directed to the body of a male in the uniform
of HM Waterguard whom CPO Vermeulen identified as a
junior colleague named APO Evans. I was asked to express
an opinion as to time of death and if there were any injuries
on the body suggestive of foul play. A full examination of the
body was not possible in the circumstances.*

*Estimation of the time of death from body temperature is
an inexact science, particularly when a body has been in cold
water. I measured the temperature of the water in the area*

*where the body was discovered, which I found to be 57°F. A
prolonged period of immersion in cold water will cause the
body to cool more swiftly, thereby incorrectly suggesting a
longer period since death. However in this case the temperature
of the body was 90°F, only 8.4°F less than normal (98.4°F)
which suggested a relatively short period of immersion,
notwithstanding the fact that according to the information I
was given, APO Evans was last seen alive at approximately
16:00 hours on the previous day, and therefore theoretically
could have been in the water for over 13 hours.*

*On the other hand, the body was fully clothed, which would
have caused it to retain its heat for longer.*

*There was no sign of rigor mortis, which usually develops
during the first 12 to 24 hours post-death. More importantly,
there was no sign of lividity or liver mortis. This patchy
discolouration usually begins within the first hour of death,
and becomes more prominent and purple in colour by 3 hours
after death.*

*Based principally on the absence of liver mortis, in my
opinion death occurred no more than 3hours before my
attendance.*

*So far as the cause of death is concerned, during the
examination at the riverside I was able to find no injuries to
the body which would have caused death.*

*The body was removed for full post-mortem examination
at the pathology lab at Charing Cross Hospital which I
conducted with an assistant at 12:00 hours later that day.*

Charles skims through the next page of findings which deals in detail with the APO's presentation, clothing and personal effects. The only evidence of acute injury was a wide area of fresh bruising on the APO's head over the right temporal bone. Charles runs his finger down to the findings of the internal examination, looking for the sub-paragraph dealing with the skull.

The scalp is reflected using standard intermastoidal incision. Overlying the right temporal bone is a thin area of fresh extradural bleeding measuring 3 inches x 1 and ½ inches. The dura is intact but directly beneath the area of extradural bleeding there is a 3-inch-long depressed fracture of the temporal bone extending by ½ inch into the sphenoid bone. The depression is significant, measuring in depth between ⅛th inch on the postero-lateral aspect and ½ inch where it extends into the sphenoid. Beneath the dura at this point is a fleshy haematoma weighing 3.8 ounces in the right subdural space, with accompanying compression and herniation of brain tissue.

Charles jumps ahead again, noting that the lungs were not full of water and that the common signs of drowning, in particular petechial haemorrhages in the conjunctiva, were all absent. So APO Evans died before he went in the water. Charles notes that nothing unusual was found in the examination of any of the other body organs, until he comes to this:

There is in addition a single unusual injury to the deceased's left side, approximately 2 inches proximal to the left kidney. I found a 2 and ½-inch-deep puncture wound of an unusual triangular shape. At its greatest depth, the width of the puncture is approximately ¼ of an inch, but at the level of the skin it is approximately ¾ of an inch. The implement that caused the wound is accordingly pyramidal shaped with a sharp point. The wound has not bled post-mortem. Immediately distal to the wound is an oval indentation from which I obtained some small flakes of rust. While at the scene I was shown a boathook from the Waterguard's launch, which has a sharp point and a curved metal projection immediately below it. In my opinion the pattern of injury would suggest that a boathook was used. There are no injuries to suggest that it was used as a weapon before death, such as linear bruising or cuts. In my opinion it is likely that a boathook was used to push the body, perhaps overboard, after death occurred. No hole was found in the deceased's tunic jacket at the point of the wound. This, and the small flakes of rust found embedded in the skin, make it likely that the boathook was used on the body while at least the upper part of the uniform had been removed. The uniform jacket must then have been replaced on the deceased's body.

Cause of death: blunt trauma to the skull.
Signed: RS Burch

Charles looks up, searching for the sound that has disturbed his concentration. It takes him a couple of seconds to place it, but then realises that although Merlin is still lying on his back on the bench, eyes closed and apparently asleep, the fingers of his right hand are drumming agitatedly on the bench. Charles studies him more closely and sees that his chest is rising and falling rapidly as if he is panting after strenuous exercise.

'Izzy?'

'What's up?' replies the lighterman, swinging his legs off the bench but remaining seated, staring at the grey painted concrete floor and fiddling with his cuffs.

'Are you feeling okay?'

'Peachey, old son,' replies Izzy with heavy sarcasm, his voice shaking slightly.

'It's not all bad news,' says Charles, softly, trying to reassure his cousin. He makes a few further notes and then puts his pen down carefully. He looks up at Merlin again and notices that he's no longer wearing his cap. Must be back in his cell, thinks Charles, or perhaps it's been taken off him.

'Do you want me to run through the evidence?' asks Charles

Merlin looks up. 'Why not?'

'Okay. The pathology evidence of time of death isn't conclusive. The man could have been in the water hours before floating to arrive near your barge. There are no signs of drowning so he was dead before he went in the water but perhaps he fell and banged his head. He was investigating by the river in pitch darkness. Perhaps he fell?'

Charles stands and starts to pace up and down in

the small cell, speaking more quickly as he warms to his task. He is vaguely aware of Merlin's right foot tapping insistently on the floor. 'Perhaps he even fell while trying to board your barge. And the confession – it's not exactly useless, but it not very persuasive as long as we can set up some case against it.'

Merlin's foot abruptly stops moving and he looks up. 'You're wasting your time, Charlie.'

Charles continues with his analysis. 'The real problem is the injury above the kidney. Even if we could show that it could have been made by something other than a boathook, he had a hole in his side but no hole in his uniform. So whoever prodded him with a boathook did so while he was undressed. That's the intriguing evidence, and it leads to some interesting questions. Why would Evans take off his jacket? To swim? Unlikely. And if so, and he died before or after swimming, who put it back on again? And why bother, unless they wanted to hide the fact that he'd been undressed. Perhaps the same person was with him both when it was taken off and when it was replaced?'

Charles turns to his cousin to find him now standing in the middle of the small room, his right hand in his trouser pocket and his left held slightly out from his side. It's an odd stance, as if the lighterman is trying to keep his balance and, as Charles looks at his cousin's expression, he's surprised to see that Merlin is now as intensely focused on Charles's words as he was indifferent minutes earlier.

'All very interesting,' he says dismissively, 'but it's hopeless, Charlie, and we both know it.'

'Nothing's hopeless, Izzy,' insists Charles. 'I've taken on cases that looked much worse than this on paper, and they've just fallen apart when I got to court. This is the best they have, the high-water mark. We haven't even started chipping away at it. And that point about taking off his jacket –' muses Charles.

'Forget it.'

'Come on, Izzy. This isn't like you.'

'You don't know me any more Charlie. Too much water under too many bridges.'

And as if to prove it, Merlin has an expression on his face which Charles doesn't recognise. The lighterman's suntanned skin looks almost grey and his eyes are over-bright and feverish. His legs tremble with suppressed energy, and behind his eyes there's another emotion which, for a second, Charles struggles to identify ... Indecision? No: fear. Perhaps the reality of his situation has finally sunk in.

'Don't give up, Izzy. This is the first time you've been here, but I've defended a dozen people on murder charges. I promise you: there's still hope.'

Charles moves towards Merlin and grasps him by the shoulders in a reassuring gesture and locks eyes with his cousin. He doesn't notice Merlin's right hand being drawn from his trouser pocket.

'You can't give up, Izzy. What about your mum? She needs you.'

'Yes,' replies Merlin, his voice shaking and a strange smile twisting his lips.

'You were my best friend. The two years I spent with

you were probably the best in my life. I will do everything I can to save you, but you've got to help me.'

Izzy lifts up his left hand and reaches under Charles right arm, putting it round Charles's back and between his shoulder blades, as if about to pull Charles into an embrace. Charles imagines that Merlin's gesture is one of thanks and affection. Then he feels something touching his chest just below his breastbone. He looks down. In Merlin's shaking and tightly gripped right hand is what appears to be a knife, its shining blade bridging the distance between the two men, its point pricking Charles's skin through his shirt. A shock flashes from deep in Charles's guts down to his knees and he feels his legs almost buckle.

Merlin whispers. 'I can't hang twice, he said.' A deep sob escapes from his constricted throat.

'What? Who said?' whispers Charles, aware somehow that a loud noise or sudden movement would be his last.

'A copper. Someone from the Dirty Squad.'

And with that, the tumblers fall into place in Charles's mind and he understands it all. The Dirty Squad; corrupt from top to bottom, and many of them on the take from the Krays.

Charles fills in the gaps. 'They told you you're certain to be hanged, so you might as well take me as well. "You can't hang twice." And – let me guess – they'll look after mum afterwards.'

Merlin nods shortly. He manages to speak, taking huge gulps of air between each phrase. 'If I don't do it, someone else will, he said. Some geezer'll come up to you in a pub, smile in your face and blow a hole in your chest. Or someone on the bus'll shove a spike into your back. But it's coming, Charlie, it's coming. You've been lucky so far but Ronnie ain't gonna give up. So it might as well be me.'

'Ronnie Kray?' asks Charles, shaking his head. 'You really gonna trust that mad cunt? He doesn't give a shit about you. Whereas I love you.'

Charles stares deep into the other man's eyes. His hands, still on Merlin's shoulders, grip tighter. Another sob breaks from Merlin's chest and now tears brim over his eyelids, blurring his vision.

'I know it all looks hopeless,' says Charles with immense intensity, measuring each word. 'And I know you want to protect your mum. But this is not the way! Think what it'll do to her, to my mother – to the whole family! Do you suppose having all the money in the world would make your mum understand? You murdered her nephew to protect her? And it'll destroy my parents too.'

Merlin is now crying in earnest, a deep moan coming from his throat between great juddering breaths. Tears splash onto Charles's white shirt.

'And in any case,' asks Charles, 'do you imagine that none of us would rally round and support your mum if the worst happened to you? Who's going to be more reliable in looking after her: Ronnie Kray – or your own family?'

Charles hears the breath catching in Merlin's throat, and his feverish stare loses some of its intensity as Charles's words percolate through the turmoil of his conflicting emotions. Although he grips the shiv as tightly as ever, and

Charles can feel a tiny point of blood – or perhaps it's sweat – running down his stomach towards his belt, Merlin's hand drops from between Charles's shoulder blades and hangs listlessly at his side. Charles still doesn't dare move. He can still feel the knife point against his skin and it would take a mere fraction of a second for Merlin to find the courage and move his right hand forward and impale Charles on three inches of sharpened metal.

'Work with me, Izzy,' Charles begs.

'You said that if I told you the truth, your rules would tie your hands in court.'

'Fuck that,' replies Charles with a trace of his familiar grin. 'We're *both* on death row! Now's not the time for professional niceties.'

'You mean that?'

Charles nods. 'On my life. I'll do whatever it takes.'

Merlin searches Charles's face, trying to read him, his sincerity – his very soul. Slowly his right hand drops. Charles releases his grip on Merlin's shoulders and steps back a pace. He reaches behind him for the tissues on the table and steps forward again. Rather than handing the tissues to Merlin, Charles himself dabs at the tears and dries his cousin's face. It's a gentle gesture between two powerful men and with it the tension in the room dissipates. Merlin sniffs and manages a weak smile. He holds out the shiv and watches as Charles pockets it.

'Now,' says Charles. 'Come and sit down with me and tell me exactly what happened. 'Start with Evans's clothes. Something tells me they're going to be the key.'

chapter 16

Today is Izzy's nineteenth birthday and, happily, it coincides with the hottest day of 1942. It was already balmy at half past six when Izzy and Charlie stepped from Tower Pier onto the deck of Union Jack's tug, *The Fairweather*, to start work, but it is now early afternoon and the temperature has climbed throughout the day. According to the thermometer on the inside of the tugboat's wheelhouse it is just touching 88°F. The lads have long since dispensed with all clothes except their trousers – in both cases rolled up to their knees – and, in Izzy's case, his cap. Both still wear heavy boots; however hot it is, they know that to move cargo and boats in bare feet is simply to invite injury.

Izzy casts off the stern ropes on each of the two barges in turn and walks for'ard across the deck of the leeward barge. Charlie waits by the head rope on the other barge. Izzy nods, and they simultaneously cast off the head ropes on both barges and swiftly lash the two together. They work well together, quickly and efficiently. Charlie is now almost as competent as his older cousin. Union Jack was at first reluctant to employ the sixteen-year-old even when shorthanded.

"'E's a big strong lad, I grant you, but 'e ain't been

doing it long enough,' he said a few times, despite Jonjo's insistence that Charlie was the brightest apprentice he'd ever had and that he picked things up very fast.

Then, a couple of months back, Union Jack's brother-in-law Ernie suffered an injury, leaving Jack in need of a lighterman at short notice, and he'd taken a chance. Since then he'd used Charles on several occasions, and while Charles loved working with Uncle Jonjo, it made a pleasant change to spend time with another Master, especially one whose family had been working the River for hundreds of years.

The skin of Charles's face, the V of his neck and his lower arms – olive coloured even after a winter covered by clothing – are now deeply bronzed by the sun. What little puppy fat he still had when he started working on the River in the winter of 1940 has now been replaced by hard, knotted muscle. While his mother, Millie Horowitz, was a competent but unenthusiastic cook, Aunt Bea lives to feed her large household in Shadwell and would happily spend her entire life in the kitchen, producing meal after meal. Whatever time of the day or night Izzy and Charles return, there is always something on the stove or in the oven keeping warm for them, often courtesy of Bea's uncle in Poplar, a kosher butcher. Despite rationing, there's always an extra chop or two or half a chicken wrapped up in the brown paper bags Charles collects for her. Since Charles started living at Juniper Street, under Aunt Bea's loving ministrations he has filled out and acquired his adult musculature.

Despite the fact that Charles has less time to go to the boxing gym, the hard work and agility required as a lighterman have left him leaner and in better condition than he has ever been in his life. He revels in his physicality; his body will do exactly what he requires of it, and at times he feels almost superhuman in his aliveness. The time has long gone when Izzy could best Charles in their playful boxing and wrestling matches, fought to while away the long hours of waiting for the tide or for permission to enter port. Charles still lets Izzy win occasionally, but the older boy is well aware that Charles is deliberately keeping something in reserve. He isn't offended; in fact, Charles's sensitivity to Izzy's pride adds one more item to the list of reasons why Izzy loves him.

Izzy raises his arm to Union Jack who waits, looking out from the wheelhouse of *The Fairweather*. Jack keeps the tug stationary, head on to the tide, its engine bubbling and chugging softly. In response to Izzy's signal he slips the gear and moves the tug forward slowly and, as the tug passes the barges Izzy jumps nimbly over the gunwales from the barge to land on its deck. With the tug still moving, Izzy throws a tow rope to Charles who catches it neatly and makes it fast to the Sampson post. Charles then leaps onto the second barge and catches the second tow rope thrown by Izzy, making that fast as well. Jack slows the engine and puts it into reverse, backing towards the prow of the barges to let Izzy rejoin Charles. The two young lightermen spend the next few seconds loosening and tightening the tow ropes in turn until they are satisfied that the barges are in perfect position, before tying them off. Jack moves the tug forward, the tow ropes tauten, the tug takes the weight, and the two barges tied astern line up like reluctant sheep and start moving.

Charles sits by the hatch of the barge towards the centre of the River, his arms around his knees. Two tin mugs of tea sit on the deck by his side. As the junior apprentice, one of his principal duties is to boil water on the tiny two-ring gas stove in the lighter's cabin to keep them all regularly supplied with fresh tea. Izzy comes over and sits next to him, his legs crossed, their knees almost touching. He reaches across Charles's bare torso to grab a mug of tea and sips noisily. They sit in companionable silence, watching the West India Docks slide by on the port side. Charles is fascinated by the hundreds of cranes bristling into the blue sky. He imagines them to be giant herons, swinging and dipping their bills as they load and unload the ships below them. He finds the work of a lighterman endlessly interesting and is sad when he acknowledges that his time on the River must soon come to an end. He has remained in correspondence with his family in Wales over the last months and has seen his father twice when he travelled to London to attend to business. Millie and Harry reluctantly accepted that Charles wanted to stay in Shadwell and, now the Blitz is over, they are less worried about him than they were. But in his last letters Harry made it clear that he expects Charles to do more with his life than be a lighterman, however much Charles may love it. Charles knows that it is only a matter of time before his father comes to reclaim him and take him back to his education and the claustrophobic Horowitz household.

Today however he is as happy as he has ever been. He loves the warmth of the sun on his skin, the wind stirring his sleek curly hair, the light dancing on the water and the screams of the seagulls as they swoop and dive in the air above him, hoping for something edible to be thrown or dumped over the back of the barges. And tonight he and Izzy are going up West to dance and spend some money. Charles has a date with the young nurse called Alison.

He looks across at Izzy's profile. He has never had a friend like Izzy, and he admires the older boy for his charm, his kindness and his sense of humour. There's always a spark of amusement dancing in those brown eyes, even when one of his adventures – usually criminal – goes horribly wrong. Like the time their getaway lorry from a night-time warehouse burglary refused to start because he'd forgotten to put petrol in the tank. They'd had to leg it, leaving a consignment of copper bars worth over £300. Charles had expected Izzy to be downcast, but he told and retold the story to his mates in the local pubs for weeks, laughing at his own incompetence.

They are heading downstream to return the barges to Greenwich where they will await the arrival of a ship from the west coast of Canada later that day. The ship will moor at the same buoys and discharge one hundred tons of timber and tinned salmon direct into the barges, which will then be towed to the River Lea via Limehouse Cut. Jack has something to attend to, so he plans to leave the lads on board the barges, just in case the Canadian ship arrives early, and return in a couple of hours. Izzy has enough experience by now to oversee loading and comparing tally cards, but Jack is confident he'll be back in good time. Izzy and Charles look forward to a lazy afternoon on the barge in the sunshine. To celebrate his birthday Izzy has a couple of bottles of brown ale in the tiny cabin and a pack of cards; Charles has *Great Expectations* to finish. In addition, in the inside pocket of Charles's jacket stowed below is a birthday present for Izzy: a fob watch Charles found on a second-hand stall in Petticoat Lane and which he has had repaired and cleaned. Izzy, always a snappy dresser when up West, likes to wear waistcoats, and Charles has spent a week's wages on the watch. He thinks it will look swanky across Izzy's chest.

They drop the barges at the mooring buoys and Jack takes his leave. The two young men settle down to wait. Despite the hooting of ships' horns and the faint noises of machinery and shouting from the wharves and docks on both sides of the river, it is peaceful in the sunshine, the barges bobbing up and down gently in the wash of passing ships of all sizes and origins.

Charles stretches out on the deck, Dickens held in one hand and the other shading his eyes from the sun. Izzy makes himself a second cup of tea and sits with his legs dangling in the water, playing idly with some pieces of cork left over from an earlier consignment and watching a pair of 1500-tonner flat-irons making their way upstream towards Kingston Power Station to unload their coal.

After a while he becomes bored and sends a piece of cork skimming through the air towards Charles. It lands just behind Charles's head. Charles doesn't notice it and so Izzy tries again with a larger and flatter piece which he sends spinning through the air with a flick of his wrist. This one catches the breeze, overshoots Charles, and lands in the water on the starboard side of the barge. Izzy stands and walks the few paces to where Charles lies, engrossed in his book, and deliberately stands between Charles and the sun. Charles still doesn't move. Then, with no warning, Charles sweeps his hand across the deck aiming for Izzy's legs. Izzy half-jumps out of the way but Charles's blow catches his departing ankle and Izzy tumbles over. Before he has time to get up Charles has dropped the book and is on top of him, laughing and grabbing for his cousin's wrists to pin them down. Charles lies across Izzy's chest, his greater weight preventing Izzy from lifting his torso from the deck and forcing Izzy's shoulder blades flat to the ground for a count of three. Izzy too is laughing, so much so that he can't summon the strength to shove Charles off him.

'One ... two ... three!' shouts Charles, and he rolls off Izzy's body and in a single movement sweeps Izzy's cap off his head, holding it aloft as if it were his prize.

Izzy jumps up, trying to retrieve the cap but although taller than Charles, is unable to get it as Charles spins and turns. Moving lightly on the balls of his feet as if in the ring, Charles bobs and weaves, throwing the cap from one hand to the other and back again, keeping it constantly out of Izzy's reach. He finally throws it up in the air, expecting

Izzy to grab it as it descends, but sends it slightly too high. A gust of wind catches it and it spins over the side and into the water. Without thinking Charles launches himself over the side of the barge and dives neatly into the water before the cap has time to sink. He surfaces after a second, the cap held aloft.

'Jesus, Charlie!' exclaims Izzy. 'Get out of there! How many times do I have to tell you?'

Charles had forgotten the filthy state of the Thames. Jonjo, Union Jack and Izzy have all warned him repeatedly that if he fell in he was likely to require a stomach pump. People die after swallowing Thames water, and had Charles's dive been seen by a policeman he would have been collared and taken to hospital whether he wanted to go or not.

Izzy reaches down and grabs Charles's wrist, hauling him back aboard.

'I was careful. I held my breath and I didn't swallow anything,' he assures Izzy. 'Here,' he says, offering the cap back.

Izzy takes it, shakes it, and puts it back in its accustomed position on the back of his head, adjusting it carefully to just the right angle. Charles runs his hands through his wet curls, shaking off the excess water, and then stands. He yawns and reaches for the heavens, stretching like a cat. He is altogether unaware of Izzy's lingering sidelong glance at his glistening torso or the longing in his cousin's eyes, and they settle down again to while away the hours.

chapter 17

Charles rings the bell to summon the redheaded prison officer. He stands in front of the door, composing himself. His jacket is back on, buttoned up to hide the dampness of Izzy's tears and his own blood on his shirt; the prosecution papers are neatly bundled and held in his hand with his blue notebook, which is now almost completely full of his angular handwriting. The shiv remains concealed in his pocket. It's taking a chance, but he has never before been searched for weapons on the way out. Blood leaks from both nostrils, and his left eye is gradually closing from a puffy bruise. Merlin looks worse: his top lip is split and dribbles blood in his mouth which, every few seconds, he spits on the floor; there's a deep gash on his left cheekbone which will probably need a couple of stitches; and his slightly laboured breathing suggests a rib or two may be cracked.

They both hear the heavy tread of the giant prison officer approaching the conference room. Charles turns back to Merlin and smiles briefly. Merlin winks at him. The door opens.

'This w— what the fuck?' exclaims the officer.

'The prisoner attacked me,' exclaims Charles as he walks through the open door.

'Right. Wait in reception, and I'll get a medical orderly to look at you,' suggests the officer. He points at Merlin and smiles threateningly. 'You're in big trouble, sunshine,' he says.

'Don't worry about that,' says Charles with an attempt at a smile. 'I can look after myself, and he came off a lot worse. I'm not pressing charges.'

'You can't let this arrogant little toe-rag get away with assaulting you.'

'I couldn't give evidence about it – it's all covered by legal professional privilege,' lies Charles. 'But you might want to have his chest x-rayed. I thought I heard a rib crack.'

The prison officer scratches his head uncertainly, looking from Charles to Merlin and back again, slack-jawed with astonishment.

'Come on, man. Stop fretting,' chides Charles. 'I'm not complaining. I've had a good workout, and now I've got stuff to do. Busy weekend ahead.'

The officer takes one last look at the two men and shrugs. Fucking Jew boys; can never guess what they'll do next. 'Suit yourself,' he says.

•

'Can I speak to Mr Kray please?'

There's a lot of noise at the end of the line. 'Which Mr Kray?'

'Mr Ronnie Kray.'

'Who's speaking?'

'Uncle Izzy from Brixton.'

'What's that? You're gonna to have to shout – oh, there you are, Ron. I think this is for you, but I can't hear 'im proper.'

The handset is passed to someone else. 'Regal Billiard Hall, Ronnie Kray speaking.'

'Ronnie, it's me.'

'About time. How'd it go?'

'Sorry Ron, but it didn't work. That brief's got nine lives. He's put Conway in the hospital wing and, let me tell you, Conway's a right mess. He's game though; Bernie on the gate reckons the lawyer's eye was closed and he had a broken nose.'

'That's no fuckin' good to me, is it?'

'No.'

There's a pause at the end of the line in the billiard hall. 'Alright,' says Ronnie. 'Thanks for letting me know. What'd you do with the shiv?'

'I think Holborne must've got it off 'im. I searched Conway myself and he ain't got it. One more thing: we've gotta produce Conway on Monday for the arraignment, but it'll probably be put off for a few days. He's in no fit state to give evidence – he can barely speak.'

'Okay. That might be as well. I'll get back to you when I've had a think.'

'Righto.'

•

Charles pushes open the street door to his apartment building. He had hoped that the reception desk would be unattended – it usually was – but on this occasion Dennis was on duty, a duster in one hand and polish in the other.

'Afternoon Mr H,' he said, seeing Charles.

'Good afternoon, Dennis. How's the family?' replies Charles as he walks swiftly down the hall towards the desk.

'Doing very nicely, thank you sir,' replies the porter cum *concierge*, bending to tidy the shelves behind the desk, and not looking at Charles. 'Brenda's pregnant again, so it looks like I'm going to be a granddad for the second time.'

'Congratulations,' says Charles. He considers calling the lift, but the ancient rattling contraption moves more slowly than a Chelsea pensioner, and so he decides to use the stairs. 'Got to run,' he calls, as he starts up the carpeted stairs two at a time.

In the flat Charles strips to the waist and, standing before the mirror in the bedroom, examines the damage. He'd instructed Merlin to make the evidence of a fight noticeable, so it was largely confined to Charles's face. There was a scratch along the line of his collar where he imagines he was caught by a fingernail, but otherwise his upper body and torso are unmarked. Just as well: it's going to be a long night, and Charles needs to be at one hundred percent.

He walks to the bathroom, grabbing the bottle of Scotch and a glass tumbler on the way. In the bathroom Charles pours himself a large slug of whisky and downs it in one. He refills the glass and puts it on the side of the enamel sink. Turning on the light over the mirror, he leans forward to examine his face. He had thought that the left eye was going to close completely, but the swelling is not as bad as he feared. Both lids look puffy and red, but he can still see.

'Good shot, Izzy,' he congratulates his cousin in absentia.

Under his nose there is a sizeable patch of dried blood on his top lip, but there appears to be little new seepage from the nostrils. Charles lifts his top lip to examine its underside. It's quite sore where another good punch crushed it against his top teeth, and there's still a little fresh blood seeping from his gum, staining his top teeth red. He reaches for the glass of whisky, takes a mouthful, and rinses it around his mouth. He's about to spit it into the basin but thinks better of it, and swallows instead. Overall, not bad. It's impossible to judge these things to a nicety.

Charles wonders how Merlin's getting on. His injuries had to be enough to fool both the prison authorities and those who would report back to Ronnie Kray; if they were enough to render Merlin temporarily unfit for trial without doing serious damage, better still. Nonetheless Charles had had to take care not to overdo it. Both he and Merlin know only too well how easy it is to misjudge such things. Sometimes with fatal consequences.

He turns over in his mind Merlin's revelations about his sexuality. Now Charles thinks about it, he isn't altogether surprised. At age nineteen Merlin was the most beautiful young man Charles had ever seen, and he was utterly charming. Whenever they were out together during the War, at the pubs in the East End or the clubs and dancehalls up West, Charles was amazed at how many glances were thrown Izzy's way, and by almost as many men as women. Merlin would laugh it off and flirt outrageously, but he always went home with Charles. In fact, remembers Charles, he couldn't recall Merlin having a girlfriend at all during that two-year period. But it was the War: many young men and women had short-lived transient relationships.

Charles inserts the rubber plug and runs some hot water into the basin. He washes the blood off his face, the water turning pink as he does so, and bathes his eyes in cool water for a few minutes. He then rinses down the sink and dries his face gingerly. He takes the Scotch into the lounge and picks up the phone. He dials most of Sally's number in Romford, but hangs up before completing it. He hears Henrietta harrumph in his head, but she says nothing.

He thinks for a moment and then goes to a drawer in the kitchen, digging until he finds something right at the bottom. He pulls out a pamphlet entitled "Port of London – Handbook of Tide Tables". It's dog-eared and stained, having been used variously as a coaster for hot drinks, a bookmark and a leveller for a wobbly dressing table since Charles purchased it. He doesn't really know why he persists in buying these handbooks, only for them to remain unread and, when out of date, stacked in order on one of his shelves. Perhaps it was in memory of those wonderful two years spent with Izzy on the River. This is the first time he's ever had cause to look at one since 1942. Charles turns the pages swiftly to the page giving details of the day's tides and runs his finger down until he finds the entry he seeks. He then returns the handbook to the drawer. He looks at his watch. Time to call in a favour from Handbag Dave and some of his mates with stalls at the Lane.

At quarter to midnight Charles slips out of the door to the apartment building on Fetter Lane. He has spent the last hour sitting at the kitchen table, a tea towel filled with crushed ice applied to his eye, and the swelling has begun to reduce. He scans the road carefully, anxious not to bump into any barristers leaving the Temple late after burning midnight oil, but Fetter Lane and Fleet Street are empty of pedestrians. Charles wears jeans, a white shirt with rolled up sleeves, a white vest underneath the shirt, and a short leather jacket, all recently acquired during the course of the evening and a quick trip to a lockup in Walthamstow. He carries David's rucksack over his shoulder. He has tried to get his thick curly hair to lie flat under a layer of Brylcreem, but with only limited success. He enjoys playing roles, submerging his identity into another's attitudes, accent and gait, but this makes him nervous. A flick knife – an old friend – nestles in a hip pocket.

A Routemaster, a number 15, rumbles along Fleet Street towards Trafalgar Square, slowing for the traffic lights at the junction with Fetter Lane. Charles jogs into the junction and leaps onto the platform as the bus moves off again. The lower deck has half a dozen passengers, four noisy teenagers and a couple of middle-aged women who are either about to finish or to start work. The Jamaican conductor leans against one of the vertical poles attached to the seats, flirting with one of the women. Preferring to be unnoticed, Charles climbs to the upper deck, taking the first empty seat at the back. By the time the bus reaches Charing Cross station the conductor has not been up to take Charles's money and Charles jumps off without paying. He darts across the cobbles of the forecourt of Charing Cross station, dodging the advancing queue of black cabs waiting for fares, and walks into the main hall. There he puts a penny into the slot of one of the left luggage lockers and stuffs the rucksack inside, slamming the door.

He walks swiftly back out of the station, across Trafalgar Square and up Haymarket towards Piccadilly Circus. The pavements are busier here, mainly with young people in high spirits and a sprinkling of tourists. At the top of Haymarket Charles ducks into the entrance of Dunn & Co. The doors are locked and the foyer is littered with windblown sheets of newspaper and used food packets. It smells of stale chip fat and, faintly, urine, but it allows Charles to remain out of sight from a vantage point to look across the road to the Rack.

Lined up against the railings surrounding the entrance to Piccadilly Tube station are half a dozen young men, in clothes not dissimilar to those worn by Charles. From this distance it looks as if most of them are half Charles's age. One, a youth with a greasy complexion, a flop of hair over his forehead and a cigarette hanging out of his mouth does not look more than fifteen or sixteen, despite his efforts to look tough. On the same pavement, but a few feet away, are three or four older men in overcoats pacing up and down, pausing and then pacing again, pretending to wait for someone, but in fact eyeing up the boys on sale. Charles watches as one, a bulky man wearing a cloth cap and smoking a pipe, leans forward and says something to one of the rent boys, who laughs in response. A short conversation ensues, the man nods, and walks off towards Leicester Square. A few seconds later the boy follows.

There is a sudden commotion across the road from the statue of Eros. A fight seems to have broken out in the queue of drug addicts waiting for their methadone scrips outside Boots the Chemist. Charles takes advantage of the distraction to slip out of the doorway and jog across the road to the railings. One of the lads looks up and detaches himself from the Rack. He's a good-looking boy, fair hair and wide lips, perhaps 18 years of age, but he has dark rings under his eyes and a hollowness to his cheeks that make him look unappetising. He might just be hungry, thinks Charles, but he doubts it.

'You looking for some?' asks the boy in a Geordie accent. He then notices Charles's clothes. 'Or are you working?' he asks, looking a bit puzzled. 'You're a bit old, eh?'

Charles leans in towards him. 'I didn't want to look like a punter,' he explains, 'but I'm not working either. I'd hoped to blend in,' he finishes lamely.

'Well, you fucked that up, then,' comments the boy, dismissing Charles and taking a pace sideways so as to re-establish eye contact over Charles's shoulder with the evening's potential business customers.

Charles steps forward again, narrowing the gap between him and the boy. 'I need some information.'

The boy looks at him sharply and mutters 'Fucking

coppers!' and makes to move off before Charles grabs his arm.

'No, I'm not the Filth. I need to find Chicken. I'm a friend of Merlin's.'

Charles sees renewed doubt and uncertainty in the boy's face.

'What happened to your face?' he asks.

'Like Chicken, I got into some trouble. Merlin's sent me to give him some money. For a ticket home if he wants, or just a safe bed for a few nights.'

'Merlin you say?'

The boy obviously knows Merlin's name, but it's not the passport Charles hoped it might be.

'He's a ... close friend,' replies Charles, avoiding the other's eyes.

The implicit confession that Charles is also homosexual appears to break the other's resistance. He nods, a curious upward jerking of his head. 'Try behind Lisle Street. Above the Wan Chai.'

Charles frowns and pulls a face as if to say he has no idea where the boy means. In fact he thinks he does know the restaurant – certainly he knows Lisle Street – but he needs to make sure he's not being given the brush off.

'Can you take me? I'll pay for your time,' he offers.

The boy scans the punters behind Charles, but doesn't apparently see any immediate business. 'How much?' he asks, transferring his gaze back to Charles.

'Ten minutes' there, ten minutes' back, so twenty minutes before you're back at work.' Charles looks round at the older men. Two have already departed and those who remain don't look keen. 'And there's not much doing here. £2?'

The boy snorts. 'You're joking. I earn more than that for a hand job.'

'£3 then. Cash in advance. No risk and no sticky fingers.' He reaches into his pocket, as if about to take out some money.

The boy steps forward, very close to Charles, and puts his right hand over Charles's while it's still in his pocket. 'Fuck's sake, mate!' he hisses. 'What're you doing? You'll get us both arrested!'

Charles had no intention of paying the boy money here but he wants to push him into a decision. He has little time to mess about.

'Okay,' says the boy. 'Follow me.'

They walk down the short stretch of Coventry Street and turn off Leicester Square by a building site, the hoardings around which announce there will be a "Swiss Centre" on the corner. Charles wonders as they pass why Leicester Square requires a centre dedicated to the Swiss nation and its industries. What will they sell – cheese maybe? Cuckoo clocks?

Lisle Street is narrow, dark and almost deserted. The thought flashes across Charles's mind that he's been brought here to be robbed, and as the boy turns to face him Charles nonchalantly loops his thumbs into his belt, making sure the flick knife is within easy reach of his right hand, but the boy turns to Charles and holds out his hand. Charles reaches into his jacket pocket and pulls out a small roll of notes. He peels off three and puts them into the other's open palm. The boy pockets them, turns round and points to a small door immediately next to a Chinese restaurant. Light still spills out of the restaurant's windows and Charles can see two or three tables occupied.

'The front door should be open. Go up to the third floor. There's no name on the door and no bell. Knock twice, and then twice again. Tell him I'll be back before dawn with some food. I've got to earn some money first.'

The boy's about to return to the Rack when he turns and peers at Charles. 'You'd better be on the up and up, mate,' he says. 'Chicken's me friend.'

The boy leans in, trying to look menacing, but Charles sees genuine concern on his young sallow face. 'I promise you,' he says, 'Merlin's a friend of mine, and he's asked me to find Chicken and give him some money. You have my word: no harm'll come to him from me.'

Charles speaks with sincerity. He hopes what he says is true.

'Fair enough,' says the other, with the same odd upward motion of his head. 'See ya 'round.'

Charles looks about himself to ensure he's not being watched and crosses the road, stepping over discarded vegetables in the gutter. He pushes against the peeling paint on the outer door which might once have been white. The door opens and Charles is immediately faced by a Chinese man sitting at the bottom of a staircase smoking a cigarette.

Both men jump. The Chinese man says something in what Charles assumes is Mandarin and scuttles past Charles, throwing his cigarette end into the street and pushing open the restaurant door.

The staircase facing Charles is in darkness and he can't find a light switch, but there is a rectangle of yellow light coming through the window at the top of the first flight of stairs and he can see tolerably well. He walks slowly up the stairs, careful to make as little noise as possible. A door opens off the first landing. It's ajar, and Charles can make out office equipment, a desk and a telephone. Perhaps the office serving the restaurant? Charles walks along the landing back towards Lisle Street and a second turn in the stairs. He feels his way up to the second floor, through increasingly complete darkness. At the top of the second flight he can see through the unpainted wooden balustrade to the third floor above him and a yellow strip of light coming from underneath a closed doorway. He creeps up the last flight of stairs and stops outside the only door on the landing. A transistor radio is playing inside and Charles can make out the distinctive electronic warbling of The Tornados' clavioline on *Telstar*. Charles lifts his hand and knocks twice, pauses, and knocks twice again. There's no reply to his knock but the radio is turned off with a distinct click. Charles waits a moment and, in case the occupant didn't hear the knock clearly, he repeats it: two and then two. This time there's movement and sound from behind the door.

'Mitch?' asks a male voice.

'No,' says Charles. 'I'm a friend of Merlin's. He sent me to see if you're OK.'

No response comes from behind the door. Charles looks at it and its frame and thinks he could probably break it down with a shoulder charge, but decides to wait.

'He's got a fucking nerve,' says the voice. 'I've not heard a word from him in weeks.'

'That's 'cos he's in prison, Chicken. He's being done for murder.'

Charles hears a squeak from behind the door and can imagine the high-pitched exclamation being cut short by the maker's own hand against his mouth. 'Look, Chicken, open the door, yeah? I don't think we should continue this conversation where we can be overheard.'

There's another pause and then the door opens slowly, a young man's tousled head appearing in the gap. He speaks with one hand hiding his mouth. 'What do you want?'

'I've got some money for you,' replies Charles, 'and I need to talk to you for a minute.'

Even allowing for the fact that Chicken is bare-footed while Charles wears boots, the boy is very short, no more than five foot four in height, and slender. He pulls a kimono dressing gown tighter around him with his spare hand, and then removes the hand concealing his mouth. He holds it out.

'I'll give you the money if you let me in. This is important, Chicken –'

'Don't call me that,' mumbles the other, keeping his lips almost shut.

'Sorry. I don't know what else to call you. That was the name I was given.'

The boy doesn't answer but he steps back and opens the door wider. Charles steps into a bedroom. He had expected something like a slum, but it is clear that Chicken – or whatever his name is – takes pride in his surroundings. The single bed in the corner of the room is covered in a purple and pink-coloured tie and dye bedspread and at least a dozen multi-coloured cushions, and there are prints of Impressionist paintings stuck with tape to the walls. A tailor's clothes rack holds a few neatly pressed clothes, and the basin in the corner of the room is clean and sparkling. A record player sits on a chair next to the bed with a small collection of LPs on the floor underneath it. If the boy has any other possessions, they're not in this room. The floor is un-carpeted, but the boards have been swept. The room smells of incense or perfume, overlaid by the Chinese cooking from the restaurant below.

The boy closes the door behind Charles and gestures to Charles to sit on the bed. Charles hesitates but there's nowhere else convenient to sit, so he accepts the offer. The boy follows suit, as far from Charles as the length of the bed will allow.

'What should I call you?' asks Charles.

'David. My name's David.'

The boy suddenly notices Charles's bruised face and swollen eye. 'Blimey, your face looks a mess.'

'Yes, it's a bit tender.'

'Tell me about Merlin.'

As the boy speaks, Charles sees why he has been hiding his mouth. The two incisors in the centre of his top gum are missing, and only one remains, at an angle, in the lower gum. Now Charles has an opportunity to examine the boy's face in the light, he can see signs of fading yellowish bruising above one eye and a healing cut in the corner of his mouth.

Charles draws a deep breath. 'The man who attacked you, Evans ... he's dead.'

David's hand once more claps over his mouth in shock. 'Oh God,' he whispers. 'I knew it didn't look good.'

'Merlin told me what happened,' says Charles gently.

David hangs his head. 'First time it's happened to me,' he mumbles into his chest, and through the lisping Charles detects a Welsh accent. The possibility that Evans may also have been Welsh crosses his mind, and he files the coincidence for further thought, later. 'Merlin had popped out to get fish and chips. I was dozing, and when I heard footsteps on the deck above me I thought it was Merlin coming back. But it wasn't.' He pauses, and Charles stays silent, allowing the boy to collect himself. 'I honestly believe that if Merlin hadn't come back when he did, that man would have killed me.'

'Did you go to hospital? Have you seen a doctor?'

David shakes his head. 'I couldn't. I left home because I couldn't tell anyone. There would be questions ... the police, and ... I'm only seventeen.' He looks up at Charles and draws a false conclusion from his clothing and his connection to Merlin. 'You know.'

Charles doesn't know. He's represented and prosecuted

several homosexual men during the course of his professional career, but he's never before been brought face to face with the reality of these young men's lives. He finds it unsettling. Nonetheless, he nods empathetically.

'But I'm getting better,' continues David. 'It doesn't bleed so much when I go ... you understand.'

Charles nods again. David is little more than a child, and nothing could possibly have prepared him for having his teeth knocked out by way of foreplay to anal rape by a large man twice his age.

'And your teeth? You're going to need some treatment aren't you – a denture or something.'

'That costs a lot though, doesn't it? And look at me – who's going to be interested now?'

'So, what are you going to do?' asks Charles softly.

'I don't know. Maybe if I can raise the money for a ticket, I'll go back home to Swansea. I don't want to. My step-dad's still there. But Mitch said he might be able to help.' The boy lapses into silence, before he attempts a weak gap-toothed smile and shrugs. 'You said you wanted to talk to me?'

'Yes. After Merlin helped you off the boat and got you into the taxi, he went back to the barge. Like you, he thought Evans was just unconscious. He was going to drag him to the bank and leave him there. He couldn't wake him. He even poked him with the boathook but he still didn't move. That's when he realised he was dead. He didn't know what to do, so he got him into his clothes and pitched him overboard. The Waterguard turned up a couple of hours later. Like I said, he's been charged with murder.'

'But it was an accident! He had to hit him to get the man off me!'

'I know that. He was preventing you being raped. That's self-defence. But he needs your evidence to prove it. He hasn't mentioned it to the police at all.'

It takes a moment for David to absorb Charles's words but slowly his eyes open wide and he shakes his head agitatedly. 'But I can't give evidence! It'll be all over the papers! My mum'll see it!'

'But you were an innocent victim,' protests Charles.

'That won't make any difference. Everyone'll know I'm gay. It's bound to come out. And the way I've been living. Isn't it?'

Of course it is, acknowledges Charles to himself. It'll all come out. If he was prosecuting he'd almost certainly cross-examine on the same basis. Despite the Woolfenden report, homosexual acts are still illegal and likely to remain that way. This poor kid would face conviction himself, despite having been the victim of a rape and a severe beating.

'I like Merlin – a lot,' says David with intensity. 'He's been very kind to me and we became very ... close.'

Charles was aware that David had been invited to spend the night with Merlin on the barge, and no payment had been anticipated between them. They were indeed close.

'But I can't help him,' finishes David, anguish in his voice.

'He'll hang if convicted.'

David drops his head again and Charles hears him

crying. 'I can't help him,' repeats David, his voice shaking.

Charles reaches inside his leather jacket pocket and comes up with a clean-ish tissue which he hands to David. He stands. This response is pretty much what he had expected. He reaches into his other pocket and takes out three £10 pound notes – much more than he'd expected to pay for information.

'Here.' David doesn't look up. 'David!' says Charles firmly, holding out the notes. David looks up, his cheeks wet with tears, and sees the money.

'There's probably enough for dental treatment and dentures,' says Charles. 'It's definitely enough to get home, if that's what you want.'

'Really?' asks David, eyes wide.

'Really.'

'Is it from Merlin?'

'No,' says Charles. 'It's from me. Now take it,' he instructs.

David reaches out tentatively and takes the money. He then launches himself from the bed at Charles, holding him in a firm embrace and kissing him repeatedly on the cheek. 'Thank you, thank you, thank you!' he says, with a kiss between each "thank you".

Charles pats him gently on the back and disengages from him.

'Can I … do anything for you?' asks David. 'I know I don't look much, but …'

He lets the kimono fall open to reveal a skinny white body and Y fronts.

'No,' says Charles. 'Thank you, but no.'

He turns to leave when David speaks again.

'I don't know, but maybe this'll help. Evans was well-known at the Rack, a regular. I was one of the few who refused him – more than once. I never trusted him, see? He gave me the creeps. I think that's why he did this to me.'

'And?'

'There were rumours about him. I don't know the details but he was caught with his pants down.'

'With one of you?'

'Yes, but there was someone else involved too. A bigwig. He got into real hot water – almost lost his job and was going to be prosecuted. We didn't see him for months. But then he suddenly reappears, as if it never happened. It was all hushed up. But everyone at the Rack knows about it, even some of the coppers – the decent ones.'

'You mean there are decent ones?' says Charles sceptically.

'A few. The ones who give us the price of a bag of chips every now and then.'

'Well I've yet to meet any – certainly on Vice. Anyway, thank you. That may be helpful.'

He turns to go again and reaches for the door handle.

'Give my best to Merlin, would you?' calls David after him. 'Tell him I'm sorry.'

Charles closes the door and returns to the street. He looks at his watch and sets off at a jog back to Charing Cross.

chapter 18

Thick fog rolls in from the Thames like a cold, damp quilt, deadening the sounds of the remaining traffic from the city to the north and covering everything in a fine layer of water droplets. The wrought iron gas lamps on the Embankment produce faint yellow globes of light surrounded by hazy halos. There are very few people around now at almost four in the morning, but every few minutes someone returning from a late shift or a desperate soul with insomnia emerges suddenly from the roiling clouds, the sound of their approaching footsteps having been undetectable until the last couple of yards.

A man waits at Embankment Pier. Water laps only a few inches below his feet and he leans out slightly over the river, straining hard to listen. He wears trousers, a leather jerkin, a short-sleeved shirt and a cloth lighterman's cap. He shivers slightly; his lightweight clothing is not appropriate for this weather, but there's a reason for that. By his feet, which wear light canvas shoes with rubber soles, is a rucksack. The fag end of a rollup, cold, damp and long-since extinguished, hangs from the corner of his mouth. He hears footsteps above him on the pavement and he crouches down. The chance of his being seen in the dark and this impenetrable fog is slim, but he is taking no chances. He waits for the footsteps to fade into the night before standing up again.

The muffled sounds of ships' horns reach him every now and then along the invisible waterway, the mournful wails of lost marine souls. For a moment the man imagines he hears the chug-chug of an engine some distance away upstream, but before he can be sure the noise disappears. Half a minute later a tugboat emerges silently out of the fog from the west. It shows no lights and its appearance out of the white clouds is so sudden that it resembles a ghost ship. It coasts towards the man's position and, out of the air, snakes a rope which falls almost on the waiting man's shoulder. He captures it neatly and pulls. The tug bumps gently against the tyres hanging from the pier edge and comes to a halt. The dark shape of a broad man looms over the gunwale, hand extended.

'Wotcha, Jonjo,' he whispers hoarsely. 'Sorry to keep you waiting.'

Charles slings his rucksack over one shoulder and takes the offered arm, gripping it wrist to wrist, and is hauled aboard.

'You still look the part,' says the skipper as he returns to the wheelhouse. 'Bet it's a few years since you wore that lot, eh?'

Charles picks up a boathook from the deck and shoves them off back into the stream.

'You're right there,' he says, climbing the steps into the wheelhouse. 'I only kept the clothes for old time's sake. I'm very grateful, Jack. I owe you one.'

'No you don't, mate. Where to?'

'Harpy Waterguard Station.'

Charles sees Jack looking sharply across at him in surprise. 'Whatever you say, boychick.'

'There shouldn't be anyone there, but can you cut the engines anyway and coast in? Just run straight past and I'll jump. I might be twenty minutes, half an hour. Then, if you can spare the time, circle round and pick me up. I've got a torch and I'll flash when I'm ready.'

'Easily done.'

Using the tide, Jack steers them into the centre of the current and then starts the engine. Charles briefly enjoys the sensation of being on the River again at night. Despite the cold and the damp that soaked into his clothes while waiting, he feels more alive than he has for ages, years perhaps. *I should've stayed doing this*, he thinks to himself. *I'd have been happier, working with honest to goodness East Enders – even the bent ones – when I knew who I was.*

The tug goes under Blackfriars Bridge and, bringing himself back to the present, Charles opens the rucksack and roots around inside until he finds what he's looking for. He pulls out a handful of sheets torn from his blue counsel's notebook.

'Can we get a bit of light in here?' he asks.

In response Jack switches on a lamp over the instrument panel and bends the flexible arm down towards Charles.

'Thanks,' says Charles.

The illumination allows Jack to see Charles's face for the first time. 'Still boxing, I see.'

Charles looks up from the sketches and frowns. 'Oh, the face. Yes, every now and then.'

'You might want to get yourself a new sparring partner,' says Jack dryly, eyes fixed forward into the fog.

Charles pores over the sketches he made at Brixton Prison. Having passed the Waterguard Station on literally hundreds of occasions while working up and down the Thames, Merlin had been reasonably sure of the layout of the lower deck. He could look into the windows to the main office and the locker rooms and, as he floated past, was often able to see the Waterguard officers in their crowded recreation room between shifts, playing cards, making drinks and getting changed. However, it's the upper deck which most interests Charles, and of that Merlin knew far less. The windows were much higher than Merlin's usual position, low in the water, and on the night he was taken there by Vermeulen he was too distressed to notice much about his surroundings. Nonetheless, Merlin's guess is that the upper deck houses both the CPO's office and the secure room for seized goods where he was interviewed.

'Coming up on London Bridge,' announces Jack.

Charles peers ahead into the foggy darkness. Custom House Quay is only a couple of hundred yards downstream of the Bridge, and it is there where the two-storey Waterguard Station is moored, its lower deck connected to the Quay by a railed bridge which slopes up or down depending on the state of the tide. Charles doesn't know what security may exist at the Customs House end of the bridge, so he plans to jump on the lower deck as the tug coasts past.

Jack cuts the engines and allows the tug to drift with the tide. Charles steps out of the wheelhouse into the moist night air and peers ahead into the dark. He can see nothing in the swirling fog. There appear to be no lights ahead – which is good if, as Charles hopes, the station is unattended. On the other hand, it's impossible to see the station as they approach; there's a real risk the tug will drift straight past it.

A gust of wind parts the fog slightly, and Jack points. 'Coming up on the port side! Get ready!'

Charles turns back to the wheelhouse, grabs the rucksack and slips it over both shoulders, tightening the chest strap as far as it will go. At the same instant as he looks up again he sees the lower deck landing and before he can move the tug is already halfway along its length. They are also at least four yards away from it – far too far for a standing jump.

'Hang on!' shouts Jack, and he spins the wheel to port. The tug heels over but turns swiftly enough to narrow the gap just as it goes past the final corner of the deck. Charles leaps into the swirling dark, reaching blindly with his hands in the hope there will be something to grab as he lands. The first thing he encounters is the rope strung between the metal posts at waist height all around the deck, but it's wet and although his hands strike it, he isn't quick enough to hold on to it. As his hands slap on the edge of the decking his lower body hits cold water. The tide is stronger than he imagined, and almost instantly he feels it pulling him away from the station. Using all his strength, he hangs on to the decking and hauls himself partially out, wriggling to get more of his body weight onto the timber. Satisfied that he is no longer at risk of being dragged off, he casts a glance over his right shoulder for a sign of the tug. It has disappeared completely and silently into the fog, taking with it Charles's sketches of the station.

Charles pulls himself completely out of the water, under the barrier rope, and onto the decking. If the Harpy is indeed occupied, and according to Merlin's information the boarding crew should at this stage of the tide – only an hour after high tide – be out on river patrol, no one appears to have noted his arrival. In any case flotsam and jetsam frequently wash against vessels moored on the Thames, clunking against their hulls and floating off again, and he doesn't think he made more noise than that would have done. Nonetheless, he remains cautious. He crouches down, sidles up to the nearest window and slowly lifts his head to look inside. The building appears to be in complete darkness. As far as he can see, the room into which he is peering is an office. He ducks down again and crawls to the next window: a changing room, with lockers along one side; and then the last two windows: a recreation room, over-stuffed with what appears to be government-issue furniture. Some of it is old enough to have been pre-War, and Charles recognises the style from his days in the RAF.

Charles steps back to the edge of the decking and cranes his neck to see the windows above him, but the walkway around the upper deck completely obscures his view. As far as he can tell no lights are illuminated. He slips off the rucksack and unties its mouth, feeling around until he encounters a pair of lightweight leather gloves. He looks up at the upper deck and changes his mind. He puts the gloves in his pocket, closes the rucksack and puts it back on his shoulders. He doubts that he would leave fingerprints on the wet decking above him in any case, but more importantly he reckons the gloves will dangerously reduce the grip he can exert when he jumps. He takes a breath, bends his knees, and with all of his considerable quadriceps strength, launches himself upwards to grab the edge of the upper deck. His hands get a good grip despite the moist conditions but at the very same moment the Harpy is struck by the wash of another vessel and rolls landward. The articulation between the lower deck and the bridge creaks loudly, and for a frightening two seconds Charles finds himself hanging in white mist over cold, black water. He waits until the station rolls back the other way and pulls himself up, grabbing the first rung of the metal railings on the upper deck. He is reliant entirely on upper body strength as his feet still dangle in mid-air, and it's harder than he imagines because of the wet clothing and the rucksack, but he is soon safely on the upper deck.

This storey of the floating building also seems deserted. Charles slips off the rucksack again and reaches in for the jemmy. This time he does don the gloves. Forcing the window, which has rudimentary locks, is the work of five seconds and within ten he's inside a small office. He tiptoes to the door, puts his ear against it and, hearing nothing, is about to open the door when he notes the uniform hanging on a hook on the inside. It has three braid rings round the cuffs: the uniform of a Chief Preventive Officer.

Charles quickly rifles through the pockets and finds a dry-cleaning bill in Vermeulen's name. Satisfied, he returns to the rucksack and takes out a small torch which he holds between his teeth.

The next ten minutes are unproductive. He opens the top two drawers of Vermeulen's desk: various shift rotas and documents passing between HM Waterguard and Customs House, blank paper, envelopes, an HM Waterguard rubber stamp and ink pad – the usual paraphernalia of an administrator. Charles moves down to the bottom drawer. This one is locked, and Charles's heart flutters in anticipation, but once it is open it reveals only a sectioned wooden tray holding a couple of fountain pens, rulers, pencils, paper clips and a bottle of ink. Why lock this away? Charles wonders. It's not impossible that colleagues keep "borrowing" pens, ink and so on; it happens in Chambers all the time, and Charles has more than once been tempted to lock his desk. On the point of giving up, Charles lifts the wooden tray. Underneath he finds a notebook. Putting the tray carefully back on the desk, he opens the book. At first glance it appears merely to contain a repetition of some of the shift patterns on the sheets in the top drawer, but then Charles notices asterisks against certain shifts. His finger travels down several pages in succession and notes that the shifts with the asterisks always contain Vermeulen himself, APO Evans and two other officers whose names keep reappearing, Butler and Kincaid. Only the first few pages of the notebook have writing on them, and Charles flicks to the back. Inside the back cover is a loose sheet of paper.

Against the initials "V", "E", "B" and "K" are careful pencil-written entries. Charles brings the torch close to the sheet. "*600 cigs*", "*2 btls brandy*", "*1 cask sherry*" ... Paydirt! Charles celebrates silently. This is the document he hoped, prayed, would be somewhere in this office: the evidence of the smuggling operation run by Vermeulen and his select group of bent Waterguard officers. For the first time since he spun round in court to see Merlin, the optimism he has unfailingly presented to his cousin has some actual substance, and Charles can permit himself a small, satisfied smile. Now they have some ammunition; something with which to fight.

Charles slips the notebook and the piece of paper into the rucksack, repacks the jemmy and torch, and pulls tight the drawstring. Then he pauses. He opens the second desk drawer, one of the two which had been unlocked, and pulls out a sheet of blank paper headed "HM Waterguard". After a moment's hurried consideration, he writes his home telephone number at the bottom of the sheet, tears off the strip, and puts it in the desk where he found the notebook. Then to make absolutely sure it will be discovered, he leaves the third drawer open half an inch. It's an enormous risk, he knows, but he has no better plan for making sure Vermeulen contacts him. He can't even be sure that Vermeulen will be on duty again over the weekend before Merlin's trial starts. What if he doesn't even come to the Harpy before going to court? Charles remembers the dry-cleaning bill in the uniform pocket, and moves hastily back to the office door. He rifles through the pockets and fishes out the bill: no address. He grimaces in the dark to himself; he has done all he can. Time to get out. Charles surveys the room swiftly to make sure he has missed nothing, and climbs back out of the window, closing it behind him. The lock is broken, but insofar as Charles can tell in the dark, no obvious damage has been caused to the window to alert immediate suspicion from outside. The puddle of water left by his dripping clothes at the desk side is another matter.

Fifteen minutes later, as the horizon behind them gradually lightens, Charles is back in the wheelhouse of Jack's tug, a towel over his shoulders and his freezing hands wrapped around a large mug of hot chocolate, as they make their way against the tide back to Embankment Pier.

chapter 19

It's daylight by the time Charles waves goodbye to Jack, and watches the tug slip back into the stream and head for Tilbury. Charles turns and climbs up the slippery steps from the pier to the Embankment, and heads back towards Fleet Street. It takes less than ten minutes to reach the flat on Fetter Lane.

As Charles pushes open the door to the apartment he hears a sliding noise, the sound of something trapped under the door, and he looks down. A note has been slipped under the front door. He bends to pick it up, pushing the door closed behind him.

"I thought you might be lonely, so I popped round. I was surprised to find you out at midnight on Saturday night, but then perhaps I shouldn't have been. Don't call me again. I need time to think. S."

'Shit,' curses Charles quietly to himself. Sally. She must have arrived just after he left. One didn't "pop round" from Romford; she would've had to make arrangements for her mother's care and then either got a night bus or, at considerable cost, a cab. She'd gone to a lot of trouble. Could she really think he was out on the razzle over *this* weekend? Or was it just her anxiety talking?

Charles reaches for the telephone and then remembers the injunction against calling. In any case, he thinks, looking at this watch, Sally will almost certainly still be asleep at this hour on a Sunday morning. The thought occurs to Charles that he should simply turn up at Romford – armed with a bag of fresh croissants perhaps – and explain everything. But he knows he can't. He's spent the night breaking the law and intends to black-mail a government officer into withdrawing evidence in a murder prosecution. He had no hesitation in doing it; his life and that of Merlin depend on it and, in any case, he believes completely that Merlin was only defending Chicken. But he also acknowledges that he had loved every second of his night's work. His heart would often thunder as the foreman of the jury rose to deliver his verdict, but that was nothing compared to the prolonged adrenaline rush he'd experienced over the last few hours. Charles recognises that he still loves the danger, the sense of being completely alive, that he had in the ring or, as a youth, running from the police. And he is miles away from being able to admit that to Sally – or to anyone, for that matter. He portrays himself – God, he even sees himself! – as "The Honest Brief", an upright member of an honourable profession, for whom integrity is the one essential stock in trade. In his own imagination he is one man swimming against a tide of corruption, criminality and prejudice. So how can he admit to Sally, who looks up to him so much, that it's all an act? That he is just as prepared to bend or break the rules as everyone else? And, in any case, Charles justifies to himself more prosaically, I've got to stay here in case Vermeulen calls.

'Why won't you trust her, Charles?' asks Henrietta's voice behind him. 'Has it occurred to you that she might love you anyway?'

'Not now, Etta,' replies Charles out loud, his exhaustion and painful face making him irritable. 'I've a lot on my plate, if you hadn't noticed.'

He strips off, leaving his clothes on the floor where they land. He spends the next ten minutes taking a long, hot shower to get the chill from his bones, gulps down the last inch of whisky straight from the bottle, and collapses onto the bed.

•

Charles wakes. He is cold and disorientated. He's face down on his bed, lying naked on a damp towel, and the curtains are open with light streaming across the bed. Then he remembers the night's activities and realises he must have simply collapsed asleep on the bed without even getting into pyjamas. A little man in his head suddenly starts work with a jackhammer. Charles groans; that slug of whisky on an empty stomach had been a bad idea. Only then does the ringing of the telephone from the lounge percolate through his muddled brain. Charles rolls off the bed and runs towards the telephone. It stops ringing as his hand reaches out to it. The tiny miner in his skull redoubles his efforts.

'Fuck!' cries Charles. 'Fuck, fuck, fuck!' but then,

instantly, the phone rings again. He lifts the receiver before the second ring.

There's a prolonged pause before either correspondent speaks.

'Who's that?' asks a male voice.

'Lost property,' replies Charles, in his most officious minor functionary cockney accent, and wondering if the response might be too elliptical to be understood.

'What?'

'I think we have something of yours. A notebook.'

'Who is this?' demands the voice. Charles can hear both suspicion and suppressed fury.

'You'll find out soon enough, Mr Vermeulen. It is Mr Vermeulen, isn't it?' Eloquent silence from the other end. 'There's enough in that notebook to send you and your chums to prison for years.' More silence. 'You know I'm right, don't you?'

'What do you want?'

'Nothing much. You'll be giving evidence against Isaac Conway at the Old Bailey sometime this week. You're going to change that evidence.'

'Ah, I get it. Does that Yiddisher little poofter think he can get round it this way? He's wasting his time.'

'I ain't no 'Yiddisher little poofter'. You've no idea the people you're dealing with. But in the end, it makes no odds who's got your notebook as long as they know how to hurt you with it. And we do, chum, we do. There's the Met, Customs and Excise – oh, and the press. Some of your colleagues might close ranks, try to protect you, but not all of them. And the press'll have a field day.'

The quality of the silence at the other end changes. Charles can almost hear the Waterguard thinking.

'I can't,' he finally responds. 'It'll be obvious. And then I'm facing perjury charges.'

'We've thought about that,' replies Charles evenly. 'All you need to do is change a particular time in your evidence. We'll do the rest.'

'How can changing a single time make all that difference?'

'Trust me,' says Charles. 'Sometimes it makes *all* the difference.'

'Why on earth should I trust you?'

'Because you don't want to go to prison. Because you don't want your picture splashed all over the newspapers. Because you don't want to lose your pension. And because if you do as you're told, you can go back to your little smuggling operation as if nothing has happened, and divide everything three ways as against four.'

'What is it you want me to change?'

'In your witness statement you say that you interviewed Mr Conway at 07:14 hours on the morning of 4 November. Change it so it says the interview occurred at 03:14 hours.'

'I can't. My original notes say 07:14 hours.'

'But where are your original notes? Not the typewritten version in the prosecution papers, but your original handwritten notes?'

'I've got them here.'

'Well then. Just rewrite them exactly as they are, but timed at 03:14 hours.'

Charles hears a deep breath being drawn at the end of the line and knows he is making progress.

'And how can I trust you to return the notebook?'

'You can't. You're going to have to take a punt on us. It's that or face the certainty of disgrace, dismissal and imprisonment.'

'I want time to think about it.'

'That's fine. You've got till tomorrow at ten thirty. But you'd better make up your mind before you step into the witness box. You'll be asked to produce the original handwritten notes, and if they're not timed at 03:14 your notebook will be shown to the judge and the prosecution. In open court, Court 4 of the Old Bailey. There won't be any way back. By lunchtime your career'll be over.'

When Vermeulen speaks again, there is no resistance or anger left in his voice; he sounds like a beaten man. 'I understand.'

'Make sure you do, sunshine,' replies Charles, breaking the connection.

chapter 20

It's Monday morning just before ten, and Charles waits for Merlin to join him in the interview room in the basement cells at the Old Bailey. He nurses a mug of tea, his elbows on the table. He stands as Merlin is shown into the room and the door shuts. The lighterman is wearing an ill-fitting dark suit which Charles had delivered to Brixton Prison from Juniper Street. Charles guesses, correctly, that Izzy has only ever worn it once before, at his father's funeral. The two men regard one another's injuries. Merlin looks like a panda; the bruising having come out under both eyes. His nose is swollen but looks more or less straight to Charles's untrained eye. The gash on his cheek and the split lip have both been stitched, and the black sutures are very obvious, reminding Charles of Frankenstein's monster.

'I don't know which of us looks worse,' says Charles lightly.

'I do. But don't make me smile, Charlie,' mumbles Merlin, try not to stretch his lip. 'It hurts too much.'

The two men sit down. 'Well?' asks Merlin.

'Well, the good news is that I got into the Harpy okay, thanks to Jack, and got a good look round Vermeulen's office. I found something – a notebook. It's not conclusive proof by any means, but it's enough to damage him.'

'And Chicken?'

Charles shakes his head. 'Sorry, Izzy. He won't do it. He's in a really bad state. He's lost most of his front teeth and he's still bleeding, you know, from his backside.'

Merlin drops his head and stares unseeing at the table between them, carved with graffiti and years of pain. Then he nods. 'I can't say I blame 'im. He's only a kid, and that bastard Evans fucked him over good and proper.' He looks up into Charles's face. 'Are we okay, Charlie?'

'What do you mean?'

'I mean, do you … do you think … well, less of me? Now you know … the sort of life I've been leading.'

Charles puts his great paw over Merlin's elegant hand on the table, and squeezes it gently. 'Of course I don't, you fucking idiot. It's how you were born, right? Part of who you are, and you can't change it. I get that. I don't think the law should interfere with what people do with their privates, as long as they're adults, it's consensual and they do no harm to anyone else.'

Merlin smiles wryly and winces as the stitch pulls. 'Not many people think that way.'

'Yes they do, Izzy. Look at the Wolfenden report. Times are changing.'

Merlin shakes his head in disagreement. 'Not where I come from. I could never have told anyone on the Thames; or at "The Prospect".' Charles is surprised to see tears glistening in his cousin's eyes. 'But I wish I'd told you ages ago.'

'Forget it. To be honest, I think I kind of knew when we were kids on the River. I just didn't think about it – having too much fun.' Charles gives Merlin a moment to regain his composure. 'Alright?' he asks.

Merlin sniffs. 'Yeah. I'm okay.' He straightens his shoulders, takes a deep breath and focuses on Charles. 'So, what's the plan?'

'Well, the first thing is, are you fit for trial today?'

'Why? Would you like more time?' replies Merlin. 'I could get a lot worse suddenly if you like, when I'm taken up.'

Charles shakes his head. 'I've been thinking about it. I think we're in as strong a position as we're ever going to be. Vermeulen's only had overnight to come up with a credible explanation. He's probably not even made contact with the two others in the team. Right now, we've managed to get a grip on a slippery snake; let's not give him time to wriggle free.'

'Good. I agree.'

'And you're okay about not giving evidence?'

'Completely.'

'I'm sure that's the right decision. I'm going to have to attack Vermeulen's credibility, suggest he deliberately fabricated the confession. Once I do that, as soon as you step into the witness box, the Crown will be allowed to put all your previous convictions before the jury which, let's face it, would be a disaster. But you do understand don't you, that if you don't give evidence, it becomes nigh on impossible for us to raise self-defence? You're putting all your eggs in one basket – discrediting Vermeulen.'

'I know. But even if I go into the witness box and tell the jury that... you know...the type of man I am, it's not going to be enough is it?'

Charles shakes his head sadly. 'No; not without Chicken, and maybe not even then. Chicken would have to be warned against self-incrimination. He could end up in prison. And once they know that you're both gay, the jury may not be sympathetic.'

'That's what I thought.'

There's a bang on the door, and it opens immediately. 'Time to take him up,' announces the gaoler. Charles stands and offers his hand to Merlin. Merlin takes it, and a silent look, laden with meaning, passes between the two men.

'I'll see you in court,' says Charles, fixing a smile in place which he hopes is reassuring.

Charles is checked out of the cell area and goes through the formal processes deep in thought. He climbs the stairs to the beautiful marbled hall on the ground floor. He's not a superstitious man but he makes sure, as he does before the start of all his cases, to look up at the mural depicting the building following the Blitz in December 1940. He knows that the ritual is unconnected to his forensic successes but, as he tells himself, now's not the time to take chances. His father, back in London for a fortnight to arrange storage of some of the surviving family furniture, had offered himself for duty that terrible night. Together with his fire warden colleagues he helped put out the fires and had carried the dead and wounded out of the rubble to waiting ambulances, as bombs and pieces of burning building fell all around them. Remembering the courage of his father, that quiet little East End tailor, always stiffens Charles's resolve.

Charles climbs the stairs to Court 4, pushes open the polished oak doors, and walks down the carpeted aisle between the benches to the well of the court where the barristers sit. Two robed barristers await him, one on the bench for juniors whom he does not recognise and, on the bench in front and slightly closer to the judge's high position, Collin Montgomery QC. Montgomery is busy scrawling incomprehensible notes in his counsel's notebook, all arrows and scribble and, as always, his wig is on askew and scraps of paper protrude from several jacket pockets.

Traditionally Queen's Counsel sit on the front bench with their juniors in the row behind, but in a case of this sort, where a junior barrister such as Charles is not being led by a QC, the opposition QC sometimes invites the junior to sit in the front bench, thereby doing him the courtesy of according him equal status. That is exactly what occurs in this case.

'Good morning, Charles,' says Montgomery, as Charles makes to slide into the bench behind him. 'Why don't you join me here? Much more room.'

Charles inclines his head in acknowledgement. 'Very kind.'

'Not at all, dear fellow.'

Montgomery then looks properly at Charles's face and

does a classic, almost cartoon, double-take. 'Good God! What on earth happened to you?'

'It's nothing. I've a new sparring partner and he's a little over-enthusiastic. It looks a lot worse than it is.'

'If you say so,' replies the QC, doubtfully. 'Now, about this: are you applying for an adjournment? I think it's a bit rough on you, having so little time to prepare for a capital case, and I shan't oppose any application too vigorously, despite my instructions.'

'Thanks, Collin, but I think we're ready.'

Montgomery raises an eyebrow in mild surprise. 'Very well. Do you know Simeon O'Connell?' and he gestures to his junior.

Charles turns and regards the junior barrister. He looks very young, certainly no older than twenty-five or twenty-six. He's either very bright or very lucky, thinks Charles; to be instructed for the Crown, even as a junior, on a murder trial at only two or three years' call is quite an achievement. 'No, I don't think so. Pleased to meet you,' says Charles.

He puts his papers on the bench and looks around the court. People are still filing in but the press benches are already full and the last few seats are being filled in the public gallery. There's an anticipatory buzz in the court, as there always is in cases of high public interest. Charles knows there will have been a queue going round the block for places in the public gallery, and he notices that there are now more barristers sitting on the benches behind him than normal. Usually when a trial is listed for a complete day or more the only barristers in the benches are those representing the parties, but in this case the benches behind Charles are half-full with barristers who have no business to attend to in that court. Charles can guess what's happened, imagining only too well the gossip that raced round the Temple at the end of the previous week: 'Did you hear? Holborne's picked up a dock brief ... in *a murder!* And guess who his judge is: Fletcher J!' So, with fireworks anticipated, barristers with nothing on that morning have decided to come and be entertained by Charles's discomfiture.

Charles's eye travels back to the public gallery, looking for someone in particular. He thinks it unlikely that the Krays will attend in person but he knows what to look for. Ronnie's scouts divide into two groups: the first are little more than scruffy street urchins, teenagers or younger, who pass on titbits of information picked up in the back alleys, markets and billiard halls of the East End. The second are usually pretty young men, very well-dressed, violent young men with whom Ronnie enjoys a much closer relationship. Charles expects that the man who attacked him in the telephone box is still being kept well out of the way, but he knows Ronnie's type. Sure enough, there, in the top row right at the end, looking down on the barristers and the still-empty dock, is a young man with blonde hair, long eyelashes and a full pouting mouth, wearing an expensive dark suit and gold rings on most of his fingers. Just Ronnie's type, thinks Charles. Charles stares at the man and, for a fleeting second, makes eye contact with him before the man suddenly finds interest in the newspaper he's carrying, and looks hastily at it. Gotcha, thinks Charles.

The clerk, a large woman in her middle years with a bosom that projects almost a foot forward of her shoulders, descends the steps from her seat beneath the Judge's position and walks across the well of the court to the barristers.

'Are you ready, gentlemen?' she asks.

Montgomery looks across at Charles, who nods his assent. 'Yes, thank you.'

'Are we proceeding direct to arraignment and trial?' she asks, directing her question more at Charles than at Montgomery.

'Yes.'

'Excellent. I'll inform the Judge and then bring him in.'

The clerk returns to the Judge's bench and, wheezing slightly, climbs the stairs leading to his chair. A door opens in the panelling behind the Judge's bench, and she disappears. Two minutes later there is a loud double knock on the panelled door and the clerk reappears.

'All rise!' she calls.

Everyone in court stands and the shuffling and whispered conversations cease. Mr Justice Fletcher enters in his black and red robes and stands in front of his seat. He bows to the Bar, and all the barristers – now numbering at least fifteen – bow in return like well-trained penguins. The Judge takes his seat, placing his red book on the bench before him, and all the other occupants of the courtroom sit.

'You are in the wrong bench Mr Holborne,' says Fletcher.

Without a word Charles collects his papers, turns, places them on the bench behind him, and walks round to join them. Attention on Charles's belittling is suddenly switched to the dock, as a clanking of metal doors and keys heralds the arrival of the prisoner. Merlin appears up the steep stone steps flanked by guards.

'You may put the indictment,' the Judge orders the clerk.

The clerk stands. 'Are you Isaac Conway?'

'Yes.'

'You are charged with a single count on this indictment, namely, that on or about 4 November 1963 you did murder John Huw Evans contrary to common law. How do you plead?'

'Not guilty,' responds Merlin in a firm voice.

The clerk turns to the Judge. 'May the prisoner sit, my Lord?'

'Yes. Mr Holborne.'

Charles rises. 'Yes my Lord?'

'I was going to ask you if your client is in a fit state to proceed, having regard to his obvious injuries, but I see that I should be asking the same question of you.'

'We are both fit to proceed, thank you, my Lord.'

Charles can see the Judge hesitating, wondering whether to delve further into the odd coincidence of both prisoner and his assigned counsel suffering from facial injuries acquired over the weekend. In the end, he decides to let the matter drop. He turns to Montgomery.

'Is the Crown ready?'

Montgomery stands. 'Yes, my Lord.'

'Then bring in the jury in waiting.'

Sixteen potential members of the jury file in through a different door and sit in the places reserved for them. Most of them look nervous, some looking around in surprise at the packed courtroom. Charles has a maximum of seven challenges without cause – in other words he can challenge off the jury up to seven people, even if his only reason is he doesn't like the look of their faces, their hairstyles or the newspapers they carry. In cases involving alleged sexual transgressions, Charles had been known to challenge off vicars, very young women and anyone carrying *The Telegraph* – the last as a matter of principle. The risk is always that the remaining jurors wonder what you're hiding or why the jury make-up is being manipulated, and so Charles has learned that the trick is to do it only when he has a strong adverse intuition about a potential juror. He has also learned that the complexion of a jury is less critical when you know in advance that your client is not going to give evidence. Jurors are less likely to be prejudiced for or against an accused by reason of his marital status, accent, education or sexuality when they have no opportunity to dissect his evidence from the witness box.

Charles scans each of the potential jurors in turn, looking for anything which suggests that any of them may be ill-disposed to Merlin or, at least, ill-disposed beyond the fact that he's charged with murder. He also looks to see if any of them might have particular difficulty accepting that a Crown witness could be dishonest. On this occasion however he can see nothing obviously "wrong" with any of the jurors and nor apparently can Montgomery, as the first twelve called are those who are sworn, and the court is left with a jury of eight men and four women.

'Mr Montgomery, you may proceed with your opening,' says Fletcher.

Montgomery rises, turns to the jury with a smile, and introduces Charles. As he tells the jury the charge faced by Merlin, they all look sharply across at the dock and study the accused murderer dispassionately. Merlin, looking uncomfortable in the suit, studies his hands. Montgomery then reminds the jury that the burden of proof lies at all times on the Crown and that before they can convict they have to be sure beyond reasonable doubt that the accused killed APO Evans, intending to kill him or to do him serious harm. Then he summarises the evidence the jury are going to hear so they can understand it in context, reminding them that his words are not, in themselves, evidence. Finally, he reminds them that whatever impression they might have of the opinions of the barristers or indeed the Judge, the factual decisions are for them alone, after receiving guidance on the law from the Judge.

His opening speech lasts just over forty minutes and is a model of scrupulous, careful, fairness. Montgomery is one of the new breed of Crown prosecutors, a prosecution advocate who takes seriously his obligation not to strive officiously for a conviction but to lay the evidence fairly before the jury. It is largely because of that scrupulous approach that juries trust him so completely and he is so successful.

He secures Fletcher's permission to call the first witness,

Vermeulen. When called, a tall fleshy man of about fifty years, with fair hair, a short bristling moustache and a pale complexion walks down the aisle from the back of the court and steps into the witness box. He carries his hat tucked under his arm and he is in full uniform – blue serge and a lot of gold braid round the cuffs. To someone unfamiliar with the differences in the insignia and braid, he would be taken for a ship's captain.

Charles studies the Waterguard carefully as he takes the oath. Vermeulen places his hat carefully on the bench beside him, takes the New Testament handed to him by the court usher, and brandishes it at head height. He disdains the offer of a card on which the oath is printed, and recites it in a loud voice from memory. His demeanour proclaims that not only does he know the oath perfectly, but it is engraved on his heart. Charles watches the direction of the man's gaze, but he appears to be unconscious of Merlin sitting in the raised dock across the court, the barristers below him in the well of the court or the banks of newspapermen and members of the public. He hands the Bible back to the usher and stands with his hands clasped at his waist, half-turned towards the Judge, awaiting the first question.

Montgomery takes him methodically through his evidence, his questions producing, almost to the word, answers which follow the text of Vermeulen's deposition. Charles notes that the time given by Vermeulen for Merlin's interview remains at 07:14 hours. So, the gloves are off.

Montgomery tells Vermeulen to remain in the witness box, and sits. The Judge has not uttered a word since

Vermeulen entered the witness box. Charles moves his blue counsel's notebook to one side, picks up the Waterguard's notebook, and stands. If Vermeulen notices his notebook or recognises it for what it is, he makes no sign of it. You *are* a cool customer, thinks Charles. This might get nasty.

'With my Lord's leave?'

'You may proceed, Mr Holborne,' replies the Judge.

'It is your evidence, CPO Vermeulen, that APO Evans had been keeping Mr Conway under surveillance for some time. Is that right?'

'Yes, my Lord, that is correct,' replies Vermeulen benignly, answering in the manner of an experienced witness, by addressing the Judge and not the barrister asking the questions.

'How long had this operation been running?'

'Some months I would guess.'

'You would *guess*?' asks Charles. 'Are you not the Waterguard officer in charge of Harpy Station?'

'I am, my Lord, which is why I wouldn't be able to remember the precise details of every operation we are undertaking.'

'Yes, Mr Holborne,' intervenes the Judge. 'You can't expect this witness to remember the details of every operation undertaken by his subordinates. How many people work at the Harpy Waterguard Station, Mr Vermeulen?'

'Between thirty and forty over the course of a week. We have a five-week shift roster, with three shifts spanning eight in the morning to eleven at night. In addition to the three crews covering London Port and the Upper Coast each evening, there are rummage crews and others.'

'You see Mr Holborne? Please don't waste this witness's valuable time by asking pointless questions.'

'I shall try not to, my Lord. So, to be fair to you Mr Vermeulen, you wouldn't be able to tell us precisely how long Mr Conway had been under surveillance without looking at the records?'

'Exactly so.'

'What records would those be?' asks Charles, ingenuously.

Between the two of them, Vermeulen and the Judge had allowed the Waterguard to walk directly into Charles's first trap. Charles knows that any formal operations would have to have been logged – if for no other reason than ensuring that the Austin Mini, the only vehicle at the disposal of Harpy Station, could be used by the officers needing it most. Yet the prosecution evidence did not list a single document dealing with the supposed investigation that took APO Evans out that night.

For the first time Vermeulen doesn't respond with an immediate answer. 'Records?'

'Yes. You have just explained that you could only inform us when surveillance began on Mr Conway by looking at the records. So I asked: what records?'

'Well, my Lord, firstly there would be APO Evans's shift records. Then there would be his personal logs. And if he was using the Station's vehicle, the car would have been booked out against his name.'

'Where are those records?' asks Charles, mildly.

'Erm, well … they would be back at the Harpy.'

'Have you looked at APO Evans's personal logs, Mr Vermeulen, to confirm that he was indeed engaged in watching Mr Conway on the night of his death?'

This time Vermeulen's pause is even longer. He had not thought to check the filing cabinet in his office to see if Evans logged his proposed visit to Conway's barge. The awful possibility occurs to him that whoever stole his notebook may have taken the logs as well. If he says he checked the log, Defence counsel is certain to follow up and ask what it contained, and then someone may suddenly produce the log, like a rabbit out of a hat, to prove him a liar. On the other hand, if he says he has not checked the log he may fail to prove that Evans was indeed out watching Conway that night.

Before Vermeulen has finished weighing the advantages and disadvantages of either answer, Fletcher steps in again to help him.

'Mr Holborne, I don't see the relevance of this line of enquiry. Whether the unfortunate Mr Evans logged his surveillance at your client's barge or not that night, we know he was found very close to it, and your client has admitted to killing him. What can it possibly matter what the records show?'

'My Lord, APO Evans's job was to investigate all the tugs, barges and lighters on the Thames for smugglers. His duties could have taken him to numerous other vessels moored all along that stretch of the Thames, from any one of which he might have fallen.'

'Are you suggesting that this unfortunate man's death was an accident?'

'It's not for me to suggest anything my Lord. It's the Crown's job to prove that it was *not* an accident, that he was killed, and by my client. But even if the Crown proves it wasn't an accident and *somebody* did kill Mr Evans, the jury has to consider the nature of APO Evans's dangerous work. His job involved him specifically *looking* for criminals at work on the River and in the course of his shift he could have stumbled across any number of unlawful enterprises, the participants in which might have had a motive for violence. It is for that reason –' and Charles looks across at this point at the jury – 'that in my submission it is entirely relevant for the jury to know on what investigations APO Evans was engaged that night.'

Several members of the jury return Charles's glance and one or two nod slightly. They have already been told that Merlin made a confession, but they are still awake enough to want to know what else Evans might have been doing that night. Who else might he have seen? Good, thinks Charles.

Charles's answer and the response of several of the jury members is enough to stymie the Judge for a second and Charles leaps into the silence to repeat his last question.

'Have you looked at APO Evans's work logs?' he asks of Vermeulen.

Now that Vermeulen has had a few moments to think courtesy of the time bought him by the Judge's intervention, he has made up his mind which way he wants to jump. 'No, my Lord, I did not. But I knew from conversations with APO Evans that that is what he was proposing to do.'

'I object to that answer,' says Charles. 'It's hearsay, as this witness well knows. And in any case, what Mr Evans *proposed* to do before the event is not evidence of what he actually did.'

'Of course it's hearsay,' says Fletcher with an evil grin, 'but you did persist in asking the question, despite the fact that I hadn't ruled on it. You only have yourself to blame, Mr Holborne.' He turns to the jury. 'Ladies and gentlemen, witnesses can only tell us what they perceived with their own senses. What someone else told them is hearsay and is not admissible. CPO Vermeulen's last answer falls into that category.'

But the damage is done and both Charles and the Judge know it; whether the comment was hearsay or not, the jury heard it.

'Shall we continue, Mr Holborne?' asks the Judge.

Charles swiftly weighs whether to leave the issue alone or to try and recover the situation. He launches in. 'You didn't see Mr Evans before he started work did you? His shift started at four in the afternoon and you didn't come in until eleven at night.'

'That's correct, my Lord.'

'So if Mr Evans discussed with you what his proposed movements were on the night of third and fourth November, that must have been some time earlier in the week?'

'Yes.'

'Your workload changes hour to hour, doesn't it, as new ships enter the Thames and you have to check them out for smuggling.'

'Yes, that's true.'

'You have jurisdiction over hundreds of ships travelling up and down the Thames every day.'

'Yes, my Lord.'

'So your daily duties have to be very flexible. Whatever the plans, you may have to shelve them to accommodate searches of new ships arriving.'

'Yes. But that doesn't prevent us from carrying out ongoing surveillance operations, my Lord.'

'The area where Mr Conway's barge was moored is a busy part of the River is it not?'

'No more or less than any other part. It's all busy.'

'Did you count the number of barges moored there?'

'No, my Lord I did not.'

'Over the weekend, I counted fifty-five moored along that bend in the river, to the west of the golf course. Do you suggest that would be an unusual or unrepresentative number?'

'No, my Lord, that would be about right. There are quite a lot of barges moored overnight in that area.'

'Any one of which might have attracted APO Evans's attention?'

'It's possible I suppose.'

Charles looks down at his notes, as satisfied as he can be in the circumstances. The last passage of cross-examination had not achieved much in concrete terms but Charles hoped that it had at least watered down the link between Evans and Merlin's barge; the dead Waterguard would most likely have been involved with dozens of vessels during his shift, and there were plenty of others in the immediate vicinity that might have been of interest to him. Charles changes the subject.

'Now, Mr Vermeulen: you told us that you didn't check APO Evans's personal log for that day. May I take it that you didn't check the log relating to the Station vehicle?'

'That is correct, my Lord,' replies Vermeulen, having now regained his composure.

'So you don't actually know the time at which APO Evans left the Harpy?'

'N … no. That's right.'

'And you didn't come on duty until 23:00 hours.'

'That's correct.'

'So Mr Evans might have left the Harpy at any time during his shift which began at 16:00 hours. His body wasn't discovered until sometime after five in the morning on the following day, over thirteen hours later.'

'That's also correct, my Lord. He is an experienced officer, and would be expected to come and go as he thought necessary.'

'But not normally alone?'

'Sorry?'

'I said, "*Not normally alone*". Waterguard officers usually work in crews of three. Members of the river patrols and the specialist rummage crews never go out on their own. It's too dangerous, for a start.'

Vermeulen looks slightly ruffled again. 'Yes, my Lord that is right.'

'Yet APO Evans was out on his own, potentially for more than thirteen hours, a period during which he would have had time to investigate scores of vessels and potential smugglers,' asserts Charles.

'Yes.'

'And you are not able to tell us what he was doing during that time, are you?'

'I'm sure he was going about his proper duties, my Lord.'

'Of course Mr Vermeulen, you would say that. You're his superior officer. But it's only an assumption, isn't it? You don't know the time he left the Harpy; what vessels he investigated during the following thirteen hours; to whom he spoke, or – and this is perhaps the most important – why he went alone; do you?'

'That may all be true, but I don't agree with your conclusion. My Lord, I knew APO Evans very well and he was a conscientious and sensible officer. I am confident he was carrying out his proper duties.'

'"*Conscientious and sensible*"? It is true, is it not, that APO Evans was suspended last year over allegations of homosexual assault?'

So surprising is Charles's change of direction and so shocking the allegation that there is an audible sharp intake of breath from the public gallery and the jury benches. Before Vermeulen can gather his wits, Charles ostentatiously takes out a sheet of paper from his bundle and holds it up in front of him as if reading.

'He was accused of sexual molestation of a rent boy working at Piccadilly Circus, together with another man over the age of twenty-one, was he not?'

This is a dangerous game and under normal circumstances Charles would never have played it. The sheet of paper from which he is pretending to read is not documentary proof of the allegations made against Evans; in fact, it is one of the pages of the pathologist's report which Charles picked up at random. But Vermeulen doesn't know that. What Charles is doing is not unlawful; is not even professionally improper. Counsel is allowed to put anything to a witness in cross-examination, and even put a piece of paper in a witness's hand for his comment, without the piece of paper going into evidence. But he knows he's taking an enormous gamble, playing what poker players call "a snow" – a bluff based on a worthless hand. Charles is risking everything on the assumption that Vermeulen hasn't checked – or can't remember – whether any documents relating to Evans's suspension were in his office, and so might have been stolen at the same time as his notebook. A thin film of perspiration now stands out on Vermeulen's pale face, which is now slightly pink about the cheeks.

'An allegation of that sort was made against APO Evans, my Lord,' he answers, slightly flustered, 'and he was suspended for a period. No charges were brought, and APO Evans resumed his duties.'

'APO Evans was in his thirties I understand?' asks Charles, apparently changing the subject.

'That is right, my Lord.'

'And he was not married?'

'Not to the best of my knowledge.'

'I suggest that the allegation you referred to a moment ago, about a homosexual assault by APO Evans, was not the first such allegation ever made against him during his career.'

Montgomery rose. 'My Lord I object to this line of enquiry. It is improper for Mr Holborne to attack the credibility of a deceased person who, far from being a witness in this case, is the victim. The prior criminal or sexual history of a victim of murder is of no relevance to the question whether he was murdered and, if so, by whom.'

'Mr Holborne?' asks Fletcher.

'But I don't put these questions to damage the *credibility* of Mr Evans. It is the Defence case that many of the barges moored overnight on the Thames are unlocked and unattended and they are frequently used for liaisons between homosexual men. The purpose of these questions is to establish whether Mr Evans might have had other reasons for being in that area, reasons completely unconnected to his duties in the Waterguard or Mr Conway.'

'Unproven allegations against this deceased officer as to his sexual proclivities will not get you even close to suggesting that he might have been engaged in such a liaison on this occasion. I will not permit the question,' orders Fletcher.

'So be it,' says Charles, but he's content enough. Although he didn't quite invent the suggestion that the barges were used for gay men to meet at night – he knew after all what Merlin and Chicken were doing – it's a long stretch from that to alleging a pattern of behaviour by homosexual men generally in which APO Evans took part. Charles is in no position to call any evidence about the use of the barges at night; it remains only an assertion from counsel's benches: worthless – at least in theory; in reality, he hopes that a seed has nonetheless been planted in the minds of the jurors.

'Is that a convenient moment for us to break, Mr Holborne?' asks the Judge.

Charles turns and looks at the clock on the wall. The time is just one o'clock.

'Yes, my Lord.'

'Members of the jury,' says the Judge. 'We will now adjourn for lunch until five past two. You have not heard much of the evidence yet, but I shall give you a warning now which will apply throughout the rest of this trial. You are not to speak to anyone about this case outside of your own number, and while in the jury room. The decision must be one for you twelve alone, and if you start talking to members of your family or friends about the evidence you've heard, they are likely to make some comment which could affect your mind or draw you into conversation. And that's what must be avoided. So the best thing is to say nothing until the trial is over. Do you understand? Thank you. Five past two, gentlemen. Take the prisoner down.'

'Court rise!'

Charles makes hand gestures towards Merlin as he is taken down, indicating that Charles will join him in the cells in five minutes' time. As the Judge disappears through the oak panelling and the members of the press stand and stretch, Charles looks up at the public gallery. The young man with all the gold rings has disappeared. No guesses as to where he's gone, thinks Charles to himself.

chapter 21

Charles grabs the wig off his head and runs up the staircase two stairs at a time towards the Bar Mess, barging like a prop forward through protesting slower-moving barristers heading to lunch.

The swing doors bang open as Charles charges into the Mess and walks swiftly to the window sill at the far side of the room. He parts the net curtains, lifts the dusty receiver off the old Bakelite pre-War telephone perched on the sill, and dials "0". After a moment, an operator picks up.

'Outside line, please,' demands Charles and after a few further seconds he hears the familiar purr of the dialling tone.

Charles dials the number for Chancery Court, a number he knows so well, frustrated at the inordinate speed it takes for the dial to return to its resting place after each rotation.

'Chancery Court,' says Sally, picking up the call.

'Sally! Thank God I caught you.'

'Yes, Charles, you did, but I'm just leaving for lunch.'

'Please, Sally give me just a moment! I'm so sorry I wasn't there Saturday night. I had to go out and do some digging on Izzy's case. I was out most of the night.'

'That's fine, Charles. You don't owe me any explanation.

But I really don't want to have this conversation now.' Her voice is calm but there is a chill in it which causes a hollow feeling in the pit of Charles's stomach.

'Just listen to me, please, Sally. You've no idea what I'm up against.' Charles looks round to see if he can be overheard, but all the other barristers are busy taking off their wigs and gowns, chattering about the state of their cases and moving quickly to order meals before the main rush starts. Nonetheless Charles lowers his voice. 'It's not just Izzy's life on the line. It's all connected with Ronnie Kray, and his List.'

'Oh, really? Good of you to warn me,' replies Sally with sarcasm thick enough to toast and cover in butter. 'I wondered when you'd get round to it.'

'I'm telling you now!' insists Charles with intensity.

'I've known for months, Charlie, like everyone in the East End. Didn't it occur to you that I might be worrying?'

'I'm sorry,' replies Charles defensively. 'I was trying to protect you.'

'No, you weren't,' says Sally, dropping her voice. 'You were doing what you always do – and what you did with poor Henrietta; you put it in a separate box and dealt with it on your own. It's *impossible* to get close to you, Charlie. You don't let anyone in. Anyway, I've told you I don't want this conversation now. In fact, I don't want this conversation at all.'

'What? Are we breaking up?'

'Breaking up what? In my book a series of shags doesn't count as a relationship,' she says, her voice dropping almost to a whisper and her new cultured diction slipping a bit. 'I've got to go. I hope the trial goes well.'

She hangs up, leaving Charles once again with the soft purr of the dialling tone.

Charles puts the heavy receiver back on its metal rests, and looks at his watch. He has forty-five minutes left to grab a bite to eat and get down to the cells to see Merlin, but he has suddenly lost his appetite. He collects his wig from the window sill, bashes it against his leg to get the dust off it, and heads for the cells.

By the time he is booked in, Merlin has abandoned his meal, a rather unsavoury-looking plate of sausages, soggy chips and peas, drowning in lumpy gravy.

'Well?' asks Merlin. 'How do you think it's going?'

'Not too bad. About as well as we can expect at this stage,' says Charles ruefully, allowing his customary optimism to slip slightly.

'You don't sound very happy,' comments Merlin.

Charles sighs. 'The deal I made with Vermeulen was that if he changed the time on the interview, I wouldn't mention his smuggling. But, I'm beginning to wonder if I'm going to have to break the deal and go in with both feet on his notebook.'

'You think he's going to backtrack, then?'

Charles shrugs. 'I don't know; maybe. But even if he doesn't, I'm not sure it'll be enough to discredit the interview.'

'What's the problem? Hit 'im with it, both barrels!' Charles stares at the lighterman, looking worried. 'You've got a funny sense of priorities, Charlie. You've done a deal with a bent Waterguard to hide from the rozzers the fact that he's been on the take for years. And the reason you've done it is to prevent me from being hanged for a crime I never committed, and you from being shivved simply for doing your best to represent the Krays' bent brief. And you're worried about keeping your word to this arsehole?'

Charles smiles. 'Well, put like that ...'

'Get your head round it Charlie: unless you get me off this, one or both of us is going to die. You said it yourself at Brixton: we're *both* on death row. So you use anything, *anything* you've got. And you've got that notebook.'

Charles nods slowly, letting Merlin's words sinking in. 'Yeah. Got it.'

•

'Mr Holborne?' says Fletcher, inviting Charles to resume his cross-examination.

'Thank you, my Lord. Mr Vermeulen, my questions so far have concerned APO Evans's movements that night, and what he might have been doing. I now want to turn to Mr Conway. You told us that he had been under surveillance as a result of "information received" that he may have been involved in smuggling spirits. Do you know from whom that information was received?'

'No, my Lord, I don't. I understood that it was from one of APO Evans's informants.'

'Do you agree with me, Mr Vermeulen, that informants

come in all shapes and sizes and levels of reliability?'

'They do indeed, my Lord.'

'Some are reliable and some are not?'

'I think I would put it differently, my Lord: all regular informants are reliable some of the time, or else we wouldn't continue using them. But even regular informants are wrong sometimes.'

'You don't know who this informant was at all?'

'No I don't.'

'So it might not have been a regular informant at all. It might have been someone else, someone new?'

'It might.'

'It might even have been an anonymous informant?'

'Yes, it might, my Lord.'

'Do you agree that informants are people who are themselves sometimes on the wrong side of the law?'

'Yes, my Lord, I do agree. We often have to rely on other villains "in the business" as it were, to inform on their colleagues.'

'And such "other villains" may have their own motives for informing on, for example, a competitor.'

'Yes, my Lord, that is the case.'

'Or they may simply want to be paid for information?'

'I think almost all informants want to be paid for their information. Not many will do it out of love of the authorities – especially the taxman,' jokes Vermeulen, prompting a sprinkling of laughter around the court. He looks confident, and Charles is happy for that to remain the case until he strikes.

'So, to summarise, an informant whose identity you don't know, who *may* himself have been a criminal with his own motives or *may* simply have wanted to make himself some money, *may* have pointed a finger at Mr Conway, saying he *may* have been involved in something illegal.' Charles emphasises each "may" because when it comes to his speech he wants to take the line that the prosecution is speculative, a bunch of "mays" with no substance.

Vermeulen shrugs. 'HM Waterguard have to deal with all sorts of lowlife, my Lord, and we have to get down in the dirt with them sometimes. It's inevitable.'

Mr Justice Fletcher nods sadly.

'But whatever the nature of the information,' continues Charles, 'HM Waterguard was never able to establish that Mr Conway had done anything wrong at all.'

'Well, investigations were continuing.'

'Your statement says that the information received was that the accused "may" have been involved in smuggling,' Charles reminds him.

'That is correct, my Lord.'

'But despite the Waterguard's investigations for "some months", you weren't able to put together sufficient evidence to make a case against the accused, or put the matter in the hands of the police?'

'That is also correct, my Lord.'

'Thank you Mr Vermeulen. I come to the last issue on which I would like to ask you some questions, that of the alleged confession you say Mr Conway made. Before dealing with the document itself, may I ask why you chose to interview the accused?'

'Well, my Lord, I was the senior officer there at the time, and I had discovered my colleague's body.'

'The Waterguard is part of her Majesty's Customs and Excise, isn't it?'

'Yes.'

'If I can put it this way, it is part of the country's tax collection machinery, but operating on the water.'

'We have investigatory functions as well, my Lord.'

'Certainly you do, Mr Vermeulen, but those investigatory functions relate to the payment or evasion of tax revenues. Your remit does not include murder, does it?'

'Not directly, no.'

'Do you have any experience investigating murders?'

'No, my Lord, I do not. These were unusual circumstances.'

'You don't have any training in investigating crimes like murder, either, do you?'

'Not directly no, but –'

'The appropriate step is to call in the police, in this case the Metropolitan Police.'

'Yes, and that's what I did.'

'Exactly. You called the Metropolitan Police, and they were on their way, and yet you decided to conduct an interview in an investigation which was not within your experience, training or remit. In those circumstances, I want to ask you why you chose to conduct an interview with the accused, when the police were only a few minutes' away.'

The Waterguard doesn't answer for a moment. 'I don't know. It was very shocking, finding John's body in the water like that, and I was sure that Conway was responsible. When I first saw him, he was crying, and I thought perhaps there was an opportunity to get the truth out of him while he was upset.'

It's a good answer. Merlin didn't deny making the confession, but Charles is in no position to explain the background or the fact that he was acting in self-defence.

'You were sure that Conway was responsible?'

'Yes, it just seemed obvious, my Lord.'

'Just pause there, please, Mr Holborne,' instructs the Judge. '"*It just seemed obvious,*"' repeats the Judge in an exaggerated way as he slowly writes verbatim Vermeulen's evidence in his red book, while glancing over at the jury to make sure they had got the point.

After a moment the Judge looks up, his hand now still, and nods to Charles that he may proceed.

'I suggest, Mr Vermeulen, that your "certainty" – based on nothing more than the coincidence that Mr Conway's barge was close by – led you to fabricate that confession.'

'Fabricate?'

'Yes,' says Charles raising his voice for the first time. 'You were sure that Mr Conway was guilty, and you took the opportunity offered by being alone with him before the police arrived to fake a confession, to make sure of a conviction.'

'I certainly did not, my Lord. What I wrote down in that interview came directly from the accused's mouth.'

'You may not be familiar with police procedure, Mr Vermeulen, but I suggest you "verballed" Mr Conway,' says Charles.

'That is quite untrue, my Lord.'

'Why didn't you get him to sign the confession then? There could have been no doubt about its truthfulness then.'

'I … I didn't think to, my Lord.'

'I see. So you're telling us that you conducted a genuine and honest interview with Mr Conway at 07:14 hours back at the Harpy, in the few minutes before the police arrived?'

'Yes, that is exactly what I'm saying,' asserts Vermeulen, his face flushing bright red.

'And you are quite certain about the time of that interview?'

Charles notices a fractional hesitation in Vermeulen's response as he realises the direction Charles's questions are about to take. 'I am, yes.'

'And you wrote down the words spoken by both of you at the same time as they were being spoken?'

'Yes.'

'So you are sure that the interview occurred at 07:14 hours?'

'Absolutely sure.'

'Mr Vermeulen: counsel and the Judge have a typewritten version of that interview. Where are your handwritten original notes taken at the time?'

Another fractional hesitation, and Vermeulen pulls a pocketbook from his uniform pocket. 'Here.'

'May I see that pocketbook, please?'

Slowly Vermeulen raises his hand and holds out the pocketbook to the usher, keeping his eyes fixed at all times on Charles's, while a faint smile plays about his lips.

Charles's heart thunders as the usher, with an infuriating lack of urgency, collects the pocketbook and walks to counsel's bench. Charles takes the pocketbook and opens it to the last page on which there is any writing. Charles knows that the alleged interview is likely to have been the last thing Vermeulen wrote in the book because it would then have been handed over for transcription. In fact, it is also the first thing in the book, and that gives rise to a flutter of anticipation in Charles's chest. It would have to be the only entry in the book if Vermeulen had rewritten it as demanded. His hands shaking slightly, Charles's finger travels to the top of the interview, and he reads: *"This interview of Isaac Conway consisting of 1 page in length was taken by me Vincent Vermeulen on 4 November 1963 at 03:14 hours ...!"* 03:14! He's changed it! Charles reads it again, and then a third time, to be absolutely sure, and to allow him time to exert an iron grip over his facial expression. As professional courtesy requires, he bends down and shows the entry to Montgomery. By the time he looks up he is calm and his face bland.

'Usher. Please would you hand this pocketbook to his Lordship?' asks Charles.

Charles waits for the pocketbook to be handed across and for the Judge to look at it, but he does not allow the Judge enough time to leap in with his own helpful intervention.

'According to your pocketbook,' continues Charles, 'which you tell us was written at the very moment when the confession was given, the time when you started the interview was 03:14 hours, and not 07:14 hours. There is a four hour difference. Mr Vermeulen: which of the two is likely to be accurate: the one that you yourself wrote contemporaneously with the so-called confession, or the typewritten version written by, no doubt, a Metropolitan Police secretary several days later in an office in London?'

Vermeulen turns to the Judge. 'I'm very sorry, my Lord, I don't know how this mistake can have occurred. The note in the pocketbook on your Lordship's desk was the note I wrote at the time.'

'You're not likely to have got the time wrong by four hours, are you, Mr Vermeulen?' asks Charles.

'No, my Lord, I can't see how that could have happened. I can only assume that the typist made a mistake. Perhaps she couldn't read my writing.'

'But if you did write the interview at 03:14 hours, how could Mr Conway have possibly confessed? You told us yourself in your evidence that the body was not discovered until over two hours after that, at 05:30, and you didn't return to Mr Conway's barge until 06:10. So how could he have confessed at 03:14?'

Even though Vermeulen had been expecting this line of questioning he clearly hadn't anticipated how damaging or embarrassing it would be. His face is now bright red and trickles of sweat can be seen emerging from his fair-haired sideburns and sliding down his cheeks.

'Well, obviously, he couldn't, but … I did interview him, my Lord, and that was after the body was discovered, obviously. I'm afraid I can't explain it.'

'The explanation, surely Mr Holborne, is very simple,' says the Judge, intervening yet again. 'CPO Vermeulen made a mistake when writing the time in his notes. Your client could not have confessed before Mr Vermeulen returned to the barge.'

'Thank you for making that suggestion, my Lord. There is of course an alternative: CPO Vermeulen has, as I suggest, made up the confession altogether and by the time he came to do so he got the time wrong.'

Charles looks at the jury. They are all staring hard at the Waterguard. Charles cannot at this stage predict whether they believe him or not, but the intensity of their gaze suggests at least that they are uncertain about his evidence – and that is all Charles needs, because "uncertain" cannot mean "sure".

Charles looks down at Vermeulen's notebook, the one he stole from the Harpy. Despite Merlin's words, he's undecided. He has just got in a nice clean punch, which will certainly score. On the other hand, he's not sure about the contents of the notebook because, despite Merlin's urging, Charles has thought of several "honest" explanations Vermeulen could deploy, if he thinks of them. For a start, he could deny the notebook is his; he might accept that the notebook is his, but deny authorship of the pencil annotations, and that would require a handwriting expert on a collateral issue, which would certainly be denied by this

Judge; he might equally say that the references to alcohol were merely a list of seized goods from other smugglers. Indeed, while in bed the night before, Charles had woken in the wee small hours with the best false explanation yet: each of the rummage teams at the Harpy were in competition with the others as to how much they could seize, and this was Vermeulen's way of keeping a score of his team's successes.

So there are many ways in which Vermeulen can muddy the waters. While his fear of exposure might have induced him to alter the time on the interview, that didn't mean the notebook offered a knockout opportunity. If Charles became involved in a complicated series of questions and answers about the stolen notebook and got nowhere, the power of the clean punch he has just landed will have dissipated in the minds of the jury. Better, he concludes, to sit down now, with the impression left in the minds of the jury that this man may be lying to them over the interview.

And so, with a regretful look across to the dock, one which he hopes Merlin will interpret as a sensible tactical decision rather than cowardice, Charles resumes his seat. As he does so he looks up at the public gallery. The young man in the expensive suit is scribbling furiously on a pad, casting worried looks towards the door. With a final look down into the court where Vermeulen is sitting almost directly below him, the man stands and slips quickly out of court.

Charles pays only half attention to Montgomery's re-examination. The QC explores for a while the possible explanations for the differences in time, but Vermeulen can come up with no better answer than he has already offered. The Judge has no questions, deciding to leave well alone, and Vermeulen is allowed to stand down.

'With your Lordship's leave,' says Montgomery, 'I will call the next witness, Adrian Peter Keeley.'

'Yes, Mr Montgomery, thank you.'

APO Keeley is a short dark man full of nervous energy. He bustles to the witness box, takes the oath, and stands with his hands clasped behind his back. Charles can see that his right foot taps, incessantly and quickly, throughout. Charles leans forward to Montgomery, and speaks softly.

'You can either lead or tender this witness. There's nothing in dispute, and I only have one question for him.'

'Thank you.' He addresses the Judge. 'My learned friend has said that I may either lead or tender this witness as none of his evidence is in dispute.'

'Thank you Mr Montgomery. The decision is yours.'

'I think it will help the jury if they hear Mr Keeley's evidence, my Lord, but I will take it swiftly.'

The QC takes Keeley through his statement, asking leading questions and obtaining the evidence set out in the statement. In Charles's opinion, Keeley says nothing of any significance in his witness statement and he only wants to ask the Waterguard one question about the missing boathook. He rises to do that a few minutes later.

'Mr Keeley, you were unable to find a boathook on Mr Conway's barge during the course of your search.'

'Correct.'

'And that surprised you?'

'Yes. It's standard equipment on every vessel working the River.'

'And like all pieces of small equipment on a boat, it can get lost easily.'

'I suppose so.'

'The barges are not locked or secured at night, are they?'

'Insulated barges, like those used to carry cheese or meat, and customs barges, which have alcohol in them – they are locked. But ordinary hatch barges like this one, for general cargo, no, not usually.'

'Do you know when Mr Conway's boathook went missing?'

'I couldn't say.'

'Do you know how many boathooks there would be on the River Thames?'

'Thousands I would guess. Probably tens of thousands.'

'Thank you Mr Keeley. That is all.'

There is no re-examination by Montgomery and the Judge has no questions, and Keeley leaves the court altogether.

'The final witness for the Crown, my Lord,' says Montgomery 'is the Home Office Pathologist, Dr Burch. Page 19 in your Lordship's bundle.'

Dr Burch is called by the usher. The doors open and a potbellied little man with a yellow waistcoat and bowtie waddles down the aisle. He is in his sixties and wears old-fashioned pince-nez on a short, upturned nose. He takes the oath in a surprisingly deep sonorous voice, enunciating each word very carefully. Montgomery takes him through his evidence carefully and with precision, paying particular attention to his calculations regarding time of death, and then resumes his seat.

Charles rises slowly. 'Dr Burch, is this a fair summary of your evidence? APO Evans suffered a blow to the head which caused his death. We don't know if he was wearing his tunic at that time. However, at some point after his death, before he went into the water, he was prodded or stabbed with a boathook at a time when he was *not* wearing his tunic. At some point after that, somebody *replaced* his tunic. And finally, at some point after that, his body was placed or fell in the water. Have I understood your evidence correctly?'

The little pathologist thinks carefully through Charles's summary, point by point, and then nods. 'Yes, my Lord. That is a fair summary.' He takes off his pince-nez, extracts a bright yellow handkerchief from his top jacket pocket, and polishes them vigorously.

Charles relishes cross-examining scientists. They think logically, which means they can be trapped by logic in a way which other witnesses cannot, and they are less likely to "massage" their evidence to support one side or the other. Charles had had cause to cross-examine dishonest experts in the past, ones who would fight to the death to uphold a theory even when presented by incontrovertible evidence to the contrary, but they were, happily, relatively rare.

'Let's start with the blow to the head,' he says. 'You cannot say if it was administered delibcrately or sustained during a fall.'

'That is correct.'

'So there is no scientific evidence to prove that the blow was *administered*, in the sense that a third party did it.'

'Correct.'

'Now let's look at the jacket. One sequence of events would be that Mr Evans died while fully dressed, someone took off his tunic, poked him with a boathook, replaced the tunic, and then, somehow, he ends up in the water.'

'Yes, my Lord. That sequence would fit my findings, but I cannot imagine any reason why someone would take off his tunic after he was dead just to poke him with a boathook, and then get him dressed again.'

God bless you! shouts Charles internally. That is exactly the point I wanted to make, but it comes so much better from a prosecution witness.

'With great respect doctor, I completely agree. A much more logical sequence would be that he suffered his blow to the head while he was undressed, partly or completely; he dies; he is then poked with the boathook; and then someone redresses him.'

'That might be more logical, but I cannot possibly say if that's what occurred.'

'How easy or difficult is it for someone to put a tunic such as this onto a dead body?' asks Charles.

'It is surprisingly difficult to dress or undress a corpse. We cut clothes off deceased persons for that reason. We don't want to do damage, to their skin or ligaments for example, by struggling with tight clothing, which might affect the scientific findings. This jacket was tight-fitting and, by the time Mr Evans was taken out of the water, buttoned right up the front. Because Mr Evans had a hole in him which was caused post-death, but the tunic did not, we know it was put back on him after he died. Whoever did that would have struggled and would have to have been quite strong.'

'That suggests, does it not, somebody who was very concerned that APO Evans was not found in a compromising position?'

Montgomery leaps to his feet but the Judge is ahead of him. 'Pure speculation, Mr Holborne. Don't answer that please, doctor. Members the jury, we cannot possibly know what was in the mind of the person who re-dressed Mr Evans, and it is wrong of Mr Holborne to speculate with this witness. Mr Holborne, you will be entitled to indulge in these wild theories during the course of your speech, if you think it will get you anywhere. But not during the evidence.'

'Very well, my Lord. Dr Burch let us turn to the way in which Mr Evans found himself in the water. We know from the absence of any significant water in his lungs that he did not drown.'

'Yes, my Lord, that and other findings.'

'So we know that after he had died and was re-dressed by someone, he came to be in the water. Am I right in believing that none of the scientific evidence helps us establish whether he was put in the water deliberately or he just fell there.'

'That would be correct.'

'Thank you. Now let me move to the issue regarding time of death. There are several difficult factors at play in this particular case when attempting to calculate the time of Mr Evans's death, are there not?'

'Yes.'

'Again, perhaps you will let me list them and you can correct me if I make a mistake. Firstly, there is the fact that he was in cold water. One of your techniques for determining time of death is the degree to which a body has cooled since the heart stopped beating. But if a body is put in cold water, that will lower its temperature quickly, thereby falsely suggesting an earlier time of death than in fact occurred. Correct so far?'

'Yes.'

'Then there is the fact that Mr Evans was wearing quite thick clothes. That would tend to keep his body warmer, a factor which would pull in the opposite direction to the cold water.'

'Yes, although I think that factor would be very much less important than the cold water.'

'Thank you. Then there is the issue of rigor mortis which, you tell us, usually starts in the first twelve to twenty-four hours and was absent in this case. In view of the fact that Mr Evans was last seen by his colleagues some thirteen hours before his body was found, that bracket is not very helpful in this case.'

'Yes, I agree with that. But I didn't place any weight on the absence of rigor mortis in reaching my conclusion.'

'Exactly. You placed most of the weight in your analysis

on the absence of *liver* mortis. Can you explain to the jury again what that is, please?'

'Certainly. When a body is still, without the heart pumping blood around the circulatory system, the blood tends to pool in the lowest part of the body. So if a body is supine – that is facing upwards – which is the case here, the blood will tend to pool in the back and buttocks. In such a case, you would see early discolouration in the skin, a purplish patchy discolouration, within an hour of death, becoming more prominent by three hours of death. There was no such discolouration in this case, which is why I concluded that death had occurred relatively recently, no more than three hours before the body was found.'

'Thank you. You look for liver mortis signs on the part of the body to which the blood will fall.'

'Yes, my Lord. As I said, when I arrived at the tow path the deceased was lying face up, and I was told that he had been taken out of the water in the same attitude. I therefore looked for liver mortis signs on his shoulders, back and buttocks, and there were none.'

Charles pauses before his all-important question, the one to which the entire cross-examination has been leading. 'If anybody were to be repeatedly turned during the period when liver mortis would emerge, the blood would not pool in any particular part of the body, would it?'

'No, probably not. I've never had a case where a body has been turned post-mortem, as if rotated on a spit, but in principle that would be right.'

Charles watches some of the faces of the jurors as they

recoil in revulsion at the thought of turning the dead APO Evans on a spit, but he presses on.

'And do you agree Dr Burch that we cannot exclude the possibility that Mr Evans's body was indeed turned by the waves and by the effect of passing ships in what is one of the busiest waterways in the world?'

Dr Burch considers this by taking off his pince-nez, staring at the ceiling of the courtroom and then closing his eyes. After a full ten seconds, during which Charles's heartbeat almost doubles, he opens his eyes, looks back across the well of the court to Charles, replaces his pince-nez and answers.

'I cannot exclude that possibility.'

'In which case the absence of liver mortis would not throw any light on the time of Mr Evans's death.'

'Yes, that must follow, my Lord.'

'Thank you Dr Burch. Would you like to review your conclusion that death occurred no earlier than three hours prior to your arrival on the scene?'

The little pathologist turns towards the Judge, a look of sadness on his pudgy face. 'My Lord, I think I must. I think this is one of those rare cases where the evidence is just inconclusive. I cannot give you even an approximation of the time of death; certainly not one about which I can be satisfied so as to be sure.'

chapter 22

'You lost your bottle!' shouts Merlin as Charles walks into the basement conference room, the Judge having risen for the night.

'No I didn't,' replies Charles calmly. 'I took the view that we were better off leaving it with his last answer, rather than getting into a long inconclusive fight over the notebook. Did you see him sweating?'

Charles explains his reasoning, but Merlin doesn't look convinced. He paces up and down the tiny room.

'You're just going to have to trust me, Izzy. I've been doing this a long time, and I think I am a better judge than you of what has an impact on a jury and what doesn't.'

Merlin finally settles on the wooden bench, his feet still tapping. 'Okay. It's done now. So, what's next?'

Charles sits down next to his cousin, takes off his wig and scratches his scalp. 'Tomorrow morning I tell the judge that were calling no evidence. Then Montgomery closes his case; he gives his closing speech; I give mine; the Judge sums up.'

'Right. Do you need anything from me?'

Charles puts his hand on his cousin's shoulder. 'No. Try to get a decent night's sleep, that's all.'

'Fat chance.'

•

Court sits again at half past ten the following morning. Within forty-five minutes, Collin Montgomery QC has completed his closing speech for the Crown and resumed his seat. The speech was a model of fairness. Having run through the important parts of the evidence, he concluded by inviting the jury to convict the accused on the basis that Evans was known to be watching his barge; Evans's body was found only a few feet from that position; and although there are some unexplained features of the evidence, for example the fact that Evans appeared to have suffered his posthumous side injury while not wearing his jacket, the accused had made a clear confession.

'Mr Holborne?' invites Fletcher.

All eyes in the court turn to Charles. He puts his hands on the bench in front of him, preparing to stand, but for a moment he pauses. He is about to rise to make the speech of his life. No, he corrects himself: the speech *for* my life. He cannot prevent his eyes flicking to the public gallery above him, seeking out the well-dressed young man, but he's no longer in the seat he has occupied so far and Charles has no time to look for him. He looks away swiftly. No, Charlie, he instructs himself; get the Krays out of your mind and *focus*. Your job now is to woo those eight men and four women sitting on the far side of the court. Nothing else matters; nothing. He stands.

He can tell immediately how difficult his task is going to

be. Of the twelve jurors only two or three make eye contact with him. The rest are…not quite hostile, but *uninterested*. Charles can always tell from their body language how much work he still has to do, from their willingness to look at him, the ease with which they will nod or smile when he makes a point. In any other case this would be the part of the proceedings he loves the most, the time when he can engage with these twelve strangers and drag them round slowly but surely to his way of seeing things as he sells his client's version of the truth – which, of course, always means selling himself. The jury have to like him or, if not "like", *trust* him; trust him to be an honest guide through the evidence and its different possible interpretations. He has to get inside their heads, read their thoughts and address their concerns about the evidence; understand what may be preventing them from accepting the truth as *he* sees it, and assuage their worries; turn the evidence on its head so they see it all differently, and through his eyes.

So Charles starts with the thing that would be worrying him most if he was sitting in those uncomfortable jury benches. He yanks his black gown up by the area where the lapels would be, if barristers' gowns included lapels, to settle it perfectly in place on his shoulders, and he smiles.

'Ladies and gentlemen. I'm prepared to bet that some of you are sitting there wondering: why haven't we heard Mr Conway's version of event? "*If he has nothing to hide, why won't he go into the witness box? Isn't that suspicious?*"

Charles notes that three of the jury members, a woman on the back row and two men sitting next to one another on the front row – one of whom is in the foreman's seat and so may be an important person to persuade – look at him briefly as he says this. Okay, thinks Charles. His next sentences are directed particularly at those three jury members.

'The law prevents Mr Montgomery QC for the Crown and his Lordship from drawing attention to that fact, but let's be straight with one another: if I was sitting in those benches, without my experience of the law, I'd be asking the very same question.'

The woman in the top row gives Charles a grudging smile. Bull's-eye! thinks Charles.

'Well, the reason is very simple. One of the great hallmarks of our English system of justice, one of the things we can most be proud of, which goes back centuries, is the fact that the accused is never, *ever*, required to give evidence. Back in the fifteenth century the Court of the Star Chamber was allowed to torture good and honest Englishmen into giving false confessions and so, for centuries since then, the law has protected any person who has the misfortune to be in that dock' – and Charles points dramatically to where Merlin sits – 'and say: they shall not be compelled to utter a word. Until relatively recently the accused was not even *allowed* to give evidence on his own behalf. It's the task of the Crown to put evidence before you which satisfies you, so you're *sure* of the accused's guilt. Anything less won't do, and the accused doesn't have to go into the witness box to explain himself. Our constitution guarantees him the *right* to point at the Crown and say: *"The evidence you've called doesn't come close to proving guilt beyond reasonable doubt, and I'm entitled to ask the jury to throw the case out without a word."* Of course, when you pause for a moment, and realise that a man's life is at stake here – you'd imagine nothing less: unless the Crown's evidence makes you *sure* – beyond all reasonable doubt – that Mr Conway killed APO Evans, how could you, in conscience, convict him and send him to the gallows? And that is why neither the Judge nor Mr Montgomery is allowed to criticise or even draw attention to the fact that Mr Conway has not given evidence. Because they know that the constitution of our country gives him that inviolable right.

'So, with your permission ladies and gentlemen, I invite you to look with me at the evidence the Crown has put before you so that you may decide for yourselves – because it is a decision that only you can take, not me, not Mr Montgomery and not the Judge – whether the evidence put before you by the Crown is enough to make you satisfied so you're *sure beyond reasonable doubt.*'

Charles watches with a faint spark of satisfaction as the woman in the top row and one of the two men in the front row – although not, unfortunately, the putative foreman – nod fractionally, if perhaps a little reluctantly, in response to his explanation. They are far from persuaded yet, but the door is not quite so completely shut as when Charles first rose to start speaking. From now on he will refer to Merlin as "Mr Conway". To use the term "accused", "defendant" or, worse still, "prisoner" is to distance the jury from the real human being sitting a few feet away from them, to dehumanise him. Charles wants them to remember throughout that they are dealing with a real person and, what is more, a "Mr": someone deserving of respect and dignity.

'The Crown's case rests on, essentially, three things.' Charles holds up his left hand and counts them off. 'Firstly: the fact that Mr Evans's body was found near to Mr Conway's barge, and that Mr Conway was under surveillance. Secondly, the pathology evidence, particularly that Mr Evans had only been dead for a short time when his body was discovered, suggesting he had been killed somewhere nearby. And lastly the fact that Mr Conway is said to have confessed.'

Charles notes with satisfaction that all but a couple of the jury members are at least looking at him and are interested in what he has to say. Two of them are scribbling furiously, making notes. On the other hand, one of the two who still refuses to make eye contact is the man in the foreman's seat, a broad man in his forties with wobbly jowls like a bulldog's, a red face and broken purple veins on his nose. A drinker? wonders Charles. Perhaps he'll be more amenable after a pint or two at lunchtime.

'Let's look first at the suggestion that Mr Evans was in fact watching Mr Conway at all immediately before his death. Mr Vermeulen tells you that Mr Conway was under surveillance as a result of a tipoff from some informant. We only have his word for that – and I'll come back to the value of Mr Vermeulen's word in a while – but we have not heard from the informant or seen any documentary evidence about the surveillance operation. Of course, you will say, you can't expect a confidential informant to give evidence. Fair enough – but not a single document? Think about that for a moment, ladies and gentlemen. HM Waterguard is part of Her Majesty's Customs and Excise. They are tax collectors and enforcers. Have you ever heard of a government department that doesn't keep records – in duplicate, triplicate, all signed, dated and filed? We all know the government's love of forms – above all, the tax authorities!'

Charles sees several jury members smile with him.

'And we know from Mr Vermeulen that several such documents would normally be completed to record what Mr Evans was doing, the shift rotas, his own personal log, the document recording the use of the vehicle. Doesn't it strike you as a bit odd that the Crown has not been able to produce a single document supporting the suggestion that Mr Evans had been conducting surveillance on Mr Conway for some months? And even if the surveillance of Mr Conway was genuinely occurring in a general sense, where is the evidence that Mr Evans was engaged on it *that night*? Is it really being suggested that he left the Harpy when his shift began at four o'clock the previous afternoon and watched Mr Conway's barge for the next thirteen hours? Of course not. Apart from anything else, these barges are in use, day in, day out. You've heard no evidence to suggest that for some inexplicable reason Mr Conway sat on his barge doing nothing for the whole of that period. So, the most likely scenario is that both Mr Conway and Mr Evans were off doing other things for large parts of that period.

We've heard from Mr Vermeulen how busy a Waterguard's life is, and how their schedules have to change at no notice in response to whatever may enter the Thames.

'So, what are we left with? The coincidence that Mr Evans's body was found close to Mr Conway's mooring. And, as soon as you think about it for a moment, you realise it may just have been that – a coincidence. Mr Vermeulen didn't disagree with my estimate of fifty-five barges in the immediate area. Any one of them may have attracted Mr Evans's interest. He may have slipped, fallen or been struck on any one of them. And then there is the issue of the barges being used for liaisons between homosexual men at night. We will never know if Mr Evans went there for business or – and forgive me for the indelicacy – for pleasure. But we do know that he had been accused of such behaviour in the past, and the Crown did not dispute the assertion that some of these barges are used at night for such purposes.

'So far I have assumed, in the Crown's favour, that Mr Evans body was found at a place close to where it went into the water, but that is not an assumption we can make, is it? His body was found in one of the busiest tidal waterways in Europe. The Crown has called no evidence to suggest that Mr Evans's body actually went into the water close to where he was found. You are perfectly entitled to ask yourself: why not? We all know that things put into moving water do not stay in one place. They're moved by currents, tides, by the passage of other vessels. But you're being asked to assume that, because Mr Evans's body was found where it was, it must have gone into the water sometime during that thirteen-hour period at the same place. I suggest to you, ladies and gentlemen, that that's not an assumption it's reasonable to make. Indeed, over the course of the thirteen hours during which the Crown cannot account for his movements, he could have entered the water miles upstream, and drifted to where he was found. So, the Crown cannot prove, beyond reasonable doubt, that Mr Evans went into the water at that point.

'And of course, it would have been so easy to call such evidence, had it existed. With all the resources at the disposal of HM Waterguard, HM Customs and Excise and the Crown? HM Waterguard would, you might think, be *perfectly* placed to provide expert evidence to explain the movement of the tides and currents on the Thames. Who better? Don't you think that, had it been possible to prove that where Mr Evans was found, is *where he went into the water*, we would have heard some evidence on that subject?

'So, on the issue of what Mr Evans was doing in the thirteen hours after he was last seen and what conclusions can be drawn from the position of his body at the end of that thirteen-hour period, you are being asked to make some very big assumptions. Firstly, that he and Mr Conway were both in the same place at the same time when Mr Evans went into the water; secondly that he came into contact with no other person who might have been involved in his death – someone working on the River or someone there for more immoral purposes; thirdly that his death was not simply an accident such as slipping or falling and banging his head; fourthly that his body remained in the same place as where it fell in up to thirteen hours earlier. Remember that, members of the jury: the Crown cannot prove any of these essential features. They ask you simply to make assumptions. And I suggest to you,' and Charles delivers the next words with a tiny pause between each for emphasis 'that just won't do.'

Charles's eyes scan across the top row of jurors and back along the bottom row. They are now all listening to him. He has learned not to read too much into the facial expressions of jurors but at least half of them look concerned, as if Charles's arguments bother them. Charles drops his voice a little as he comes to the central point on this part of the evidence. He wants them to have to lean forward to listen; it creates a more intimate conversation. He doesn't want to be a barrister making a speech to a packed and hushed public courtroom; he wants to be the jury's honest guide, talking to them directly and confidentially. And they all do lean forward.

'The point is this, members of the jury: unless you're *sure* there cannot be an alternative explanation for Mr Evans's being found where he was; unless you are *sure* no other reasonable explanation exists; unless you are *sure* this cannot have been a coincidence; then you cannot convict consistently with your oath, because you cannot be sure beyond reasonable doubt that Mr Conway killed him.'

Charles lets a few moments pass to let this final point sink in. The eight men and four women of the jury sit back in their seats and Charles can almost see the cogs in those twelve heads clicking and whirring as they think about

Charles's words. Two members of the jury, one at each end of the top rank, smile grimly at him and nod slowly. They may not like it, but they are no longer sure they are sure.

Charles moves onto his second point, his voice brisk and more business-like. He has learned over the years that it is essential to vary the pitch and tone of his voice. There is nothing worse than a barrister droning on in a monotone, regardless of the content of his speech. This is a performance, and Charles knows it.

'Next, we have the pathology evidence. I can deal with time of death quickly: you heard Dr Burch give his careful and considered evidence. He was, you will remember, a witness called by the Crown, and therefore someone the Crown says will give you truthful and accurate evidence. And as you know Dr Burch retracted his earlier view that Mr Evans probably died within three hours of his body being discovered. He agreed that, in short, we have no idea at what time Mr Evans met his death; it must have occurred between four o'clock in the afternoon of the previous day and shortly before the discovery of the body. I accept that the relatively small drop in body temperature suggests that it was probably the second half of that period, but we can get no closer than that. So the link the Crown asks you to draw, that Mr Evans had been dead only a short time, and therefore is likely to have been killed near to where he was found, is broken. Mr Evans could have been killed half a day earlier, and simply drifted to the point where his body was found.

'Then there is the head injury. Dr Burch cannot tell

you whether it was inflicted deliberately or it might have been caused by Mr Evans falling and striking his head on something hard. Let us recall the sort of work Mr Evans and other members of the Waterguard do. They board dozens if not hundreds of vessels every week while still on the water. Vessels which move, which have slippery gunwales, and which have ropes, chains and other obstacles littered across their surfaces. Mr Evans was doing this in the dark. How can we possibly exclude *accident* as the cause of death in those circumstances?'

Charles pauses to make eye contact with several of the jury members. All twelve are now looking intently at him, waiting for him to speak again.

'But the evidence which I find most odd, and I suspect you will too, is this hole in poor Mr Evans's side. We know it must have been created after he died, but while the top part of his body was unclothed. And the question I keep asking myself is: what on earth was Mr Evans doing taking his clothes off? He's a uniformed officer of the Customs and Excise. You saw Mr Vermeulen's uniform. Mr Evans wore the same uniform – although with less braid round the cuffs. Mr Evans's job didn't require him to swim, in the middle of the night, across the Thames! Which does make me think, bearing in mind the allegations made against Mr Evans in the past: perhaps he was engaged in activities which had nothing to do with his duties. If he *was* indulging in sexual activity with another man, which we all know is against the law and carries all sorts of dangers with it... well, that opens up an entirely new set of possibilities which would have had nothing whatsoever to do with Mr Conway. None of us will ever know what Mr Evans was doing that evening, but I do ask you to keep well in mind the fact that prior to his death, this bachelor – against whom homosexual allegations had been raised in the past – was not wearing any clothing, at least on the top part of his body. We will never know if whoever took the considerable trouble to get him dressed again just put on his jacket or *all* of his clothing. But consider this: whoever did that, they did not want Mr Evans found in a state of undress, did they? And you are entitled to ask yourself: why? And if you consider that Mr Evans was engaged in sexual activity, *or might have been*, there is absolutely no evidence whatsoever to link that with Mr Conway.'

Charles watches as several of the jury members turn to look at Merlin and ask themselves if they think he is the sort of man to have clandestine homosexual liaisons with a member of the Waterguard on a dark barge moored at night on the Thames. As if Charles had arranged it, right on cue Merlin sits up straight from his slouched position and lets the jury members examine his strong handsome face, his tanned features and his broad shoulders. Even tired, drawn and worried, he still looks like a matinee idol. Charles waits for the jury members to return their attention to him and notes with satisfaction that it is the four female members of the jury whose consideration of Merlin lasts the longest.

'I respectfully submit to you ladies and gentlemen that far from the pathology evidence helping the Crown prove the case beyond reasonable doubt, it throws up more questions than it answers. One thing is sure: there is no scientific evidence to link Mr Evans's body with Mr Conway, his barge, or a deliberate assault. As Dr Burch concedes, the blow which killed him could have been an accident, it could have occurred almost anywhere and not just by Mr Conway's barge, and – if it was deliberate – it could have been administered by anyone with whom Mr Evans came into contact both in pursuance of his Waterguard duties or in pursuance of more nefarious objectives.'

This time Charles notes several members of the jury nodding fractionally, including even the putative foreman.

'And so, ladies and gentlemen, I turn to the last piece of evidence, and the one I'm sure will concern you most: the alleged confession. It is of course the cornerstone of the Crown's case. But it is *fatally flawed*. Firstly, the timing problem. Mr Vermeulen was initially absolutely certain that the time that he undertook the interview was 07:14 hours in the morning, which would tie in perfectly with all the other parts of the investigation. But when I pointed out that his handwritten notes were timed at 03:14 hours he was equally convinced that he wrote that time down at the same moment as he conducted the interview. But we know he cannot be right about that, because he could hardly have been obtaining a confession to a murder even before he discovered that a murder had occurred. His Lordship postulated one possible explanation: the secretary typing the notes simply mis-read the time. Well you will have a chance to look at the handwritten notes when you retire to the jury room, and you will see that they are very clearly written and it would have taken a very short-sighted secretary indeed to have made such a mistake. But I have an alternative explanation: Mr Vermeulen made up the confession subsequently, forgetting the time when he actually carried out the interview. Why? Because he put two and two together to reach five; he was sure he'd got his man, and he was going to make sure he got a conviction. I suggest, ladies and gentlemen, that you cannot exclude that as a possibility, which means you can't be sure that the confession is genuine.

'Is there any other piece of evidence which helps us decide if the confession is genuine? Well, yes; there are three.' Again Charles lifts his hand and counts them off. 'Firstly: why was Mr Vermeulen conducting this interview at all? It's not his job. He has no training or experience in conducting interviews of this sort. This is a job for the Metropolitan Police who had already been called and who were on their way. He had only a very short time to wait, and yet he hurries to conduct an interview which, for all he knows, he could completely muck up. Doesn't that smack of a man trying to bolster the evidence while he had time, rather than a man sticking to his duty?

'Secondly, where's the detail? Please can I ask you to look at the typewritten version of the interview in front of you?'

Charles waits while the members of the jury find the document from the small pile of papers in front of them. There are six copies, so each pair of jurors sitting next to each other leans in, sharing a copy.

'Now, put yourself in Mr Vermeulen's position. Imagine for a minute that you're conducting the interview of the murderer of one of your colleagues and, against all the odds, your suspect simply confesses that he did it: *"We had a fight and I killed him."* Wouldn't you ask why? Wouldn't you ask for details? I suggest to you that if the interview occurred as Mr Vermeulen says it did, it would have carried on for longer than this simple, bland confession followed by Mr Vermeulen telling Mr Conway: *"I am ending this interview now to await the arrival of the Metropolitan Police."* The mark of a genuine confession is that it contains details that could only have come from the accused. That way, the accused can't get out of it later. There is absolutely no such detail here, is there? I suggest this –' and Charles picks up the document, holding it delicately between his thumb and forefinger as if trying to avoid being contaminated by it – 'is "a verbal" – a dishonest account of an admission that was never made.

'And lastly, why didn't Mr Vermeulen get a signature from Mr Conway? Isn't that obvious, even if you're not trained in conducting interviews with alleged murderers? Wouldn't you have thought to yourself: *"Well I never, he's just admitted to it. But there's only him and me here so, just to make sure he doesn't go back on it, I'm going to get him to sign the notes."*

At this point, with immense satisfaction, Charles watches the putative foreman nodding his ruddy face up and down, his jowls wobbling. He at least likes that point.

Charles again looks up and down the two lines of jurors. He feels like a circus performer spinning plates on sticks. Up and down the lines he runs throughout his speech, making eye contact here, grinning there, raising his eyebrows at a third, looking for a response, persuading them, one by one, that his version of the truth is the right one, keeping them with him, building the momentum so that none of the jurors, once captured, falls away.

'The question you have to ask yourselves, members of the jury, is this: am I satisfied so I am *sure* that the interview was taken in the manner and at the time Mr Vermeulen says it was? If you think that my suggestion is correct – or that it *may be* correct – your duty is to acquit Mr Conway. If you think that Mr Vermeulen may have made up the confession because he was desperate to get the man he was sure was responsible; if you think he may just have added two unconnected events – the finding of the body near Mr Conway's barge, and the fact that Mr Conway had been under surveillance – and assumed Mr Conway was guilty; if you think he was so angry at the loss of his colleague that he might have been prepared to bend the rules; if you think he may have taken the law into his own hands and embroidered the evidence to make it more compelling – then again, you cannot convict. If any of this evidence doesn't feel right to you; if you are left wondering and doubting – then you only have one course.'

Charles pauses. There is complete and total silence in the courtroom. Every member of the jury is now following him intently. He has them, and the rest of the court for that matter, in the palm of his hand. He slowly closes his grip around them.

'I return to the comments I made right at the beginning of my address to you. The Defence has to prove nothing. The Crown has to prove everything – and to a very high standard: so you are sure. If you think these alternative explanations for the evidence *might* be correct, your duty is to bring in a verdict of "Not Guilty".'

Charles smiles, and the tension in the courtroom eases a little. 'Ladies and gentlemen, thank you for listening to me with such patience and attention. I'm sure that when you retire to discuss the evidence between you in the jury room, you will give it just the same careful attention and analysis, and on Mr Conway's behalf I can ask no more. Having done so, I suggest to you that on the evidence you have heard, the only verdict that you could reach consistent with your oath and with common sense is to find Mr Conway not guilty of the charge of murder.'

Charles remains standing for a few more seconds, his eyes once again travelling up and down the faces of the two banks of jurors, and then resumes his seat. Got them! he thinks.

'Thank you, Mr Holborne,' says the Judge. 'I think the jury might like a few minutes' break before I start my summing up. I shall rise until twelve twenty.'

'Court rise!'

The occupants of the public gallery and the press benches disperse quickly, rushing out to get a cup of tea, run to the toilet, or have a quick smoke. Charles now looks up and squints at the gallery to see if he can locate Ronnie Kray's eyes and ears. There, slipping out of the door, is the young man.

Back in the cells five minutes later Merlin gives Charles a bear hug. With his mouth close to Charles's ear, he whispers: 'Well, you persuaded me. And I know I did it!'

Charles disengages from Merlin and throws himself on the bench, suddenly exhausted. 'Let's not count our chickens,' he says. 'It felt good, and they looked as if they were with us, but you never know.'

Merlin watches him for a while. 'What's the matter, Charlie? You've done everything you possibly could.'

'Yes. Most of it unprofessional, and a good part of it illegal. I feel like I've thrown away everything I've worked for, for the last fifteen years. I feel grubby.'

'Better alive and grubby, than dead and clean.'

Charles smiles ruefully. 'True,' he admits. 'But if you're acquitted, that's the end of the story for you. I've still got to get Ronnie Kray off my back. And as you pointed out, he's not going to stop.'

chapter 23

Mr Justice Fletcher takes just over an hour to direct the jury as to the law, summarise the evidence, and go as far as he can to persuade them to convict the accused without tempting the Court of Appeal to intervene. Considering the identity of the judge, thought Charles, the summing up isn't as bad as he'd feared. Fletcher instructs the jury to ignore speculation about nocturnal homosexual liaisons or why APO Evans appeared to have received an injury to his side after he was killed and while he was partially undressed. In the learned Judge's opinion, precisely what APO Evans had been doing before he met his death is irrelevant. The only issue for them is whether the prisoner killed him. Echoing Montgomery's speech, he directs them that the fact of the surveillance, the location of the body and the confession are ample to prove beyond reasonable doubt that the prisoner is guilty. He repeats the point that the mistaken time as to Vermeulen's interview is insignificant if they believe, as he urges them to do, that a Chief Preventive Officer of HM Waterguard is most unlikely to make up such a confession. Nonetheless, because Charles had called no evidence, Fletcher is unable to put the boot into Merlin or the Defence case, and so much of what Charles had said to the jury is still in everyone's mind when the jury rises for a late lunch at half past one. Counsel are released until no earlier than half past two.

Charles spends half an hour in the cells with Merlin, but everything has already been said and they sit in virtual silence, each lost in his own thoughts. Finally, Charles says he will wait in the Bar Mess, and Merlin agrees. Charles leaves Merlin with his *Daily Sketch* and walks upstairs.

Two or three other barristers are also awaiting verdicts and Charles joins them at one of the tables, having ordered tea and shortbread biscuits. Over the years he has tried numerous strategies for passing this time. He has taken papers relating to other cases and envies other barristers who seem capable of putting their current jury out of their minds and concentrating on writing an Advice on Evidence or drafting an indictment in a different case, but he can't manage it. He has tried taking a novel, but finds that even that degree of concentration on something else is beyond him. Even when he has no personal involvement in the outcome, when he is acting for a defendant, particularly one in whose innocence he believes strongly, Charles finds himself jumpy and unable to settle. This time is the worst of all. More than once he stands to go to the telephone to see if Sally will speak to him, and more than once he forces himself to sit down again, to pace once more around the room or to pick up a newspaper. The jury in the case of one of the other two barristers returns with a verdict and he jams on his wig and scuttles downstairs. The other gets on the Bar

Mess telephone and starts a long conversation, apparently with his clerk, leaving Charles to his own thoughts.

Since his first conference with Merlin at Brixton, when he left with the prison-made shiv in his pocket, Charles has not spoken to Merlin about what will happen if the lighterman were to be convicted despite all Charles's efforts. Merlin's breakdown and his handing over of the weapon suggest that, come what may, he won't attempt to kill Charles, but they haven't actually discussed it. In any case, thinks Charles, even if the worst-case scenario occurred and Merlin went to the gallows without honouring his agreement with the Krays, Ronnie's retribution is still coming. Charles knows enough about the Krays to be certain that they won't just give up. So, some long-term solution is still required.

The enormous wooden clock on the Mess wall ticks the minutes past with interminable slowness. The other remaining barrister finishes his call and disappears into the lavatory with a newspaper, leaving Charles alone in the room. On impulse he walks to the telephone on the windowsill. He uses the back of his hand to clear a space amongst the collection of flies which battered themselves to death against the windowpane, and perches on the edge. He requests an outside line, and dials.

'David Horowitz, please,' he asks when the call is picked up. 'Charles Holborne,' he adds, in response to the question as to his identity.

He waits for a moment and then hears his brother's voice. 'Charles? Everything alright?' David sounds concerned; Charles almost never calls at work.

'Yes. At a bit of a loose end, waiting for a verdict, so I thought I'd call.'

David chuckles, but is still surprised. 'That's nice. I hoped we'd see you on Friday.'

'Yes, I know. Something came up at work.'

'On Friday night?' chides David, gently. Charles doesn't answer. 'You know how important it is to Mum and Dad. Friday nights are sacred.'

'Don't have a go at me, Davie. I phoned to hear a friendly voice. Anyway, this *is* exceptional. I'm representing Izzy Conway.'

'What?' replies David, astonished.

'You knew he'd been arrested, charged with murder?'

'Yes, of course, despite the fact that Mum's still not on speaking terms with Aunt Bea. Yet another subject we all avoid. But how're you involved?'

'Long story.'

David pauses. 'Well, at least one of the family is standing by him. I'm glad. Can you do anything?

'I'm not sure. Maybe.' Charles lapses into a silence pregnant with unarticulated communication.

'There *is* something wrong, isn't there, Charles? Something else.'

Charles draws a deep breath, twitches aside the net curtains from the dusty windowsill on which he sits and gazes, unseeing, down at the top of the black cabs and other traffic rumbling along below.

'It's a tricky case,' he says, finally.

'Are you sure that's all? You sound as if your mind is

miles away – from me and from your case.'

'I've been thinking about what you said about Henrietta,' says Charles quietly. David waits. 'Actually I've been talking to her.'

'What do you mean, you've been talking to her?' asks David, perplexed.

'Well, to be accurate, she's been talking to me.'

'Charles? Should I be taking this seriously? You're beginning to worry me.'

It takes a while for Charles to respond, but when he does his voice is brighter and stronger, as if he had indeed been joking. 'No, I'm not serious. This case is just getting me down. Remember Dad told us he knew the Krays father, Charlie Kray, the pesterer?'

'Yes, when we collected him from hospital at the end of last year. What of it?'

'I followed up the lead he gave me and I managed to get in touch with them. I tried to straighten out the problem over Robeson.'

'And?'

'I wasn't successful. I'm still apparently on Ronnie's "List".'

'What's that mean?' asks David, concern loud in his voice.

'I don't really know yet. It's tied up with this case.'

'For God's sake, Charles, go to the police. Why do you always think you need to manage everything without help?'

'You forget what job I do, David. Half the police in the Met are corrupt, and some are hand in glove with the

Krays; I wouldn't know who to trust. And of those who haven't got their snouts in the trough, most them think I killed Henrietta, or I've been working for the Krays already and therefore deserve it – or both. I've turned this over in my head for months, but I can't think of a way out.'

'Surely there must be one decent copper in the whole Metropolitan police force you could turn to?'

'Sure there is – but which one is he? Look I've got to go.' Charles has seen the usher from Court 4 waving urgently at him from the door. He stands up and retrieves his wig.

'But Charles, you've got to do *something*.' David's voice is insistent, and he doesn't want Charles to break the connection.

'I know. I'll come up with something. Got to go.'

Charles hangs up. The usher, seeing Charles finish the call, approaches. 'We have a verdict.'

Charles walks silently down the carpeted stairs in the company of the usher, his heartbeat picking up speed. It's always like this – the surge of adrenaline and anticipation – exactly like walking from the dressing room and climbing into the ring for a fight or, when he was a teenager, manoeuvring a barge under the hail of a Luftwaffe bombardment. The times when he feels most alive.

The usher holds open the double doors into the courtroom for Charles to precede him down the aisle. It appears that Charles is one of the last to resume his place because the court is packed, the public gallery full, and there are half a dozen journalists standing with their backs to the panelled walls who have been unable to find seats.

Montgomery and his junior sit in their respective benches, surrounded by extraneous barristers who have returned to hear how Charles got on with his dock brief, and the clerk of the court stands by the door behind the Judge's seat, waiting for Charles to reach the barristers' benches. The courtroom crackles with tension.

'Ready, gentlemen?' asks the clerk.

'Yes,' Montgomery and Charles reply simultaneously.

The clerk slips through the door but it does not close completely and it is evident that the Judge has been waiting in the corridor outside to enter. The clerk knocks on the door.

'All rise!' calls the usher, and there is the rumbling threat of over one hundred people getting to their feet.

Mr Justice Fletcher enters the courtroom and takes his seat, and the clerk places the Judge's papers and notebook on his bench before him. Fletcher waits for the shuffling and banging of seats to finish before addressing counsel.

'I understand we have a verdict. Is there anything either of you wishes to say before I call on the jury bailiff?'

'No, thank you, my Lord,' answers Montgomery, half-rising from his seat. The Judge looks across at Charles, who shakes his head.

'Very well.'

The usher knocks on the door leading to the jury retiring room and it opens almost instantly. The jury members file into their benches. With some surprise Charles notes that the person first to take her seat in the front bench, in the foreman's position, is not the ruddy-faced man but one of the women who formerly sat in the top row. Some barristers assert that it's impossible to predict the jury's verdict from the jurors' facial expressions, but Charles has a rule of thumb which, although not infallible, is usually reliable: if the jurors, in particular the foreman or forewoman, are prepared to make eye contact with him, it is usually a good sign. Particularly in a capital case, it is very hard for jurors to make eye contact with either the accused or his counsel when their next words will sentence the prisoner to death. On this occasion however, the forewoman flashes a glance towards Charles and they make eye contact for a fraction of a second before she takes her seat, notes gripped tightly in her hand. Charles's heartbeat quickens further still, and his hands tightly clench the top of the bench. He notes his white knuckles and removes his hands to his lap where they can't be seen.

The court settles again, this time into absolute silence. The clerk stands and picks up the indictment.

'The accused will stand,' she orders Merlin. Merlin complies, pushing the light brown locks off his forehead and setting his face, ready for the worst.

'Will the foreman or forewoman of the jury please stand?'

The woman at the end of the front row rises hesitantly and the clerk addresses her.

'Please answer the following question "Yes" or "No". Have you reached a verdict on which all twelve of you are agreed?'

'Yes,' says the woman, her cheeks and ears burning red.

'On the charge of murder, do you find the accused guilty or not guilty?'

There is an awful moment's hesitation as the woman takes a deep breath and then announces: 'Not guilty!'

The tension breaks and there is a buzz of conversation and movement in the public gallery and the press benches, but Charles is oblivious to it. He turns to Merlin in the dock. All the strength appears to have left the lighterman's body. His fists grip the rail of the dock and his arms, rigid and locked at the elbow, continue to hold him upright but his knees are bent and he stares at his feet, taking great gulps of air. His face is as white as a sheet of paper. He manages to look up and lock eyes with Charles for a moment, a weak smile on his pale handsome face.

Montgomery turns to Charles's bench and leans across. 'Well done, Charles. I hope your client realises just how lucky he was to have got you – and on a dock brief. Terrific piece of advocacy.'

Charles smiles his thanks, and is dimly aware of other barristers clapping him on the back and congratulating him, but he can't make eye contact with any of his celebrating colleagues. If only they knew, he thinks to himself. To secure this acquittal he has committed burglary and blackmail and broken half a dozen professional rules, the discovery of which would certainly end his career and lead to imprisonment. He doesn't deserve plaudits bought at such a price.

The Judge ploughs on through the commotion, ordering that the prisoner be discharged, and immediately rises.

Counsel stand but the court is too full of excitement for anyone else to heed the usher's shout of "All rise!"

Charles turns and looks up at the public gallery. The watchers are busy putting on coats, talking animatedly to one another and queuing to leave the courtroom, but as far as Charles can tell, Ronnie's spy is nowhere to be seen. Charles doesn't know what this signifies; probably nothing.

Merlin is being escorted back down to the cells to collect his belongings and complete the final paperwork. Charles calls across to him.

'I'll be down at the cell doors!'

Merlin nods and disappears.

Charles pushes his way up the aisle through the crowds and makes his way to the basement cells, constantly looking about him for the young man or any other sign of danger. Merlin is waiting for him when he reaches the steel door. The cousins embrace.

'Thank you!' whispers Merlin with intensity into Charles's ear. Charles pats his back. 'What can I ever do to repay you?'

'I've no idea. Stay out of trouble?'

Merlin disengages and holds Charles away from him by the upper arms.

'I'm gonna have to. The Waterguard'll be all over me like a rash from now on. And that Vermeulen's not likely to forgive and forget.'

'Not just him. Don't forget the Krays.'

Merlin frowns. 'I think you've got more to worry about on that score than me. What're you going to do, Charlie?'

'I really have no idea, Izzy. Emigrate, maybe?'

'Don't joke about it Charlie.'

'I'm not sure I was joking. Anyway, we need to get you to a phone. Your mum'll be tearing her hair out with worry.'

Charles starts to move off when Izzy grabs his upper arm tightly, dragging him back. 'Keep your eyes peeled when you leave, Charlie,' he instructs.

'Why? Do you think something's going to happen immediately?'

'I've no idea, but Ronnie's eyes and ears have suddenly disappeared, and it's going to be crowded out there. You'll be vulnerable.'

Charles nods. 'I think I know someone who can get me out a different way.'

Twenty minutes later one of the ushers from Court 1, whom Charles has known for fifteen years, opens a side door usually reserved for members of the judiciary, checks outside, and allows Charles to slip away unnoticed by the crowds of journalists and onlookers waiting in the Great Hall and on the court steps. Charles walks swiftly towards Holborn Viaduct – the opposite direction to the one he would usually take – his shoulders hunched, his hat pulled down over his eyes and his collar up.

chapter 24

It is two weeks later, and Charles crosses the damp cobbles of Kings Bench Walk and walks towards Chambers, pulling his raincoat tighter about him with one hand and holding his hat firmly on his head with the other. The blustery wind which has been blowing all day has left shifting drifts of litter in the gutters and against the wheels of the parked cars. It is late afternoon but the light is already failing, with dark clouds scudding up the Thames from the east bringing an early sunset. A thin band of orange sky is still visible at Charles's back, behind the dome of St Paul's and the silhouetted buildings of the City, but in the direction he is walking the horizon is dark purple, despite the fact that it is not yet five o'clock. On the corner of Crown Office Row Charles passes the uniformed officer of the Honourable Society of the Inner Temple with his long pole – Charles always imagines it to be a six-foot matchstick – struggling against the wind to light the gas lamps.

Charles hurries up the worn stone steps into Chambers and pushes open the door to the clerks' room. Barbara is in the act of replacing the handset of the telephone and sees Charles enter.

'Afternoon, sir,' she calls. 'Have you got a minute?'

Charles hasn't spoken to Barbara in person in the days since Merlin's trial finished. In fact he has barely talked to anyone, having virtually imprisoned himself inside the apartment at Fetter Lane. He had managed to re-establish some dialogue with Sally, but only by telephone, and even then Sally was guarded and cool. He had explained to her that, having secured Izzy's acquittal, he now had to sort out the problem with Ronnie Kray, and suggested that Sally and he didn't meet until it was safer. She had not demurred. Quite where that relationship was going he would have to sort out in due course.

He told the clerks that he needed a few days out of court to address the backlog of paperwork, which was true enough, but the real reason was Ronnie Kray and his List. He left the apartment only when absolutely necessary, when he was unable to persuade the local shopkeepers to deliver for him or when he had need of a book from Chambers, and in those cases he would disguise himself as well as possible with his raincoat and hat, and rush out and back as quickly as he could, constantly looking around for signs of danger. On the one occasion he had no choice but to go to court he arranged to travel with a colleague and had spent the entire time distractedly looking over his shoulder. The only reason he was out of the apartment on this occasion was because urgent completed work had to be taken back to Chambers before being posted to the solicitors.

'Yes, what's up?' asks Charles, handing over to Barbara the Instructions now bearing his endorsements.

Barbara takes the files offered by Charles, puts them on the desk without glancing at them, and collects some papers from the filing cabinet behind her. 'Would you mind coming with me, sir?' she asks.

Without waiting for an answer, she walks past him and leaves the clerks' room. This is unusual; Barbara rarely leaves the clerks' room at this, the busiest time of day. Charles follows Barbara as she runs lightly upstairs to the first floor, her skirts rustling and leaving an inviting wake of perfume. Barbara knocks on the door of the first room she comes to, that of another barrister, pushes the door open and tentatively puts her head into the room. Satisfied that it's empty, she flicks on the light and holds the door open for Charles.

Barbara closes the door behind Charles and turns to regard him steadily. 'You've been very difficult to contact over the last few days.' It's a statement, but her intelligent blue eyes seek an explanation.

Charles nods. He is reluctant to lie to Barbara. Leaving aside the fact that his career depends on her continued support and goodwill, he likes her efficiency, her quick brain, and her complete unflappability. But he cannot tell her the truth.

'I know. I'm sorry. My personal life has become a little … complicated.'

Barbara waits to see if anything further will be forthcoming but Charles looks down at the carpet and it's clear that she will get no greater explanation.

'In that case, do you want me to give these away?' and

she holds out several pristine sets of instructions tied in pink ribbon.

'What are they?' asks Charles.

'Three sets of new instructions, all murders. Only one has a silk in place, and the implication from the Instructions in the other two is that you can either recommend a silk to lead you or do the cases solo. Everyone in the Temple is still talking about your success in the dock brief.'

'I hadn't realised.'

'Well, if you'd been in Chambers a bit more or perhaps picked up the phone, I would've told you. One of these is urgent as they want you to do the committal, and the solicitor's been on the phone every day for the last four days.'

Charles holds out his hand and Barbara passes the papers to him. He looks briefly at them. 'Wow,' he says. 'A prosecution. And a defence from Kingsley Napley.

'Indeed.'

Barbara watches Charles carefully as he puts the other papers on the desk behind him, unties the ribbon on the Kingsley Napley instructions and scans the list of enclosures on the first page.

'This could be your big break, sir. As long as you don't muck them up completely, you might even be applying for silk next year on the back of this surge.'

Charles looks up. 'Really?'

'Yes. But you need to focus. You can't go disappearing for days on end.'

'Understood.'

'And one other thing …' she hesitates, apparently

having difficulty finding exactly the right words to use. 'The influx of work has been the subject of some comment in Chambers. Naming no names, but one of the silks saw the briefs coming in and has already been onto the solicitors trying to persuade them that you're too inexperienced for this level of work.'

'What? Trying to get the case moved to him?' demands Charles, disbelieving.

'I don't think it was quite as blatant as that, but that was the implication.'

'I'm going to bloody report him!'

'No, sir, you're not. Firstly, I'm not going to tell you who it was –'

'I could hazard a guess –' interrupts Charles.

'And secondly, it was a lot of hot air. You know what it's like. There're a lot of insecure members of the Bar, and they're often jealous of others' success, especially young juniors coming up on the inside. But unless you start work on the papers now, you do risk losing them. And the bigger prize.'

Charles nods in agreement. 'Okay. I get it.'

'So, no more disappearing off the radar, okay? If you need a holiday – and I'd be the last to stop you taking one – book time out of the diary for over Christmas or perhaps just into the New Year. Get some conferences with these new clients under your belt, and we'll try to fix the trial dates according to your availability.'

Charles had intended returning directly to the flat, but instead goes to his room and starts work on the three new briefs. Now out of his self-imposed confinement he finds he is able to concentrate better and fret less. Nonetheless, he decides not to remain in Chambers too late and so, at just before seven, with the Temple still quite busy, he clears his desk, replaces his coat and hat and descends the stairs. Clive, the junior clerk, is locking the huge outer oak door to the clerks' room and sees Charles.

'Oh, 'allo, sir. I didn't know you was in. I got something for you.' The young man holds out a slightly crumpled piece of paper. 'Sorry. I was gonna post it through the door over the road earlier, but it was so busy I never got the chance.'

Charles unfurls the paper. It's a note of a telephone call, recorded as having arrived at quarter past six that evening. *'Meet me after work tonight? Been making enquiries and I've got an idea. 7:30 at New Fresh Wharf. I'll be on the General Grant towing up from Greenwich.'*

'Did you take the call?' asks Charles, suspicious. The last time he had received a note of a telephone call left with the clerks, it had ended up with a knife fight in a telephone box.

'Yeah.'

'What did he sound like?'

Clive shrugs, and glances at his watch, clearly anxious to be away. 'Young I guess? Local – I mean 'e sounded like me. Cockney, like.'

'But he didn't give a name?' persists Charles, suspicious.

'Well, yeah, 'e did, but I thought it was a joke, so I didn't write it down. Now, what was it? Some wizard or other ...'

'Merlin?'

'Yeah, that's it. Merlin. Sorry, sir, but I'm going to miss me train.'

'No, that's okay. You get off. Thanks.'

Clive turns and runs off, leaving the front door banging. Charles reads the note again. The detail contained in it – the reference to New Fresh Wharf and the name of the tug – are reassuring. Charles looks at his watch. It's a thirty-five-minute walk or a twenty minute jog from Chambers to New Fresh Wharf, just past London Bridge; it is one of Charles's favourite training routes and he knows it well. But if he's going on Merlin's oily old tug he doesn't want to do it in his suit, and he doubts he has time to return to the apartment, change, and then run to London Bridge in sufficient time. There's no way he can rely on getting a taxi without a prolonged wait at this time of the evening. He reaches a decision and runs back upstairs to his room. He deposits the newly-acquired briefs on his desk and removes his coat and jacket, followed by his waistcoat and tie. He then re-dresses with his raincoat over his shirt sleeves. He is now free to move more easily. He looks down, but there is nothing he can do about his striped barrister's trousers and black polished shoes. He hangs the removed clothing carefully over the back of his chair. He considers his hat, still on his desk. He wants to wear it for the purposes of disguise but it will almost certainly blow off if he runs. Undecided and under pressure of time, Charles picks it up, locks the doors again and goes back downstairs.

He puts the hat on his head and peers out of the doors onto Crown Office Row looking for any signs of danger.

It seems clear: a few barristers and clerks walking swiftly towards their trains or buses, but no one hanging about. Charles pulls up his collar and joins them, walking towards Middle Temple Lane and then turning left to emerge on the Embankment. He crosses the road, preferring as always to get as close to the water as possible, takes off his hat again, and starts running eastwards towards the City.

It is now completely dark and Charles feels the first drops of rain against his face as he runs. Leather-soled shoes are not ideal for running, particularly on damp pavements, and he slows to make sure he keeps his footing. Buses occasionally pass him travelling towards Westminster, the light from their windows creating a series of fast-moving yellow rhomboids on the pavement, each illuminating Charles briefly as if he were on a roll of film. He sees one or two passengers turn to look at the odd sight of a barrister jogging in a raincoat and clutching a hat in his hand along the Embankment in the dark.

By the time Charles reaches London Bridge the shower has stopped, and it is seven twenty. He turns right off Lower Thames Street and runs lightly down the steps beside Adelaide House towards the river and away from the sound of traffic. Reaching the bottom, he pauses to get his breath back, wisps of steam rising from his warm, damp clothing into the cool night air. Charles hasn't been down on the wharf for over twenty years and had forgotten just how large it is. Stretching westward as far as his eyes can penetrate the gloom are piles of crates, barrels and boxes, huge coils of rope thick as his arm, vans and lorries parked for the night facing out over the water and, towering above all, half a dozen travelling cranes reaching a hundred feet into the air, water dripping off their steel skeletons. Taking care to avoid slipping on the tracks set in the concrete, Charles follows the line of the cranes along the waterfront, letting the sounds of the river wash over him: water lapping, steel cables clanking against superstructure, the whip of a pennant against a mast and the mournful far-off hoots of ships' horns. A cargo ship moored at the wharf rocks gently on the high tide, surrounded by its acolytes of lighters, but both it and the wharf itself are dark and deserted. As he passes the cargo ship the scent of fruit reaches Charles's nose. Pineapple, he thinks, his stomach suddenly rumbling.

Charles continues walking westwards, passing a couple of steamers, and looks for a vantage point from which to see the *General Grant's* approach. The wind is picking up again as another squall approaches, and small waves now wash over the wharf edge. Rain starts to fall again and Charles jams his hat firmly on his head. He sees a bright red telephone box outside the new warehouse and takes shelter inside. He feels for his cigarettes only to remember with disappointment that he has left them in his jacket pocket, hanging over the back of his desk chair.

'Bugger,' he curses softly to himself, and he leans his back against the wall of the cubicle to wait.

chapter 25

By eight-fifteen the *General Grant* is still nowhere to be seen, and Charles is wondering if he has missed it. On the other hand, Merlin may simply have been delayed. A dozen or more vessels have passed Charles, tugs both with and without barges in tow, steamers and, heading for the upper reaches of the Thames, flat-irons with their hinged funnels which can be lowered to permit them to pass beneath the low bridges further upstream.

By the time Charles had spent ten minutes inside the telephone box its windows have steamed up, and he has no choice but to abandon it if he wants to continue to keep a lookout. He paces up and down the edge of the wharf trying to keep warm, straining his eyes downstream into what is almost complete blackness, looking for lights. His stomach grumbles with hunger. Finally, he sees a light approaching. At first Charles concludes that wherever the vessel is bound it's not for the wharf where he stands, as the ship is too far out towards the north bank of the river, but it suddenly corrects its course and heads towards him. He hears the familiar chug-chug of the diesel engine of the reliable old tug inherited by Merlin from his late father. As the tug approaches the wharf, Charles recognises its familiar outline and he waves. The masthead light flashes off and on quickly in response. Charles frowns as the tug fails to slow when he expects and he wonders why Merlin's in such a hurry. Only then does he realise that the *General Grant* is towing a barge, on a line that looks a bit too short to Charles's eye.

The engine pitch changes as it is slipped out of gear, but too late. The tug is still moving fast towards the wharf side and just when Charles fears a collision it is belatedly thrown into reverse gear. Although Merlin brings her round in time, her port bow strikes the wharf side with quite a thump, and the prow of the barge bumps the stern of the tug.

'Throw us a line, you idiot!' shouts Charles genially at the silhouette of the man descending from the wheelhouse. The man turns. It's not Merlin. This is a huge man, well over six foot at Charles's guess, and shaped like a rugby ball, wider at his waist than anywhere else. He has a shock of straight dark hair sticking up almost vertically from his forehead and a widow's peak. He wears a heavy overcoat over a voluminous suit, and a tie which stops at the third button of a white shirt straining to cover an enormous midriff. In his hand is a revolver, which is pointing directly at Charles's head. Charles knows who this is: "Big Pat" Connolly, eighteen stones of mean Glaswegian, and one of the Krays' trusted enforcers.

'Get on,' orders Connolly.

For a split-second Charles wonders if he could duck and run. He's never met Connolly but he knows the Scotsman by reputation and at that moment Charles is struggling to remember if the reputation extends to the use of a handgun. But Charles is standing in twenty yards of open space and he concludes that, even allowing for the poor light on the wharf, his chances are poor; even a bad marksman would have time for two or three shots before Charles made it safely behind the nearest pile of packing crates. And then there's Merlin: Charles doesn't believe the lighterman would have betrayed him or that he would have voluntarily handed over his beloved tug to the Krays. So there is a chance he's aboard somewhere, and needs help.

Another man steps from behind the wheelhouse, also in a dark overcoat. He's almost a foot shorter than Big Pat but still solidly built. Charles knows who this is too: Ronnie Kray.

'Come on, Horowitz, don't keep us waiting,' he calls. 'I'd rather Pat didn't shoot you where you stand, but if you leave me no choice, that's what's going to happen.'

The tug has begun to drift back out into the stream. Charles reaches a decision, takes a deep breath and runs, leaping over the widening gap and landing on his hands and knees on the deck. Before he can stand up, Ronnie aims a kick at his face. The blow lands on Charles's forehead and skids off and although he's not badly hurt, Charles is thrown by the force onto the floor, his back against the wheelhouse.

'Stay there,' orders Ronnie. Connolly moves to stand in front of Charles, the gun pointed at Charles's chest. Ronnie looks up into the lit wheelhouse. 'Okay, let's go,' he calls to whoever is piloting the vessel.

'What direction?' comes a reply. Not Izzy.

'How the fuck do I know?' says Ronnie. 'Just keep going the way we were.'

Charles hears a series of clunks, grating noises and curses as the pilot struggles to engage gear. The tug lurches forward, slows, and then moves off again, the wheel dragged violently to starboard. The two men standing in front of Charles each grab hold of something to keep their footing, but the gun remains pointing at Charles throughout.

'I could drive this fucking thing better than this,' shouts Ronnie to the wheelhouse.

'Sorry!' comes a call from above as the tug picks up speed.

'I thought you said you knew what you were doing,' Ronnie says furiously.

'I thought I did, but it's not the same as what I'm used to.'

Charles hears a faint whistle carried to him on the wind. To anyone who had never worked on the River it would have sounded just like a bird call, but Charles recognises it immediately. Every firm of lightermen has its own distinctive call. Such calls have been in use for centuries and, according to Union Jack, probably were modelled originally on bird calls. With up to a score of lighters, barges and tugs all bustling about unloading a single cargo ship or working a specific wharf in the Port of London, and large expanses of water across which to communicate, such distinctive calls are essential for lightermen trying to work together. To the untrained ear the whistles used by different groups of lightermen could sound almost identical, and it took

Charles some weeks of listening and practice to be able to recognise and reproduce the call employed by uncle Jonjo, Jacob and Merlin. Once learned however, they are never forgotten.

The call is repeated, and this time Charles can place its origin: Merlin is somewhere behind him, presumably locked on the barge being towed by the *General Grant*.

A stronger gust of wind catches the brim of Charles's hat and his arm shoots out in an attempt to catch it, but it flies overboard.

'I wouldn't worry about it,' says Ronnie. 'You ain't gonna need it.'

'So, you're just going to shoot me, are you?' asks Charles focusing on the man standing before him.

'You've got it coming, Charlie Horowitz, or whatever you call yourself now. You've caused me no end of trouble.'

As if to prove it, at that very moment the tug dips into a wave and sends an arc of water over the prow directly onto Ronnie, drenching his expensive overcoat and spreading a pool of water over the deck which he is too slow to avoid and which floods over his shoes.

'Fuck!' he exclaims, dancing and splashing out of the way too late. 'First there was Robeson,' he continues. 'D'you have any idea how long it took us to set him up? Twelve years' work thrown away! And then Terry – that cost me the best part of a monkey for quack's fees and getting him out the country – and he's still snorting like a rhinoceros.'

'Terry?' asks Charles.

'The bloke whose nose you broke outside the Bailey.'

'Oh, I broke it, did I? Good.'

A shout comes from the wheelhouse above them. 'Do you want me to pull in somewhere?'

'Anywhere quiet.'

'It's all wharves and warehouses along here, Ronnie.'

'Then keep going till you find somewhere quiet, you useless cunt!'

'I always knew you were a coward,' says Charles, shaking his head sadly.

'Say that again,' says Ronnie, unsure if he's heard correctly over the sound of the engine, the wind and the splashing prow. The water is getting choppier as the wind picks up again. For the last while Big Pat Connolly has been fighting back belches, and although Charles can't see the man's complexion in the half-light, the way his big moon-face distorts every now and then suggests that it won't be long before he's vomiting.

'I said I always knew you were a coward, and now you're about to prove it,' says Charles.

'And how d'you make that out?' challenges Ronnie, taking a step towards Charles threateningly.

'You were a coward when we sparred at the Rupert Browning, and you were a coward on that Wembley card. Charlie Simms always said you had no guts. Not like your brother. Now Reg, there's a man who commands real respect,' says Charles with as much disdain as he can command. 'He's worth two of you,' he spits.

With a growl Ronnie takes another step forward and aims a vicious kick at Charles's head. Charles covers up and the blow lands on his upper arm, but this time it hurts and he feels the whole arm down to his fingertips go dead. Nonetheless Charles looks up and smiles at his attacker.

'It's easy, isn't it Ronnie, when you've got Big Pat standing there pointing a gun at me. But you haven't got the balls to do it man-to-man.' Charles shrugs. 'Like I said: a coward.'

'Shall I do 'im now, Ronnie?' asks the huge Glaswegian, aiming carefully at Charles's forehead, but unable to prevent his gun arm swaying with the movement of the tug.

'Fucking coward is it? Fucking coward? Stand up you cunt. Here –' Ronnie calls up to the man in the wheelhouse – 'put that light on over here!'

The engine note drops as the pilot looks for the for'ard searchlight. The foredeck is suddenly floodlit.

'Pat, back off a bit. Keep the gun on 'im, but don't shoot 'im till I tell you. I'm going to teach Mr Horowitz a lesson to take with 'im.'

Ronnie takes off his black-rimmed glasses, folds them closed carefully and slips them into the top pocket of his coat. Then he takes off the coat, followed by his suit jacket, and hands them one at a time to Pat, who takes them and folds them over his free arm. Ronnie takes off his tie and puts it in his trouser pocket, opens the top button of his shirt and rolls up his shirt sleeves. Still seated, Charles pulls off his raincoat, shoes and socks. He's going to have to move fast, and leather-soled shoes on a wet deck will hamper him.

'Stand up!' orders Ronnie, getting into his fighter's stance, fists held close to his face and left shoulder leading.

Charles stands slowly, assessing his surroundings. The foredeck is about three quarters of the size of a boxing ring, but it's cluttered. To Charles's right, at about three o'clock, is the bridge ladder and, only a yard or so behind is a coiled line. Further round, at about ten o'clock, is the capstan and the bitt. Charles realises that he's going to have to be very careful with his footwork, but he might nonetheless be able to make use of the obstacles. He could find them with his eyes closed, but once Ronnie is concentrating on boxing he'll be much less aware of them.

Charles tries to remember what he knew of Ronnie's fighting style. Pound for pound the odds are on Charles's side. The two men are of almost equal height but Charles is substantially heavier, and if he can get in a good punch he thinks he can knock Ronnie down. Charles is noted for fast footwork, especially for someone of his weight, but Ronnie's lighter build means he is probably quicker – or at least he was when he still trained regularly. Charles has no idea if that's still the case, but he doubts it; the gangsters enjoy a lifestyle of late club nights, good eating and heavy drinking. On the other hand, despite his taunts, Charles is aware of Ronnie's reputation as a "game" fighter, a slugger who would keep going despite heavy punishment, especially when watched by Reggie. He never could face the shame of not being equal to his brother, and it's this vulnerability on which Charles has gambled to provoke him. So, once he gets inside Charles's guard, Ronnie could be dangerous and Charles will need to keep out of range.

Charles drops into his fighting stance. He bends his

knees, absorbing the pitch and roll of the tug. He notes that Ronnie is less able to predict the ship's movements and is having greater difficulty keeping his balance. Another advantage. Charles shuffles forward and backwards, keeping his head moving, his bare feet on the deck feeling secure.

Charles launches a step jab off his lead foot but the roll of the tug takes Ronnie almost out of reach and the jab merely touches Ronnie's cheek. Ronnie launches an immediate flurry of blows, a jab and cross double followed by an attempted left hook. Charles covers up, sways back to avoid the hook and moves straight back in to land a forty-five-degree jab, rolling his hips at the same time to generate more power. It's a good shot and it connects squarely with Ronnie's jaw. Ronnie is surprised and hurt, and forced into attempting a clinch, but Charles pulls away out of reach. He keeps Ronnie at arm's reach with flicker jabs, waiting for the next roll of the tug. When it comes he attempts a step-through jab but he's too straight on and makes an easy target. Ronnie powers an uppercut through his guard and onto Charles's chin. Charles's head rocks back and, before he can react, Ronnie's inside and thundering body blows into his abdomen, taking Charles's breath away. Charles wraps his arms round Ronnie, trying to lessen the space available to the gangster to work his arms but it barely makes a difference. Charles grips his fingers together behind Ronnie's back and squeezes hard in a bear hug. He's so close he can smell the aftershave on Ronnie's smooth cheek and the Brylcreem on his wet hair. Charles then lifts and heaves, spinning clockwise on his right heel and forcing Ronnie into a collision with the bridge ladder. Ronnie's left knee strikes one of the lower rungs and as he tries to keep his balance he stops punching Charles, and Charles is able to back off, his guard raised once more.

Charles forces himself to keep his footwork going, backwards and forwards and side to side, trying not to display any weakness, but the blows from Ronnie have hurt him and sapped his strength.

Ronnie comes forward again and Charles dances further backwards to gain himself a few seconds' further respite. Ronnie's next attack is a lightning power jab from the back foot followed immediately by an uppercut. The jab gets partially through Charles's guard and strikes Charles's forehead, but most of the power has been taken off it on the way through. Charles immediately sways to his left just in time to feel Ronnie's forearm brushing his face as the uppercut misses him by quarter of an inch. Charles steps inside and with a grunt connects with a right-handed body jab, giving it as much power as he can muster. The breath whooshes out of Ronnie's lungs and as his chin drops slightly Charles sways back and hits him with a perfect left-handed uppercut, catching the corner of his chin. Ronnie staggers back, trying at the same time to move sideways and avoid the right-handed punch which he knows is coming, but his left foot slips at the same moment as the tug rolls slightly to starboard. All of a sudden Ronnie is sitting on his backside, looking surprised. Before he can clamber to his feet, Charles straightens up, takes two quick steps forward, plants his left foot solidly and swings his right foot hard at Ronnie's exposed head. He imagines Ronnie's chin to be a rugby ball and kicks through it as he was taught at university. His ankle connects solidly under Ronnie's chin, and the blow snaps the gangster's jaws shut with such a "Clack!" that the sound would have been heard on both banks of the river. Ronnie falls spread-eagled onto his back, his suit trousers and shirt soaked through. His eyes are open but he's only semi-conscious.

There is a sudden crack from the pistol behind Charles and he freezes for a millisecond, expecting immediate pain, but none comes. He leaps over Ronnie and grabs the line coiled by the capstan behind the fallen gangster, looping it round his neck and pulling hard. Ronnie writhes and kicks and his fingers scrabble at the rope, but Charles pulls with all his might, closing Ronnie's windpipe. Charles looks up at Connolly. Connolly's gun arm is outstretched, supported by his other hand, and he's within an instant of pulling the trigger again, but now Charles is kneeling behind Ronnie and the big Scotsman no longer has a clear shot. He hesitates. With the movement of the tug making his arm sway and only half of Charles's body for a target, he can't be sure what he'll hit.

'Put it down, or your boss is a dead man!'

Connolly doesn't obey, but he does lower the gun fractionally.

'Throw it down!' screams Charles, pulling tighter still.

Ronnie's face is going purple and his eyes look as if they are popping out of his skull. His clawing fingers and frantic leg movements are becoming weaker. Connolly drops the revolver carefully by his feet.

Charles looks up sharply, trying to gauge from the almost black riverbanks where they have reached. They are coming up on Hammersmith Bridge. He searches his memory for a trick he and all the other apprentices used to do on sunny afternoons during the war. It might just work, but not if the tug goes through the centre arches. He spins round to look at the silhouette of the looming bridge and then turns back to Connolly.

'For God's sake not through the centre arches!' screams Charles, eyes wide with simulated fear.

'What?' mumbles Connolly, confused.

'Haven't you heard of the sandbanks? For God's sake man, we'll run aground and all drown!'

A head appears out of the wheelhouse and Charles sees the pilot for the first time – a young man, little more than a teenager, with a thin face and wild eyes. 'What's he saying?' he demands of Connolly.

Connolly shrugs, and gestures at the bridge, only sixty feet away.

'Sandbanks or something in the centre arches.'

Charles shouts to the young pilot. 'Steer to the right for God's sake! Go through the lowest arch!'

The boy's head disappears back inside the wheelhouse and the tug lists suddenly to port as he spins the wheel too violently to starboard. Charles watches as Connolly's revolver slides several feet across the foredeck towards the gunwale, where it stops. At the very same moment as

Connolly steps across to retrieve the gun, the tug enters the lowest arch of Hammersmith Bridge. Charles drops Ronnie's torso, stands, turns, and runs the six feet towards the tug's prow. With his first leap his left foot is up on the gunwale and with all the strength in his powerful legs he launches himself into the night sky, arms reaching upwards towards the underside of the bridge. He makes good contact, grips the steel girder, and the tug continues in its angled journey through the arch. Charles lifts his legs to let the wheelhouse pass beneath him and waits for the barge. By the time Connolly has retrieved the gun the tug is already emerging from the other side of the bridge. Connolly looks at the foredeck, puzzled at Charles's absence, and then spins round but everything behind the wheelhouse is pitch black. Charles waits another second and then drops onto the flat roof of the barge behind its tarpaulin-covered load.

He remains still for a few seconds, listening intently. Ahead of him from the deck of the tug come shouted orders and Charles hears the engine note drop, but behind him he hears, much louder than before, Merlin's whistle. Charles crawls to the hatch and slides it open, dropping down into the hold. There is only one place Merlin could be confined: in the tiny cabin at the back, and as Charles picks himself up he hears thumping on timber.

'Izzy?' calls Charles.

'Charlie?' comes Merlin's muffled voice. 'Is that you? I thought I heard a gunshot.'

'He missed. Keep talking and I'll follow your voice.'

It is so dark at the bottom of the barge that Charles can't

even see his hands in front of his face. He moves forward cautiously, his arms outstretched in front of him, lifting his bare feet carefully so as not to trip on any invisible obstacles. His hand encounters the wooden cabin door and, by feel, he identifies a plank of wood propped at an angle jamming the door shut. He lifts it out of the way and pulls the door open to find Merlin, a lit match in his hand, almost burned down to his fingertips. The two men embrace, and the match burns out.

'How'd you get away?' asks Merlin.

'Remember that trick we did when we were kids, hanging off the underside of the bridge? Come on, let's get out of here. We're going to have to swim, but we're close to the bank.'

'Fuck that!' replies Merlin, pushing past Charles. 'I'm not leaving them with my tug. It's everything, my entire livelihood.'

'There's three of them,' says Charles, but Merlin is already about to pull himself out of the hatch. 'And they've got at least one gun!' he calls, in vain. Merlin's feet disappear through the slightly lighter rectangle of darkness and Charles can hear him crawling above his head on the deck.

'Shit!' swears Charles to himself, but he follows.

He joins Merlin crouched behind the load.

'Listen!' says Merlin.

Charles strains his ears. 'The engine's been cut.'

'Yes. We're drifting with the tide. Can you see where we are?'

Charles looks to port but can't see well enough to recognise any landmarks. He points to starboard. 'Isn't that The Old Ship?'

Merlin peers in the direction of Charles's pointed arm. They're approaching a brightly lit pub on the north bank of the river from which can be heard the faint sounds of music. 'Yes, I think you're right. Which means ...'

Merlin leans out slightly from behind the packing cases and looks for'ard. He can see the outline of Big Pat Connolly, backlit by the yellow light from the wheelhouse, standing at the stern of the *General Grant*, peering into the dark. The big Glaswegian appears to be facing the lighter and the revolver can be seen in his right hand, hanging loosely by his side. The young pilot has left the wheelhouse and is standing over Ronnie Kray, who sits on the bottom step of the wheelhouse ladder. The boy is examining Ronnie's neck.

'Those fucking idiots – there's no one at the wheel! Look – we're going to run aground on Chiswick Eyot! She'll beach and capsize!'

As the lighter slides past the pub on the northern shore, Charles peers out from behind his side of the packing crates. Ahead of them, less than fifty yards away, is a low dark island covered in trees. The tug is drifting on the fast tide with the wind behind it and the eyot is approaching fast, four points off the starboard bow.

Merlin half-stands but Charles hauls him back down by the sleeve. 'What d'you think you're doing?'

'I'm gonna rush them and try to get her under power

again. The barge is on a short line, only five or six feet; I can jump the gap.'

'That's suicide. You'll never make it to the tug: you'll be dead before you even get off the lighter!'

'But I've got to do something!' hisses Merlin, wrenching his arm free of Charles's grip.

'Wait a sec – let me think!'

Merlin stops and Charles makes some rapid calculations. Kray and his colleagues had not found the light that would have illuminated the stern of the tug and so everything abaft the wheelhouse, including the lighter, remains in complete darkness. They might just be able to take them by surprise if they're quick enough.

'Have you got anything we can use as a weapon?' asks Charles. 'What's under here?' he whispers, lifting up the corner of the tarpaulin.'

'Nothing; just empty packing cases. And the sweep.'

The sweep is an eighteen-foot long oar or paddle used by lighterman to steer the unpowered lighters on the tide and, when occasion demands, to paddle. Using them is extremely hard work and with every lighterage firm having at least one tug, they are now used relatively rarely.

Charles feels underneath the tarpaulin and his hand encounters the blade. He slides it out behind him quietly.

'It's going to be fucking heavy,' says Charles. 'Do you think you can swing it?'

'I don't know. You were always stronger than me.'

'Yeah, but you still work the River every day; I'm just a desk jockey. Okay, let's give it a go. You go down the starboard side and try to distract them; I'll need the port side to give me enough room to swing. But we've got sixty feet to cover.'

Charles hefts the sweep, passing it through his hands until it is balanced, and then readjusts it, moving as much of its length ahead of him as is possible to lift.

'Ready?' asks Charles.

'Yes.'

'Good luck.'

The cousins creep out from their opposite sides of the crates. The three men ahead of them in the light are completely unaware that the tug is only a couple of seconds from running aground. Charles and Merlin manage to get half the way to the tug's stern before being seen.

Then: 'Hey, boss!' calls Connolly, half-turning towards the wheelhouse. 'They're here!'

Time slows almost to a halt over the next few seconds, as everything happens at once. With an inarticulate war-cry, Merlin sets off at a sprint, covering the remaining distance and leaping into the air to clear the six feet of black water between the prow of the lighter and the stern of the tug. Charles too runs the last few feet, raising the sweep to his right shoulder as he moves. One pace short of the prow, Charles plants his left foot like a hammer thrower and pivots around it, extending his arms and swinging the sweep in a horizontal anticlockwise arc towards Connolly's head. At precisely the same moment Connolly turns and raises his gun arm towards Merlin who is, simultaneously, in the air between the two vessels. The wooden pole thrums in Charles's hands like the wings of an enormous insect as it sweeps round. Then, with a satisfying "thud" and a violent jarring of the timber which sends a juddering vibration all the way up to Charles's shoulders, the blade cracks heavily against Connolly's skull. A split-second later, and the gun fires.

Charles completes his three-hundred-and-sixty-degree spin just in time to see Connolly's corpulent body entering the water, coat-tails flailing, and the glint of the revolver leaving his hand and describing a separate arc before it too disappears beneath the surface.

Charles's elation lasts less than a heartbeat as the *General Grant* beaches on the eyot and immediately lists precipitously to port. He watches as the deck turns into a forty-five-degree slope. His eyes frantically sweep across the tug seeking Merlin but he can see only the white shirt-clad Kray twin and the thin-faced youth, both tumbling and rolling across the wet deck towards the water. Then, for a split second, he spots Merlin's muscled forearms hanging off the stern gunwale of the *General Grant*, up to his neck in turbulent water. And then Charles knows, with complete and prescient clarity, exactly what's about to happen, and he is utterly powerless to prevent it.

'Izzy!' he screams, as the momentum of the lighter carries it inexorably into collision with the stern of the beached tug. Merlin is lost to Charles's sight and there is a horrific crunching sound. The lighter rebounds slowly. Charles watches, open mouthed, as Merlin's hands release the gunwale and sink beneath the waves.

'No!' cries Charles.

He jumps feet-first into the water and swims to the point where he last saw the lighterman. He dives blindly, repeatedly, frantically, feeling in the black water for his cousin. He doesn't know how long he searches, ten minutes, twenty perhaps, and he doesn't know how he ends up lying on his back in the mud, gasping for breath and sobbing. He has no idea what has happened to Ronnie Kray, Big Pat Connolly or the pilot, and he doesn't care. He stares unseeing at the clouds scudding above him and the patches of starry night sky between them, oblivious to the cold creeping stealthily into his bones and into his heart.

chapter 26

Charles stands by the graveside, shoulder to shoulder
with his brother. On Charles's other side is his father,
Harry Horowitz and Raynor Conway, Izzy's younger
brother. Opposite, amongst the women, is his mother,
Millie, holding the hand of her sister-in-law, Aunt Bea.
On the other side of Aunt Bea is David's wife, Sonia. It
has taken Beatrice nearly twenty minutes to get from the
Memorial Chapel in the cemetery to the graveside. She
had abandoned her wheelchair and insisted that she would
walk, but her breathing difficulties had required her to stop
every few steps. By the time she reached the open grave,
all the other mourners had been waiting for some time and
were beginning to get cold.

It hasn't rained for a couple of days but the area around
the graveside is still sodden, and Charles looks at the shoes
of the mourners opposite him, all caked with muddy clay,
picked up from the recently refilled graves on either side
of Izzy's. Charles's mind wanders as the rabbi intones the
ancient prayers in Hebrew. Wonderful things had been
said about Izzy during the funeral service, by the rabbi who
knew him slightly and by several of the mourners who knew
him better. All had particular anecdotes to relate concerning

Izzy's mischievous sense of humour; his acts of kindness to all who needed him; his attractiveness to women; and, of course, his steadfast support of his ailing mother. Charles had not spoken. He knew that the well-intentioned words did describe the man he knew – at least in some respects – but he was also acutely aware that Izzy had led a half-life, of which most of those around the grave were completely ignorant. Charles cannot help feeling that he is taking part in a charade, ironically, just as Izzy had done all of his adult life.

Charles becomes aware that his mother is staring intently at him, and he smiles sympathetically at her over the open grave. She continues to gaze at him without smiling and, after a moment, looks down. *What have I done this time?* wonders Charles. Charles considers his mother's grey hair, fluttering free from under her scarf, and the ever-deepening lines around her eyes and on her forehead. *She looks old*, thinks Charles. *I wonder how long it will be before I'm burying her?* Then he corrects himself: *How long it will be before she's burying* me?

'You never came to see *me*,' chides Henrietta's voice, close to Charles's right ear.

Your family wouldn't let me come to the funeral, he answers silently.

'But you never came to see me,' she insists.

Are we going to have a row about this, now? asks Charles. *Really?*

For once Henrietta does not answer back.

The service by the grave is short. A small clean trowel

is handed around the menfolk, and each stoops in turn to lift a small quantity of soil from the fresh pile heaped at the graveside to drop it onto the coffin. Clods of damp earth and stone strike the coffin lid, and as always Charles wonders if they might wake the occupant. With every "thud-rattle" Beatrice utters a quiet moan, each one signifying the deepening and irreparable tear in her heart. She was, of course, delighted to see Raynor who returned from Canada for the first time in years to attend the funeral, but everybody knows it: Izzy was her favourite, her friend and her carer. In any case Raynor will soon depart to return to his business, his wife, and his two children in Toronto, and then Beatrice will be alone.

When all the men have dropped their trowels-full of soil the mourners line up again for the recitation of *Kaddish*, the ancient Aramaic prayer for the dead.

'*Yis-gadal, v'yis-kadash, sh'may raboh,*' – Exalted and hallowed be His great Name – say Raynor and Beatrice, the principal mourners, and all present, including Charles, answer with "*Amen*". Charles finds himself reciting all the responses along with everyone else, despite the fact that he tells himself he believes in none of it. Nonetheless, there is power in these words – the ghosts of a dead language spoken so many thousands of years before – a sort of irresistible magic that sweeps him along despite himself, and to his complete surprise and embarrassment, he feels tears leaking from his eyes and his breath catching deep in his chest. Charles, who usually has an iron control over his emotions, has cried only once since Henrietta was murdered. Millie and Beatrice look over at him. Beatrice's expression is one of sympathy and shared grief; Millie's expression is more impenetrable.

The prayer reaches its end, as always, with a plea for the God who makes peace in his heavens to make peace for all the world – albeit with a special mention for Israel – and the congregation says "*Amen.*"

Charles is still trying to stifle his sobs when a tissue appears in front of his face, offered by David. Charles takes it and wipes away his embarrassment.

The rabbi shakes hands with members of the close family and those of his congregation whom he knows well from his Sabbath services, and the mourners begin to move in twos and threes back up the muddy path where they will wash their hands at the tap outside the Memorial Chapel, in accordance with Jewish custom.

Charles takes a few steps away from the graveside to compose himself. After a moment he feels a solicitous hand on his back.

'You okay?' asks David, one hand holding the yarmulke on his head to prevent it being dislodged by the light breeze.

Charles nods. 'I didn't think I'd get so upset. It took me by surprise.'

'What do you expect, Charles?' replies David, sympathetically. 'You and Izzy were once very close. And then, as fate would have it, you reconnect with him in order to save his life —'

'Only for him to lose it weeks later. I let him down.'

'That's not what the police say. Nor the way you tell it.'

The story Charles had given to the police, the coroner and to anyone who asked was that there had been a problem with the rudder of the *General Grant* which Izzy had been trying to fix when both tug and lighter were blown onto the eyot. The tug had seen many years of service and had been known to develop such faults before. Furthermore, after the collision, its stern was badly damaged and the rudder had been destroyed, so no evidence was likely to be found to gainsay Charles's account. He hadn't mentioned the presence of Ronnie Kray or his associates. He assumes they must have got away – no other bodies had been found and there'd been nothing in the press – but he has heard nothing from that quarter in the interim.

'That's not what I mean. Forget it.'

David's penetrating blue eyes regard Charles carefully for a moment. Then, perceptive as ever, he asks: 'Heard anything from Henrietta of late?'

Charles smiles. 'Yes, actually, just now. She sends her regards.'

'Now, why doesn't that surprise me?' replies David.

'What, her sending her regards?'

'You know precisely what I mean, Charles. Has it occurred to you that your loss of control just now might have something to do with Henrietta?'

Charles shakes his head, eyes closed, while at the same time answering reluctantly 'Yes, of course it has.'

'Well,' smiles David, 'that's a start, then. Come on.'

They turn together to walk back up the path, but soon catch up with Beatrice, who is struggling, a young woman at each of her elbows. In accordance with Jewish tradition, they both wish her long life.

'Davie, would you mind if I had a word with Charlie in private?' she asks.

'No, of course not. I'll see you in a moment,' he replies, and walks off.

'Thank you for your help, girls, but Charlie can take over from here.'

'Are you sure, Aunty Bea?' asks one, glancing at Charles from under her eyelashes and finding in his dark good looks a reason to stay.

'Perfectly, thank you. You run along.'

The two young women move off, leaving Charles supporting his aunt by one elbow. She doesn't move for a moment but allows the others to get out of earshot. When she speaks, she stares into the distance.

'He loved you, you know?'

'I loved him too,' Charles answers, feeling his throat tighten again.

'I know you did. But not in the same way.' Charles glances sharply at his aunt; so she knew all along. He nods slowly to himself, but remains silent. 'It took him a long time to get over it, when you lost touch,' Beatrice continues sadly.

'Don't, Aunt Bea,' pleads Charles. 'You've no idea how bad I feel about it now.'

'Don't feel bad, Charlie, love. Seeing you again and you

making up with him, even with the strain of his court case – you can't know how happy it made him.'

Despite Charles's best efforts, he finds his eyes leaking again, and he sobs. 'Really? I feel there was so much unsaid.'

'No, Charlie, not at all. He knew how much you loved him even if it couldn't be ... well ... in the way he hoped. In the few days he was home after the trial, I've never seen him so contented. At ease, you know? Lighter of heart, he was. And it wasn't just the trial.'

Charles bends and gives his aunt a hug, the sobs coming thick and fast now.

'There, there, Charlie, love. We'll both have to make do without him.'

•

Two weeks later, and Charles stands by a different grave in an altogether different cemetery. West Ham Jewish Cemetery where Izzy was interred is populated by a century of dead East End Jewry. Jewish tradition prohibits ornate headstones, grand sepulchres, statues and flowers. To mark the fact that someone has visited a grave, a small stone is picked up from the path or from the graveside, and left balanced on top of the simple gravestones, which are engraved only with their Stars of David and their brief lettering in Hebrew.

This cemetery however is very different. It is private, and Charles has had to seek express permission to enter. It lies behind the beautiful family chapel at Viscount Brandreth's country seat and is the final resting place of eight generations of that illustrious family, including the Viscount's eldest daughter, Henrietta. It backs onto open fields, and the traffic sounds in West Ham are here replaced by birdsong and the wind rustling the leaves of two enormous horse chestnut trees which hang over the well-maintained grass paths and colourful flowerbeds which decorate the graveyard.

Charles had half-expected his request to be refused, as it was when Henrietta was originally buried, but perhaps something had cracked or softened the lump of granite the Viscount called his heart because a handwritten letter had arrived in Chambers giving him permission to visit on the date sought. His erstwhile father-in-law informed him coldly that none of the family would be present, but the gate would be left unlocked for him. So too would the door to the chapel, presumably in case Charles were belatedly to see the error of his ways, decide to change teams and switch allegiance to the Viscount's God.

Charles has done more crying in the last few days than he can remember in any period of his adult life, and he has no tears for Henrietta or for himself this beautiful afternoon. But he has something to say, as he stands in front of the headstone marking his wife's grave.

'About time,' says Henrietta, still keen to get in the first blow even from the afterlife.

'Yes, I know. I'm sorry Etta; I let you down.'

'Yes, Charles,' says Henrietta by his elbow, sighing deeply. 'You did. But, to be fair, it wasn't all your fault.'

'I won't do it again.'

Silence.

'I said, I won't do it again.'

Still silence.

chapter 27

Charles and Sally sit in Charles's Jaguar outside the suburban house of his brother and sister-in-law. Sally takes Charles's huge hand and holds it in both of hers on Charles's thigh.

'Second thoughts?'

'About being with you – absolutely not. About introducing you to my parents – yes. Second, third and fourth thoughts.'

It is a month after Izzy's funeral and three weeks after Charles had made his peace with Henrietta. Or so he hopes. His late wife has not felt impelled to comment any further on Charles's conduct of his personal life, and so he assumes she approves – or perhaps doesn't disapprove sufficiently to continue haunting him. That hasn't prevented him talking to *her* whenever the mood takes him, but the sensation that she is there, listening, is fading.

On the previous Sunday, Charles had risen, showered and shaved carefully, donned his new sports jacket, and driven to Romford with the huge bouquet of flowers he had bought the previous day and which had taken up most of his bath overnight. There he laid siege to the Fisher household. He was told repeatedly, both by Mrs Fisher from the front door and by Sally from her bedroom window, to go away, but he had steadfastly ignored them, prompting some neighbours to point at him and laugh and others to consider calling the police. He loitered outside on the pavement for over three hours, sitting on their garden wall and reading *The Sunday Times*. Then it had started raining heavily. Charles would have remained where he was, but Mrs Fisher finally took pity on him and invited him in to dry off and have a cup of tea. Sally had remained in her room for another hour, but after Charles had told Mrs Fisher what he proposed saying to Sally, she let him go upstairs.

Sally reluctantly opened her door and he had sat on her bed for nearly two hours, trying to convince her that he wanted to be different and that, with her help, he could be. He told her about his conversations with Henrietta, and David's opinion that he had completely failed to deal with his grief following her murder. He told her he was belatedly beginning to realise that if you love someone you need to make time for them and let them in. He also told her that he was quite sure he was in love with her. Finally, Charles told her the entire story involving Ronnie Kray. She'd suspected that Ronnie was behind the attack in the phone box but she'd known nothing about the events which led to Izzy's death. Charles honestly admitted that, short of emigrating, he had no idea how he was going to get out of the fix he was in, but for some reason it was this last admission – the confession that he was vulnerable and scared – that finally persuaded Sally to give him a second chance.

Sally insisted that Charles agree to return to Snow Hill Police Station and push for an investigation into the attack on him outside the Old Bailey. She accepted that he couldn't tell the police how he had manufactured the evidence to secure Izzy's acquittal, or the circumstances of the events on the River, but the knife attack had been witnessed by third parties. Charles thought it was a waste of time; even if by some miracle the police were interested enough to try to identify the attacker, there was no evidence to link him with the Krays, and so the twins would still be on his back.

Nonetheless Charles telephoned Snow Hill Police Station on two occasions to make an appointment, and left messages for DC Miller or any of his colleagues involved in the investigation of the knife attack, asking for a call back. He heard nothing in response. He went to the police station twice, but on neither occasion was there anyone available on the team to speak to him. The message was clear: the police weren't interested in investigating further.

Charles and Sally had resumed their relationship and had seen one another every couple of days, twice going to the cinema – once with her friends and once with his – and walking, slightly ostentatiously, hand-in-hand during their lunch breaks in the Inner Temple Gardens. If any of Charles's colleagues disapproved, none said so.

Then Charles had at last accepted his parents' regular invitation to come for Friday night dinner; on condition that he could bring a guest. That appeared to be a step too far for Millie Horowitz, but David and Sonia had resolved the difficulty by inviting everyone to their home for "proper tea" on Sunday, a neat solution to the difficulties likely to be prompted by a Friday night Sabbath meal laden with a religious significance that would only exclude Sally, who so much needed and wanted to be included.

Charles flicks his eyes up from Sally's hands wrapped around his to the rear-view mirror. He checks around himself so frequently now that it's become almost unconscious. The suburban street is lined with stationary vehicles but empty of both moving traffic and pedestrians.

'So, how terrible can it be?' asks Sally. 'Even if they hate me, it's one tea, right?'

Charles shakes his head. 'You don't understand,' he explains quietly. 'David and Sonia would never hate you. It's not them, it's Mum and Dad … well … to be honest, it's Mum. Dad mostly agrees with anything she says for a quiet life.'

'I haven't been frightened of *my* Mum since I was twelve.'

'It's not fear of *her*, Sally.' He swivels in the leather seat and turns to her. 'I'm just exhausted by the battle. And I'm worried for my father. Look, I can't explain all of it but in really simple terms: I've been fighting a war with my mother since I was born. The battle ground shifts, but it's always the same war. I'm a terrible disappointment to her, and she can't hide it – she doesn't *want* to hide it. It's her not-very-subtle way of trying to make me be something … someone, different.'

'But you're a success. You started in the East End, on

the streets, and now you're a successful barrister.'

'I could be bloody Prime Minister; it'd make no difference. When I was little, it'd be because I didn't finish my greens, or spilled some paint or something. Usually I wouldn't even know what I'd done wrong; all of a sudden she'd no longer be my loving mother, but an iceberg. She'd act as if I was a stranger, and she could carry it on for days. Wind forward twenty years and I committed the ultimate offence, a rejection of her and everything about her: I married out. The punishment for *that* crime was a permanent withdrawing of love. Nothing less would do. They shut the door on me – literally shut the front door in my face – acted as if I was dead, sat *shiva*, said prayers for the dead, the whole thing. So I was out of it for a while. It was a relief, to be honest. I missed Davie a lot, and my Dad, but …' Charles shakes his head sadly. 'Then Henrietta was murdered …I went on the run, and a friend –'

'Rachel? Your girlfriend?'

'Yes, Rachel – though she wasn't a girlfriend at that time. But she got us back together.'

'Which is good, right?'

'Yes, sort of, but Mum's attitude hadn't changed. Then Dad had his heart problems. Which, of course, was my fault.'

'How does that work?' asks Sally, not entirely sure how seriously she should take the comment.

'It's not as bonkers as it sounds, actually. He's been the main casualty of this war. He's spent the last forty years trying to separate two of the people he loves the most, at first arbitrating, then trying to shame us into behaving and, now, just watching and hurting. In the year since his operation there's been an undeclared truce: we speak on the phone, but for the most part I stay away. According to David, Mum's finally laid off me, 'cos she's frightened it'll kill Dad.'

'What started this all off, Charlie?'

Charles shakes his head. 'I don't know. The way she was brought up, maybe? I think it was my job to make her happy, and I didn't. I couldn't. She's a disappointed woman. Not just in me, but in her marriage, her life. At least she felt secure in the East End. Out here in the suburbs she feels isolated. This innocuous little house of David and Sonia's –' Charles jerks his thumb towards the darkened semi-detached behind them – 'and me – we're the terrifying face of assimilation.'

'Hendon? The place is crammed with Jews,' Sally points out, looking quickly at Charles's expression to see if he's offended by the remark.

'I know.'

'And is that why she won't like me: 'cos I'm not Jewish?'

'Yes. And because we're not married.'

'But wouldn't it be worse if we were married?'

'Oh yes.'

'It'd be worse if we were married –'

'Yes.'

'– Or it's worse because we're not?'

'Yes.'

Charles explains: 'That's my mother in a nutshell. Ever hear the story about the Jewish mother who buys her son two ties, a red one and a green one?' Sally shakes her head. 'Well,' continues Charles, 'the first time the son sees her after his birthday, he thinks: "I'd better wear one of those new ties" and he chooses the red one. Then his mother opens the door to him, looks him up and down, and says: "So, what's wrong with the green tie?"'

Sally laughs.

'That's my mother,' continues Charles. 'Logic's not her strong suit. In fact, it'd be a positive disadvantage to her.'

They sit in silence. Charles looks at his watch. 'Come on,' he says, letting go of Sally's hand and opening the car door. He scans the street quickly before stepping out, but it's still deserted. 'Let's get this over with.'

Sally follows Charles out of the car and they walk together down the garden path. David and Sonia have been married for a year and this is their first home together. Unlike Charles, David married a "nice Jewish girl" and now lives within three miles of his parents' home. He'd not turned his back on his religion or his culture, nor committed the sin of anglicising his name. Having lived in Charles's shadow for the whole of his young life, he now unexpectedly finds himself the favoured son, a position he finds uncomfortable. As a boy he worshipped his tough, clever older brother and as an adult he respects him, despite his life choices. He hates being used by his mother as a goad to taunt Charles.

The door opens just as the visitors reach it and Sonia

and David stand on the threshold. Sonia holds out both her hands and takes both of Sally's.

'You must be Sally. It's so lovely to meet you,' she says with a broad and sincere smile, '*at last*,' she adds mischievously over Sally's shoulder at Charles.

God bless you, thinks Charles.

Sonia is not a beautiful woman by most people's reckoning but she's handsome, with a full figure and thick black lustrous hair, usually tied in a scarf. What draws men to her are her dark eyes, from which shine a wonderful infectious warmth. She grew up in a strictly orthodox home, and whereas the Horowitzes lived in the melting pot of London's East End for generations, until she met David she had encountered no one at all from outside her own Jewish community. Indeed, marrying David had caused waves of disapproval in *her* family.

Sonia is acutely aware of her mother-in-law's relationship with Charles and had seen with alarm how the catalyst of her marriage to David has exacerbated his problems. She understands very well why Charles remains at a distance. Although no one in the family speaks of it, she reads the newspapers and knows what Charles has been through, and in her charmingly simple way, she thinks he's due some happiness. For Sonia to live in sin with a non-Jew, worse, to marry one, would be totally alien; unthinkable. But if Sally makes Charles happy and is a good person, Sonia will make her as welcome as she can. From Sonia's straightforward standpoint, everyone is a good person until they prove conclusively to her that they are not.

She draws Sally into the hall. 'This is David,' she says, and David shakes Sally's hand.

Sally is astonished at the differences between the two brothers. David is slim and over six feet tall, with a broad brow, light grey-blue eyes and a shock of light brown hair. But then he smiles, and his eyes crinkle in just the way Charles's do; and when he speaks, his voice is just a lighter version of his older brother's.

'I'm pleased to meet you after all this time,' says David, looking over her head with light-hearted disapproval at Charles.

'Come into the lounge,' says Sonia. 'Mr and Mrs Horowitz aren't here yet,' she adds quietly.

•

Over an hour has passed at the Horowitzes but Millie and Harry, usually sticklers for punctuality, have still not arrived. Sonia supplies Charles and Sally with cups of tea and tries not to look repeatedly at the clock. The food laid out on the dining room table – smoked salmon, olives, pickled and salted herring, fried fish balls, baskets of bagels, Danish pastries, two large home-baked cheese-cakes – a real high tea, as Charles had commented admiringly – has been re-covered with its greaseproof paper. The brothers conspiratorially sneak occasional titbits from under the coverings when they think the women aren't watching. Charles starts to relax. It's obvious that David and Sonia like Sally – she and Sonia have been in fits of giggles more than once – and with a bit of luck his parents have either forgotten or, more likely, decided not to come.

When the doorbell finally sounds they are all startled. There's a moment of silence as they brace themselves. Then Sonia forces a smile and rises to open the door. David and Charles remain seated, Charles staring at the carpet. Sally stands, smooths her hair, paces nervously, and finally perches on the edge of her armchair behind the door. She clasps her hands together, marvelling that one old Jewish woman could cause such trepidation.

They hear voices in the hall and the lounge door opens. Millie Horowitz enters. She is in her early seventies, her permanently waved hair largely grey and her hearing beginning to fail, but her backbone is still ramrod straight and her head proudly erect. She is short and slim, simply and elegantly dressed in a floral cotton two-piece, a blue handbag over her arm and a matching velveteen hat with fine netting over the crown and side walls, a cluster of rhinestones forming a teardrop to one side. It's a striking confection and Charles knows, with certainty, that it's his mother's own work. He stands.

'Hello, Mum,' he says, and hugs her. She permits the gesture without quite taking part. 'How are you?' he asks solicitously.

'Hello, Charles. I'm getting by. And you?'

She appraises her elder son swiftly, her eyes, undimmed by sixty years of close millinery work, missing nothing.

'Very well, thank you,' answers Charles formally. 'Mum, I'd like you to meet my girlfriend, Sally.'

Millie turns to Sally and looks unexpectedly surprised.

Her brow furrows. Sally had politely risen from her chair when the older people had arrived. Now she too wears a peculiar expression.

'Mrs H?' she asked. 'Is it you?'

'I know you, don't I?' replies Millie.

'I'm Sally, Mrs H. Nell's girl, remember?'

'You two actually know one another?' asks David incredulously.

Sally laughs in relief and disbelief. 'Yes we do! A long time ago now, but still.'

She and Mrs Horowitz embrace with more warmth, notes Charles, than was demonstrated to him.

'You've grown into a fine girl, Sally. How's your mother?'

'Just a minute,' interrupts Charles. 'How the hell do you know each other?'

At that moment Harry enters, in conversation with Sonia. 'Harry,' said Mrs Horowitz, putting a hand on his arm, 'look who it is. It's little Sally.'

Harry Horowitz peers at Sally and a slow smile creeps across his face. 'Well, I'll be! *You're* Charles's Sally?'

Sally turns to Charles. 'My Mum was an outworker at your Mum's millinery shop, years ago,' she explains. 'I used to go with her on the bus to take her finished work down every Sunday morning.'

'She was such a good girl,' says Millie. 'She'd play with the buttons for hours. And pretty too, like a picture!'

'She's not changed,' said Harry approvingly. 'Still lovely.'

Millie looks at her for a while, nodding slowly in agreement. 'Is your mother still alive? And your sisters? All married now, I expect,' but she doesn't allow Sally to answer. 'So what about this tea, then?' she continues without pause. 'We've come half way across London and been here half an hour already, and no one's offered me so much as a cup of tea.'

Sonia smiles at the "halfway across London" but takes her cue and slips out to the kitchen.

Charles inclines his head to Sally's. 'You knew?'

'Of course not,' whispers Sally. 'I was six. She's was just this woman my Mum called "Mrs H".'

Millie takes Sally's arm. 'Help me sit down over there at the table,' says Millie, who has never had trouble walking or sitting in her life. This isn't acceptance by Millie, but it's a start. Sally half-turns towards Charles, and winks. Charles grins, looks at David, and shrugs lightly. David shakes his head ruefully at his older brother, but he knows that Charles will need time to decide how he feels – if he ever gets round to exploring it at all.

The telephone in the hall rings and David slips out to answer it. He returns a few seconds later with a puzzled frown on his face. He speaks softly to Charles so as not to disturb Millie and Sally's conversation.

'It's for you.'

'How can it be for me? I don't live here,' replies Charles, his confusion prompting him for once to state the obvious.

David shrugs, and gestures with his open palm towards the hall.

Charles steps out into the hall and walks to the telephone sitting on the small semi-circular walnut table near the front door. The receiver is lying on the glass which protects the table top, and Charles picks it up.

'Charles Holborne?'

'Who's speaking?'

'Don't you recognise my voice?'

And Charles does recognise the voice, and as he does so he holds his breath in anticipation of what's about to come. 'Ronnie Kray. What can I do for you?'

'It's not Ronnie, it's Reggie. Now you listen to me carefully, Mr Holborne. We've had a long chinwag, Ron and me, about what to do with you. I've been getting a bit pissed off about the amount of time, money and effort it's taking to put you in your place, and Ronnie and me have other business to attend to. So we've decided to take you off the List.' Charles's heart soars as he hears this. 'But there's a catch, see?'

Reggie pauses, and Charles hears papers being shuffled at the end of line.

'Here in front of me are two different versions of a hand-written interview by Chief Prevention Officer Vermeulen. I also have a statement from Mr Vermeulen, explaining how you threatened him to make him change his evidence. It's all signed and sworn and so on – I even got a solicitor in the Firm – you might know 'im – to draw it up and witness it. And I've got a piece of paper with your home phone number written on it, in your handwriting verified by an expert.'

As Reggie Kray continues the list of the evidence that

would destroy Charles's career and have him thrown into prison, Charles's ears burn and sweat appears on his forehead.

'Now, I ain't going do nothing with all of this for the mo. But you better understand this: we own you. You got Harry Robeson potted, which set back our business plans for a long time. Now I know you can't do the same job as he did. He was a bent solicitor, company fiddles, tax and all that, whereas you're a bent barrister, courts and judges and so on. But that still gives rise to some interesting opportunities for the Firm. So there'll come a time when we call in this debt. And if you want to stay off the List and out of prison, you'll do exactly as we say. Have I made myself clear?'

'Yes,' replies Charles softly.

'Louder, so's I can hear you.'

'Yes,' repeats Charles, more loudly.

'Good. You see Charlie, you give yourself these airs and graces, but I always knew you was as bent as the rest of us. And now you know it too. Enjoy your Sunday tea.'

The connection is broken, leaving Charles standing in the hallway, the telephone receiver to his ear. He slowly lowers it to its cradle, oblivious to the clink of tea cups and the chatter from the adjoining room.

Charles feels numb. Being on Ronnie's List would have meant constantly looking over his shoulder, but he could have dealt with that. *It would've required action, probably violence, but that's okay, I'm good at that; I can do cold, unemotional, decisiveness. That's what you'd say, Etta. But this...this* debt *hanging over me? Over my whole career, and forever?*

What shakes Charles to his core are Reggie's last words. Could that slimy thug really have put his grubby finger on the doubt lurking in Charles's soul? How can Charles remain the honourable barrister, the man of integrity, from inside the Krays' silk-lined pockets?

I've lost everything, haven't I? Everything I've ever worked for.

'Who am I, Etta?' he whispers to his late wife. 'What am I going to do?' he pleads.

Silence.

If you enjoyed *The Lighterman* and would like to
keep up-to-date with the adventures of Charles Holborne;
if you would like to receive freebies, advance notification
of Simon's bookshop and library talks about life at the
criminal Bar, his newsletter or other utterly unmissable
information, please sign up here:

http://www.simonmichael.uk/newslettersign-up/

Acknowledgements

As I learn my trade, I find that more thanks are now required than in the first two books of the series. I owe a debt of gratitude to the following: to Roger Madgett, sailor extraordinaire, and Barrie Tyson, ex-lighterman now living in Australia, for assistance with boats and life on the River; to Ian Pears (herein knighted) and Caroline Sumeray, both HM Coroners; and to Cathy Helms, Neil Cameron, Helen Manley, Carly Jordan and Emma Riddell for design, proof-reading and other invaluable thoughts. Finally, to my wonderful agent, Lisa Eveleigh, whose dedication to, and belief in, me go far beyond the call of duty (or, indeed, the prospect of remuneration).

Simon Michael was called to the Bar by the Honourable Society of the Middle Temple in 1978. In his many years of prosecuting and defending criminal cases he dealt with a wide selection of murderers, armed robbers, con artists and other assorted villainy. A storyteller all his life, Simon started writing short stories at school. His first novel (co-written) was published by Grafton in 1988 and was followed by his first solo novels published here (by WH Allen) and in the USA (by St Martin's Press). In 1991 his short story "Split" was shortlisted for the Cosmopolitan/Perrier Short Story Award. He was also commissioned to write two feature screenplays.

Simon then put aside writing for 25 years to concentrate on his career at the Bar. A firm believer in second chances, in 2016 he retired early to write full-time, and thus the

Charles Holborne series of thrillers was born. *The Brief* was published in the autumn of 2015 and the second in the series, *An Honest Man,* the following year, both to widespread acclaim and 5-star reviews. *The Lighterman* is the third in the series, in which at least two further books are planned.

Simon lives in Bedfordshire. He is a founder member and former chair of the Ampthill Literary Festival.

the
brief

Book 1 in the Charles Holborne series.

BOOK 1 – THE BRIEF

ISBN 9781910692004

1960s London – gang wars, corrupt police, vice and pornography – ex-boxer, Charles Holborne, has plenty of opportunities to build his reputation with the criminal classes as a barrister who delivers. When his philandering wife has her throat slashed, Holborne finds himself on the wrong side of the law and on the run. Can he discover the truth of the brutal slaying and escape the hangman's noose?

BOOK 2 – AN HONEST MAN
ISBN 9781911129394

Can Charles extricate himself from a chess game played from
the shadows by corrupt police officers and warring gangs
without once again turning to crime himself? Based on real Old
Bailey cases and genuine court documents, **An Honest Man** is
the second in the series of Charles Holborne novels by barrister,
Simon Michael, set in the sleazy London of the 1960s.